HELL
BAY

Kate Rhodes grew up in London, but now lives in Cambridge with her husband, the artist and writer Dave Pescod. Kate began her career as an English lecturer and still works part-time as an educational consultant. Before becoming a crime writer she produced two award-winning poetry collections. In 2015, Kate was awarded the Ruth Rendell Short Story prize.

Also by Kate Rhodes

Blood Symmetry
River of Souls
The Winter Foundlings
A Killing of Angels
Crossbone's Yard

HELL BAY

KATE RHODES

**SIMON &
SCHUSTER**

London · New York · Sydney · Toronto · New Delhi

A CBS COMPANY

First published in Great Britain by Simon & Schuster UK Ltd, 2018
This paperback edition published 2018
A CBS COMPANY

1 3 5 7 9 10 8 6 4 2

Simon & Schuster UK Ltd
1st Floor
222 Gray's Inn Road
London WC1X 8HB

www.simonandschuster.co.uk
www.simonandschuster.com.au
www.simonandschuster.co.in

Simon & Schuster Australia, Sydney
Simon & Schuster India, New Delhi

A CIP catalogue record for this book
is available from the British Library

Paperback ISBN: 978-1-4711-6542-9
eBook ISBN: 978-1-4711-6541-2
eAudio ISBN: 978-1-4711-7375-2

Typeset in the UK by M Rules
Printed and bound by CPI Group (UK) Ltd, Croydon, CR0 4YY

MIX
Paper from
responsible sources
FSC® C020471

For my mother Wendy Rhodes,
a brilliant English teacher,
who taught me to read and inspired
my passion for books

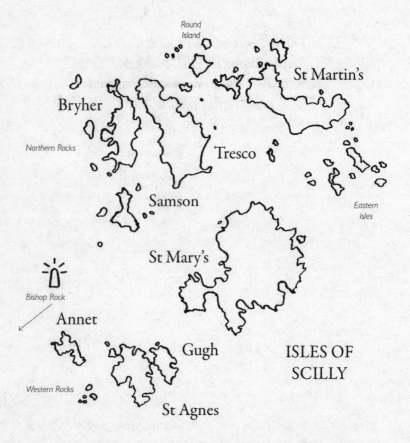

Round
Island

St Martin's

Bryher

Northern Rocks

Tresco

Samson

Eastern
Isles

St Mary's

Bishop Rock

Annet

Gugh

ISLES OF
SCILLY

Western Rocks

St Agnes

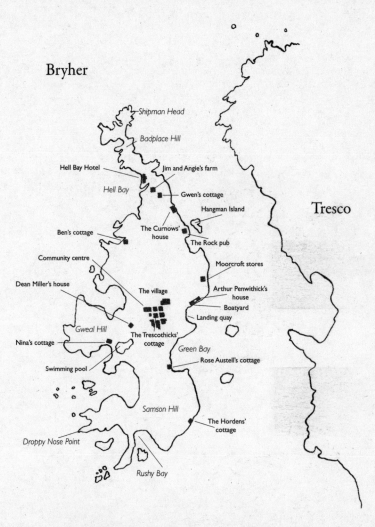

Bryher

Tresco

Shipman Head

Badplace Hill

Hell Bay Hotel

Jim and Angie's farm

Hell Bay

Gwen's cottage

Hangman Island

The Curnows' house

Ben's cottage

The Rock pub

Community centre

Moorcroft stores

Dean Miller's house

The village

Arthur Penwithick's house

Boatyard

Landing quay

Gweal Hill

The Trescothicks' cottage

Nina's cottage

Green Bay

Swimming pool

Rose Austell's cottage

Samson Hill

The Hordens' cottage

Droppy Nose Point

Rushy Bay

Bryher is the smallest inhabited Scilly Island. It is approximately one and a half miles long, and half a mile across at its widest point. The island has ninety-eight permanent residents, most of whom make a living from fishing, boatbuilding, or summer tourism at the island's pub, hotel or campsite.

Laura steals out of bed while the rest of the island sleeps. By 6 a.m. she's in the kitchen, cramming toast into her mouth, staring out at the late winter darkness. North wind batters her face as she leaves the cottage, a whiplash of blonde hair streaming across her shoulders. All of her sixteen years have been spent here; she only has to glance at the sky to second-guess its moods. A line of pink is gathering over Gweal Hill as she climbs its sharp incline, careful not to snag her tights on the bracken and coarse grass. Her mood improves when she catches the scent of brine. A water baby, her mother called her when she was small, happier splashing in the waves than toddling on dry land. The view from the crest of the hill is endless: two thousand miles of ocean, whitecaps skimming its vast expanse. She opens her mouth to taste the salt, lungs filling with ozone while breakers pummel the beach below. Soon she'll say goodbye to this place, just one more summer before she can spread her wings. In August, there will be parties and dancing on the beach, the drunken relief of leaving home, but for now she must focus on the task in hand.

She collects the torch from its hiding place under a rock, but when she stares at the bay a hundred feet below, the water is too treacherous for boats to land. Huge breakers arrive and retreat, the crash of water against granite as loud as applause. It's only when Laura spins round that a figure appears in the half-dark. That smile is so familiar, her lips curve in reply. She's still smiling when pain sears through her chest, the torch dropping from her hand. She reaches out, even though there's nothing to grab as she plummets backwards. The last thing she sees is not the ocean, but the black island where she was born. Its jagged outline imprints on her retinas four seconds later, when her skull smashes against the rocks with the dry crack of an eggshell fracturing. The riptide drags her away, long hair flailing as dawn arrives. Her body rolls with each wave. The killer watches from the clifftop, certain that she is more beautiful dead than alive. From this distance, she could almost be a mermaid.

1

I'm not at my best when the taxi drops me at Penzance quay. My headache has followed me from London to Cornwall on the overnight train. I've tried dunking my face in cold water, a fistful of Nurofen and a full English, but lights still flash whenever I shut my eyes. The sea air is so icy it's hard to believe this is the first day of March, spring just weeks away. Shadow gives me a baleful look as I slump on a bench; rucksack, camera bag and holdall strewn at my feet. The dog I inherited six weeks ago is behaving himself for once, sitting on his haunches, tongue lolling. There's a ticket for St Mary's in my pocket, but the 9 a.m. ferry hasn't arrived, which is no surprise. Storms often disrupted the service to the Scilly Isles when I used to travel home from school on the mainland. My family has scattered far and wide since then. Only my uncle Ray lives on Bryher now, famous for his long silences. I spent my teenage summers in his boatyard, until the lure of the mainland grew too strong to resist. It still mystifies me to be going home. There's no reason, apart from the obvious one: to fix what's broken. I need the island's peace to make a decision that will change the rest of my life.

Penzance harbour looks the same as when I was a boy, the church still lording it over the town, pale and dominating on the skyline. The quay's limestone crescent has its arm raised, defending itself against high tides. The place is still ridiculously pretty; fishermen's cottages in pastel shades, dories bobbing on the water as the dawn light hardens. It takes a Cornishman to know that life here is harder than it looks. In winter, when the blow-ins leave, the place dies on its feet. The only people stirring today are lobstermen, preparing their creels for the first catch of the season. In the distance, there's a chug of smoke as the ferry arrives to carry me to St Mary's, before the last leg of my journey home to Bryher. All I can hope is that no one familiar gets on board – the threat of conversation makes my head pound even harder. The *Scillonian* pulls into harbour half an hour late, and my first port of call is the bar, instead of the crowded café. A teenage brunette in a cheery red uniform is polishing the counter, but there's no sign of a smile when I request coffee.

'Sorry, I'm not allowed to serve for another hour.'

I pull out my warrant card. 'That's okay, I won't arrest you.'

Her jaw drops. 'There's no way you're a cop.'

'Trust me, I am.'

I can see why she doesn't believe me. I've worked

4

undercover so long, anonymity has become second nature. The mirror behind the bar shows a shambling giant with a blue-black beard, mud-green eyes sunk deep in their hollows. The girl studies the details on the back of my card in amazement.

'Detective Inspector Benesek Kitto, thirty-four years old, Metropolitan police. That's an island name, isn't it?'

'Born and raised.'

'What kind of dog is that?'

'He's a Czechoslovakian wolfdog.'

'Lovely coat on him. What's his name?'

'Shadow.'

The girl gives me a considering look. 'Promise you won't tell anyone I opened early?'

'Cross my heart and hope to die.'

When she emerges from behind the bar with a bowl of water, Shadow wags his tail shamelessly, hungry for female affection. I retreat to a window seat and knock back strong black coffee, hoping to annihilate my migraine. Once the mug's empty, I walk on deck with the dog slinking at my heels. The sea's surface shifts and turns as we pass Land's End, a restless sleeper, eager to shrug the night's weight from its shoulders. I'm already missing my London existence: a cool flat in Hammersmith, my vintage motorbike gathering dust in a lock-up, mates I drink with every weekend, who never ask questions.

I alternate between the deck and the bar as the ferry

chugs towards its destination. The journey feels end-less. Trying to read the Steinbeck novel that's stuffed in my pocket only worsens my headache, so I stare out of the window as the waves grow taller. The *Scillonian* docks in St Mary's harbour at midday. The island is a smaller version of Penzance: fishing smacks bellied on the low-tide mud, houses running in grey terraces, connecting the hills to the sea. Already the scale feels stifling, despite miles of clean air overhead. St Mary's is a throwback to the fifties, cars travelling along the coast road at a sedate pace, but this place is a metropolis compared to where I'm going. It used to amuse me that the islands are owned by royalty. Charles and Camilla would never deign to visit Bryher, even though their ancestors bought it for loose change. Shadow's whining for food, so I haul my bags to the waiting room and go in search of dog biscuits. He looks unimpressed when I hold out my palm.

'Take it or leave it,' I say.

He gives me a killing look before claiming the pellets with a single lick. No doubt he'd hop on the first train back to Hammersmith, given the chance. He accepts another handful, then turns his head away in disgust.

The young bloke in the ticket office is reluctant to sell me a fare. Apparently the Tresco passage is so rough, the boat may not arrive; none have sailed from the outlying islands in twenty-four hours. I hunker beside the harbour wall, my headache lifting around 2 p.m., the vice around my skull gradually loosening. By the time the *Bryher Maid* appears, the sea is churning, waves coming to a rapid boil. I don't know whether to be relieved or afraid when the boat finally docks. The crossing doesn't bother me. After so many hours on the Atlantic, my gut's immune to motion sickness. It's the idea of arrival that brings a cold sweat to the back of my neck.

The skipper greets me with a single nod of acknowledgement. Arthur Penwithick is always sceptical about people who desert the island. He's still captaining the clinker jet boat my uncle built for him twenty years ago, licensed for fifteen passengers. His appearance hasn't changed since I was a kid. He must be close to sixty now, dressed in yellow oilskins, a frizz of brown hair under the cap he never removes, buck teeth protruding from his upper lip. After we set sail, Arthur offers a low grumble of conversation. It's been a tough winter on the island, only a handful of tourists at the hotel, some blow-in renting a holiday cottage. He looks more relaxed when Bryher rises into view. It's a speck of rock, less than two miles long, exposed to everything the Atlantic chucks at it. Slowly it transforms into a black row of boulders. From here it's easy to see why its name means 'the place of hills'; the high incline of Shipman Head Down overshadows its only village. When I look back towards the mainland, one of the passengers is bent over the rail, studying the wake's jet stream or trying to retain her lunch. The dog is struggling too, the boat's heaving motion making him shiver.

At Tresco everyone disembarks, leaving just me and Arthur to cross the sound to Bryher. I've dreamed of this place for months, longed to breathe its salted air, but my childhood empire looks smaller than my memory painted it. Straight ahead I can see my uncle's boatyard, the doors of his workshop hanging open, the ferry-man's narrow house beside it. A hundred metres north along the shore stands the island's shop, which doubles as a Post Office. It's a detached stone cottage freshly painted white; the words 'Moorcroft Stores' inscribed in red above the porch. Behind the buildings, the land is a rich, unbroken green, with Gweal Hill looming in the distance. The ferry docks on a quay designed for small craft and fishing vessels. If a millionaire's yacht ever tried to land here, they'd be out of luck. The jetty would be metres too short. Bryher's familiar odour hits me before I've set foot on dry land: boat diesel, fish guts and woodsmoke drifting on the breeze.

My uncle is waiting on the beach, straight-backed and watchful. Ray is thinner than last time, thick hair whiter than before, face so hard-boned it looks cast from metal. Sun and salt air have turned his skin to sandpaper, his cheek grazing mine when he offers an awkward one-armed hug. Ray's smile arrives slowly as I dump my bags, the dog leaping across the shingle. If he's concerned about my ragged state, or the huge grey wolf trailing behind me, he's too poker-faced to admit it. I glance around to orientate myself; the island's east coast is sinking long granite fingers into the sea, as the quiet between us deepens. I could tell him why I'm here, but I don't want sympathy today. All I need is help carrying my bags to my parents' cottage and a quick goodbye. It's my uncle who breaks the silence first.

'Back for long, Ben?'

I shrug. 'A month, maybe two.'

'Work can spare you that long?'

'I'm using up leftover holiday.'

He gives me a sceptical look but doesn't reply, setting off down the path with my rucksack slung easily over his shoulders, even though it must weigh thirty kilos. My father used to greet me and my brother in the same way, pleased but wordless, carting our kitbags home every Friday night. The silence allows the landscape to fill my senses, my feet sliding on the rain-soaked ground, gulls sailing over Shipman Head as we cut a line through the centre of the island to my childhood home. Even at ambling pace, the journey doesn't take long. Bryher is half a mile across at its widest point, but nothing moves fast here; no cars or motorbikes, just a network of paths riddled with rabbit holes.

'Bad weather,' he comments. 'A girl's been missing all day.'

'Who's that?'

'The Trescothicks' older daughter.'

Jenna and Matt Trescothick were two years above me at school. He captained the five islands football team and she was the May queen. I watched them surfing with their friends each summer, gripped by hero worship. They were tanned, good-looking and impossibly cool; the island's golden couple. When they married at eighteen, everyone turned out to throw confetti and watch them start their charmed lives. I saw their oldest girl at a bonfire last summer, a pretty blonde teenager with an infectious smile; but even in a place this small, kids drive their parents crazy. One time, my mum's nagging pissed me off so badly I hid in a friend's barn for a whole weekend, until everyone believed I'd drowned on a midnight swim.

We're passing through the hamlet at the island's centre now; two dozen small, slate-roofed cottages built from local stone, resting in a hollow. Beyond them the community hall is painted a virulent yellow. The old schoolhouse stands on the outskirts of the village, still named for its educational past even though its last pupil graduated forty years ago. Most of the island's buildings are clustered in the valley, sheltered from the wind by the surrounding hills. My grandfather should have built here too, but he preferred solitude. We skirt round Gweal Hill until a different kind of sea greets us, waves strong enough to toss boulders around like marbles. The house where I grew up stands on Hell Bay. It's a simple stone box under a sagging roof, windows filmed with brine. The only other building in sight is the island's hotel, ten minutes' walk away, its white outline resembling a row of sugar cubes scattered along the horizon. I'm grateful when Ray dumps my bag at my feet, refusing to come inside.

'Maggie cleaned the place and put food in your fridge,' he mumbles. 'I'd better get back to work. Come by the yard whenever you like.'

The door is unlocked, even though my last visit was six months ago, for my mother's funeral. I only spent a couple of nights here then and the place looks shabby; the air in the hallway smells of mildew, dust motes hanging on the cold light that spills through the door. The kitchen cupboards are crammed with boxes of Cornflakes and packets of rice, as if my godmother is afraid I'll starve without her assistance. I scoop food into a bowl for the dog then lie on the rough woollen blanket that covers the settee, poleaxed by my long journey, but it's impossible to sleep. Water drips too loudly from the tap, storm petrels arguing outside. Who would think a one-storey building could hold so much of the past? Ghosts arrive as I stand by the sink. I can smell my mother's lavender scent, the salt that clung to my father's skin until his fishing boat capsized on the Atlantic Strait. Today, even the living seem like spirits. My brother is two thousand miles west in New York, yet I picture him sprawled beside me in his favourite chair. Evidence of my half-finished attempts to modernise the place for my mother are everywhere I look: new tiles on the kitchen floor, sage-green paint peeling from the walls. The bathroom is no better. I installed a sleek shower cubicle, but never got around to fitting a decent bath and sink.

If I stay here I'll end up climbing the walls, so I

grab my coat again when evening comes. I try to leave without waking the dog, but he noses out of the door, determined not to be abandoned.

'You'll get trodden on,' I warn him.

He vanishes down the path, confident as a native islander. I stand in the porch to tuck my scarf deeper inside my collar, torch in my pocket. When I was a kid I knew every bump and crater, fleet-footed in the dark. No one gets hurt here, unless they make a stupid mistake. Every few years someone breaks an ankle, tripping over a molehill or rabbit hole; then it's a short but agonising boat ride to the field hospital on Tresco to get it cast. But tonight it's stars that catch my eye, not the pockmarked ground. Without street lights, they're free to dazzle. There's a 180-degree view of the northern hemisphere, pinholes of silver light piercing the sky's surface. The beauty is almost enough to drop me to my knees, and it takes me several minutes to drag my eyes back to the ground. Once I've returned to the quay I follow the island's eastern coast towards the pub, until an ugly man-made glare rises from the beach below.

Voices drift up as the tide rolls closer. Judging by the flare of torch beams, half the island's population is braving the cold. It doesn't take a high IQ to know that Laura Trescothick is still missing. It's tempting to revert to type and jog down to lead the search, giving orders in a loud, no-bullshit voice. I remind myself that I'm taking a break from being a cop, but feel a twinge of guilt as the Rock looms from the dark. The pub is a wide two-storey building, facing New Grimsby Sound. I pass the island's only phone box and head indoors. The place reeks of the past: woodsmoke from the ingle-nook fire, brandy, home-cooked food. A few punters are relaxing on sofas by the hearth. Luckily, they're too busy chatting to turn round. Dean Miller sits at a corner table, immersed in his newspaper. The island's only pro-fessional artist looks more eccentric than ever, grey hair shaved close to his skull, a yellow cravat knotted around his throat, jeans so paint-spattered there's no clear denim. He's been producing ugly abstract seascapes ever since he came over from America thirty years ago.

My godmother, Maggie Nancarrow, is behind the bar, the sight of her making me feel like I'm ten years old again, buying cider for my dad. She doesn't spot me at first, too busy opening a bottle of wine, tortoiseshell glasses perched on the tip of her nose. Her bird-like form is wrapped in a scarlet jumper and faded jeans, wild grey curls surrounding a face as round and pol-ished as an apple. The welcoming grin she produces soon fades into concern.

'I've been expecting you all day.' She dashes round for a hug, the crown of her head level with my chest. She tilts her face back to inspect me more closely. 'You're still ridiculously handsome, Ben, despite the beard.'

'You say that to all the boys. Thanks for looking after the house.'

'Only you inspire me to scrub floors.' She looks down at Shadow. 'What's this? I thought you hated dogs.'

13

'I inherited him.'

Maggie's eyes brim with questions she's too wise to ask. 'You're too skinny. Stay there, I'll bring you some food.'

'Let me come and see Billy first.'

Billy Reese is one of the island's stalwarts, preparing pub grub with occasional flashes of brilliance for the past decade. Appetising smells hit me when I enter his kitchen: fish frying, lemon juice, the sharp reek of garlic. He's sitting at the stainless-steel counter, chopping parsley at a hectic pace with a red-handled knife, one heavily bandaged foot resting on a stool. He's a tall, bald-headed man in his fifties, who wears a bandana when he cooks, like the elder statesman of a motorcycle gang. His sombre face creases into a grin when he sees me.

'Come to arrest me, Ben?'

'Depends how many laws you've broken.' I clap him on the shoulder. 'What happened to the ankle?'

'I tripped going home, Saturday night.'

'Nine sheets to the wind?'

'Eight, maybe.' His smile reveals rows of tobacco-stained teeth. 'Help yourself to grub.'

'Maggie's sorting me out.'

By the time I return to the bar she's produced a bowl of fish chowder, French bread and a glass of apple juice. Not asking what I want is her way of showing she cares. Maggie's only fault is assuming she knows everything, from the island's history to the dietary needs of every regular. When she answers the phone, her thin hand races across the pad as she scribbles down a fish order. The Rock isn't just a pub; fishermen store their catches here, in the kitchen's huge industrial fridges, leaving Maggie to broker deals with restaurants on the mainland. Over the years, she's developed a winning technique: charm alternating with contempt. The chowder's even better than I'd remembered, a smoky tang of haddock laced with cream, a hard kick of salt. The bowl soon empties, which returns the smile to my godmother's face. She props both elbows on the bar, chocolate-brown eyes watching me.

'What's new, Ben?'

I attempt a relaxed shrug. 'Not much. I'm just taking a break.'

'I don't see you for six months, and that's all you've got to say?'

'You know me, Maggie. Conversation's not my best skill.'

I'm not ready to explain that my DCI has given me three months to decide whether my ten-year career as an undercover officer with the Murder Investigation Team should come to an end. The boss refused to accept my resignation, insisting on a cooling-off period, when I would rather have walked away. Maggie's stare is so clear and unblinking, she seems to have guessed my predicament without being told.

'Did you hear Laura Trescothick's missing?' She leans closer, elbows resting on the bar. 'The kid didn't show up for work this morning. No boats have sailed all day, except the *Bryher Maid*. She must be on the island somewhere.'

'With some lad, probably.'

'Her boyfriend hasn't seen her. She's not the type to let people down.'

An odd feeling crosses the back of my neck, as if someone has let in a blast of cold air. When I turn round to locate the chill, a woman is sitting alone by the fire, hands folded in her lap. Her face is a pale-skinned oval, sleek brown hair falling to her jaw, neat as a medieval pageboy. I turn away before she catches me gawking.

Maggie carries on talking about the missing girl. It's a reminder that in a community of a hundred everyone knows your crises, whether you like it or not.

'There's a meeting at the community hall tomorrow,' she says.

Her gaze is a direct challenge, but I don't reply. The kid's probably hiding in a mate's attic to give her family a scare. After an awkward moment, the conversation switches to her son Patrick, a close friend when we were kids. He's a vet now, in St Ives, married with a family, running a smallholding. An hour passes before she slides a single shot of rum across the bar.

'One for the road, young man,' she says, turning away to load the dishwasher.

I'm eternally grateful that she hasn't asked how I'm coping. I toss the drink back, then fetch my coat, taking care not to stare at the brunette again. Dean Miller is still buried in his paper, a fresh beer at his elbow, oblivious to his surroundings. The dog falls into step by the door, giving a bark of irritation, as if I've dragged him from more important pursuits. The sound of the wind rises from a whisper to a shout as the door shuts behind me.

Back at the cottage, I pull off my boots in the porch and try to ignore the ghosts that press in from the walls. Instead I think about Laura Trescothick. She was on the verge of teenage beauty last summer, flying a kite on the beach with her friends, long hair streaming in the breeze. The cold in the bedroom makes me shiver as I undress, then the place suddenly plunges into darkness. I grope through the black air for candles. The generator should kick in immediately, but nothing happens. The island is reminding me that even basic amenities like heat and light can't be trusted out here. It's harder than ever to silence the questions that flood my head, as the candle gutters in the draught.

2

Rose Austell's cabin lies on the far side of the island, closer to the sea than any other building. It's no larger than a wooden caravan, but she could never leave it behind, despite floods and vicious draughts, the holes appearing in its corrugated-iron roof. She's alone in her kitchen when the lights flick out. Shock makes her release a muffled scream. Darkness scares her almost as much as visits from strangers, and official letters from the world outside. At fifty-five, she has only left Bryher a handful of times. She scrabbles for matches, and soon the space is lit by the orange glow from her paraffin lamp. The kitchen is lined with boxes of seeds and roots that she forages for all year. Sachets of valerian, sea-spurrey and bittersweet lie on her table, waiting to be made into ointments for muscle pain and arthritis. Rose pushes the ingredients aside, too distracted to work. She stares at the mobile phone her son Sam gave her, willing it to ring.

The news about Laura Trescothick has upset her all evening, a toxic cocktail of guilt and anxiety burning the pit of her stomach. Sam dated Laura for the best part of a year, but it ended badly. Rose can't help picturing the girl's face under the water, blonde hair shimmering, her beauty a fierce reproach. When her eyes blink open again, the ocean is battering the shore outside, grey and relentless. She has seen the granite coastline in all weathers, fifteen-foot waves somersaulting across the beach. Rose understands that the sea steals more than it gives. When she was a girl, her father told tales of Bryher's wild history and the lawless men who ruled the Isles of Scilly for three centuries. Their fearless spirits seemed romantic, until she realised that her island still lay in the smugglers' grip. She has good reason to hate them now.

Rose peers from the window again, praying that Sam will return, but seeing only Tresco's dark outline, the moon blinded by clouds. She presses her fingers over her lips to stifle another cry. Laura is missing, and so is her only child, but there's nothing she can do.

3

Terns are squealing when my eyes open. My headache has made a comeback, the day starting with a stream of curses as I haul myself into the cold, but at least the power supply is working again. The cottage looks worse by daylight: cork tiles on the bathroom floor curling at the edges, the generator in need of a service, and weeds covering the allotment where my mother grew spinach and potatoes. The waves outside hiss like playground bullies, slapping and jeering as they assault the beach. Shadow's doing his best to trip me up, a blur of excitement whirling at my feet, barking at full volume, desperate to greet the day.

'Bloody hound,' I mutter, yanking up the zip on my coat.

It's clear no ferries will sail this morning. The tide is battering the shore, reminding me that Hell Bay was named for good reason. For nine months of the year the water is tranquil, but winter's infernal storms blow in from the west until it requires muscle to wrench open your front door. Hell Bay Hotel glitters with prosperity at the end of the sweeping beach. A night in an ocean-view room in high season retails for a small fortune, with the guarantee of impeccable food and accommodation. If I screw up my eyes I can see Zoe Morrow standing on the terrace, small as a stick figure in the distance. She's dressed from head to toe in electric blue, short hair dyed platinum since we hit our teens. I shade my eyes to view her more clearly. She's giving an enthusiastic two-handed wave, beckoning me over. In her glory days at college she planned to join a rock band and conquer the world, but her talent has been reduced to a hobby. After her dad's heart attack, she put her singing career on hold. Her parents retired to Mevagissey, while her two brothers pursued careers on the mainland, leaving her to run the hotel alone. It would be polite to trot over to give her a hug, but I set off in the opposite direction. Shame, I suppose. I'd rather my best mate from school didn't see me in a foul mood.

Fresh air is reviving me by the time I reach Droppy Nose Point, the rocky spur that juts into the Atlantic from Bryher's southern point. It was my favourite place as a kid, for its daft name and huge granite outcrop that resembles an elephant's head, trunk raised. The rocks here are bright green with algae, mussels clinging to them like clusters of grapes. It crosses my mind to search the beach to look for the missing girl. Maybe some boy brought her here, a row between them escalating into violence, but I have to remind myself that someone else is in charge. Cutting round Samson Hill brings me to the eastern side of the island, sheltered from the fierce breeze. The channel is calm as a mill pond, revealing the island's split personality, the lush green outline of Tresco visible across New Grimsby Sound. The dog vanishes into a field of bracken as I skirt past South Cottage, hoping to avoid being spotted, but a man's harsh voice calls out, loud as a drill sergeant's.

'Who's that skulking behind my hedge?'

'Ben Kitto, Tom.'

After twenty years, it still feels odd to use his first name, instead of Mr Horden. He was my form teacher at secondary school until he resigned in a hurry, for reasons unknown. His feet crunch rapidly on the gravel, but his appearance has changed. He stands with shoulders back, wearing a shirt and tie under his V-necked sweater, his face carved with deep lines. One of his eyes is as cloudy as milk, the other giving me the fierce grey stare that could reduce kids to tears in his maths lessons. The man's house is uncompromising too, a block of raw stone, window frames painted black.

'Come inside, boy. Say hello to my wife.'

'I can't today. Ray's expecting me at the boatyard.' It's a lie, of course, but the bloke has always given me the creeps.

'Let him wait.'

Horden seizes my elbow and propels me inside. A stream of unpleasant smells greets me: cabbage from last night's dinner, bleach and overheated air. The odour reminds me of hospital corridors and suddenly I'm longing for a quick exit. He leads me into a kitchen lined with floral tiles that must have clung to the walls for decades, pots and pans gathering dust on the shelves.

'Someone to see you, Emma. You remember Ben Kitto, don't you? Mark and Helen's youngest.'

Emma Horden used to be a smartly dressed woman with a placatory smile, always rattling a bucket for good causes outside Tresco church. She vanished for a few months after her husband's resignation, and now she's almost unrecognisable, overweight and stoop-shouldered in a drab pinafore, grey hair in rats' tails. She looks me up and down, taking in my five o'clock shadow and ancient leather jacket, then shakes her head firmly.

'Benesek sings in the choir. He's the only boy that can hold a tune.'

'That was a while back, Emma.'

'Leave me alone, I don't want strangers stealing my treasures.' She seizes a ceramic bowl from the window ledge and cradles it against her chest. 'Whoever you are, go home before the storm comes.'

'That's good advice. I just wanted to say hello while I was passing.'

The bowl she's holding is filled with objects that glitter in the light filtering through the curtains; key rings, coins and seashells. Mr Horden looks awkward when we return to the hallway, his kitchen door closed to protect Emma from more confusion. 'You'll have to forgive her, she's having a bad day.'

'We all get those sometimes.'

'Are you still fond of reading? You always had a book under your desk in my lessons.' It's hard to tell whether he's joking, or blaming me for poor classroom behaviour twenty years ago.

'Guilty as charged.'

His milky eye rolls in my direction. 'Come by one evening, there's a fine collection of novels here. No one uses them now.'

'I'll do that, Tom.'

'Have you resigned from the police force?'

I shake my head. 'Just taking a holiday.'

'Pressure got too much for you, did it?'

'I'm on leave, that's all. I'd better get on.'

My ex-teacher's questions leave me brooding. A fatal error has pushed me from my job, not the pressures of work. Most of my colleagues have forgiven me, but acceptance is a milestone I've yet to reach. Memories of school catch up with me as I follow drystone walls along the winding path towards the quay. We used to laugh at Horden's expense, pupils spinning ridiculous stories because of his razor-sharp voice and the girls' claims that he leered at them. It's a relief to escape the loneliness emanating from the couple like a bad smell, Shadow at my heels as I walk north along the shore. The view of Tresco banishes my bad mood, its fields and gardens stretching out like miles of crushed green velvet.

Ray's workshop doors are wide open, but there's no sign of him. Sunlight is leaking through holes in the tin roof when I find him in the covered yard. The frame he's building is twenty feet long, a traditional fishing boat, with keel and bass boards already in place. He looks up from his bandsaw to offer a smile of greeting.

'It's a lapstrake,' he says. 'For a lobsterman on St Mary's.'

'You're using cedar?'

'Built to last,' he replies, nodding. 'Finish it with me, if you like.'

I can't find a reply. When I was a teenager, Ray offered to take me on as his apprentice; I loved spending time in the yard, but lacked his patience. It still bothers me that I left Bryher at eighteen without apologising properly for letting him down. The work he's offering would take a month at least, but it's impossible to imagine the boat's hull forming under my hands after neglecting my skills for so long. Shadow seems to be waiting for my decision, pale eyes alert to every movement. I pick up a broom to gather wood shavings while my uncle carries on working. Sweeping was my childhood punishment for getting under his feet, but I do it willingly now, the flow of movement clearing my mind. It amazes me that Ray has coped here alone since his last workman retired. I spend an hour sorting materials into drawers: tacks, twine, half a dozen caulking irons. When I look at the quay again, the sky is a solid wall of cloud. Fishermen have brought their vessels round from the west to shelter, clinker boats lining the jetty. Some of them are familiar, names unchanged for generations: *Clara Belle*, *Destiny*, *Scilly Lass*. All I want is to close my eyes until the world settles again. But the boats are soothing to watch, floating in a shoal, colourful as children's toys. It crosses my mind to tell Ray my dilemma, but personal chat has never been his forte.

After a few hours, my uncle switches off his saw and removes his goggles. I assume he's breaking for lunch, but he reaches for his padded jacket.

'Coming to the meeting? The police are over, from St Mary's.'

'I think I'll skip it.'

He holds my gaze. 'Everyone'll be there.'

Avoidance isn't an option; ignoring the meeting would be like announcing that I don't give a damn whether a young girl lives or dies. I trudge after him reluctantly, Shadow chasing ahead of us on the cinder path.

The community hall looks smarter than when I was a kid, a large one-storey barn with new windows, Day-Glo-yellow walls even uglier now the clouds have lifted. Like most things on the island it's multi-purpose, serving as scout hut, wedding venue, bingo hall and theatre. The interior smells of dust and floor polish, new blinds hanging at half-mast. Its high windows and pine floor resemble a school gymnasium, folding chairs laid out in ranks, but today there's standing room only. I recognise most of the people here: Zoe's a few metres away, spiky blonde hair ruffled by the wind, chatting to Maggie and Billy. Angie Helyer, a pretty, doll-faced redhead, flashes me a wide smile from the other side of the hall. She was a couple of years below me at school, but now she's the owner of a small goat and chicken farm, the latest baby slung across her chest in a sling, her toddler crawling at her feet. Her husband Jim, one of my oldest friends, must be tending their animals. Even Rose Austell has emerged for the occasion, standing apart from the crowd, her face half hidden by a veil of witch-like black hair. Everyone looks expectant, waiting for instructions.

When Matt Trescothick takes the stage you could hear a pin drop. He was so much cooler than my older brother when I was a kid, his football skills and ease with girls filling me with envy. Even now there's a glimpse of his teenage charisma, when he used to swagger down to the quay with Jenna on his arm. His rangy build, dark eyes and strong features would suit a movie star, mid-brown hair cropped close to his skull, but today he's gaunt with exhaustion. It feels wrong to be sitting in the audience when I'd rather be next to him, observing the crowd for suspicious behaviour, even though I've known most of them all my life. The cop at his side is close to retirement age, showing his respect by wearing full uniform, epaulettes slick with gold brocade. He's small-framed, with a narrow intelligent face, expression grave as he surveys the crowd.

'I'm DCI Alan Madron, I'll be co-ordinating today's search. I'm sure the family are grateful so many of you have turned out. Is there anything you want to say before we get started, Mr Trescothick?'

Matt's gaze skims the crowd without connecting. I know that blank-eyed stare too well; concentration is the first thing parents lose when they realise a missing child might not return. His voice is deeper than I remembered, roughened by cigarettes or booze.

'Jenna wants me to thank you all; she was too upset to come. It means a lot that you're all helping to find our girl.'

The muscles in Matt's face are working overtime when he sits down again, with people murmuring their support. If this was a press call, his image would be smeared across the nation's screens already, millions of viewers assuming he's guilty. It's a proven fact that most murder victims are killed by a family member, or someone they know well. I silence the thought before it takes root. All of my instincts are telling me to help the uniforms organise the crowd, even though the kid's likely to be hiding somewhere, brooding about some secret grievance. Silence settles over the room when the DCI speaks again.

'The island will be divided into quarters, one group sweeping each area. My officers will co-ordinate the search.' He scans the room again. 'Laura went up to her room around ten-thirty on Sunday night. Her mum heard her leave yesterday, Monday the first of March, around 6.15 a.m. She was due to start the breakfast shift at the hotel by seven. We know for a fact that she couldn't have left the island by boat; the sea was too rough for crossings until midday. If anyone has any information about Laura, please talk to me or a member of my team.'

Madron's statements make me grit my teeth. If I was in charge, I'd hold immediate interviews with the family to rule out suicide; the girl may have been facing pressures we know nothing about. Ray and I are first out of the hall when the meeting ends, Shadow in the distance, sheltering by a gorse bush. The island's population is emerging into the fresh air, expressions ranging from gloom to determination. The DCI wastes no time in dividing us into groups. My heart sinks when I see that my team includes the Hordens. My old teacher's eyes look even more disturbing from a distance; one pale as ice, the other dark and focused as a laser. When I turn round, the brunette from the pub is ten metres away, circled by a pool of cold sunlight. She's taller than I imagined, long legs clad in tight jeans and red wellingtons, dark hair glistening. This time she catches me staring. She returns my gaze, unsmiling, before walking away.

The young PC leading my group is called Eddie Nickell. He looks like a sixth-form prefect, his face surrounded by a crop of blond curls, cheeks shiny with pride at being given special duties. He instructs us in slow monosyllables, as though he's calming a gang of unruly five year olds. It sounds easy enough: search the beaches, lift manhole covers, check buildings and paths. When I look up again, Shadow is slinking into the distance, and for once I'd like to keep him company.

The only saving grace is that Zoe is in my team. We haven't seen each other since her visit to London at Christmas, when she dragged me from one music venue to the next, ending our day riotously pissed in a tequila bar. She's one of the few people I know who manages to stay consistently upbeat, her laughter always the loudest in the room, unwilling to let disasters dent her optimism. She looks as good as ever, with that Amazonian build, shock of white-blonde hair, almond-shaped dark eyes and freckles dusted over glowing skin. The wild curves of her figure would set my pulse racing if I hadn't known her since I was three. She flings her arms round my neck to give me a hug. It's been so long since anyone touched me that I make the most of it, then have to remind myself not to cling.

'How are you, big man?'

'Alive, last time I checked.'

'What's that on your face?'

'A fashionable beard.'

'What's wrong with a decent close shave? You should have told me you were coming home, I'd have hung out the flags.'

'It wasn't planned.'

She narrows her eyes. 'You travelled all night on a whim?'

'Pretty much.' Shadow appears at my side, unwilling to be left out.

'That's one hell of a dog. Is he yours?'

'By default, yeah.'

'I wouldn't fancy meeting you in a dark wood.' The dog responds ecstatically to Zoe's petting, with a frenzy of tail-wagging. 'But you're a cutie, aren't you?'

'Keep him, please. I can't stand dogs.'

'You're mean. He just needs some love.'

At last we set off to search the north-eastern quarter of the island. We're a motley bunch, ages ranging from late teens through to seventies, representing every local family. Dean Miller is traipsing behind us, a white streak of paint marking the sleeve of his jacket, his eyes fixed on the horizon. The artist seems more interested in finding inspiration for his paintings than looking for the missing girl. The party walks north at a snail's pace. It falls to me to lift the manhole cover behind the shop, then lower myself into the black hole until my feet hit the concrete storm drain at the bottom; my torch reveals nothing except a stream of black slurry, and a few rats vanishing into the distance. I hold my breath, trying not to inhale the ripe stench of sewage. Zoe's smile has vanished when I climb out again, as if the girl's absence has finally hit home.

'Do you really think Laura's been hurt?'

'Let's hope not, but it gets more likely as time passes.' I lower the manhole cover back into place. 'How long has she worked for you?'

'Since last July. She's saving to do a drama course this autumn.'

'A star in the making. What's the kid like?'

'Great, actually. I thought about laying her off with the other casuals, but she was desperate for cash, so I found bits of cleaning and decorating, to pay her a few quid over the winter. She's got this wicked sense of humour, imitating people all the time.'

'Has she got a boyfriend?'

'Danny Curnow, but his parents don't approve.'

I raise my eyebrows. The Curnows are the island's wealthiest family, made welcome because they invest in local businesses. Jay Curnow owned a building company on the mainland, then got a divorce and married a woman twenty years his junior, had a late child. It seems unlikely that the pampered son of a millionaire would resort to violence, even though young women are more likely to be attacked by their partners than anyone else.

We've reached a row of fishing huts. There's nothing inside except nets and crab pots, air still tainted by last season's catch. We progress slowly along the footpath, sweeping the beer garden behind the Rock, grass rough underfoot as we head north. Cromwell's Castle looms over the coast of Tresco; it looks impregnable, high grey turrets protecting it from attack. Hangman Island almost fills the narrow channel between the islands. No one knows how it got its name, but the locals think it was used for executions. It certainly looks ghost-ridden today, a raw outcrop of granite jutting from the sea.

'I used to swim out there with Steve Parfitt for crazy teenage sex,' Zoe says.

'You minx.' I carry on scanning the ground, not telling her that it's old news. Her boyfriend bragged about it to every lad at school. 'What happened to Steve?'

'Bank manager, in Truro.'

'I seem to remember you hating his guts.'

'Ancient history.' She smiles widely. 'I'm off men, since my last romantic disaster. Singlehood suits me better.'

'Each to their own. Celibacy isn't my idea of fun.' I pick up a carrier bag but find it empty, the plastic billowing like a streamer in the wind.

'It beats dealing with the misfits I always choose. Come back to the hotel later; I'll tell you how I've been channelling my energies.'

After another hour, we reach the island's northernmost point, Badplace Hill rearing over us. Our search has provided a tour of sites famous for shipwrecks and smuggling. We've turned over stones, checked potting sheds and empty holiday cottages, but the return journey reveals nothing except the fading light. PC Nickell's face has lost its veneer of excitement by the time he commends our efforts then sends us on our way.

'Come for that drink.' Zoe grabs my sleeve then grinds to an abrupt halt, staring up at me. 'Why not tell me what's bothering you on the way?'

'There's nothing to report.'

'I've got eyes, Ben. Is work getting you down?'

'Just something that can't be changed.' I've grown so used to lying about my job, it's easier to stay quiet.

'You're still as open as a razor clam.' She prods a finger at my chest. 'I know you, remember? Sooner or later you'll have to talk.'

'Later, preferably, but thanks for the offer.'

Describing a hole in your life doesn't make it vanish, it just makes it deeper than before. She threads her arm through mine as we carry on walking.

Zoe updates me about life at the hotel as we leave the search party. It's been a profitable year, but her dreams of becoming a professional singer are still out of reach. Soon the hotel will close for two weeks of refurbishment, before the spring rush, leaving her free to contact agencies on the mainland and persuade them to offer her gigs. Now she's blathering about interior design styles she's keen to try in the hotel bedrooms. I zone out when she waxes lyrical about distressed woodwork and modernist furniture.

'What happened to that solicitor you were seeing, on St Mary's?' I ask.

'The guy was way too keen. Pity, he was a brilliant cook.'

'That was his biggest virtue?'

She releases a quick laugh. 'Your mind's still in the gutter, Ben.'

I feel a pang of guilt. For the first time in weeks I'm teasing someone and letting myself be teased in return. Laughter activates unused muscles, an ache in my chest when I try to speak. Something catches my eye as we trudge back to Hell Bay. On top of Gweal Hill a thin figure stands alone, looking out to sea. He slips a pair of binoculars into the pocket of his dark coat, the light spilling from his torch quickly extinguished.

'Who's that on the hill?'

Zoe looks up quickly, but the figure has vanished. I'm left to wonder who would stare out at the empty waves late on a winter afternoon, when the wind's strong enough to lift you off your feet.

The hotel's panoramic windows are lit up to greet us, around a dozen guests visible inside the Atlantic Bar. Zoe rushes inside to check that the reception area is running smoothly while the hotel operates on skeleton staff. A gaggle of punters is grouped round a single large table, Angie Helyer serving drinks from a silver tray. She must have dropped her kids at the farm then raced back to start her waitressing shift. It's a fact of life that most of Bryher's inhabitants need two jobs to survive. Angie bounces over, her frame as diminutive as a pixie, features delicate when she peers up at me.

'It's good to have you back. Jim wanted to come on the search, but someone had to mind Noah and Lily.'

'You still look like a sixth-former, Angie. They can't be your kids.'

She rolls her eyes. 'You old charmer. What's your poison these days?'

'Grolsch, please. But I can't stay long, my brother's skyping later.'

'Have you heard Zoe's new songs yet?'

'She's been saving them for me.'

'Find yourself a table and I'll put on the CD. You're in for a treat.'

There's still no sign of Zoe when music filters through the speakers at low volume. Her voice is always a pleasure to hear, a smoky version of Adele, tugging at the heartstrings, but the new melody beats anything she's written before. It sounds like she's tapped into the island's frequency. When I close my eyes I can see the cliffs at Shipman Head pleated in granite folds, and the treeless face of Samson, pitted with ancient graves. She's conjured the islands' moods perfectly, the rocky headlands silhouetted against an infinity of sky. It's so absorbing that I'm still lost in the music when Zoe reappears.

'Trust Angie to embarrass me,' she mutters. 'I never play my own stuff in the bar.'

'Your voice sounds better than ever. It's the first time you've written about the islands, isn't it?'

'I'm not all froth and nonsense, you know.' Her smile widens with relief. 'Thank God you like the songs. I've already sent them out to agencies.'

'How would you juggle gigs with running this place?'

She shrugs her shoulders. 'I love it here, but this place has taken enough years of my life.'

We carry on talking about her escape plans until I drain the last of my beer, then lean over to kiss her cheek. 'I'd better move. Catch up soon, Zoe.'

When I scan the bar again, Angie is busy chatting to a

guest, so I wave goodbye across the half-empty bar then launch myself into the cold. The light from the hotel weakens as I trudge home. There's no sign of Shadow, even though I whistle for him; maybe he's cut his losses and found a better place to stay.

My brother skypes at precisely eight o'clock, a ritual he's followed twice a week since our mother died. It's always a jolt to see his face; a healthier version of mine with the same black hair, except his is carefully groomed. He leans forwards to study me.

'Jesus, you look like shit. What have you done to yourself?'

'Thanks for the reassurance, bro.'

'Exercise and get some sleep, for fuck's sake.'

'Is this your famous bedside manner?'

'Just being honest. How's the old place holding up?'

'Take a look.' I circle the room, letting the camera on my laptop pick up details.

'It could be worse. Anna wants to bring Christy over soon, to check out her Cornish roots. You'll have to decorate the bedroom.'

It would never occur to Ian to lift a paintbrush. While I was chasing girls and staring out of the window, my brother applied himself to every lesson. He met his American wife at medical school, then relocated to upstate New York. We talk for another ten minutes about football. Even though he's two thousand miles away, he still obsesses over the FA Cup. Ian's face softens when he mentions that his daughter is enjoying playschool, then he looks embarrassed, like he's spoken out of turn.

'Give Christy a kiss from me.'

I assume he's about to say goodbye, but his face looms closer. 'Did they hold the inquest for your work partner yet?'

'The coroner needs another week.'

'Are you okay?'

I nod. 'Getting there.'

'Remember the best way to survive: sleep, eat, exercise.'

'Really? I've been existing on thin air.'

'And have sex, if you can find someone desperate enough.'

My brother's grin fades from the screen, and I imagine him in his lakeside house, feeling guilty about revealing his happiness. I'm about to rummage in the cupboards for some of Maggie's food when a sound stops me in my tracks. The keening is so desolate it makes me fling open the door. Shadow is sitting on the beach, head back, baying at the sky. Random fits of barking without any obvious cause are his most annoying habit. I'm certain the creature does it for the sheer pleasure of pissing me off.

'Pack it in, drama queen,' I say, as he slinks inside.

The conversation with my brother has turned my mind back to Clare's death six weeks ago. The thing that hurts most is that I could have prevented it. Judgement hung in the air at the station; voices falling silent when I reported for work. If it had happened to someone else, I'd have felt the same, torn between pity and blame. More than anything, I miss her raucous laugh, the kindness she preferred to hide, endless, crude one-liners slipping from her mouth. I wrench the front door open again and step outside, cold air scouring away my frustration. A half-moon hangs overhead, hazed with brightness. I taught myself the names of the shadows on its face during my stargazing phase: the Sea of Tranquillity, Ocean of Storms, Sea of Clouds. Except they're illusory, of course. The lunar surface is arid, marked by lava fields or impact craters after shielding Earth from countless fatal collisions with asteroids. The moon looks ghostly tonight: a paper semicircle, cut out and pasted to the sky. Light spills down like alchemy, turning the ocean silver. A pulse of anger sends me back indoors. It's too late to help Clare, but Laura Trescothick may still be alive. I flip open my notebook and scribble a list of islanders' names until the words start to blur.

4

Rose keeps her torch switched off, eyes slowly acclimatising to the moonlight. There's been no word from Sam since Laura went missing, but she's too scared to approach the police. Her only option is to hunt for him herself. Up ahead, the outline of Badplace Hill blocks out the stars. Drystone walls lead her across open fields to the island's northernmost beach. The sea's beauty is undeniable – miles of black water, glittering like onyx – but the history of the place burdens the air. Smugglers and seamen fought terrible battles here, until it was named 'bad place', for countless massacres. Blood has soaked every stone. Wreckers set false fires on the hillside, luring ships to founder on the rocks. The survivors were slaughtered as they swam ashore, smugglers claiming their bounty.

Rose forages here by day for oarweed and bladderwrack, but at night the shore is haunting. She wishes she could return the island to a time of innocence, before her son was snared by promises of easy money. A plastic bag lies hidden in the place he described, under a white boulder by the path. She's tempted to hurl it into the sea, let the waves swallow it, but loyalty makes her hide the package inside her coat.

She feels even bleaker when she gets home. Sam confessed weeks ago that missing a collection would put him in danger. She's tempted to unwrap the parcel and discover what he's been carrying to the mainland, but whatever it contains, her home isn't a safe enough hiding place. The wind is rising to a gale as she digs a hole in the sand, sheltered by the ramshackle walls of her cabin. Placing the package at the bottom, she tamps the surface flat with her boot, then marks the spot with a piece of slate.

Rose calls her son again once she's back inside, but the only reply is silence. Anxiety makes her pull open the door to his room. The familiar football posters line the wall, nothing out of place, but her breath falters when she sees a small, silver item on his bedside table. He never leaves his phone behind, its flat battery explaining why her calls have gone unanswered. The window reveals acres of cold black sky, the sight of so much emptiness making her shiver.

5

My libido can't seem to accept that physical contact is so unlikely, it may as well give up the ghost. I wake up aroused again this morning, even though my sex life has dwindled to a handful of one-night stands over the past year, days too full of work to allow anything more. I take a cold shower, then head for the boatyard. The texture of the sea has changed; small, choppy waves, scudding closer as the tide rises. Drizzle wets my face as I walk inland, with the dog at my heels.

Ray looks unsurprised when I reach his workshop at eight thirty, as if my arrival was inevitable. I don't bother to ask if the girl has been found; he'd say if there was news. It's beginning to look like the kid slipped into the sea, either by accident or design. Rain clatters on the tin roof of the covered yard, loud as fingertips on a cymbal. The work he gives me is back-breaking. Splinters spike through my gloves as I lift the boards, hours spent doubled over, forcing strands of wool greased with lanolin between the planks. In the past I could master any new skill, but now my hands feel weakened, fingers failing to keep up. A low buzz of sound drifts from the radio, melody drowned by hammer blows. The smells are familiar too: white spirit, varnish, Ray's bitter French coffee stewing on the burner. It takes me forever to remember how to hold the caulking iron, but my teen-age summers labouring in the yard must have lodged in my memory alongside the island's geography. By midday the knack has returned. I hold the caulk loosely in my hand and tap it lightly with the hammer, to avoid jarring my wrist.

'Time for a break,' Ray says, as I drive wool into another seam.

It's one o'clock, the morning gone in a blur of physical labour. I study the structure again to see what we've achieved, yet it looks no stronger than before. It's still just a few raw lengths of wood, braced together by twine, but it beats staying at the cottage blaming myself for a tragedy I can't fix.

'Want a sandwich?' Ray pulls out a grubby package wrapped in greaseproof paper.

'Not now, I need some stuff from the shop. I'll be back in an hour.'

He gives a crisp nod. 'Leave the dog with me then.'

Shadow curls deeper into a pile of wood shavings, nose buried under his paws. The rain is falling more heavily when I head for the shop, so I jog fifty metres north along the shore. From the outside, Moorcroft Stores is a typical Scilly Isles cottage, with a low-slung slate roof and miles of shingle beach for its front garden. But Pete and June Moorcroft have turned their front room into a well-stocked grocery, with a tidy desk in the corner for Post Office business. It's clear the place is still their pride and joy, postcards arranged in decorative rows either side of the door, Rose Austell's sachets of herbs and jars of honey displayed on a high shelf. The couple are drinking tea at the kitchen table that doubles as a sales counter. They're as neatly groomed as mature models in an expensive clothing catalogue, both in their early fifties. Pete and June escaped from London twenty years ago, where he worked as an accountant and she was a chef in a top city restaurant, but they still look too smart for island life. Pete is a portly figure in a striped shirt, deck shoes and well-pressed jeans, ginger hair thinning. His skin is a little too florid, as if he's been overindulging in the good red wine he always keeps in stock. The shopkeeper's wife rises to her feet before him, her silvery hair cut into a chic crop. June has always been the outgoing one, compensating for her husband's shyness with a kiss of welcome. She looks thinner than before, dark circles under her eyes, probably because she moonlights as Zoe's cook most evenings in low season.

'How's the big smoke been treating you, Ben?'

We slip into conversation about the last time they visited relatives in Putney and how glad they were to return to Bryher. June does most of the talking, in her gentle west-London drawl, her husband nodding in agreement but never meeting my eye. Their range of stock has widened considerably since I was a teenager. The room holds everything a household could require, from tins of sardines to knitting yarn, local cheeses and luxury Belgian chocolate. They've even invested in a fancy new refrigeration unit. I wander around, taking care not to trip over sacks of potatoes and a pile of day-old newspapers. Once my groceries are piled on the table, Pete scribbles the total in his notebook, then offers an awkward smile.

'Pay us later if it's easier, Ben.'

'It's okay, I've got money on me.'

The routine never changes. I chuck fifty quid into the cash box on the way out and help myself to change. My box contains shampoo, razor blades, coffee, milk, a bag of vegetables and a hunk of frozen steak; enough staples to last all week. Something about the transaction reminds me why I've missed the island. It would be easy to cheat, but the system works because people play fair. I feel calmer on my way home, even though rain has seeped under the hood of my jacket, dripping down the back of my neck. The dog appears out of nowhere as I cross the beach, scenting the possibility of food.

Back at the cottage I eat my sandwich at the kitchen sink. It feels better to stay on my feet than sit down for a solitary a meal. Over the years, Clare and I must have eyeballed each other over a thousand grubby tables in McDonald's, Subway, run-down pizza joints and curry houses, always taking care not to be seen. How did I screw up so badly? I brace my hands on the counter until her face fades from view. The truth is, Ray's doing me a favour by providing me with enough hard labour to switch off my guilt.

Rain is falling in horizontal sheets when I leave the cottage again, the sea spitting its contempt at the land. Kittiwakes bawl overhead, the roar of the shingle deafening as the tide drags it away. I'm about to turn onto the footpath when something catches my eye. A black-clad figure is running across the beach, his movements jerky. He's approaching at speed, arms flailing like he's running a race, the dog's ears pricking as he draws closer. It's a boy not a man, wet fringe plastered to his forehead, dressed in sodden jeans and a thin shirt. He stops two metres away, panting for breath.

'You have to help me, please.' Danny Curnow has grown up since we last met; thin-faced and handsome, his boyband haircut dripping with rain.

'What's wrong, Danny?'

'Laura.' The word spills out in a sob. 'I can't leave her there.'

The boy turns and sets off again, feet dragging on the sand. My only option is to follow. Lights from the hotel beam down as I jog past, rain half blinding me. The building looks pristine against the cliff's backdrop, and I'd rather be locked inside one of Zoe's luxury rooms than facing the elements. We scramble over the rocks and drop down into the next bay. My brother and I spent our summers swimming here, but there's nothing welcoming about it now. The boulders are sharp as broken teeth, surfaces slick with sea moss. Abruptly the boy comes to a halt, breathing ragged as he points ahead.

'Over there.'

Her blonde hair is unmissable, standing out against the cliff's dark face. The girl is lying face down, the tide dropping her at the point where shore meets land. Instinct surfaces fast and in a heartbeat I'm an investigator again. I put my hand on the boy's shoulder as tears stream down his face, a trail of snot dangling from his nose.

'Take some deep breaths, Danny. Then tell Zoe to call the police, and bring Matt and Jenna here. Can you do that?'

He's wide-eyed with shock. I'd rather escort him back to the hotel, to make sure he doesn't keel over, but the girl can't be left alone. Shadow seems to have understood the gravity of the situation for once. He stays at my side rather than chasing ahead, waiting for instructions. Danny clambers back across the rocks, running again as soon as he hits the shore, but my own pace slows. Sprinting won't help the girl now. Her limbs sprawl across the sand, letting the rain wash her skin clean, not much bigger than a child. The boy has covered her torso with his jacket and when I pull it back, the sight stops my breath. I don't know whether she went into the sea naked, or the tide has stripped her bare. I've seen drowned victims' bodies before, their bloated skin a dull grey, but the cold water has preserved Laura's beauty. One of her arms is raised high, the other at her side. Apart from some raw grazes on her shoulders, she's a perfect life-sized doll, a bluebird tattoo at the base of her spine. The opening at the back of her skull is deep enough to reveal fragments of bone. Otherwise no serious injuries, or ligature marks. The only saving grace is that the kid hasn't been locked in a basement somewhere. With a wound like that, her life must have ended before she could scream for help.

'Go home now,' I snap at the dog, then point at the horizon. Shadow slinks away, tail between his legs.

He could pollute the crime scene by getting too close, churning the sand with his paws. I pull the coat over the girl again, taking care not to touch her skin. Then all I can do is keep the gulls away; they're circling overhead already, hoping for a free meal. My stomach clutches uneasily. The feeling worsens when Jenna and Matt appear on the beach, running across the sand. From a distance, Jenna looks just as she did years ago, when she starred in the fantasies of every boy on the island. Tall and long-legged, a typical surfer girl, hair the same raw gold as her daughter's. It's only up close that shadows of time and anxiety appear on her face.

'Let me see her, Ben.'

I tell her not to touch, but she snatches the coat away. When she cradles her daughter in her arms the incision at the centre of the girl's chest is revealed for the first time. I've seen enough stab wounds to identify it straight away, but it's just as well that Jenna hasn't noticed. Her raw cry of disbelief makes me turn away; it feels intrusive to watch. Matt's expression is blank as a new sheet of paper. My experience of murder scenes has taught me that grief comes in all shapes and sizes. Some people keep it battened down, while others put their heads back and wail. There's something pure about the way Jenna's crying, distress pouring out at high volume, while her husband remains glassy-eyed, arms rigid to his sides.

'Like a mermaid,' he mutters.

It's an odd comment, yet it makes sense. Even in death the girl's form is perfect, long hair rippling down her back. I'm still standing with them when a stone skitters down the cliff face. My head jerks back in time to catch sight of someone too close to the edge, peering down through binoculars, gone before I can identify him. Part of me wants to chase up the stone steps cut into the rock. If it's the same bloke that was hanging around on Gweal Hill on the day of the search, I want to know why he's spying on a murder scene. But I can't leave until the investigators arrive. Jenna is still holding her daughter, whispering so quietly her voice is drowned by the waves. She no longer looks like a high-school sweetheart as the wind batters us. Her hair's shorter, frown lines bisecting her forehead. Matt is on his knees, not moving a muscle, while his wife croons over their daughter's body.

6

A procession of islanders arrives to offer help. Zoe comes first with umbrellas, a flask of brandy and a dark blue bedspread covered in fine embroidery. Only she would choose something so beautiful for a shroud, the gesture a reminder of her kindness. My godmother and Billy Reese appear next. The chef's limp is still pronounced as they cross the beach, his bulky form wrapped in his old biker's jacket, but he's first to put his arm round Jenna's shoulders. Maggie manages to persuade the couple to wait for the police at the hotel. By now Jenna is too broken to refuse. Rain has soaked us all to the skin, but her strength seems to have melted away, even though she's flanked by supporters. She leans heavily on her husband's shoulder as they cross the beach, Zoe's arm supporting her waist.

Then it's just me, guarding Laura's body. At least her face is covered now. I don't have to confront those empty china-blue eyes. My godmother stands at my side, trembling in the breeze.

'Go back, Maggie. I'll be fine.'

She hooks her arm through mine. 'I'd rather stay.'

'You'll catch your death out here. Get on home.'

'God, you're hard to help,' she mutters. 'Promise you'll come for a meal later?'

'There's no need to keep feeding me.'

'You're not superman, Ben. Accept some support for once.'

'Stop fussing.'

I drop my head to kiss her goodbye, and she touches my cheek, brown eyes holding mine. 'Life will get easier. You know that, don't you?'

'Can I have it in writing?'

'Be at the pub by eight, or there'll be hell to pay.'

I nod my agreement, then watch her stride away, bright red waterproofs blazing a trail across the dingy sand. It still seems odd that such a powerful persona is trapped inside that tiny physique. Now that I'm alone, thoughts reposition themselves inside my head. It's time to stop feeling sorry for myself; this is my chance to make amends.

DCI Madron surprises me by attending the scene himself, instead of sending a minion. He looks different out of uniform – a small, neat figure, sheltering under a striped golf umbrella, watching the pathologist kneel beside Laura's body. Two female paramedics hover close by, ready to take her to St Mary's morgue.

'My granddaughter's the same age,' he murmurs, then turns to me. 'What's your name, young man?'

'Ben Kitto.'

His gaze sharpens. 'I know your uncle. An inspector with the murder squad, aren't you?'

'Not for the time being. I'm on extended leave.'

'Why's that?'

Something about his direct manner demands the truth. 'I resigned, but my DCI asked me to reconsider.'

'Yet you stayed here alone, guarding the girl's body?'

'Her parents are in no fit state. It's clear she was attacked.'

'That's conjecture.' He shakes his head sternly. 'The post-mortem will confirm cause of death. Debris in the sea may have cut her, or she could have fallen from the rocks.'

There's no point in arguing, but I know he's wrong. Deep stab wounds always look the same; a clean incision, then puckered skin where the blade exits. 'The press'll be on this like jackals, sir. Dead blonde teenagers sell papers, don't they?'

'I won't let them past St Mary's.'

'If you need more officers, let me know.'

He gives me a sharp look. 'Is that a serious offer, Inspector Kitto?'

'I've got the right experience.' There's no point in twisting his arm; I can tell he's the kind to make every decision himself.

'Thanks, I'll keep it in mind.'

He taps my number into his phone, then nods goodbye. When I turn back, all four adults are clustered round the girl's body, screened by a blue plastic wind-break. It goes against the grain to walk away, my concern growing as I trudge back across the beach. The post-mortem may not happen for days. Until then, Madron seems happy to pretend the kid died by accident, leaving whoever stabbed her on Monday morning wandering around Bryher at liberty. I'm certain that no one on the island force has experience of murder investigation, so the chances of the girl getting justice are slim to none. My anger is still bubbling when I see Danny Curnow, curled in a ball inside my porch, arms clasped round his knees, Shadow hunkering beside him. I've never been great at giving comfort but now there's no choice.

'You'll freeze out here, Danny. Come inside.'

The cop in me is curious to observe the boy's behaviour. It seems too neat that he found his own girlfriend murdered on the beach, when statistics say that he could have put her there. The kid doesn't move a muscle, forcing me to pull him to his feet. Once we're indoors I sit him at the kitchen table. If he's pretending to be in shock, he's doing a good job. His teeth are chattering, pupils pinhole small, hands jittering in his lap. Conventional wisdom calls for sweetened tea, but I offer him two fingers of vodka in a tumbler instead.

'Get that down you.'

Danny throws the drink back, then gives a rasping cough. I notice the watch on his wrist when he lowers the glass: TAG Heuer, top of the range, with a wide silver face. The expensive timepiece is the only sign that he's a millionaire's child – the rest of his clothes are low-key. After five minutes his eyes come back into focus. He's watching me build a fire in the grate to get him warm.

'Want me to call your family?'

He shakes his head in silence. Shadow's taken a liking to my guest, sitting at his feet while tears leak from the kid's eyes. I steer Danny towards the hearth, throw on another couple of logs. He starts talking in a raw monotone while I'm collecting more wood from the basket by the door.

'Someone killed her, didn't they?'

'We'll have to wait till she's been examined to know for sure.'

'I'll kill him.' His jaw clenches as he stares at me. 'I won't rest till I find who did it.'

'That won't help Laura now. What were you doing, when you found her?'

His eyes blink rapidly. 'I've been looking for her, at every high tide.'

'When did you get together?'

'A year ago.' He wipes his eyes with the back of his sleeve. 'She could have had anyone, but she chose me.'

Her parents' charisma must run in the genes. 'Did she get on with your family?'

A dull laugh slips from his mouth. 'My parents tried to stop us seeing each other.'

'How come?'

'They say she's holding me back.'

'She wanted to act, didn't she?'

'We both do. We're starting a course in Falmouth in September.'

His use of the present tense worries me. The boy hasn't begun to accept his girlfriend's death, even though her corpse lay right in front of his eyes, but that could be part of his charade. 'When did you hear she was missing?'

'Zoe rang on Monday morning. I was waiting for a ferry to work on Tresco, I'm a groundsman at the Abbey Hotel.'

'You should call your folks, Danny. They'll be worrying.'

He shakes his head. 'I'll text them.'

The boy fumbles with his phone, face pale as bleached cotton. It's tempting to fire out questions, to discover exactly what he knows, but I have to remind myself that it's none of my business, unless the DCI includes me in his team. I focus on keeping the kid warm instead, banking more logs on the fire. Ten minutes later there's a loud rap on the door.

The man standing in the porch is wearing expensive jeans and a designer woollen coat. Jay Curnow appears to have grown younger in the past year. He must be in his sixties, but there's no grey in his chestnut-brown hair, skin oddly free of wrinkles. It looks like he's paid for more than one surgical intervention since he attended my mother's funeral. His smile is artificial too, several kilowatts brighter than the situation requires. I could be reading him wrong, but the expression on his face appears to be relief.

'Thanks for looking after my son,' he says.

'He's very shaken, I'm afraid.'

'Never mind, I'll take care of him now.'

Danny's body language speaks volumes when his father strides into the lounge. Even though he's falling apart, he flinches when Jay's hand skims his shoulder.

'Come on, son, let's get you home.'

'Happy now, dad? You hated her guts, didn't you?'

'That's not true. We want the best for you, that's all.'

The boy's voice rises to a shout. 'You don't give a shit about what I need.'

Danny's face is rigid with anger as he barges past, the front door slamming. I expect his father to pursue him, but he stays put, sighing heavily. 'Another bloody disaster.'

'Sorry?'

'We tried to keep them apart, for his own sake, but the boy wouldn't see sense. First he quits school, now this happens.'

'I don't suppose his girlfriend chose to end up dead on a beach.'

'Of course she bloody didn't. That's not what I meant.' His stance changes, hands balling at his sides, ready to throw a punch.

'Your son's had the shock of his life, Mr Curnow. He needs your help.'

'Who the fuck do you think you are?' he snarls. 'Keep out of my family's business from now on.'

I watch him march away, torn between pity and judgement; anyone with common sense would know that obstacles only strengthen teenage love affairs. Curnow's aftershave lingers on the air, strong enough to leave a sour taste in my mouth.

The thoughts rushing at me are so exhausting, I lie down on the sofa without removing my trainers. My sleep is troubled by blank-eyed mermaids, swimming through my dreams. It's pitch dark when I wake up, my phone buzzing loudly, Shadow whining to be let out. There are half a dozen texts from Maggie, threatening to send out a search party. I swear quietly as I pull on my coat, but human company and a square meal are what I need. I fill Shadow's bowl with food and this time he takes the sensible option, staying behind, instead of facing the cold.

The pub is almost full when I arrive. The atmosphere reminds me of the night my father's boat capsized, when I was fourteen. People waited for news from the coast-guard with the same quiet anxiety. Faces turn towards me, full of questions, hoping I'll explain the girl's death. The afternoon's events will have circulated from house to house, but I'm in no mood for a public broadcast.

The only free seat is at Dean Miller's table. The artist is wearing his usual paint-spattered clothes, hair shaved to a grey stubble. I don't know whether he chooses to be solitary, or people have made the decision for him.

He glances up from his beer to study me. His face is keen-eyed and oddly youthful, even though he must be sixty-five, deep vertical lines bracketing his mouth, like he's forgotten how to smile.

'Okay to sit here?' I ask.

'Sure. But I'm not in the best mood.'

'Me neither. I won't disturb you.'

I take off my coat then head for the bar. Maggie raises her eyebrows when I ask for lager, levering the top from a bottle of orange juice without saying a word. She's single-handed tonight, doing a brisk trade while the islanders numb their shock. I make an effort not to catch anyone's eye. If one person asks a question, there'll be a free-for-all. I carry my drink back to the table and absorb Dean's silence, as he stares blank-eyed at his crossword puzzle. Billy is dressed in chef's whites when he delivers a plate of fish and chips to the table. The chef is still walking with a limp, the look on his face concerned.

'You all right Ben? You've had one hell of a day.'

'It wasn't my best. How's the foot?'

'Standing on it's not helping. The bloody thing looks like a puffball, but her ladyship needs me here.'

I gaze at my plate. 'That's your idea of health food?'

'Cornwall's finest, mate.'

He gives my shoulder a light punch then hobbles back to the kitchen. I'm halfway through the meal before Dean speaks again.

'Are you going to finish those chips?'

'I doubt it. Help yourself.'

'Don't tell my cardiologist.' His fingers are covered in faint blue and yellow stains as he reaches for a chip. 'Sorry I'm not the best dinner companion. Laura was a friend of mine, it's hard to believe she's gone.'

'You saw her often?'

'She came by every few weeks to pump me for information about LA, after she heard I grew up there. The girl dreamed of being in the movies.' His voice is a slow Californian drawl as his eyes swim out of focus. I can't guess why a teenager would befriend a man of retirement age with few social skills, but unlikely bonds develop on a small island, when choices are limited.

'Do you know much about acting?'

'My first job was painting backdrops in Hollywood, before special effects took over. I got to see plenty of stars misbehaving. Laura didn't care that Tinseltown has a million bartenders waiting for a break; kids don't hear negatives. We often chatted about it when she sat for me.'

'You painted her?'

'I do portraits sometimes, to take a break from the sea.'

'Did her parents know?'

'That was her concern, not mine. We did a straight trade: I paid her a few pounds, she picked my brains.' Another chip dangles from his fingers, as though he's forgotten it's there. 'Laura was so full of life.'

The thought of her waterlogged body kills my

appetite, food still heaped on my plate. 'What else do you know about her, Dean?'

'Something had her scared. She said my studio was the one place where she felt safe.'

'Was it boyfriend trouble?'

'I'm the wrong person to ask.' His lips seal in a hard white line.

Dean may be an incomer, but he understands the island's rules. If people speculate about each other's problems in a place this small, it would tear itself apart. By now I've had enough of the artist's tense company. I scan the room for the brunette, but there's no sign of her, which is a mixed blessing. A glimpse of that serene face would be a reward after a horrible day, but complications won't help me. When I look back, Dean seems relieved to be alone, picking through my leftovers. I give Maggie a quick salute then hurry out into the cold. My frustration builds as I check my phone. I've been hoping for a text from Madron, but nothing's arrived.

The sea is at low tide on the way home, water whispering to the land. I stand still, absorbing silence and cold, the last molecules of London atmosphere lifting from my skin. When I start walking again, a figure sways out of the mist. At first it looks like a man's lumbering outline, but it's my old teacher's wife, Emma Horden, wearing a black anorak, shambling over the rough ground. She's muttering to herself, round face marked by tears.

'Let's get you home, Emma. Tom'll be worried.' I

touch her arm, but she jerks free, her hand battering my chest. For someone with reduced mental capacity, there's surprising force behind her punch.

'The girl was on the beach. Is she still there?' Her words are as quiet as a prayer.

'Laura, you mean?'

A look of fear crosses her face. 'Was it you that hurt her?'

'I'm a policeman, Emma, one of the good guys. Come on, I'll take you home.'

'Maybe you're lying.'

'It won't take us long. You'll be fine, I promise.'

Now her outburst is over, she lets me lead her along the path, docile as a child. Tom Horden is waiting at South Cottage. The teacher's expression is so furious, I remember how he used to yell at us to finish our work, but this time his anger is directed at his wife, one of his eyes ice-cold while the other burns.

'Where've you been, Emma? I hope you haven't been causing trouble again.' She crosses the threshold, stumbles upstairs. 'Thanks for bringing her back. She slipped out through the back door; I've spent the past hour searching.'

'Does she go wandering often?'

'All the time. I'm afraid she's getting harder to control.'

'What did you mean about Emma being in trouble before?'

He looks embarrassed. 'Last summer a tourist

accused my wife of harassing her on the beach. She said Emma threw stones, but I'm sure she was mistaken. She gets confused sometimes, but she would never hurt anyone deliberately.'

'Your wife said she'd seen Laura Trescothick's body on the beach.'

Horden shakes his head firmly. 'That's not possible, Emma was indoors with me when she was found.'

He barks out a quick goodnight as I turn away. His wife's behaviour is a reminder that the islands are home to some vulnerable souls, living on the margins. I remember reading that patients with Alzheimer's can grow violent as their illness worsens, making me wonder if Emma ever lashes out at her husband. I spent my school years fearing and disliking Horden in equal measure, but the only emotion he triggers now is pity.

7

Rose hasn't slept since hearing of Laura Trescothick's death. Anxiety has driven her from the cabin at dawn, to the last place the girl visited. Now she's standing on Gweal Hill, watching the sea race inland, the pink sky speckled with gulls. The earliest women on the island must have stood on the same spot, waiting for the fishing smacks to return, with the cold north-easterly breeze tugging their clothes. She needs some of their resilience now, but it's centuries out of reach. Rose stares down at the yellow spume coating the rocks. Its lacy texture can't disguise the granite's raw edges, capable of tearing a drowning man's skin to shreds. The image destroys her reverie. Suddenly her son's face floats above the waves, his dark stare pursuing her. If he's met the same fate as Laura, her life will be impossible to mend. The boy has been her world for nineteen years.

She sinks onto a boulder, limbs weakened by anxiety, shutting her eyes tight to picture where Sam might be hiding. If the police find him first, he'll go to prison. The boy has always been delicate, for all his rough good looks;

locking him up would break his wild spirit. It would have nowhere to run, the prison's concrete walls stunting his dreams.

There's no information Rose could report, if she contacted the police. The men who haunt the island's coastline may have caused the girl's death and Sam's absence, but they arrive in rusting boats as dusk falls, anonymous as the tides. It terrifies her that soon they will demand payment for the package she found, even though she can give nothing in return. She's still staring down at the sea when footsteps crunch across the gravel. Danny Curnow is approaching the peak of the hill, hands buried in his pockets, his expression desolate. She rises to her feet, falls into step beside him.

'You should be at home, love. Have you been out all night?'

He keeps his face averted. 'I have to keep my eyes open, Rose. The nightmares are killing me.'

'Laura wouldn't want you to suffer like this, would she?'

'It's my fault she's dead. If I'd stayed away, she'd still be alive.'

Rose rests her hand on his arm. 'Come back to the cabin. I'll give you herbs to help you get some sleep; there's no need to talk, unless you feel like it.'

The boy hesitates, then follows her down the path at a slow pace, too broken to argue.

8

Thursday morning starts in front of the bathroom mirror. I've always hated shaving, even though it's a necessary evil; the skin I'm scraping clean is winter pale after months under wraps, but the ritual steadies me. It feels like I'm returning from a spell in the wilderness as my beard disappears down the plughole, until a whirring sound sets my teeth on edge. The sound builds to a grating motorised roar as I leave the cottage, a drone buzzing twenty metres overhead. Madron has placed an embargo on press visits, so the hacks have bought themselves an alternative. Shadow howls at the unwelcome noise, but it will make no difference. Aerial shots of the beach where Laura was found will soon fill every front page. I feel like shaking my fist at the sky, but turn up my hood instead, following the dog towards the boatyard.

There's no such thing as a solitary walk in a place this small. Time-lapse photography would show islanders constantly meeting as they go about their business.

The first person I bump into is Angie Helyer, pushing a buggy loaded with shopping bags. She looks different from the sassy waitress I saw at the hotel, dressed now in an ancient duffel coat with her three-year-old son Noah clinging to her sleeve. She was always popular at school, one of those kids who never made enemies. Her copper-coloured hair is cut in the same pixie-like crop she wore then, fine-boned face a little too pale. It's still hard to believe she's married to my oldest friend on the island, mother to a baby and a toddler, even though I was best man at their wedding. She grins at me, but the pale blue smudges under her eyes show she's running on empty.

'Need a hand with those bags?'

'If you don't mind, Ben. That would be great.'

'You're saving me from hard labour at the boat-yard.'

'Are you okay?' Her smile fades. 'It must have been terrible for you, finding Laura like that.'

'Her parents are the ones that are suffering. I'm trained to deal with it.'

'Jim'll be so pleased to see you, he's not been right since we heard she was missing.'

Her husband was a loyal mate at school; a scrawny, tow-haired lad, too sensitive for his own good. He was bullied mercilessly in the playground, despite my efforts to defend him. Things improved when he fell for Angie on prom night and never looked back.

'Did you spend much time with Laura?'

Angie nods vigorously. 'We did shifts at the hotel together, when the place was hopping. She babysat for us sometimes too, to give us a night at the pub. Such a lovely girl.' She stops speaking abruptly. 'Jim's under a lot of pressure with expanding the business, I worry about him sometimes. We've borrowed so much money for the new building, he hasn't been sleeping right.'

'Lily must keep you awake too.'

'You can say that again. My back's killing me from lifting her; sciatica, I think.'

'Sounds nasty.'

'Sorry, I shouldn't moan. I'm not exactly a yummy mummy, am I?'

'You look pretty good to me.'

She shoots me another tired smile as we approach North Farm. It's a typical Scilly Isles farmhouse: pale stone ringed by granite walls extending to the field behind. The Helyers have grown their stock along with their family. There must be fifty goats tethered in the field, a brand-new outbuilding behind the farm. I stop by the porch to help Angie carry her shopping inside, but she touches my arm instead.

'Go and see Jim. He's in the chicken shed.'

'Can you mind the dog? Chasing birds is his favourite hobby.'

She rolls her eyes. 'Sounds like a typical male.'

Shadow follows her eagerly, no doubt hoping for food. When I open the barn door, dozens of chickens are pecking the dusty floor, early light spilling through the windows. Jim's kneeling by the roosting house, carefully placing eggs in a straw-lined box, so focused on his task that he doesn't see me arrive. I can't help smiling at the sight of him scrabbling in the straw. He's filled out a little since the old days, but his untidy hairstyle is still more suitable for a poet than a farmer. My mind fills with the long days of summer, when we used to scour the beaches in his canoe, looking for girls and adventures. When he finally swings round, his face breaks into a grin.

'Trust you to creep up on me.' He rubs loose straw from his hands, then slings his arm round my shoulder. 'How's life, Ben?'

'Mustn't grumble.'

He studies me again. 'You've been overdoing it.'

'Works been tough lately, that's all.'

'Let's go to the pub one night, drown our sorrows.'

'Sounds good to me.' The sympathy on his face makes me smile, it's always been his default reaction. 'This place has grown, man. I need a tour of your new enterprise.'

I should be at the yard by now, but the pride on his face won't let me walk away. He shows me round the newly built barn, then the cheese house. An industrial churn stands beside a steel table and refrigeration unit, dozens of round cheeses stacked on a shelf, wrapped in muslin.

'Smells great in here,' I say. 'Makes me want to sample the produce.'

'Take some with you. Local restaurants buy our stuff now; any more orders and we'll be taking on staff.'

'You'll be the island's richest tycoon.'

'I doubt it. We've borrowed cash from everyone with money to loan, and we've got the mother of all mortgages.' The anxiety in his voice grows clearer with each word.

'It must have hit you and Angie hard, about Laura.'

He shakes his head. 'She was so young, sweet-natured too. The kids loved her. How could something like that happen here?'

'Someone must know. It has to be an islander.'

'Who'd hurt a girl that age?' He studies me again as if I should have the answer at my fingertips.

Even though he's a family man running his own business, Jim's face is childlike, hazel eyes round and questioning. He and Angie rarely leave the islands; Laura's death must feel like losing a relative.

'Got time to see Lily and Noah?'

'I'd love to, mate, but another day. Let's have that drink soon.'

Some of the tension slips from his face. 'I promise to be better company then.'

He returns to work immediately, so immersed in collecting eggs he's forgotten me already. I whistle for the dog as I leave, waving goodbye to Angie as Shadow barrels down the path. The couple's reactions prove that Laura Trescothick's death is having a ripple effect, with even Bryher's happiest families feeling the impact.

Ray is waiting for me in the yard, spooning coffee into the battered pot he's used since I was a kid. He gives me a sober glance, but doesn't mention the drone still buzzing overhead. There's no way of knowing whether his solemn expression is a response to my lateness or Laura's death. His silence is a saving grace, although it makes me wonder where his emotions have been hidden all these years. Maybe a lifetime of hammering copper nails into decking board has helped to vent them. He leans down to scratch the dog's ears, then hands me a mug of black coffee, strong as battery acid.

'Jesus, that's foul.'

'Only way to drink it.' He looks amused. 'Help me with the steamer, can you?'

We spend the next hour lifting wood from the coffin-shaped metal box. Ray tests each piece for pliancy with the flat of his hand before deciding whether to return it to the heat. The wood needs to be supple, but not so saturated it will splinter when it's shaped. He examines each plank closely, checking it's absorbed enough moisture. My phone buzzes loudly in my pocket as I close the lid. It's Zoe, inviting me for a lunchtime drink. I fire off a quick acceptance, then text Madron to request a meeting. The dead girl is still at the front of my mind, so I may as well repeat my offer. With any luck, the DCI will buckle under pressure. When I glance through the open doors, a delivery boat is mooring on the quay.

'That's the oak,' Ray says. 'Want to bring it in for me?'

'What did your last slave die of?'

At least the rain's stopped, the sea as flat as sheet metal, etched by a ripple of waves. It takes an hour to haul the strakes and planks inside. I've always loved the smell of untreated oak; heavy as tar, not sweet and cloying like cedar. The task makes my shoulders ache, the back of my neck slick with sweat as I regret cancelling my gym membership. Ray produces his usual grease-proof lunch, which is my signal to leave. Shadow trots ahead, tail wagging; he's adjusting to island life more easily than me, happy to roam where he pleases. The curtains in Matt and Jenna's windows are still drawn as I pass through the village. Laura's younger sister Suzanne must be sitting in darkness with her parents, too fragile to return to school. Tupperware boxes are stacked by their front door, as if the islanders believe that food is the antidote to grief.

I call at the cottage to clean up, selecting a fresh T-shirt and my only decent jacket. At the hotel, I leave Shadow on the patio, giving him a stern warning to behave. Zoe's behind the bar, charming the last few guests of the season, while another group eats lunch by the panoramic window. It's easy to see why visitors spend a fortune to wake up here, beside acres of uninterrupted sea. From the seating area there's a view of the bay where Laura was found. I'm still wiping the image from my mind when Zoe appears at my side. She's wearing black trousers and a glittering silver blouse, hair slicked back from her face. She looks calm enough, but on closer inspection I can tell she's preoccupied.

'Look at you, handsome.' She runs a fingertip along my newly exposed jaw.

'What are you after, Zoe?'

'You're the hero of the hour, that's all. Like the old Ben, all dominating and in control. I almost fancied you.'

'Careful,' I say. 'You'll break the habits of a life-time.'

'Don't worry, I'm off relationships.'

'Pity, I chose my best clothes, just to seduce you.'

She wrinkles her nose. 'If those jeans are your best effort, you'll be single a long time.'

'You do wonders for my ego.'

We find a table by the window, a waitress bustling over with glasses of beer. The routine between us has lasted all our lives, affectionate insults strengthening a friendship that becomes more ingrained each year. After teasing me about my shoddy clothes for another few minutes, Zoe's face turns serious.

'Are you okay?' she asks, her eyes glistening. 'I feel like crap and I didn't even see Laura's body.'

'I'll survive.' After ten years of murder investigation, death no longer seems shocking, just sad and wasteful. 'Danny got there first, not me.'

'How is the poor kid?'

'Desperate to get his hands on the killer, rowing with his mum and dad.'

'That's no surprise.' Her face tenses. 'Laura's sister must be in a bad way. She and Suzie were like twins.'

'Nothing can help the family right now, except time passing.'

She gazes down at her drink. 'We should all seize the day, if something like this can happen to someone so young. It sounds selfish, but it's got me thinking about the future.'

'How do you mean?'

'Maybe I should get mum and dad to sell the hotel, chuck myself into singing, body and soul. It's the one thing that really makes me feel alive.'

'You've made a start, contacting agencies. It's a good way to test the water.'

'It's high stakes, Ben. If they reject me, I'll be in bits.'

When I look at her again, it's impossible to imagine Zoe's confidence waning. She faces every situation with her chin up, ready for battle. She carries on chatting at high volume about her musical plans, the overload of information distracting me from brooding about finding the girl's body. The next time I glance through the window Shadow is chasing a stick through the air. The tall brunette is standing on the shingle, making me wish she'd turn round and show her face.

'You're not listening,' Zoe complains.

'Who's that woman?'

She peers out as the dog bounds after the stick again. 'Forget it, sunshine, she's married. I was asking you whether I should do a press release for my new album.'

'What's her name?'

'Nina Jackson, but leave well alone.'

'Give me a minute, can you? I'll just check on Shadow.'

My friend's mocking laugh follows me to the exit. The dog races across the beach in my direction, but the slim woman is already vanishing into the distance, leaving me with mixed feelings. I wanted a close-up of that fine-boned face, but I'm no position to act. My phone rings as I prepare to face Zoe's ribbing. DCI Madron's voice addresses me with calm authority.

'Are you free for a meeting today, DI Kitto?'

'The last ferry left at two, sir.'

'Be on the quay in half an hour, our launch will collect you.'

He rings off before I can reply. It crosses my mind that he may just be agreeing to meet me out of politeness; he's probably appointed someone already to lead the case, the battle far from won. I turn to wave a quick goodbye to Zoe, then take Shadow back to the cottage and collect my thickest coat.

It's a bumpy ride through the Tresco channel on the police launch – an old speedboat with a grinding outboard motor. The skipper is the young PC who led the search party two days ago, Eddie Nickell. He explains that he's new to the job, pink-cheeked with excitement as the boat scuds into St Mary's harbour.

My last trip to the station on Garrison Lane was twenty years ago, to be cautioned for tombstoning off the sea wall. The small grey building appears unchanged; an empty desk in the reception area and a rubber plant wilting in the corner. I wait by the door while Nickell dashes ahead to announce me. Judging by the photo board, DCI Madron has just six full-time officers to administer law and order to the entire Scilly Isles; four on St Mary's, two more on Tresco. Time seems to be winding backwards to the days when bobbies knew every local's name. I can't help thinking about the station in Hammersmith, crammed with state-of-the-art computers, a high-end café and a gym used by two hundred officers.

The DCI's office is ten-foot square, the phone on his desk antique. His pinboard holds pictures of community events, including one of him opening the Tresco gig race, rowing boats lined up at the starting point. It's impossible to imagine myself in his shoes, being the friendly face of law enforcement. Madron sits behind his desk, giving me a shrewd grey stare, his blue tie tightly knotted. The word dapper was invented for men like him, making me feel huge and dishevelled by comparison.

'Tell me why you're so keen to be involved, Inspector Kitto.'

'I thought your team might have a skills gap in murder investigation.'

'That's certainly true,' he says with a brief smile. 'Your DCI's worried about your mental health.'

'Sorry?'

'I called Sarah Goldman today. She says you were awarded a Queen's Medal for the undercover work you did with your partner, before she died. Your boss thinks you should spend your time here recuperating, not working on another murder investigation.'

'I'm fully recovered. The counsellor signed me off with a clean bill of health.'

'Goldman warned me you can be obsessive.' He flips open his notebook. '"Arrogant at times, inclined to ignore procedure." If you worked for me, I'd remain in full control of the case.'

'Of course, sir.'

'The island community is so small, every arrest happens in plain sight.' He gestures round the room, which contains only a filing cabinet and a shelf full of manila files. 'You probably couldn't cope with our primitive facilities anyway.'

'That's not a problem. I was born here, remember.'

'I suppose that would be an advantage. The islanders need someone they can trust; a stranger might make them close ranks.' He gives me an expectant stare. 'Are you serious about leading the investigation into Laura Trescothick's death?'

'You're offering me the job?'

'I haven't decided.'

'Has the pathologist filed his report?'

'The post-mortem's later today. If you want to be SIO, you should attend. His initial findings suggest foul play.'

The memory of Jenna weeping over her daughter's body and Matt too broken to speak makes me give a brisk nod. 'I'll go, if you give me the case.'

'We'll talk about that after the autopsy. I need to phone the hospital first – let Dr Keillor know you'll be attending.'

It's only when Madron lifts his phone that I realise I've been manoeuvred. His expression is calm as he speaks into the old-fashioned receiver in his quiet West Country burr. He probably expected just this outcome. Not only has he offloaded the investigation, he's saved himself the trauma of watching a young girl being sliced apart.

The post-mortem takes place in St Mary's hospital. The humble building looks like a row of Portakabins, a middle-aged receptionist pointing me down the corridor with a look of distaste, as if she recognises me as the type of man who enjoys ogling dead bodies. In reality, the thought of seeing Laura Trescothick's corpse again is inducing a cold sweat.

Dr Keillor is mumbling to himself as I push open the door. He looks well past retirement age, sparse grey hair barely covering his bald patch, a shirt and tie under his brown corduroy suit, as if autopsies are just another day at the office. His black-rimmed spectacles magnify his eyes so powerfully, his gaze feels like being placed under a microscope.

'I can't dawdle today, Inspector Kitto. I'm booked on the six o'clock ferry.' His voice sounds regretful, as if he'd rather spend all night dissecting the girl's body. 'You can ask questions when the procedure ends.'

'Fine by me.' I take up my position, leaning against the wall opposite.

He smiles as he slips on his white coat. 'A man of few words, I see. That's good, I prefer to work uninterrupted.'

Keillor seems to forget my presence when he removes the sheet from Laura's body. The girl's golden hair is the only bright thing left in her possession. Her lips are a deep blue, reminding me again of mermaids. I blink rapidly, clearing away my flight of fancy; she's just a slender teenager lying dead on a slab, cloudy eyes stretched wide open. Scratches on her ribcage and legs show where the sea has handled her too roughly, dragging her across the rocks.

It's only when Keillor cuts open her chest to perform the Y section that my legs feel unsteady. I've attended dozens of post-mortems without embarrassing myself, but this girl is little more than a child, fingernails coated in chipped red varnish. I breathe slowly to stop my head spinning, focusing on details. Now that the girl's hair is pulled back from her face, I notice a bright pink, heart-shaped earring dangling from her left earlobe, the other one missing. Keillor is still hunched over her torso, using a probe to measure the wound in her chest, his movements deft and methodical. I try to remember how she looked when she was alive, while he removes her heart, liver and spleen. Last summer she was just a young girl playing on the sand, like summer would never end. By the time he's weighed her organs and sewed up her chest cavity, my breathing steadies again. The pathologist frowns as he peels off his gloves, washing his hands thoroughly with surgical soap that stains his skin yellow.

'This young woman met a savage death, Inspector. She was stabbed through the thorax, the blade piercing her intercostal muscles, then the left ventricle of her heart. There's a massive impact wound to the back of her head and most of her ribs are shattered, but the knife wound alone would have killed her. The cuts on her right palm suggest she tried to remove the blade, before falling a considerable distance.'

'Could she have stabbed herself?'

'Not in this case. Suicides rarely inflict chest wounds, because they research methods and learn that cardiac wounds are agonising. The blade penetrated her body by eighteen centimetres. Her assailant probably had to run at her to drive it that deep.' Keillor looks apologetic, as if he's embarrassed by such unpleasant news.

'Can I take her earring?'

Keillor looks startled but places it in my hand, a questioning look on his face. I'm not sure why it seems right to keep one of the girl's possessions, but I drop it into my pocket, before thanking the pathologist for his help and making a quick exit. The blast of cold wind that greets me feels like a blessing, scouring away the last hour. Madron has played a good hand by challenging me to attend the autopsy. Now I'm committed, whether I like it or not, a piece of Laura

Trescothick's jewellery burning a hole in my pocket. Someone used a long blade to put a sixteen-year-old girl through agony, and the bastard's still wandering around the island. The severity of her injury makes me certain that she was killed by someone she knew intimately. Such terrible crimes normally occur when a relationship sours, in a moment of madness. When I call at the station again, Madron confirms my position as his SIO. He advises me to hold a public meeting bright and early tomorrow, to inform the islanders of the state of play.

'I can only spare one officer from my team,' he says quietly. 'We can bring more uniforms over from the mainland.'

'That won't be necessary.'

A gang of officers scouring the island would send the community into blind panic. I need to start by interviewing everyone who was on Bryher on Monday morning; talking to a familiar face might relax the killer enough to make a mistake. I lean forwards to catch Madron's eye.

'Where do I send forensic evidence, sir?'

'The lab in Penzance.'

'That could slow us down.' The only transport to the mainland is the passenger ferry, or the Sky Bus from St Mary's to Land's End, both journeys taking time and effort to co-ordinate.

'You're on Scilly Isles time now, Inspector,' Madron says, observing my reaction. 'One piece of advice; treat the family with respect. You probably know that Matt Trescothick won a bravery award, just like you, a few years ago.'

'No, sir. I'm out of touch with island news.'

'He's had his troubles recently, but he's a volunteer captain on the local lifeboat. Matt saved a father and son from drowning, when they were swept from the rocks at Shipman Head.'

'You want me to treat him with kid gloves because he's a local hero?'

His face blanks. 'You'll get nowhere by placing his family under immediate suspicion. I'm asking you to meet them regularly, and respect the islanders' loyalties.'

'I'll bear that in mind.' I feel like reminding him that murder investigation is my speciality, but his advice is sound, and it's best to humour him.

A different officer ferries me home, middle-aged and calmer than Nickell. The journey is silent, apart from the boat's motor labouring through the waves as Bryher's rough outline appears. It dawns on me that the work I should be ignoring has followed me home. A twist of fate has made me senior investigating officer on a murder case I never anticipated, but there's no other choice. People I care for are at risk until the killer's found.

When I unlock the cottage door, Shadow emerges like a high-velocity bullet. He tears across the beach in a wild break for freedom, barking at high volume, while the knot in my stomach twists like a steel hawser.

The case has got me hooked already. It fascinates me that someone living inside such a tiny community could suddenly turn murderous, after the island has been crime-free for decades. Pictures of Laura on the internet news sites don't help me relax. Some idiot's posted one of her sunbathing in a white bikini, more like a pin-up than a murder victim. I'm still working on constructing a timeline at midnight, but my progress is slow. On my last murder case I had a team of thirty detectives, crime scene officers and the chance to hit the ground running. This time nothing's pinned down. The girl's body spent forty-eight hours in the brine, most of the forensic evidence washed away. The pathologist says there was no rape or molestation, just a stab wound to her heart and a massive impact injury. I close my eyes and picture the scene. Someone dragged Laura to the top of the cliff or she went there by choice. Why would a young girl climb a hill at dawn on a cold and blustery day, except to meet a boy? Danny Curnow's shock looked genuine when he was shivering in my kitchen, but he's keen to study drama; he could be a consummate actor. One thing I know for sure is that frontal stabbings are normally carried out by angry male killers. It takes rage, physical strength and bravado to look someone in the eye then stab them to death. Laura's injury is the kind you see after a pub brawl, fuelled by booze and testosterone, not on a small island on a sober winter morning.

Statistics are still bothering me when I drop into bed.

More than ninety per cent of female victims are murdered by their partners. I stare at cracks in the ceiling. Danny may be the obvious suspect, but nothing about this case has been convenient so far. Any male islander could have nursed feelings towards her. Names and faces of the people I've known all my life filter through my head, until sleep claims me just before dawn.

9

My new deputy arrives on my doorstep by 8 a.m. I was
hoping for a reliable old hand, but the officer Madron
has sent is Eddie Nickell, presumably because he lives
on Tresco and can be present every day. The constable
is six inches shorter than me, blond curls framing a
cherubic face, his voice reedy as a choirboy's. He offers
his life story as soon as I place a mug of coffee in his
hands. He went to Plymouth University to study law but
returned after a year, preferring a more practical job.
My heart sinks even further when he explains that he's
twenty-three years old.

'This is a great opportunity for me, sir. I'm keen to
hear about the Murder Squad.'

'Don't call me sir, Eddie. It makes me feel ancient.'
He carries on gabbling until I hold up my hand to
slow him down. 'I've arranged to see the family before
today's meeting. It's important that the islanders see us
supporting them. Remember, they're newly bereaved.
Let me do the talking, okay?'

Shadow's nowhere to be seen as we walk inland, but I can hear him barking cheerfully in the distance. It irritates me that I let him out for some fresh air, only for him to run amok when I'd rather he stayed out of mischief. It takes less than ten minutes to reach Matt and Jenna's cottage; the building is modest but freshly painted, earthenware pots full of flowers beside the front door. Two decades have passed since the pair were high-school icons; since then he's been a lifeboat captain and crewed on trawlers, until he was laid off, his wife working for a holiday company on Tresco. It's Matt who answers the door, his face solemn, no sign of his old swagger when he shakes my hand.

'Thanks for helping us, Ben. I'm glad you're in charge.'

'Anyone would do the same.'

'Suzie's in a bad way. Is it okay if she stays here, with my mum?'

'Of course. But can I see her first?'

The hallway is filled with framed photographs, smiling family portraits that already look historic. The living room smells of coffee and trapped air, curtains still drawn. Suzanne is slumped on the settee, her grandmother, Gwen Trescothick, beside her. The old woman is petite and formally dressed, her grey hair cropped short. Her calm expression reveals that she's so focused on helping her granddaughter, her own grief has been suppressed. Suzanne doesn't lift her head when I offer my condolences, breathing uneven as she tries not to cry.

When her father flicks on a sidelight she gives a moan of protest.

'You need to hear what Ben's got to say, love.'

Matt's eyes lock onto my face expectantly, as if Nickell doesn't exist. Distrusting outsiders is an island tradition: my new deputy is Cornish born and bred, but he's not from Bryher. I speak in a low voice to avoid panicking the girl.

'We'll have to work fast to find who hurt Laura. I'll need help from all of you.'

Suddenly the child's face looms closer, her skin blotchy with tears, long hair a shade darker than her sister's. When she grips my wrist, her nails mark my skin. 'You know what happened to my sister, don't you?'

'Only her injuries, Suzanne. We don't have any more details.'

'Would she have been in pain?' Her eyes are pleading.

'Laura probably didn't even know what was happening.' The white lie is all I can offer by way of comfort.

When I look up again, Jenna has appeared, her hand skimming Matt's shoulder. She walks to the window to open the curtains. Her dark clothes are as sober as her movements, but even now she looks striking, a tall blonde with perfectly symmetrical features. The dim light shadows her high cheekbones and wide-set blue eyes, but it's her expression that concerns me: I've seen that Valium stare before, bereaved relatives getting by on tranquillisers.

'It's time to get on with it,' she says quietly. 'We need to find the bastard who did this to Laura.'

'I can't believe it was an islander.' Matt's face contorts with anger.

'I'm afraid it looks like it must have been. No ferries ran the day before,' I reply. 'If you're ready, we should get started.'

No one says much on the short walk to the community centre, the couple arm in arm, as if they're providing each other with a lifeline. The atmosphere is charged when we go inside. Last time, people were hoping Laura would be found alive, but now the air's fizzing with anger. The killer is almost certainly in the room. Around seventy people are sitting on the folding chairs, talking in hushed tones, until I rise to my feet and silence falls. All of the faces here are familiar: Maggie and Zoe in the front row, Ray at the back, arms folded.

'Most of you know me already. I'm DI Ben Kitto, from the Metropolitan Police. I'll be running the investigation. I want to reassure you that we'll find Laura's killer, but in the meantime, you need to stay safe. We believe the murderer is still on the island, so keep your houses secure, and don't go out alone. No one leaves Bryher without my permission for the time being. We'll be using this hall as our headquarters. Before you go today we need to check our list to see who was here on Sunday night and Monday morning.' I scan the room again. 'Any questions so far?'

Dean Miller puts up his hand. 'Why do you think Laura was attacked? Maybe her death was an accident.'

'The murder weapon hasn't been found yet, but we know she was stabbed.'

The crowd draws a collective gasp of panic. Silence returns as I explain that everyone must provide the name of someone to verify their whereabouts on Monday morning, when Laura went missing. A few of the older islanders look shocked. The crime rate here is negligible, most houses left unlocked all year round. The only theft I remember as a child was a man's underwear taken from a washing line, then returned on April Fools' Day, sprayed baby pink. When I scan the crowd again, the tall brunette is alone at the end of a row. The hall is warm, but she's still wearing her coat, her expression distracted as I bring the meeting to a close.

I leave Eddie collecting details from the crowd milling by the door. My first task will be primary-stage interviewing, to rule out those closest to Laura. Secondary stage will include friends and distant relatives, the ripple effect spreading out to acquaintances. But the standard stages of detection mean little in a place where lives are so tightly intertwined.

It's not easy to stay objective when I return to the Trescothicks' house. Jenna, Matt and Suzanne huddle at the kitchen table, clearly exhausted. I've sent Gwen home, so I can focus on immediate family members first.

'I need to speak to you separately, please, before things are forgotten.'

Jenna looks concerned. 'Can't we stay together?'

'You'll remember more this way; I need every detail.'

'I'll go first,' Suzanne whispers. 'To help Laura.'

'Is it okay to talk here?'

The girl gives a timid nod. 'I suppose so.'

Her parents leave the room reluctantly. Their younger daughter is pale in the morning light, a few pimples dotting her face, but she'll be a beauty soon. At fourteen she's got her mother's tall, athletic physique and classic bone structure, her dad's wide-set brown eyes. Right now, she looks more like a terrified child than a fully fledged teenager, dressed in black jeans and an oversized jumper. I feel a quick burst of sympathy; the kid seems so shaken it could be weeks before she's fit to return to school. Behind her on the wall I spot a framed certificate with her name printed at the bottom.

'What did you win?' I ask, pointing at it.

'The Three Islands junior race, last summer.'

The annual swimming race is a local rite of passage. Every summer hundreds of islanders thrash through the waves from Bryher Quay to the west coast of Tresco, then back via Hangman Island at breakneck speed. To have won the teenage category the girl must be stronger than she looks.

'That's impressive. How long did you take?'

'Just under two hours.' My attempt at small talk has little effect, her shoulders still hunched with tension.

'That's good going; it almost killed me when I tried. You must be one hell of a swimmer.'

'Dad taught me, but I'll never be as good as him.' A flash of pride crosses her face then fades away as I put the Dictaphone on the table. 'You're recording what I say?'

'It'll be the same for everyone. Just as well actually, my handwriting's lousy.' I try to keep my smile reassuring. 'Let's start with anything you remember about Sunday night.'

She drops her head, twisting a silver ring on her thumb. 'Laura went out in the afternoon. I heard her singing in her room when she got back, around seven.'

'Do you know where she'd been?'

She shrugs. 'For a walk, probably.'

'With Danny?'

'She wasn't meant to see him.' The girl looks away. 'His parents didn't like her. Dad said she should forget about him.'

'But you think she met up with him on Sunday?'

'I don't know.' She still won't meet my eye. 'They went to the fishing huts sometimes.'

'Laura told you that?'

She blushes to the roots of her hair. 'They had nowhere else to go.'

The sheds are always empty on Sundays, the perfect place to take a girl when privacy's hard to find. I did it myself, back in the day.

'She never brought him here?'

'Dad's always around, they couldn't even talk in private.'

'Do you think Laura and Danny argued on Sunday?'

'She seemed okay when she got back.'

'Was Laura really keen on him?' The girl gives a single nod in reply. I can see the yearning in her face, a reluctance to accept that her sister's gone. 'Who was she seeing before Danny?'

She hesitates. 'Sam Austell, but she chucked him last year.'

'He's a footballer, isn't he?'

'Not anymore, he's back living with his mum.'

'How did he react to Laura ending it?'

'Not great at first. He kept texting and calling her for weeks.'

'Was there anyone before him?'

'Nothing serious.' Suddenly Suzanne's eyes are brimming. 'She used to be home more, with us.'

'You spent a lot of time together, didn't you?'

'Since I was small.'

'Did you hear her leave on Monday?'

'My alarm went at seven, but she'd already gone. She often took a walk before work, to have some time alone.' Suzanne wipes her hand over her face, smearing tears across her cheeks. 'The boat to school was cancelled, so I came back from the quay about half past eight and made Mum a cup of tea.'

'You've done well, Suzie, but let's stop there. If you remember anything else, we can talk again, any time.'

I can see she wants to say more, but isn't quite brave enough, despite my encouragement. When I lead her out into the hall, Jenna's waiting. She probably heard the entire conversation. In a standard murder investigation family members would be kept apart, to stop them copying each other's stories, but Madron is adamant that they will be more co-operative if they're treated as innocent bystanders.

Jenna sits opposite, only her hands revealing the strain. Her fingers are knotted, like a mountaineer clutching a guide rope.

'Tell me about Sunday night, Jenna.'

'Laura ran back up to her room straight after dinner. She's at that stage where she guards her privacy.' Her voice peters out like she's just realised that her daughter's wish has been granted in the worst way possible.

'She sounds the independent type.'

Jenna's face flickers with pride. 'Laura's always been a go-getter. She was ambitious and confident with boys too. She didn't take any crap.'

'How do you mean?'

'A lad she was seeing flirted with someone else, so she ended it, just like that.'

'How did he react?'

'She didn't let him come crawling back. My daughter never took any nonsense.' Her voice breaks as she struggles for breath. 'She was so headstrong, we clashed sometimes.'

'You argued?'

'Only because we're alike. I don't know what I'll do without her.'

She carries on answering questions, her voice breaking. The two sisters had been laughing and playing music on Sunday night, everyone in bed by eleven.

'Was Laura happy at home?'

'Of course. Why wouldn't she be?'

'No reason, I just need all the details you can give me. Did you know Dean Miller was painting her?'

'Laura loved going to his studio.' There's a note of panic in her voice. 'You don't think he hurt her, do you?'

'I'm just checking what people knew. What do you remember about Monday morning?'

'I heard the door shut twice, so I knew both girls had left. Monday's the one morning when I can lie in for an hour before work. I followed my usual routine until I heard the ferry wasn't running.'

'What time did Matt get up?'

'I don't know. He slept at his mum's on Sunday night – Gwen's been struggling since his dad died last year.'

Her voice is matter-of-fact, but the statement sets alarm bells ringing. Until now the family have presented a united front, but the loss of her father-in-law could have put them all under strain. She copes with the rest of the interview, but gives me a solemn stare when it ends. 'I knew you'd help us, Ben. That's why we wanted you in charge.'

'Sorry?'

'You were always smart and determined. If anyone can find out who hurt Laura, it's you.'

It amazes me that she's composed enough to offer encouragement, but it's a pity Matt chooses this moment to appear. His expression darkens at the sight of his wife's hand on my arm. I can almost smell the jealousy coming off him. I keep my movements slow and deliberate, to prove that her gesture is casual, but anger still surrounds him like a force field when his wife leaves the room. Once we're alone he fixes me with a fierce glare.

'I'll comfort my wife. You stick to finding the bastard that killed our daughter.'

'I intend to, Matt, but I need more information about Laura. She wanted to be an actor, didn't she?'

'Her drama teacher said she was a natural. She had charisma too, always popular at school.' I recognise the clench-jawed set of his face. The toughness of island life prepares you to handle your emotions, but Matt's stoicism seems to be demanding a high price today.

'What do you think of Danny Curnow?'

'His dad's a prat.' He spits out the words. 'Jay Curnow's buying up Bryher, inch by inch. He thought Laura was unworthy of his son and heir.'

'He told you that?'

'The whole island knew.' The anger on his face raises my curiosity, but his dislike for Curnow will have to be explored another time; right now there are more pressing concerns.

'What time did you get up, the day Laura went missing?'

'About ten. I'd been in the pub the night before, so I took my time.'

'Gwen can vouch for that, can she?'

'Go ahead and ask her.' He stares back at me. 'What are you getting at, exactly?'

'Nothing, I just need to know where every islander was, the morning Laura died. Can I take a look at her room, Matt?'

'Why? She hated people touching her things.'

'It could give us clues.'

He leads me upstairs then backs away, as if he can't bear to breathe the jasmine perfume still hanging on the air. The room seems too sophisticated for a sixteen-year-old girl, with dove grey paintwork and monochrome New York skylines on the walls. Dean Miller must have been right about her yearning for a more glamorous existence. Her wardrobe holds exotic clothes she probably bought second-hand on the mainland: a red feather boa, dresses in metallic fabric, a fake leopard-skin coat. I pull on sterile gloves before opening her bedside cabinet. It holds tubes of lip gloss, a silver charm bracelet and a copy of *The Fault in Our Stars*. It's the only book in the room, but there are dozens of DVDs. A few are vampire and zombie movies, but most are Hollywood classics – *The Big Sleep*, *Casablanca*, *Rear Window*.

There's no sign of a diary, letters, or anything to

explain her state of mind. Her phone is probably at the bottom of the ocean, but her laptop sits on a desk in the corner. I pack it into an evidence bag, for the IT guys to process, then pull the bed away from the wall to check for secret hiding places. All teenagers have one, so I carry on searching. Eventually the breakthrough comes by chance. Something rattles when I bump against her wardrobe and I hear the clatter as an object falls to the floor. It's a tin box, six inches square, decorated with a picture of Polperro Beach, in chipped enamel paint. The lid is so tight it takes effort to prise it open. Inside there are two photos of Sam Austell. They show him as a burly, dark-haired youth, giving the camera an irritable stare, as if he resents anyone stealing his image. I don't know much about the boy, apart from his sporting prowess and the fact that his mother keeps bees. Tucked beneath the pictures is a neat silver package. When I peel back the foil, a chunk of cannabis resin releases its distinctive smell of bitter chocolate and tobacco. A piece that size would retail for several hundred quid in London. Laura's personality is starting to make sense: a girl who loved to dress up and escape reality, by any means possible. It's too soon to guess if she was still in love with Sam Austell, but the cannabis stash could be the first of many secrets. I'll have to scour the island to find the rest.

10

Leaving the cabin takes all of Rose's courage today, hunger finally forcing her outdoors. The winter sun feels fierce enough to singe her skin, gulls screaming out warnings, the sea's drumbeat hammering the shore. She screws up her eyes to search for her son's outline, but sees only the *Bryher Maid* crossing the sound to Tresco, a thin stream of smoke trailing from its engine.

Rose tries to steady her thoughts as she walks. She taught Sam self-sufficiency as a child. He knows where to find edible herbs and berries, even in winter. The boy watched her dress his scrapes and bruises with dock leaves, capable of identifying nature's antiseptics in any hedgerow. But what if he's alone somewhere, unable to move? Her panic is still simmering when she reaches Moorcroft Stores. Luckily, June is alone, tidying shelves, the shopkeeper offering her a smile of welcome, the radio playing quietly in the background.

'Good to see you, Rose. Got time for a cuppa?'

'Not today, I've got things to do.' She puts her cardboard box on the table, filled with sachets of wild camomile and meadowsweet, jars of autumn honey.

'This is perfect,' June says, poking through the contents. 'Guests from the hotel bought the last lot. One woman said your calendula oil helped her eczema.'

'It cures most skin complaints.'

'Sit for a while, please. I could use some company.'

June's soft voice helps Rose relax. She listens in silence to her small talk, watches her place bread, eggs and cheese in a bag, along with pasta, coffee, tins of tomatoes. When the shopkeeper puts the bag at her feet, she feels the usual surge of embarrassment.

'That's too much.'

'We owe you from last week.' June's calm eyes study her face. 'Are you okay? You don't seem yourself.'

Rose is about to explain, but June's husband rushes in from the back room, making her fall silent. Pete Moorcroft looks out of place as usual, more like a bank manager than a shopkeeper. He has no respect for the old remedies, offering a brusque greeting before telling his wife about a late delivery. Something cold in his far-seeing eyes makes Rose shiver as she tightens her coat. She scoops up the bag of groceries and hurries away without saying goodbye, but the man follows her outside.

'Rushing off so soon, Rose? That's a pity. It's time we had a chat, isn't it?' The man's florid face presses too close, but his gaze never meets hers.

'Nothing to talk about.'

'That's not true. I'll drop by soon, we've got plenty to discuss.'

The sneer on Pete Moorcroft's ruddy face makes Rose back away. She clutches her supply of provisions closer to her chest, before stumbling home across the shore.

11

Laura Trescothick's parents look shocked when I show them the cannabis, both claiming that she never used drugs. Either they had no idea, or they're putting on a convincing show. But why would a kid who was desperate for money suddenly blow hundreds on a stash that size? Someone must have given it to her, or she was involved in small-scale dealing. It's noon when I leave their house with the laptop and tin box wrapped in evidence bags. All the girl seems to have left behind is a room lined with dreams and a distraught family. I trudge back home to look for Shadow, but there's no sign of him, making me grit my teeth in frustration. At the community hall, Zoe is keeping Eddie company. He seems to have fallen under her spell already, cheeks reddening as she focuses on him.

'I hope you're not distracting my officer, Zoe.'

'I came to offer you a flask of coffee. It's bloody freezing in here.'

'That would be great, thanks.'

She disappears in a flurry of long limbs and canary-yellow jeans, Shadow seizing his moment to slink through the open door.

'You should be at home,' I tell him.

'He's beautiful.' Nickell leans down to stroke him. 'I've always fancied a wolfdog.'

'Solve the case and he's all yours.'

'Seriously?'

'Cross my heart.'

The constable looks like a child at Christmas, and it dawns on me again that my only helper is as excitable as a boy scout, but at least he's keen. Eddie has been busy checking the names of the seventy-two permanent residents present on Bryher at the time of Laura's death. Twenty-six more were absent because they leave the island each winter. Most of them take factory or labouring jobs until the tourist season starts again at Easter. Few of the people listed have any reason to harm anyone, let alone a sixteen-year-old girl. The party of elderly American historians staying at the hotel have already been ruled out; the security camera above the desk would have captured them exiting the building. I've already given the go-ahead for them to leave when their visit is due to end in a few days' time.

'Have Organised Crime made many drug-related arrests in the past year?' I ask.

Eddie shakes his head. 'Contraband goes through the islands fast, but there was a big coup a few years back. A yacht sailed into St Mary's harbour with five million quid's worth of heroin on board, bold as brass. The National Crime Agency are running another big marine surveillance operation, but they keep their cards close to their chests.'

'So where did this come from?'

Eddie's eyes widen when he studies the piece of resin that almost covers my palm. 'That's enough for one hell of a party.'

'We need to find out where Laura got it.'

'I'll contact the NCA.' He scribbles another note on his pad, like a secretary taking dictation.

'I want to see Sam Austell too. He was dating Laura last year, but she ditched him.'

'People saw him and his mum on Sunday,' he says. 'I bet they're both hiding in her cabin. She's a recluse, isn't she? The kids on Tresco are scared of her.'

'Rose is an expert on the island's plants and flowers; my mother swore by her remedies. I haven't seen Sam for a couple of years. What do you know about him?'

'He's nineteen, living at home, the apple of his mum's eye. He nearly broke into the first team at Plymouth last year, till they released him for attitude problems. He's gone off the rails since then. I nearly arrested him last month, for drunk and disorderly.' Eddie glances down at his notes. 'Laura called him half a dozen times in the month before she died.'

'I doubt he'd wait a whole year to get even for being dumped, but we need to rule him out. Have you had any luck with other calls Laura made?' Even though her phone's missing, her provider has issued a printout of numbers dialled and received in the past six months.

'I've traced them all.'

'That's quick work, we can check the list later. I need to visit Danny Curnow first.' Something about Laura's boyfriend has been nagging at me, ever since I found him huddled on my porch.

'Can I come along, to see your interview technique?'

'Find the Austells first, Eddie. You can take the dog.'

I reach the Curnows' place in just fifteen minutes. The house lies beyond the pub on the north-eastern shore, nothing like the rest of the island's low stone cottages. It's a sleek glass box with a metallic roof, windows shimmering with light. Jay Curnow is wearing the same expensive clothes as before, but this time he greets me with a handshake, instead of clenched fists. His reason for keeping the years at bay becomes clear when I meet his wife. Patty Curnow looks young enough to be his daughter, blonde stripes in her long chestnut hair, skin glowing from a sunbed tan, even though her smile barely rises above freezing. The Curnows' hallway could feature in *Grand Designs*, with a cathedral-height ceiling and a marble staircase rising in a sinuous curve.

'Danny's not himself,' Patty says. 'He's hardly been out since it happened.'

'Can I speak to you both before I see him?'

She leads me into a living room designed to impress, high heels clacking on the wooden floor. A glass wall provides panoramic views over the sound to Tresco. It doesn't require expert knowledge to guess that the furniture and artworks cost serious money.

'You've got a beautiful place here,' I say.

'So I should hope,' Jay's reply is deadpan as he gestures for me to sit down. 'The construction was a nightmare. The house is anchored on a steel platform, so we could build on sand.' He looks in my direction. 'I've seen your place on Hell Bay. Ever thought of selling it?'

'Never. It's been in my family three generations.'

'Let me know if you change your mind.'

Jay Curnow's knowing smile suggests that most people can be persuaded, with the right cash offer. I glance around the room again, surprised that he's comfortable talking about property deals so soon after Laura's death. One of Dean Miller's seascapes hangs over the fireplace, a riot of turquoise waves, beside several family photos taken when Danny was small. The Curnows are immaculately groomed in each shot, the child's hair combed smooth as he beams for the camera. Even in that setting, Jay's expression is combative, as if winning battles is his sole reason for getting out of bed each morning.

'How's Danny been?' I ask.

'Beside himself, as you can imagine.'

'It must be hard for you all.'

'The kid seems haunted.' Curnow's gaze shifts to the view outside, lingering there until his wife's staccato footsteps break the silence. She deposits a coffee tray on a glass table. Up close, her eyelashes are soot black, patches of dark pink make-up glittering on her cheeks, her perfume too sweet for my taste. She's studying me closely now, like I'm an unpleasant substance on the sole of her shoe.

'Did you spend much time with Laura, Mrs Curnow?'

She hands me a cup and saucer. 'We hardly saw her. Danny took her to Tresco some evenings, but it was awkward, because of the cottage.'

'How do you mean?'

'I own several properties on Bryher,' Jay replies, 'including Tide Cottage.'

I stare at him. 'But Jenna grew up there. It belonged to her parents.'

'The Trescothicks rent it off me now. They're not great tenants.'

The reason for Matt's contempt suddenly crystallises. 'Why did you stop your son seeing Laura?'

'She was holding him back. Until she came along he was planning to do business studies at uni, then suddenly he's starry-eyed about some drama course. I put my foot down, obviously. Right now he thinks we're the bad guys, but he was chucking his life away.'

'We wanted Danny to stay at school to finish his A-levels,' Patty agrees. 'Studying acting at college would never get him a job.'

'So he wasn't allowed to see Laura?'

'He can do as he likes,' she snaps. 'We're not

monsters. We let him go wherever he wants, but she wasn't welcome here.'

'Did you know that they were planning to live together, in Falmouth this autumn? They'd paid a deposit on a flat.'

Patty gawps at me, her husband releasing a hiss of disbelief. 'There's no way he'd go behind our backs.'

'We've gone through Laura's bank records, and the landlord confirmed it yesterday. What was Danny doing the morning Laura went missing?'

'He tried to get to Tresco, but the ferry was cancelled, so he came home till it started running again. I was here the whole time.' Words spill from Patty's mouth, but Jay remains silent, eyes trained on Dean Miller's painting, like he's measuring every wave.

'Did either of you notice what time your son left in the morning?'

Jay's gaze slips to the floor. 'I was having a lie-in, after working late the night before.'

'I made breakfast for him, around eight,' Patty says. 'Then he rushed straight out. He didn't talk much, to be honest, but he seemed fine.'

'That's helpful, thanks. Can I speak to Danny now, please?'

The couple's actions baffle me. Surely anyone with two brain cells would know that separating teenagers is the surest way to unite them? They're slow to comply with my request to see their son, but silence works in my favour. After a long waiting game, Patty leads me up the lavish staircase, with its glass and chrome balustrades. The interior is too ostentatious for my taste, but the outlook is dazzling. The tide is so far out, the beach appears to be coated by a thin silver glaze.

Danny's room smells of fetid air and the sharp tang of hair gel. The kid is hunched on his bed, in jeans and a crumpled sweatshirt, a rime of stubble covering his jaw. There's a hunted look in his eyes, making me wonder again if his panic at the murder scene came from fear of discovery, instead of shock.

'How are you, Danny?'

'How do you think?' he snaps back.

'I need to ask some questions. Is that okay?' He gives a rapid nod, arms braced round his knees. 'Can you tell me about the last time you saw Laura?'

'Sunday afternoon, we went for a walk.'

'Where did you go?'

His gaze slips from mine. 'Just round the island, I'd been waiting to see her all week.'

'Did you argue?'

He shakes his head blankly. 'We were making plans. She was excited about us leaving this autumn.'

I want to ask more probing questions, but the boy's rigid body language shows he's not ready to open up. 'What time did you leave here on Monday morning?'

'Early, but there were no crossings, so I came home.' His story echoes his mother's a little too perfectly. 'I reached Tresco by midday. My boss was pissed off, but it wasn't my fault.'

'Can you prove you stayed here till then?'

Danny stares at me, round-eyed. 'You think I hurt her?'

'Everyone has to account for themselves at the time Laura died.'

'Mum saw me leave, both times.'

'Not your dad?'

'I don't care what you think.' Suddenly his face contorts with anger. 'I loved her more than anyone. I'll find the bastard that killed her, whatever happens.'

'Don't do anything stupid, Danny.' I study him again. 'How do you get on with Laura's family?'

'I hardly know them. She was all that mattered.'

The boy retreats into silence, refusing to look up. His cavernous room is full of creature comforts: a sound system in the corner, bench press and free weights, shoe rack loaded with designer trainers. Everything is shiny and new, but the only personal items are the photos on his wall. They all seem to be of Laura: outside a café in a patch of sunlight, or lying on the beach, giving the camera a dreamy smile. His focus on her seems obsessive, adding to my concern.

'You really cared about her, didn't you?'

'We'd have got married.' A muscle ticks in his jaw. 'All I wanted was a fresh start, away from here. We'd have told our parents after it was too late for them to interfere.'

I'm sure plenty of teenagers would love to trade places with a pampered only child, getting his parents' undivided attention, yet the lad seems to view his luxuries as a trap. It feels cruel to bait him when he's at rock bottom, but it's my job to check his reactions.

'Laura was two-timing you, Danny. Did you know?'

'What?' His head jerks back.

'She kept photos of Sam Austell in her room.'

'That ended a year ago. He treated her like crap.'

'She called his number plenty of times. Laura still cared about him.'

He scrambles to his feet, face reddening. 'That's bollocks.' Danny grabs a wad of dog-eared envelopes from his chest of drawers, then brandishes them at me. 'She sent me these. It began before we started seeing each other. I'd get home from school and find a message in my pocket. The last one came the day she was found; she posted it from the mainland on her day off.'

'Why did she send letters instead of emails?'

'She thought it was more romantic.'

Laura Trescothick's handwriting is round and child-like, hearts and flowers drawn on the envelopes. There's no sign of the budding sophisticate, just an infatuated girl, pouring out her emotions. The package must contain fifty envelopes.

'Can I borrow them?'

'No way. They're private, between us.'

'They could explain why she died, Danny.'

He hugs the letters to his chest before finally handing them over. 'She sent texts every day too. I hate not getting them anymore.'

'We think she climbed Gweal Hill, the morning she died. Why would she do that?'

'To be alone probably, we had no privacy.'

'There were drugs in her room, Danny. Did you give them to her?'

'Of course not. She hardly even drank; I never saw her take anything.'

The boy's anger hangs over him like a cloud as I repeat the question, then his head bows and it's clear he's too drained to continue.

I mull over his answers when I leave the Curnows' house, with Laura's letters wrapped in an evidence bag. If Danny is telling the truth then the girl made all the running; she could have been texting him the morning she died. But it's equally possible that they'd argued, and he followed her there in a jealous rage. The more I discover, the more they seem like star-crossed lovers, the future constrained by circumstances. Laura's family were forced to sell their home, only to rent it back from the Curnows, but the teenagers ignored their parents' conflict. Back at the cottage I leave the letters on the table to read later. When I emerge again, Shadow is sitting in the porch, tongue lolling in expectation.

'Will you never leave me alone?'

His glacial eyes are impossible to read. I dump food in his bowl and grudgingly accept that I must copy his behaviour. To find Laura's killer I'll have to pursue the islanders hard, until one of them cracks.

12

Eddie is hunched over his laptop for most of the afternoon, hitting the keys like a fledgling journalist filing a late story. My old sidekick would laugh her head off if she could see me now. Clare was a hard-bitten Glaswegian with a black sense of humour, well-versed in every trick in the book. I've never believed in the afterlife, but if one exists, she must be tickled by the sight of me floundering, with only a well-mannered schoolboy to help. Eddie's frown reveals that he's got his own misgivings. Maybe murder investigation is less glamorous than he'd hoped.

'Tell me about Laura's phone,' I say.

'Most of her calls were local; to her mum, nan, sister and Danny Curnow. But I can't see why she called Dean Miller three times in the week before she died. One call lasted half an hour. Why would a young girl phone some weirdo artist in his sixties?'

'Let's go and find out.' The dusk is thickening outside the window. 'Then it's time you went home.'

'I don't mind staying.'

When he reaches for his coat I have to stifle a laugh. It's an old-fashioned gabardine like the ones primary school kids wear over their uniforms. We set off down the path with Shadow at our heels.

'Do you want me to do anything else tomorrow, sir?'

'Train yourself to stop calling me sir, then find out if any islanders have form.'

'I've already put most of their names through the PNC.'

'That must be testing your patience.' The Police National Computer holds details of every arrest, but works at a snail's pace, sometimes taking hours to spit out results.

The old schoolhouse lies on the outskirts of the village – lights glow inside its windows, the door to Miller's workshop hanging open. It's a mystery why a single man would choose to live in such a big place, with so many rooms to accentuate his loneliness, but the artist doesn't seem in a rush to accept company. We have time to read the school's motto still engraved on a stone lintel: 'per aspera ad astra', before he answers the bell. Miller has swapped his paint-stained overalls for a dark blue apron, tied around his waist. His quick gaze darts from Eddie's face to mine.

'Here to see me, gentlemen? You're welcome, but the dog stays outside. Those creatures give me allergies.'

I leave Shadow whimpering in the porch, Miller's house intriguing me as we follow him down the hall. My father was a pupil here in the sixties. I catch a glimpse of the high-ceilinged living room, with original floor-boards and wood-burning stove still in place and some of the classrooms left intact. The kitchen has survived since Victorian times with few alterations; quarry tiles on the floor, a cast-iron range and a wide porcelain sink. Miller's only concession to modern times is a trompe l'oeil painting on the wall, its wild swirl of blue making me feel like I'm trapped underwater at high tide. The artist must have been in the middle of cooking his dinner – red and yellow peppers lie on his chopping board, waiting to be sliced.

'We won't keep you long,' I say. 'Laura called you several times just before she died. Can you describe those conversations?'

'She wanted to let off steam.' Miller wipes one of his hands across his apron. 'You know how teenage girls are. Emotions overwhelm them; she wasn't having an easy ride.'

'In what way?'

'Home, love, ambition, the whole nine yards.' His penetrating gaze fixes on my face again. 'Surely you remember the trials of growing up, Inspector?'

'Of course, but I need specific information about Laura.'

'My memory's not that reliable, but her story never changed. She wanted to be with Danny, living a different life.'

'Was she scared of anyone? Surely she gave you more details?'

'We were pals, strange as it may seem. Often she just called to chat about something she'd seen on TV. It may surprise you, but the island's young people gravitate here. They sit around the house, or in my studio, treating the place like a glorified youth club.' He picks up one of the peppers and holds it to the light, inspecting the gloss on its skin. 'They're lucky to have somewhere to hide. My parents were so strait-laced, I had nowhere to hang out at their age, so I never turn them away.'

'You sound like a social worker.'

'Hardly, Inspector.' Miller looks amused. 'I'm more like a vampire. Being surrounded by all that youth and beauty stops me getting old.'

I carry on asking questions, but meet with a wall of generalities. Eddie's keen eyes inspect my face after we leave, clearly expecting me to unlock the old man's riddles. The artist's odd manner leaves me convinced he's hiding something, but it will take more than one visit to unlock his secrets. I walk Eddie down to the quay, then wait on the jetty as the small craft heads across the sound for the five-minute journey to Tresco, leaving a reek of diesel. My new recruit has impressed me more than I expected, showing plenty of initiative. Maybe his optimism will stop getting on my nerves after a while. When I turn round, Ray is standing on the quay.

'Hungry?' he asks.

'If you've got enough to spare.'

I follow my uncle upstairs to his living quarters. His kitchen contains only the bare essentials: a wooden table he built himself, rudimentary cupboards, oilskins hanging behind the door. Ray's food is basic too, a hunk of bread and beef stew, which he ladles into a bowl without saying a word. Shadow gives a loud bark of appreciation when my uncle sets another bowl on the floor. Ray nudges a glass of whisky towards me when we sit down.

'You look in need of a pick-me-up,' he says, the corners of his mouth twitching.

We eat our meal in silence as the waves darken, but my appetite has deserted me. I swallow the food for Ray's sake. When I look at him again, his eyes are a calm turquoise, as if nothing could unsettle him.

'Did you see much of Laura, Ray?'

He shrugs. 'Not really. I showed her and Suzie how to catch crabs from the quay when they were small.'

'And lately?'

'I saw her sneaking into the boat sheds with the Curnow boy now and then.' His smile appears then fades again.

'Who'd want to harm her?'

'No one, far as I know. But her dad's got a temper, after a few drinks.'

'You've seen him fighting?'

Ray rises to his feet abruptly. 'Maggie's the one to ask. I never go to the pub on a Saturday night.'

Out in the kitchen I hear him clattering plates in the sink. His living room is even more austere than I remembered, nothing on the walls except tide tables and a nautical map of the world, shipping lanes picked out in red. Maybe Ray keeps it as a reminder of his decade in the navy. My eyes drop to the table beside his rocking chair; it holds rolling tobacco, cigarette papers and a pair of binoculars. I feel a quick twitch of discomfort as I remember the distant figure on the cliff, peering down at Laura's body. When Ray returns with two cups of vile-smelling coffee, I point at the spyglasses.

'I didn't know you were a birder.'

He shakes his head. 'Boats, not birds.'

'Do you watch from Gweal Hill?'

'No need, I can see them from here.'

Ray studies the horizon while he sips his coffee. Silence returns as we watch the sea's surface, flecked with moonlight. When I was Danny Curnow's age, my uncle fascinated me; the only islander to have travelled the world, a naval officer, fighting battles in faraway countries. He never parted with his secrets, always keeping his cards close to his chest. These days I'd like to understand him better, to know why he's always been alone, but direct questions never get past his defences.

'Thanks for the meal, Ray.'

'No problem.' There's a half-smile on his face. 'Pay me back in labour tomorrow.'

'That could be tricky. The case is keeping me pretty busy.'

'One evening, then.'

'God, you're a slave driver. I'll see what I can do.'

The cottage is cold when I return. Shadow sits on

his haunches, waiting expectantly while I pile kindling with dry logs onto the fire, but the warmth fails to relax me. It seems odd that Laura wrote to Danny in an age of digital communication, but it could have been a gimmick stolen from the heroes of the old-fashioned movies she loved. The chronology's hard to follow when I leaf through her letters, most are undated, but themes emerge straight away. The girl was longing for escape. She describes both sets of parents as 'monsters', her only tender words reserved for her sister, who she seemed sad to leave behind. Each note begs for meetings, makes sexual promises, enticing him like a siren. They all carry the same hand-drawn picture at the end; a heart pierced with an arrow, like an old-fashioned tattoo. Given how she died, the symbol makes me wince. I gather the envelopes back into their pile. The memory of Laura's autopsy triggers a dull pain at the base of my skull, my regular headache making a comeback.

I drop another log onto the fire, sparks flying, and notice Shadow scratching at the door. A blast of sea air rushes in as he slinks outside. Hell Bay stretches out in a crescent, lights from the hotel glinting in the distance, no other sign of humanity. I close the door then warm my hands by the fire. It strikes me again that despite failing Clare in the worst way possible, it lies in my power to keep the island safe. This is my chance to clear the slate. The overhead light flickers wildly, announcing that another blackout is on its way. I grab my torch and carry on studying my notes, determined not to be distracted.

13

Rose is too agitated to focus on her herbal remedies tonight. She stands in the doorway of her son's room, hands clasped. There's a chance Sam has fled the island, like his father, who sailed away without looking back. But why would the boy leave so suddenly? She looks at a photo of her son after scoring his first goal for Plymouth. Other pictures from his brief sporting career are plastered across his wall; he loves to relive those moments of glory. The idea comforts her. Surely he will return soon, to claim his trophies? Rose returns to her kitchen, breathing deeper to steady herself. The air is sweetened by familiar smells of campion, lily of the valley and asphodel.

She feels calmer as she stands at the sink to wash up. There's nothing outside the blackened window except the sea retreating from the land. But suddenly something moves directly ahead. A man's face appears from the dark, making her cry out in shock. Her heart is beating too fast when someone hammers on the door. Pete Moorcroft stands on the threshold, staring at her.

'What do you want?' she stammers.

'Just a little conversation, Rose. You owe me that at least.' Moorcroft barges past, then wastes no time dropping into a chair. 'Someone on the island has a business proposition for you.'

'I'm not interested.'

'He'll pay a hundred and fifty grand for this place and the land behind.'

'Jay Curnow sent you, didn't he? Tell him to get lost.'

'The council want you out. Better sell while you can, buy yourself a little flat on St Mary's.'

'Does June know you do his dirty work?'

'What choice do I have? He paid for our place to be refitted, after the flood last year.' Moorcroft shifts awkwardly in his seat. 'Remember we provide your food. How would you survive if our little arrangement ended?'

'I want you out of here.'

'Curnow says to keep away from Danny too. He doesn't want his boy polluted by your mumbo-jumbo. It's anti-depressants the lad needs, not witchcraft.'

Rose flings the front door open, waiting for him to go, her whole body trembling. She knows it's important not to show weakness. Moorcroft buttons his coat slowly, his tone colder than before.

'He won't stop till he gets what he wants, Rose. I discovered that years ago. Do as he says, before you get hurt.'

When he's gone, she slumps onto a stool, head bowed. It's a few minutes before she can reach for a remedy to soothe her anxiety: foxglove, lavendula and feverfew. She dabs the oil on her throat and temples, but her nerves refuse to steady.

14

Sleep eludes me when I finally go to bed. I read *Of Mice and Men*, feeling more like Lennie than George, slow and lumbering, none too smart. I'm just drifting off when a noise comes from outside. The wind must be rattling the door; Shadow is barking frantically. I switch the light back on to investigate, but nothing in the lounge has been disturbed. When I look outside, something is lying on the step; a plastic bag with a rock weighting it down. There's no one in sight, but the dog is circling the house, refusing to come inside. When I shake out the bag onto the table, it contains fragments of paper. It doesn't take long to reassemble the photo of Laura Trescothick, which has been cut into five jagged pieces. I rub my hand across the back of my neck. Someone has gone to the trouble of leaving me a gift, and the message is clear. Laura's existence was torn to shreds, the killer reliving his moment of glory; or someone else wants to scare me away. He must have loved or hated her, to desecrate her image so viciously. I use the plastic bag to gather the fragments, taking care not to leave fingerprints.

When morning comes, I leave Shadow and the sliced-up photo with Eddie at the hall, then head for Green Bay to see Rose Austell, to find out why she avoided the last public meeting. Smoke puffs from the tin chimney of her cabin as I drop down the path. The place stands on the cusp between beach and land, her garden a tangle of overgrown lavender bushes, beehives clustered round an apple tree. It's a cross between a shack and a beach hut, with a corrugated-iron roof and woodwork daubed in a rainbow of colours, as if someone has been using up paint samples. The steps from the beach creak ominously, threatening to splinter under my weight. When I tap on the front door there's a rustling sound inside. Eventually a dark brown eye inspects me through the inch-wide opening.

'Can we talk, Rose?'

'Not today, I'm busy.'

'Don't you remember me? My mother was a friend of yours.'

The door opens another fraction. 'Helen Kitto's boy?'

'Five minutes, please. That's all I need.'

Rose's front room explains why some locals view her as a witch. Bundles of blackened roots, twigs and leaves are stacked to the ceiling on drying trays. The atmosphere is musty, as if the windows have been closed all winter, the cloying sweetness of honey and aniseed

scenting the air. Bunches of bracken and grasses are sus-
pended from the rafters, turning the walk to her kitchen
table into an obstacle race. Rose is a thin woman in her
fifties, wearing a woollen dress that looks home-made,
dyed black hair pulled back from a face that must have
been striking once, with a Roman nose and high aris-
tocratic forehead. Her necklace is made from fragments
of driftwood bound together by twine. I have a sudden
memory of sitting at her table as a child, eating bread
slathered with honey, while she drank tea with my
mother. Rose's serenity has been replaced by tension
since then, hands shaking as she makes me a drink. I
can see she's afraid of something when her hawk-like
gaze measures my face.

'Turned out handsome, didn't you? A true Cornishman.'

I smile at her. 'You're looking well yourself, Rose.'

'Helen was my friend. That's the only reason I opened
my door.'

'I appreciate it. How've you been keeping?'

'Not so bad.' She seems to be growing more close-
lipped with each statement.

'Did you hear about Laura Trescothick?'

She points at the radio on her windowsill. 'It was on
the news, and June told me about it, at the shop.'

It sounds like Rose's lifestyle is unchanged, bartering
with the Moorcrofts in exchange for food. I've never
been told who fathered her boy, only that she's raised
him alone. Her anxiety grows more obvious by the

minute, the tremor in her hands worsening as she fiddles with her necklace.

'Where's your son today, Rose?'

'I don't answer for him, he's his own master.'

'What does Sam do for a living these days?'

'Odd jobs mostly. Last summer he worked in the pub kitchen with Billy, after the football club let him go.'

'I could use his help. When's the last time you saw him?'

Her eyes narrow. 'Days ago. He'll be on St Mary's, with his mates.'

'He's not left the island.'

'Then he could be anywhere.' Her face is blank with panic as she twists a lock of hair.

'Something's upset you, Rose. If you tell me, I promise to help.'

'I fret about what the sea brings in, nothing else.'

'Can I see his room? I could get a warrant, but it's easier to do it now.'

'He's got nothing to hide.'

'So you won't mind me looking. You want to know where he is, don't you?'

It takes ten minutes of gentle persuasion, while Rose bridles, her hands fluttering in protest. Eventually she lets me inside her son's bedroom. The space is smaller than a prison cell, a narrow bed pressed against the wall, no furniture except a single wardrobe and a wooden chair laden with discarded clothes. The boy's only prized possession seems to be a row of football trophies, gathering dust on a high shelf. It doesn't take long to check under his mattress and run my hands over the items in his wardrobe. There's nothing here to implicate him in Laura's disappearance, except his vanishing act on exactly the same day. My concern only rises when I see a phone on his bedside table, plugged into a charger, beside a lighter and a packet of Rizlas. When Rose confirms that the mobile is her son's, it crosses my mind that Sam could have met the same fate as Laura, but I keep my suspicions to myself.

'I appreciate your help, Rose. When Sam comes back, can you get him to call me?' I pull a card from my pocket and leave it on her table, letting my eyes wander round her home again. There's nowhere a grown man could hide; no cellar or attic in this tiny cabin. 'How are the bees?'

'Hibernating.'

'Lucky them. Did your son ever bring Laura here?'

'Her sister's round here more often. Suzie's interested in my herbs.'

'Was Sam upset when the relationship ended?'

'Not for long. That one wanted more than he could give.' She stumbles to her feet abruptly. 'I've got work to do, Benesek. It's best you leave.'

On the way out she thrusts a jar of honey into my hands. It's clear gold, a chunk of honeycomb wedged at the bottom. I turn to thank her, but the door has already closed, making me wonder how many visitors cross her threshold. Rose's renowned eccentricity is a great defence. There's no way of knowing if she's hiding Sam somewhere on the island, but it's obvious she's keeping secrets. Something's put her on edge, yet she seems too afraid to explain. The boy's disappearance leaves a sour taste in my mouth that no amount of honey could disguise. Very few twenty-year-olds let themselves be parted from their phones. It's possible that the boy killed Laura, then threw himself into the sea, but the idea seems far-fetched. If he and Laura were both running drugs round the islands, they could have fallen foul of the same smuggling gang.

I have to make one more call before returning to the hall. Gwen Trescothick lives in a narrow cottage, the windows studding its pan-tiled roof, looking down on my friend Jim's farm. She answers the doorbell quickly, the distress of her granddaughter's death so soon after losing her husband apparent in her face. Her features are wizened, skin deeply furrowed as she attempts a welcoming smile. The place is small and neat as a doll's house, the opposite of Rose Austell's cluttered cabin. I have to dip my head to enter her kitchen, where every surface sparkles. The first thing I notice is a framed newspaper clipping on the wall. Matt Trescothick's face wears a grave expression in a black and white portrait, under the headline LIFEBOAT HERO IN DARING SEA RESCUE. She watches me expectantly and for the first time I notice that she's wearing hearing aids, head angled towards me when I ask my first question.

'What kind of girl was Laura, Gwen?'

'A sunny little thing when she was small, my husband adored her.' Her words ebb away. 'But she was ready to fly the nest. Matt wouldn't mind me saying things have been tricky since he lost his job. Laura absorbed some of the worry.'

'How do you mean?'

'They've got money troubles. Laura was trying to save, but her mum took half her wage. Jenna's never satisfied.' Her lips pucker in disgust.

'How do you mean?'

'Nothing's ever good enough to please her.'

I give a slow nod. 'Matt slept here, the night before Laura died, didn't he?'

'Can you blame him? I don't like him staying over, but a man wants to feel supported at home.' Her gaze flits towards the window. 'It's affected the whole family.'

'Do you remember what time he got up that morning?'

Her gaze slips from mine. 'Tenish, I think. He was the worse for wear when I cooked him breakfast. My son's still grieving for his dad; God knows how he'll cope with losing his girl as well.'

'He's lucky to be getting so much support.'

'I feel sorry for Danny Curnow too. I couldn't sleep last night – when I looked out of the window about three o'clock, he was wandering across the beach, like a lost soul.'

Gwen's statement puts Danny in the right place to have left the photo of Laura on my doorstep, but fails to provide a reason. We carry on talking for another half-hour, the rest of our discussion focusing on Laura. It builds my impression of an extrovert girl with big ambitions and a wide circle of friends, her grandmother unaware of any enemies.

Eddie looks upbeat when I return to the hall, the dog rousing to his feet to sniff at me before loping back to his blanket in the corner. My deputy still seems fascinated by the idea that the killer may have marched up to my front door, to leave his photographic tribute, but his excitement rises even further when I mention my concern for Sam Austell's welfare. If he's been running drugs round the islands, he might be in danger. I ask Eddie to alert the NCA and tell them that smugglers' boats could be haunting Bryher's shores.

He picks up the phone immediately, leaving me to study a printout of islanders with criminal records, downloaded from the PNC. Matt Trescothick is first on the list; despite his hero status, the guy served fifty hours of community service two years ago for punching a man outside the Rock, leaving him with bruised ribs. Then, just before Christmas, he was cautioned for affray outside a Penzance nightclub. It surprises me that the island's golden boy is losing his glitter; unemployed and picking fights, his marriage under pressure. Then my eyes drift to a record that's twenty years old. The reason for my old teacher Tom Horden's resignation finally makes sense: one of his thirteen-year-old pupils accused him of touching her inappropriately. The school gave him an ultimatum, to quit immediately or risk going on the sex offender's register if the case went to court. All I remember is his rapid departure and rumours of a breakdown. Horden has lived quietly since then, behind his high privet hedge, caring for his wife. I close my eyes and try to imagine him following Laura on a freezing cold morning, governed by impulses he couldn't control.

'Are you okay, boss?'

I rub my hand across my jaw. 'Just thinking, Eddie. Why?'

'The picture of Laura is from her Facebook page; anyone could have downloaded it.'

'It's their motive that interests me. Someone wants me afraid that I'll meet the same fate, if I pursue the case.'

The image he hands me is an intact version of the fragments in the plastic bag. It shows Laura beaming at the camera, fresh-faced and innocent. I try to imagine why anyone would destroy her image. Maybe the killer couldn't handle all of that youth and beauty being out of reach. Either her father or her boyfriend could have been afraid she would abandon them. My theories about the case are still whirling round my head when Eddie speaks again.

'A woman came by earlier. She wants your permission to travel to the mainland.'

'What's her name?'

He scans his list. 'Nina Jackson, Gweal Cottage.'

I rise to my feet slowly, telling Eddie I'll interview her while I'm there, kill two birds with one stone. My tongue seals itself to the roof of my mouth as I follow the path west from the hamlet, the dog in hot pursuit. She's the only woman to interest me in months, and now she's about to leave. The place she's renting lies at the foot of Gweal Hill, and is another of Jay Curnow's properties. It's a fisherman's cottage, adorned with features designed to lure tourists into long summer lets: pale blue shutters, rose bushes trained across the porch, a stone bench by the front door. When I glance back, Shadow is behind me on the dunes, tongue lolling as he trots to catch up. Music pulses through an open window, a hot burst of Motown, playing at full volume. I knock harder in case she hasn't heard; Marvin Gaye abruptly falls silent.

The woman stands in the doorway, in leggings and a thin white T-shirt, feet bare even though it's the end of a harsh winter. Up close, her eyes are the same colour as the honey Rose gave me earlier, pale amber, reflecting the light.

'Nina Jackson?'

'That's my name.'

'I'm Ben Kitto, you wanted to see me.'

'I know who you are. Your assistant says I need your permission to leave Bryher.'

Shadow bolts through the open doorway, making

me wish I'd left him at home. 'Sorry, he's got no manners.'

She produces a smile at last. 'I didn't know he was yours. He often comes here.'

'Scrounging for food?'

'Company, I think. We take walks on the beach.'

'Feel free to adopt him, he's hunting for a new owner. Do you mind if I come in?'

She steps back, her movements fluid and graceful. 'You need to interview me, don't you?'

I stand in her hallway, hands buried in my pockets. 'Is now a good time?'

'Not here. The kitchen's warmer.'

Her log burner's roaring in the corner, the room hot enough to make me peel off my coat. There are few personal details on show, except a copy of *Mansfield Park* lying open on the table. It's obvious she's a neat freak, as well as a fan of high-class literature. She moves around in silence, filling the kettle, not bothering with small talk. Her dark hair follows her jaw in a sleek line. I can't help admiring those long limbs and subtle curves, but after a minute I force myself to look away. Nina places a mug of tea in front of me, and it would be rude to admit that I hate the stuff. The steam smells lemony, with an odd tang of woodsmoke. I put my Dictaphone on the table and press record, but when she sits opposite, her gaze is so direct, it's a struggle to concentrate. There's no sign of warmth on that perfect oval face.

'When did you arrive on Bryher, Nina?'

'A month ago, I flew from Land's End.'

'But now you're going back to the mainland?'

She shakes her head. 'Just for a day trip. I'm staying here six months, I already do bits and pieces of work.'

I spot a violin case on a shelf by the door. 'You're a musician?'

'Only as a hobby.' She runs her fingers through Shadow's fur.

'It would help to know why you came here.'

'Sorry, you want me to explain myself.' She changes position, as if the straight-backed chair causes her discomfort. 'I live in Bristol, but fancied a slower pace. I thought I'd give rural isolation a try.'

I can almost hear the gaps in her statement. 'You came to the right place.'

'It suits me so far.'

I glance at the wide gold band on her finger. 'Will your husband be joining you?'

'I'm not married.' Her calmness falters, before her gaze steadies again. 'It's Laura you want to talk about, isn't it? We only spoke once, in the hotel bar, when I ate there one evening. She recommended places to visit on the islands, but I never saw her again.'

'You must see everyone who uses the path. Do many people walk on the cliffs?'

'Dean Miller often sketches up there. I see the Hordens, Danny Curnow and Jim Helyer sometimes.'

I could ask about her alibi for Monday morning, but

it would be pointless. Living alone, with no houses in viewing distance, who could confirm it? I turn off the Dictaphone then study her face again.

'You're visiting the mainland today?'

She shakes her head. 'Monday. My aunt will never talk to me again if I forget her birthday.'

'I'll get Eddie to put it in his log.'

'He seems very keen.'

'That's an understatement.' I run my hand across the back of my neck, pain gathering as I reach for my coat.

'You do that a lot.' Her clear gaze settles on me again. 'Your headaches probably come from a pinched nerve at the top of your spine.'

I stare back at her. 'How did you guess?'

'From the way you move. I did three years medical training, but qualified as a chiropractor. If you sit here I can release it for you.'

'There's no need, I should be going.' But the pain's suddenly intense enough to keep me standing there.

'Are you scared I'll hurt you?'

'Of course not.'

'Then let me help.'

She makes me sit on a wooden chair, her manner so matter-of-fact that resistance seems futile. Normally I'd race for the door, but the discomfort's bad enough to make me take a risk. She stands behind me, her hands cool on the back of my neck. It's so many months since a woman touched me, my senses are on overload. Her scent is a subtle blend of roses and fresh air, but her hands are more direct, fingers probing the base of my skull until she hits the site of the pain. Suddenly it's so raw my vision blurs.

'There it is. Now look ahead for me,' she says quietly.

She places the flat of her hand against my jaw, then pushes my temple hard. A starburst of pain flashes through me, then something clicks into place. When my eyes open again, she's crouching in front of me, watching my expression.

'Better?'

'You're a miracle worker. What do I owe you?'

'First session's free. I can show you relaxation exercises another time.'

Shadow gives a loud bark, as if he's tired of being overlooked. Nina leans down to stroke his head and he falls silent instantly. The expression on her face is solemn as she holds out my coat, and before long I'm on the beach again. When I stare up at Gweal Hill, I'm pain-free for the first time in weeks, but no closer to understanding who killed Laura Trescothick.

15

It's mid-afternoon by the time I reach the Rock, hoping for more information about Laura's father, even though DCI Madron would be angered by my line of enquiry. Maggie is stacking shelves behind the bar with bottles of mixers, in time for the tiny influx of regulars that counts for happy hour on Bryher. When her head pops up, her grey curls are dishevelled as she gives me a grin.

'My favourite godson.'

'Your only godson, Maggie.'

'Don't be such a pedant. I can tell from your face you've come to pick my brains. Do you want to talk here or in private?'

'Your office is the best plan.'

She bobs ahead, small and agile as a child. The office shelves are lined with books about the history and geology of the Scillies, biographies of local writers and artists. Her desk is stacked with folders labelled 'bills paid' and 'money loaned'. Maggie's finances have always sustained the fishing community, subsidising families through winter's lean times. Without her, the island's economy would grind to a halt.

'I need to know more about Matt and Jenna. What's your view of them?'

She leans back in her chair. 'Everyone respects Matt, but Jenna holds that family together. He's tried building jobs, the oil rigs, driving work on the mainland, but nothing sticks. There's not enough work on the trawlers these days.'

'I heard they sold Tide Cottage to Jay Curnow.'

'He got it cheap when the bank repossessed it.' Her face darkens. 'Jay always goes after properties when people are down on their luck. The guy isn't blessed with much compassion. Matt took it to heart, Jenna's the calm one.'

'No wonder there's no love lost between the two families. Have you ever loaned the Trescothicks money?'

'Once in a while.'

'Come on, Maggie. It's details I'm after.'

'I leant them a grand last winter. They returned every penny.' Her shrewd eyes level with mine. 'Most of the time Matt's a great guy, but if he loses it, you'd better steer clear. He's been spending too much time in here lately.'

'Tell me about the man he hurt.'

'A tourist jostled him at the bar two summers back. Normally it would have blown over, but the bloke's wife called the police.'

I recognise the regret in her voice. Islanders exercise their own form of justice, rarely involving the authorities. The warring parties cool off at home, shake hands in the morning, or avoid each other until the dust settles.

'Matt drinks too much?'

'If he was happier, he'd spend more time at home. He wants to be the breadwinner, but it hasn't happened.'

'What kind of dad is he?'

'Caring, by all accounts. Jenna guards her privacy; she's never said a word against him.'

'He doesn't push her around?'

'I bloody hope not, that girl works like a trooper. You can see the strain she's under.'

'What about Laura and Suzanne?'

'Those girls were thick as thieves. God knows what poor Suzie will do now,' Maggie says quietly.

'Do you know how Laura got on with her dad?'

Maggie gazes at her folded hands before replying. 'They seemed close, but a few weeks ago I saw them arguing on the beach. It was around midnight. I saw the pair of them from my bedroom window when I shut the curtains. He was shaking his fist at her; even with the window closed I could hear him yelling.'

'Any idea why?'

'He was furious about something.' Maggie's eyes catch mine again. 'Aren't you going to ask what I was doing the day Laura was taken?'

'You're not high on my suspect list.'

Suddenly her expression hardens. 'It could be any one of us, Ben. You should keep your eyes open.'

'Believe me, I am.' I know better than to argue when she's upset.

She shuts her eyes. 'Sorry, darling, I can't seem to forget seeing Laura on the beach. It sticks in my throat that she was killed, right in front of us. That bastard probably drinks in my pub.'

'Chances are. Can you think of anyone who'd harm her?'

She hesitates. 'Only Dean Miller comes to mind.'

'Why? He says they were close.'

'They were, but he's lived alone so long, and he's an oddball. Loneliness sours people, doesn't it?'

'He told me kids flock to his place.'

'They go there to meet their friends, that's all.'

'Dean was spotted in his studio the morning Laura went missing; it looks like he got up early to paint. Right now, I've got no reason to doubt it. Do you know if anyone wanders round the island at night?'

'Jim Helyer takes late walks sometimes, and Emma Horden runs poor Tom ragged.' She reaches up to touch my cheek. 'You were always the smartest kid here, watching people with those big green eyes. You'll work it out.'

'Run away with me, Maggie. We could fly to Vegas tonight.'

'Tempting, but one divorce is enough.'

'Pity.' I give her hand a quick squeeze. 'Is Billy around?'

'Night off. His ankle's still buggered.'

'He's got no alibi for Monday morning.'

'Yes, he has,' Maggie says in a firm voice. 'I can vouch for him.'

'How come?'

'Billy was in pain, so I let him stay over.'

'I still need to speak to him. You wouldn't have heard him leave the guest rooms.'

'He slept in my bed, you fool.'

It's a struggle to stop my jaw hitting the ground. 'Right, I didn't know.'

She laughs at full volume. 'Old people have sex, Ben, get over it. You'll be glad when you're sixty.'

'How long's it been going on?'

'Over a year. He's kind, sweet and I enjoy his company.'

'One wrong move and he's fish bait.'

'Don't worry, he's crazy about me.'

'Then he lives to cook another meal.' I pick up my coat, trying to banish an image of Maggie and Billy in the big oak bed I trampolined on as a kid. 'One more thing. Who'd give Sam Austell shelter on the island?'

Her eyebrows rise. 'No one comes to mind; his mates are on the mainland. He's another lost soul these days. Me and Jim went to see him play in Plymouth; you should have seen him sprint. The boy deserves a second chance.'

Eddie's shirt is wilting when I get back, knife-edge creases melting away. His expression is so dejected that I want to explain that the slack days of an investigation give time for reflection, until the wheels start turning again. One of the things I loved about working with Clare was her refusal to admit defeat, even when our backs were against the wall. She just ploughed on, hammering every case into submission. I push her to the back of my mind and focus again on my new underling; it's clear he's in no mood for a pep talk. Even our walk to the quay feels like *Groundhog Day*, Arthur Penwithick emerging from his house at the exact moment we reach the jetty, to ferry him home. I consider doing a last recce for Sam Austell, but my chances of finding him in the dark are negligible.

My next few hours are spent delivering my promise to Ray. Work on the boat continues late into the evening. My uncle only speaks to give me instructions, humming quietly as he measures each seam, his lack of communication a relief after filtering information all day. We're adding the lapping now, overlaying planks, tamping more wool and resin into the gaps. The boat has become a whale's skeleton, the keel its vertebra, ribs curving like cupped hands. It makes a wheezing sound in the cooling air, odd clicks and snaps like joints flexing. The work gives me enough pleasure to make me regret choosing policing over chandlery for a split second, but patience has never been my greatest virtue. When I left home at eighteen I needed the challenge of tougher questions. At nine o'clock I say goodnight, Ray emerging from under the boat to give me a quick salute. The lights are on in Arthur Penwithick's house next door when I leave, TV blaring. Eddie has spoken to the ferryman already, and I'm certain Ray would have heard him leave if he'd set out early on Monday.

Someone is sitting in my porch when I reach the cottage, making Shadow give a loud yip of greeting, the glow of a cigarette visible in the dark. In summer people often wait outside friends' houses, enjoying the weather. In a place this small it's never long before they return. But loitering on a chilly winter night means that the visit is more important than a social call. Jim Helyer unfolds himself from the bench, his smile sheepish.

'Making a nuisance of yourself, Jim?'

'I brought beer.' He brandishes a six-pack of Löwenbräu.

'In that case, you're my honoured guest.'

Jim and Zoe are my only close friends left on the island, others scattered to the four winds, chasing work or adventures, but he seems uneasy, his banter slower than normal. Jim's a typical islander, programmed to volunteer information at his own pace. Once the heat from the fire penetrates the room, he starts to unwind, tension easing from his face.

'Tell me how London's been treating you,' he says quietly.

It would be a relief to let off steam about Clare, but

no words arrive. 'The usual high pressure crap, I won't bore you with it. How's parenthood going anyway?'

He looks at his hands. 'Great most days, but juggling the farm can be a challenge. I've persuaded Angie to stop at two, but she's not thrilled. Five or six kids is her idea of a family.'

He has almost drained his second beer, and I'm getting the lie of the land. More issues are weighing on his mind than Laura's death.

'Spill the beans, Jim. Something's bothering you.'

His shoulders twitch, as if I've threatened him. 'There are no excuses, when I've got Angie and my kids. I'm the luckiest man alive.' His fingers jitter on the arm of the sofa. 'I made a stupid mistake.'

'Let me be the judge.'

'Laura kept coming round to babysit, all fresh and young and beautiful. I couldn't take my eyes off her.' His words tail into silence. 'I tried to kiss her one time, three months ago. When she slapped my face that put an end to it.'

My thoughts click into professional mode. 'Angie said you were tending the animals the morning Laura died. Is that true?'

'I'm up at five thirty every day; it takes me two hours to milk the goats.'

'Can anyone confirm that?'

'Gwen Trescothick probably saw me from her window. She's an early riser.'

I study him again. 'Why are you saying this now?'

141

'It's been messing with my head. I needed to tell someone.'

'You decided to confess before someone else blew the whistle?'

'Nothing you say can make me feel any worse. It was crazy, Ben, maybe I'm cracking up. I just wanted to be young and carefree again, like the old days.'

'Did you call or text her, after that?'

He shakes his head. 'Angie hasn't got a clue, thank God. Please don't tell her what a prat I've been. It would break her heart.'

'I can't protect you. It's a murder case.'

'Why not let me help? I know the island better than anyone.'

'That's impossible now. You'll have to come to the station, after the memorial service tomorrow. Make a formal statement for the record.'

'I wasn't thinking straight, that's all.'

'Explain it to me tomorrow.'

He looks miserable when he stands up to leave, the atmosphere thick enough to slice. Once he's gone I lean against the front door, exhaling curses. It's hard to believe that Laura's rejection might have sent a gentle soul like Jim onto the cliff that morning, with a knife in his pocket. My gut tells me that the only men close enough to commit murder were her dad and her boyfriend, but Jim's confession can't be overlooked.

Something feels different when I finally lie down. The pain in my neck has dulled to a vague throb, and I remember Nina Jackson's cold hands on my skin, that misleading wedding ring tempting me to run a search on her, even though she's done nothing wrong. I shut my eyes and wipe her from my mind. The wind is gusting across the roof, hard enough to rattle the tiles. I'm still worrying about whether infatuation could have pushed my old friend over the brink into violence when sleep finally arrives.

16

The visit from Ben Kitto has left Rose unsettled. She remembers seeing him as a tiny infant, his black hair as thick as a fox's pelt, the child's cry loud enough to raise the roof. Today she felt both glad and afraid to see him again, a giant with calm green eyes. His quiet manner almost made her spit out the truth about Sam's absence, the boatmen haunting the shores and Jay Curnow's attempts to steal her home.

To keep herself occupied, she rummages for clothes to wear at Laura Trescothick's memorial service, but finds nothing suitable. Her wardrobe contains remnants from the charity shops on St Mary's. Years ago, she chose items for their glitter, decking herself out in second-hand finery, but now every garment is threadbare. Her favourite red velvet skirt is riddled with moth holes. She rubs its soft fabric against her cheek, remembering a time when she loved to dance, get drunk, flirt with men. It would be easy to yield to self-pity, release the tears pricking the backs of her eyes. But what purpose did crying ever serve?

Rose stares at the flickering lights of Tresco's houses,

across New Grimsby Sound, wishing that she could pray. The psalms and verses she learned at Sunday school lost their meaning a long time ago. The only gods Rose believes in now are nature and the sea, elemental forces that can cure or destroy. But she remembers the ritual her mother performed each spring, to cleanse the place of bad spirits. She collects sprigs of rosemary, sage and juniper from boxes stacked against her wall. Once she has lit the herbs with a match, fragrant smoke fills the air. She wafts the smudge stick into every corner of the cabin, muttering words under her breath to complete the ritual. The air is still pungent with hope when her son's phone begins to ring. She has kept it charged since finding it in his room, and now she snatches it from the table.

'Who's there?'

The answer is a blather of words, spoken too fast, in a language she can't understand. The man's tone is bitter as his voice rises to a shout.

'Give me my son back, please,' Rose whispers into the phone.

There's another loud stream of curses before the line dies.

17

Shadow begins the new day with a fit of temper, his out-raged barks pursuing me for a hundred metres when I leave him locked indoors. I'm not looking forward to my first trip to the local church since my mother's funeral, but today there's no choice. Laura Trescothick's memorial will replace the normal Sunday morning service, and a crowd of islanders are waiting on the jetty to be ferried over to Tresco. The family have asked mourners not to wear black, so I've opted for a blue plaid jacket and jeans. Zoe is following the colour rule too; she dashes over to greet me wrapped in an emerald green coat, her vivid red lipstick an obvious ploy to make her look cheerful.

'God, this is grim,' she mutters. 'I wish they hadn't asked me to sing.'

'Matt and Jenna will be grateful so many came.' I glance around the crowd. 'Did you shut the hotel for the morning?'

'A friend from St Agnes is running the bar. I wanted to close up, but we've still got guests.'

All of the islanders have arrived, except the Austells. The Curnow family stand at the edge of the crowd, Danny's expression mutinous, as if he'd rather grieve alone. But it's Matt's body language that interests me most. So much tension is stored in his movements that one badly chosen word could ignite an explosion, reminding me of his argument with Laura the week before she died. Suzanne clings to his side, the girl's face shrouded by long hair the colour of wet straw. My eyes skim the crowd, aware that the killer must be among them. Their expressions all look the same: solemn and pinched with cold. Dean Miller has swapped his paint-stained overalls for a blazer and freshly pressed trousers. The Hordens are beside him, Emma hanging onto my old teacher's arm as if she might lose him in the melee. Jim is keeping his head down, deliberately avoiding me after his surprise confession; my old friend's pallor reminds me that he was infatuated with the girl the entire island has turned out to mourn.

The Trescothicks are first onto the ferry, Arthur Penwithick helping Jenna aboard. I ride over on a fishing smack that's been called into service for the event. The decks have been scrubbed clean but the odours of fish guts and salt still taint the air. I stare over the side as we cross New Grimsby Sound, wishing I could swim the narrow channel like when I was a kid. A searing blast of cold might open my eyes wide enough to spot missing clues. Everyone waits for the crowd to spill from the deck before climbing the shallow incline of Tresco hill.

The larger island may only be five minutes from Bryher, but it's foreign territory. The landscape looks manicured, a paddock is filled with well-groomed horses and ponies for tourists to ride in summer. Tresco operates on a grander scale, the Abbey Gardens drawing thousands of visitors each year.

By the time we reach the island's church, many of Tresco's inhabitants have joined the crowd to pay their respects. The nave's white walls are decorated with flowers, balloons and swags of ribbon, more fitting for a christening than a memorial. Most of the people filling the low wooden pews are Laura's age; some of her friends already in tears.

The service begins with 'All Things Bright and Beautiful', and time winds back to the days when I sang in the choir, more for the music than religious conviction. It seemed like a good way to meet girls until I realised that rugby players fared better than boy sopranos. My eyes scan the walls as the vicar welcomes us. The church is named after St Nicholas, patron saint of fishermen, a roll call of the drowned printed on the wall. My father's name is among them, lost when I was fourteen. My mother's visits to church grew more regular after that, as if faith could plug the gap he left behind.

The air tastes of incense and dust as Zoe rises to her feet. When she sings Laura's favourite song, 'Thinking Out Loud', her status as the islands' sweetheart is confirmed. You could hear a pin drop as she delivers each pure note, the melody heavy with longing, a reminder that even in the worst circumstances she can hold an audience in the palm of her hand.

Matt rises to his feet as the last note fades. His expression's numb, but he holds it together while photos of Laura are projected onto the wall of the nave. If he killed her, then he must have nerves of steel to deliver his daughter's eulogy. His voice fractures as he describes a talented girl with a zest for life. Heads bow as he speaks; the death of someone so young raises too many questions, the natural order crumbling. I look around to see if anyone's gloating, but the mood is sombre. Arthur Penwithick arrives late from mooring his boat. There's no room in the pews, so he stands at the back, grease-stained cap clutched in his hands. Jim is sitting across the aisle from me, eyes welling as he gazes ahead. Despite his wife's alibi that he was tending their livestock the morning Laura vanished, I still need to quell my discomfort about interviewing an old friend in connection with the girl's murder.

There's an atmosphere of relief when the service ends. Even in winter, the churchyard is picturesque – elm trees marking the periphery, gravestones so old that the names of the dead have worn away. The island has run out of burial plots. Laura will be cremated on St Mary's, like every other islander. When I look up, Nina Jackson is on the other side of the crowd, wearing a dark red coat, talking to my uncle. For once, Ray is making conversation with someone he barely knows, shoulders angled in her direction, his raw-boned face animated.

The sight brings a smile to my face; I can't remember seeing him flirt with anyone until now. Zoe appears at my side as I watch them.

'You did well. I'm not an Ed Sheeran fan, but you made that song sound half decent.'

'High praise, big man. Didn't anyone tell you it's bad taste to ogle girls at a memorial service?' she whispers.

'Tell that to Ray. I think he's smitten.'

'My arse,' she sniggers. 'Trust you to fancy the island's most troubled female.'

'Is she?'

'She's got complicated tattooed all over her.'

'Beautiful though, so who cares?'

'You're such a cliché.' Zoe digs her finger into my ribs. 'How's the investigation going?'

I give her some general details as we walk back to the quay. It's clear she's been deeply affected by Laura's death; behind her flamboyance, she's finding it hard to accept.

'You couldn't have stopped it, you know.'

'That's not true.' Her eyes glisten. 'Laura was killed on her way to work for me.'

'It's not your fault.' I shake my head. 'What do you know about Sam Austell?'

'The guy loves his recreational drugs; I chucked him out of my bar last month, high as a kite.'

We part company on the quay when she catches the first boat back, leaving me brooding over suspects. My suspicion that the girl could only have been killed by someone inside her intimate circle with powerful feelings for her is growing stronger. Her elusive ex-boyfriend Sam has social issues, but surely no one would wait a whole year to hurt a girl for ending their relationship? His disappearance could have less to do with guilt than a messed-up life. He may have walked into the sea, unable to handle his sporting dreams being shattered. I'm still puzzling over all the options when the ferry docks on the quay to carry the last islanders back across the sound.

My footsteps are leaden as I reach the village. I've arranged to give Matt and Jenna an update, the winter pansies beside their front door a blur of purple blossoms, far too cheery for the occasion. Jenna is dry-eyed when she answers the door, holding herself together against the odds. Her formal clothes have been replaced by a sweatshirt and faded jeans, the memorial's gloom stripped from her skin.

'Want me to come back tomorrow?'

She shakes her head firmly. 'I need to hear your news.'

I sit beside her on the leather sofa. A picture of Laura beams down from the mantelpiece. It's a typical school portrait, golden hair in a ponytail, smile so unquestioning it looks like she's never doubted anything in her life. My guilt about making slow progress rises by another notch. Jenna's studying me closely, eyes round with questions.

'When someone gets attacked like this, it's almost always by someone they know . . .' My voice tails into silence. 'The process must feel slow, but we have to eliminate people, one by one.'

'So long as you find him, I don't care how long it takes.' The need in her eyes is so raw, it's clear she expects a promise.

'I won't stop looking, Jenna, if that's what you mean.' She clutches my hand for a second. 'Where are Matt and Suzanne?'

'At his mum's. Gwen's too upset to be alone.'

'Have you remembered anything else about Laura's behaviour?'

'Only that she was less open than before. There'd been tension between us recently.'

'About what?'

'Her future.' There's another flicker of emotion, her eyes welling. 'It's all my fault, Ben.'

'What did you argue about?'

'She was racing to grow up, like me at her age. I thought making her pay rent might slow her down, but she was determined to leave.'

I nod in reply. 'We should search her room again, in case I missed something.'

The suggestion is more for her benefit than mine, to make her feel useful. First, we check Laura's wardrobe and cupboards, then I use a claw hammer to pull up loose floorboards. It's only when I turn Laura's desk over that my fingers touch cold plastic. A transparent folder is taped to the underside, my breath catching at the sight of a wad of banknotes. My first thought is that the cash must be linked to the drug supply she was hoarding.

'There's a couple of thousand here. Where would she get this kind of money?'

Jenna bites her lip. 'No idea. She's been so secretive lately. Her gran would tell us if she gave the girls cash. Why the hell didn't Laura say anything?' The discovery seems to have renewed her fighting spirit, anger cutting through the Valium haze as we go back downstairs.

'How's Matt been coping, Jenna?'

'Not great, he was closer to her than anyone.'

'I heard he's been having problems.'

'Rumours flying, are they?' Her face sets in a scowl. 'I bet the scandalmongers are having a field day.'

'People are bound to be concerned.'

'Winters are tough here, you know that. A man like Matt wants to contribute to the community, but there are fewer chances every year. He's been at a loose end for months.'

'Sorry to probe, but you want Laura's killer found, don't you?'

Her tone shifts from anger to misery. 'It hits a nerve, that's all. The gossips love destroying a man's reputation.'

My head's pounding when I leave the house. The meeting has given me a new set of questions. Why would a young girl hide so much money from her parents, unless she was ashamed of how it was earned? Maybe she thought her mother would demand a portion, because she took half her wage? I pause outside Gweal Cottage. A shadow moves behind the curtains, and I remember Nina Jackson's invitation. The idea of seeing her again is so tempting, I feel like marching up her path. Pain roots deeper into my muscles as I turn back towards the community hall. There's no putting it off any longer; my deputy will be waiting to witness my interview with a man I still consider one of my closest friends.

Eddie helps me set up the room for the interview, the Dictaphone ready to capture Jim Helyer's words about his relationship with the victim. But when four o'clock arrives it's his wife who enters the hall, her movements brittle with tension. She marches straight over, her eyes puffy and red-rimmed.

'Jim's ill, so I came instead.' She perches on the edge of a table.

'Is he okay?'

'A migraine hit him after the service. His sensitive bloody nature always leaves me dealing with the crap he leaves behind.' There's no trace now of the pretty, delicate girl who married Jim Helyer. Her face is harder than before, the years suddenly catching up with her.

'Is it okay to record you, Angie?'

She gives an abrupt nod, then words stream from her mouth before I can ask another question. 'He told me the truth, after he got back from yours last night. I couldn't believe it at first. She was our babysitter, for Christ's sake.' A single tear rolls down her cheek. 'He's been a fucking idiot, but that doesn't alter the facts. I heard him get up to do the milking, the day Laura died.'

'You saw him in the field?'

'I didn't look, but his pattern never changes. He came in at the normal time.' Maybe she doesn't realise it, but she's punctured her husband's alibi. He could have risen at the same time as usual, walked to Gweal Hill to kill Laura, then rushed back to his chores without anyone noticing.

'Did he ever behave strangely towards Laura?'

'He went quiet when she was around. I didn't take much notice at the time.'

Her statement makes me remember Jim retreating into his shell when he fancied girls at school, shyness getting the better of him.

'Has he ever been violent towards you?'

'Of course he bloody hasn't. He screwed up big time, that's all,' she mutters. 'This is my reward for having his kids, and working like a slave. Trust him to have a mid-life crisis at thirty-four.'

'Thanks for coming, Angie. Tell Jim to call us, as soon as he recovers.'

After she leaves the hall, Eddie looks uncomfortable, as if he's witnessed a scene he'd rather forget, but my concern about Jim's involvement remains lower than the key suspects. My suspicions are still focused on her father and her boyfriend, but neither can be arrested without hard proof.

I stay behind for hours after sending Eddie home,

flicking through hand-written reports. It's only as I walk back to Hell Bay that an odd sensation washes over me, like cold water trickling down my spine. I used to get that feeling a lot when I first worked undercover, as if a sniper had me in their sights. When I spin round, the beach is empty. I bury my hands in my pockets and keep walking, ashamed of myself for being paranoid.

Shadow almost knocks me over in his desperation to exit the cottage. The first thing I do when I get inside is email Madron to inform him about the money in Laura's room. Tomorrow morning another meeting will be called; everyone on the island will be fingerprinted, so forensics can check the banknotes. An email has arrived from my DCI in London, one of Sarah Goldman's weekly bulletins; a covert reminder that I must make a decision soon. I delete the message before it can play on my mind. When I scan the internet it's clear the press have flouted Madron's instructions, buying photos from someone at the memorial service. There's a picture of Jenna emerging from the church, white-faced and stricken, the ultimate intrusion into a mother's grief. The image makes me angrier than before, my determination to find her daughter's killer growing sharper all the time.

18

Desperation gives Rose new-found courage. When night falls, she sets off towards Shipman Head. Few stars are out tonight, the water matte black, occasional streaks of white when the clouds crack open. There's nothing here to lift her soul – just a raw waste of shingle and the ocean's endless questions. She waits behind the dunes, determined to discover the truth. An hour passes before an outboard motor buzzes across the water. There's a grinding sound as the dinghy's prow hits the shingle. One of the men jumps ashore, the other remaining in the boat, as he heads for the hiding place where she found the package. It's too dark to see his face, apart from the glitter in his eyes. She ought to remain hidden and call the police, but the feeling bubbling in Rose's chest is a mixture of fury and hysteria.

'What have you done to my son?' she yells out.

The man turns in her direction, frowning deeply, before speaking in the harsh Eastern European accent she heard on the phone. 'You must be Sam Austell's mother.'

'That's why I'm here. Did you hurt Laura Trescothick too?'

'You're talking rubbish.' He lunges forward, grabbing her arm, his eyes pitiless. 'Did you know your son's a thief?'

'Where is he? I've looked everywhere.'

'Sam owes us big money. Do you understand? When you find him, tell him I won't wait forever.'

Suddenly the man shoves her, sending Rose reeling backwards. She lands heavily on the shingle, a dull pain burning through her hip as the boat leaves the shore.

19

Sleeping past dawn is impossible while my thoughts churn like a tumble dryer, so I put myself through a brutal round of press-ups at 5 a.m. I'm not keen on exercise apart from outdoor swimming, but a frame like mine requires it; being muscle-bound is better than running to seed. A hard sweat normally releases my stress, but the thought of Sam Austell nags at me as I step into the shower. He's hiding somewhere on an island two miles long. If he's alive, he must have found shelter, and he could have valuable information. Somehow, he's kept one step ahead of our searches, advantaged by knowing the island like the back of his hand.

It's still dark when I leave the cottage and turn inland. The dog treats the early morning walk like a grand escapade, gambolling across the grass, chasing seagulls.

'Leave them alone, you bully.'

Shadow pays no attention, jaws snapping as one of the birds takes flight just in the nick of time.

The houses in the village are still shuttered. At any

other time it would be a pleasure to have the island to myself, but today I'm too focused on my search. If Austell is still alive, he would have chosen the island's sheltered side, avoiding the icy northern breeze. I peer through the windows of a cabin on the outskirts of the village. Zoe's family own it, birdwatchers renting the place each summer. There's no sign of a recent visitor, the kitchenette clean and orderly, bed still made. It takes half an hour to check garden sheds and outbuildings, then I walk down to the quay. It still bothers me that there's an outside chance that Austell killed Laura in a jealous rage. If he cast himself from the cliffs in a fit of guilt, who would know? The sea doesn't always return its dead. My mother would have been relieved if the waves had carried my father's body home for a proper funeral. All he got was his name in the local paper and a dozen white roses scattered at high tide.

I stand on the quay to gaze across the sound. Tresco has vanished behind a wall of sea mist, pillowing the water in a thick white cloud. The fog could take hours to clear; it feels like the island is conspiring against me, keeping secrets to itself. Visibility ceases a couple of metres from shore, the atmosphere so dank that I'm keen to return to the cottage for breakfast, but Shadow dashes ahead, scratching at the doors of a boat hut. I swear under my breath, because Ray's flat is close by. He won't take kindly to being woken before sunrise by me yelling at a wayward dog.

'Come here, you mongrel,' I mutter. Shadow looks

up expectantly, whining to be let in, so I twist the door handle to satisfy his curiosity.

He streaks through once it swings open. The air inside the hut is tainted by seaweed and brine, the sour tang of fish blood. When my eyes adjust to the poor light, there are nets piled in the corner, balls of nylon twine and crab pots stacked in a pile. There's a crashing sound, then I'm knocked sideways, gasping for breath. A man flails past, footsteps clattering on the concrete. I drag myself after him, yelling for Ray's help as I pass the quay. The sea mist's thicker now, swirling in front of my eyes, but his outline is still visible, thin limbs moving like pistons, ragged coat flapping in his wake. The gap's closing as he sprints north towards Shipman Head, the dog snapping at his heels. We've been running for five minutes before he makes the mistake of glancing back, falling head first onto the shingle. I throw myself across him, hearing him choke on wet sand. It's only when his arms are braced that my heart rate doubles; he could be carrying a weapon. I shift my weight to roll him onto his back. The dog is overjoyed by the drama, barking at full volume.

'Empty your pockets,' I snap.

Sam Austell's eyes are rolling, a thin beard covering his jaw. He's no longer the muscular football star in Laura's photo. He's aged ten years since then, jabbering a stream of expletives, limbs twitching as I search him. His pockets yield only a cigarette lighter, loose change and a bar of chocolate. My guess is that he's been waiting until the shop is unmanned to make occasional raids. Judging by his thinness, food isn't his top priority.

'Who were you hiding from, Sam?'

'You can't change it.' His face spasms, eyelids fluttering. 'Lost now, gone forever. The tide always steals your treasures.'

It sounds like he's reciting a poem, and I'm tempted to dunk him in the sea to bring him round. It's too early to tell what drugs he's swallowed, but I doubt whether shock tactics would help.

'Did you hurt Laura?'

'Beauty everywhere.' A foolish grin crosses his face. 'The sky, seashells, golden sand.' His tone is full of wonder, eyes chasing details. I'm still holding him down when Ray and Arthur finally appear.

'You took your bloody time,' I mutter. 'Help me get him to the hall.'

The boy's clothes are filthy as we march him inland. There's a streak of tar on his mud-spattered jeans, wet hair sticking to his skull. By the time he's handcuffed to the chair, Eddie has arrived, clearly thrilled by our first arrest.

'He needs to go to St Mary's hospital,' I say. 'Tell Madron I'm on my way.'

'Can I come?'

Eddie's face is so full of longing that I give a reluctant yes, aware that I would be breaking every protocol by transferring Austell without a second officer to restrain him. When I whistle for Shadow he slinks out of the bushes by the quay. I leave him at the boatyard with Ray, then we lead Austell onto the ferry. The young man's wrists are handcuffed, lips moving without pause, oblivious to his surroundings. Eddie asks me endless questions during the twenty-minute crossing, keen to know how I tracked him down, but it was perseverance, not detection skills, that won the day. Austell's still mumbling to himself about the sea. If he's pretending to have lost his senses, the guy deserves an Oscar; the boat heaves over choppy waves as we approach our destination, but neither the rocking motion nor the engine's drone can break his reverie.

We walk Austell to the small hospital where I attended Laura's autopsy. The treatment room is staffed by a locum today, his consulting room too small for comfort. Through the open doorway there's a hospital bed, oxygen tanks and enough kit to stabilise emergency cases before flying them to Penzance. Dr Gleeson is around my age, with a dark buzz cut, a badly cut suit and a gentle expression. He talks to Austell in a soft murmur.

'Let's get you comfortable, my friend.' The boy's monologue continues, a hiss of words too garbled to follow. 'Can the cuffs come off while I examine him, please?'

'They have to stay on, to restrain him.'

Dr Gleeson shakes his head in disapproval before starting his examination. A stench of sweat fills the room when Austell's shirt falls open, ribs protruding from his skin. He's so malnourished, it must have been days since he's eaten. The medic works with slow deliberation, like we've got all the time in the world, checking his breathing and shining a torch into his eyes. Austell's response to his questions is a tuneless hum, followed by a jumble of mismatched phrases.

'The ocean,' he mumbles. 'It drowns the past and future, wave after wave.'

The doctor's face is grave when we step outside. 'Psychotic episodes can last hours, or months. It's likely to be drug-induced. He needs emergency psychiatric care in Penzance; the toxicology report will tell us what he's taken.'

'Could he be faking it?'

'His pulse is galloping, his pupils are blown and I can smell the chemicals coming through his skin.' My frustration must be showing; the doctor leans over to touch my arm. 'Mental illness requires patience from all of us, Inspector.'

I keep my temper under wraps and thank him for his help. When I finally emerge, Madron is in the waiting area, wearing a congratulatory smile. I listen to his praise for tracking down the victim's ex-boyfriend, even though there's no hard proof that Austell laid a finger on Laura.

'It's all guesswork so far, sir. He's not under arrest.'

The DCI shakes his head. 'Her old flame vanishes the day she's killed, then you find him babbling like a lunatic. He's obviously a drug addict. I'd say that was conclusive, wouldn't you?'

I don't have an answer, but the only aggression Austell has shown so far is barging me out of the way, to make his escape. Eddie seems to agree with our superior officer. His grin indicates that he expects promotion on the back of the arrest. He's keen to accompany our suspect to the mainland, but I send him back to Bryher, to collect fingerprints and inform Rose that her son has been arrested before the island ignites with gossip.

I would prefer to use the Sky Bus to Land's End, but Austell would be a liability on a small aircraft. My only option is to take him across on the *Scillonian*, the ferry almost empty as it leaves harbour. A crew member finds us a room below deck, furnished with two easy chairs. I feel a pulse of concern as Austell begins to weep again, even though he's been sedated. I need to get him to the hospital before he has a complete meltdown.

'She slipped away,' he says. 'Now the sea's falling from the sky.'

I handcuff him to the chair, tired of his riddles. 'Sleep now, Sam. You need to rest.'

Austell's eyes close immediately. I stand by the porthole, hoping for a last sight of land, but finding only a swirl of sea mist. He sleeps through the journey, giving me time to observe him. His ticks and twitches continue, even when he's asleep, as if his brain can't shut down. He keeps calling out, then lapsing back into unconsciousness. When the boat docks in Penzance he's still babbling nonsense, unable to answer basic questions.

It's early afternoon when a squad car drives us to the hospital. Austell reacts fiercely to every noise, giving an ear-splitting scream as a motorbike passes, gunning its engine. It's a relief to deliver him to the experts. The consultant is an attractive middle-aged brunette, with a world-weary smile, her name badge informing me that she's called Dr Jen Lucas. Something about her calm manner makes me believe that she's a safe pair of hands. Her voice is sober when she fills out his admittance form.

'A third of psychosis cases are cannabis-related, but violence is rare, they're normally quite passive. We'll keep him in a secure room until he stabilises.'

Dr Lucas echoes the medical viewpoint I've already heard. The length of a psychotic episode can't be pre-judged. She raises her hand in a tired salute, before hurrying back to her duties, leaving me free to board the last Sky Bus of the day from Land's End, the journey to St Mary's taking just fifteen minutes, the sea below us boiling with dark grey waves. I should feel relieved, but the sensation never arrives. I don't believe in easy answers, even though my DCI seems convinced that Laura's killer is under lock and key in the psychiatric unit of Penzance Hospital. We have no proof that Austell has committed a crime. All we know for sure is that his football dream collapsed, yet he's had money to throw around in the pubs, convincing me that he's been running drugs around the islands. It's frustrating that no answers will be found until he can communicate. If he and Laura fell foul of the same islander, he might know the killer's name.

Ray appears on the jetty when I arrive on Bryher. It would break the habit of a lifetime for him to express concern, but he invites me in for food. I thank him before explaining that I need to get home.

'Where's Shadow?' I ask.

'He buggered off across the beach hours ago.'

'Bloody dog thinks he owns the island.'

The five-minute walk back to the cottage helps me reach a decision. Shadow's waiting in the porch, giving a quick yip of greeting as I grab a bottle of wine without taking off my coat. He stretches out on the rug, giving me time to escape before he can follow. He may have won points for tracking Austell down, but tonight he's surplus to requirements.

Nerves kick in as I follow the path to Gweal Cottage. Maybe it's because I'm not sure of my motives. All I know is that I want to see Nina Jackson again, if only to force her from my thoughts. When she opens the door, she's dressed in cut-off jeans, a low-necked blouse and severe, metal-framed reading glasses. The contrast is oddly sexy. I feel daft, standing there with a bottle of Rioja in my hands.

'You should invite me in,' I say, handing over my gift. 'It's an island tradition to offer visitors food.'

Her eyebrows rise. 'Really? That's news to me.'

Music spills from her sound system when she finally admits me. A man is singing his heart out in a language

I don't understand; Portuguese maybe, or Spanish. It reminds me that she's out of my league, but the easy route has never carried much appeal. Whatever happens next, at least I'm here in her kitchen, breathing in her scent. It's heavy with roses and cinnamon, an undertone of musk giving a kick of sensuality. I park myself at her kitchen table, too tired to care about invading her space. There's something calming about watching her handle crockery, movements deft as she pours soup into a bowl, tears a hunk of bread from a loaf.

'Did you make this?'

'Cooking's one of my pastimes.' She holds up the bottle of wine. 'Want a glass of this?'

'Only if you join me.'

She sits straight-backed, watching me eat. Behind all that composure, I can't tell whether she's irritated or amused. The soup is minestrone, spicy enough to leave a warm aftertaste; her bread's good too, crust sticky with olive oil and sea salt. The wine helps to thaw away the bone-chilling boat ride from St Mary's.

'I hear you wrestled a violent man to the ground this morning,' she says.

'The grapevine often exaggerates.'

'It's not true?'

'It was much less heroic; the guy was in a weakened state, he fell over and I jumped on top of him. Can I ask you a personal question?'

'Only if you promise to stop staring. It makes me uncomfortable.'

'Even when you're staring back?'

She drops her gaze. 'I read *Jamaica Inn* at an impressionable age. The smugglers looked like you, tall and black-haired. You're the last of a dying breed.'

'My ancestors were fishermen, but they risked their lives just as often.' I put down my glass. 'What made you visit Bryher in the middle of winter?'

'I could ask the same thing.'

'It's my home. You needed a reason to come here.'

Silence stretches out so long, it seems certain she won't answer. When she does finally speak, her tone is so jagged it sounds like she's swallowed broken glass.

'Something happened that I needed to forget. I thought being away from home would make it easier.'

'Has it?'

'Not yet.' She takes a gulp of wine. 'Why did you come back?'

'Same reason, but tonight's curing me.'

'Is that your best line?' She lets out a laugh. 'Finish your drink, then go home to Shadow.'

'You promised to show me some relaxation exercises.'

Her expression grows serious. 'How are the headaches?'

'Still there, but less painful.'

She rises to stand behind my chair. Even though I'm expecting it, the coolness of her fingers on my skin sets my teeth on edge. She eases my head forwards, then touches my jaw, slowly straightens my neck again. 'Try shoulder rolls, a dozen rotations, morning and evening. Want me to write it down?'

'I don't need instructions.'

'There's nothing else on offer.'

'Why don't we find out?' When I pull her into my lap her scent of musk and old-fashioned flowers is potent enough to taste, her skin poreless, amber eyes turning molten. My lips graze the underside of her jaw. When she kisses me back, it's tempting to carry her straight to bed, but she's already pulling away.

Nina sits on the chair opposite me, fingers touching her lips. I don't know if she's trying to wipe the kiss away or hold it in place.

'I can't get involved with anyone, Ben.'

'Don't complicate it. You fed me, so I'm returning the favour, that's all. It's an . . .'

'. . . island tradition?'

'Come to mine tomorrow, eightish.'

'I'm busy.'

'Wednesday then, same time.'

I grab my coat and leave before she can argue. The sea mist is thickening again, so dense and chilly it takes concentration to navigate the path home. After fifty metres a sound cuts through my high spirits; footsteps trailing across the shingle, like a slow echo. But when I spin round, the fog is impenetrable. The noise could be my mind playing tricks after a tough day. The killer is hardly likely to pursue me across the island, unless he's armed to the teeth. I make a deliberate effort to ignore it, white air stifling my breathing as I push on through the dark.

20

The sea's call is no more than a whisper tonight, as Rose stands in her kitchen, humming to herself. Since hearing that Sam is alive, she feels invincible. The threat of losing her home no longer scares her, or the boatmen hiding in the shadows. Soon her son will be under her roof, and her remedies will restore his health quicker than any hospital. She doesn't even care that the doctors are insisting on a police chaperone when she visits.

Rose is swaying to music that murmurs from the radio. Elvis is singing about tenderness and never letting go, but when the song finishes, her happiness fades. Soon she must board the ferry across miles of blank sea, leaving Bryher behind for the first time in years. She pushes the thought aside. Tonight, she will let herself celebrate: her boy is alive, and no matter what people claim, he must be innocent. She reaches for her pestle and mortar, to blend feverfew, burdock and vervain. The combination will purify his blood and calm his mind. She crushes the herbs into a fragrant powder, perfecting a recipe to heal her son.

She is pouring the dried mixture into a sachet when something startles her. A sound arrives out of nowhere, as loud as thunder. A fist pounds on her front door, almost forcing it from its hinges. Then the floor vibrates as someone kicks the wooden wall of her cabin, the onslaught so thunderous it sounds like her home will collapse around her ears. She presses her hand over her mouth, stifling her screams. Rose hits the light switch, then cowers in a corner, too terrified to move. Darkness might let her escape through a window if they break down the door. She's still shaking when the noise finally stops, but manages to drag herself to a window. The beach is empty, except for the gleam of moonlight, as if the men threatening her have vanished into the ether. There's no way of knowing whether the smugglers came back, or Curnow sent his men to hound her. She will have nowhere else to hide if they destroy her sanctuary.

21

Discomfort tightens the muscles across the back of my neck as I gaze down from the stage. The whole island population has packed the community hall this morning. DCI Madron stands at the back, monitoring my performance. My boss still seems certain that Laura's ex-boyfriend killed her in a drug-fuelled rage, but I can see no concrete proof that Sam Austell harmed Laura. My own suspicions remain focused on Danny Curnow and Matt Trescothick, both men staring back at me from the audience. The crowd listens attentively as I explain that money has been found in Laura's room, her parents unaware how she earned it. The memory of the chopped-up photo on my doorstep makes me advise the islanders again that security is paramount.

'If you have to leave home after dark, make sure you're accompanied. Keep yourselves safe until the killer's found.'

Some of the islanders look sceptical, as if they can't believe Laura's attacker is still on island soil.

Matt gives a grudging nod when I ask him to return in an hour for an update, then the hall clears rapidly, leaving me and Eddie to chase loose threads. My first task is to call Penzance Hospital. Dr Lucas is non-committal on the phone, explaining that Austell is still struggling to speak. The evidence supports Madron's theory that Sam could have attacked Laura, then made a failed suicide attempt by swallowing cannabis resin. But we have no evidence other than his toxicology report, which shows sky-high levels of toxins in his blood. My call to the National Crime Agency draws a cagey response. An unlicensed vessel with a Latvian crew was caught recently; no contra-band was found aboard, but the sniffer dogs went wild, suggesting that they had thrown their stash into the sea, and it's possible that a larger network is still operating in local waters. News from the IT experts is just as inconclusive. Laura's computer reveals nothing more sinister than a passion for eBay and hundreds of intimate messages from Danny Curnow. Common sense tells me that Laura's death is linked to the drugs swilling round Sam Austell's system, but so far there's no hard proof.

Matt Trescothick's heel taps out a jerky rhythm when he sits down for our meeting, his face grey with tiredness.

'We think smugglers have been running drugs through the islands, Matt. It's possible Laura was caught up in it. That's what we're checking now.'

He shakes his head resolutely. 'I told you, she never touched that shit. We raised her to keep clear of it.'

'You were seen arguing with her a few weeks ago, on the beach, late at night. Can you tell me why?'

'Are you serious?' Matt leans forward in his chair, a muscle ticking under his left eye. It looks like he's having to work hard to stop himself from punching me. 'My daughter's dead, and all you do is criticise me for giving her advice.'

'Tell me what the row was about, Matt.'

'Laura sneaked out of the house late, to meet Danny Curnow, so I followed her. I knew she'd end up hurt if they stayed together.'

'The onlooker told us you were throwing your fists around.'

'Who said that, for fuck's sake? Do you really think I'd hit my own child?' He studies my face for a second, then his expression darkens. 'You're as bad as the rest of them.'

Matt storms out of the hall, leaving me relieved that Eddie has escorted the DCI back to the launch. Madron would take a dim view of the confrontation, after his advice to treat the family with care, but we need a breakthrough soon or he'll be pressing for a quick conviction.

I set off for Tom Horden's cottage with Shadow traipsing behind me through the fields. My old teacher may not be high on my suspect list, but I need to finish interviewing everyone present on the island the day

Laura died. Eddie has spoken to him already, but I want to hear his story for myself. I feel sure that Tom Horden will have been up with the larks, mathematical brain dividing the day into neat sections, but his appearance proves me wrong. Sparse grey hair sticks out from his skull in untidy clumps when I reach South Cottage. My old teacher is in need of a shave, brown trousers creased as he gives me a muted welcome.

'Sorry I missed the meeting, my wife had a bad night.' He angles his face towards me, his good eye making assessments. 'Please ignore the mess.'

His kitchen sink is piled with last night's dishes and a stack of laundry is dumped in the corner, proving that basic household chores are a burden on top of looking after his wife. There's stiffness in his movements as he sits at the table, rheumatism or discomfort slowing him down.

'Is this an official visit?'

I place the Dictaphone on the table. 'Everyone on the island is being interviewed about Laura's death.'

'Your constable knows we were here all morning. Emma won't be able to confirm it though, her memory's like a sieve.'

'I'd still like to speak to her again.'

'Don't disturb her, please.' Horden's face sours. 'It takes hours to calm her down.'

'When's the last time you saw Laura?'

'Our anniversary meal at the hotel last month. The girl gave us a free bottle of wine.'

'People saw her here more recently.'

His hands tremble in his lap. 'She dropped in occasionally, to keep Emma company. I don't remember the exact date of her last visit. Two weeks ago, perhaps.'

I give him a steady look. 'The schoolgirl you were accused of touching was younger than Laura, wasn't she? But they were the same physical type.'

His tone is icy when he speaks again. 'Nothing gets forgotten, does it?'

'Not when it's that serious. You got fired over it, didn't you?'

'That child's allegations cost me my career. I resigned to avoid the smears, even though I'd done nothing wrong. She was intent on harming me, but Emma was the real victim. She wouldn't leave the house for months.'

'Why?'

'Shame, I suppose, despite my innocence. Some children are as violent as adults. They want to bring us down to their level, but she never got the chance.'

'What happened when Laura came here?'

'She sat with Emma, chatting, watching TV. Most times I left them alone.'

'Did you pay her to keep your wife company?'

'Of course not. The girl visited us out of kindness.'

'Can I speak to Emma now, Tom?'

'It was twenty years ago, for God's sake. The charges were dropped.'

'This is to do with Laura, not the past.'

'We should still have legal representation.'

'I'm collecting facts, Tom. Neither of you are being accused of anything.'

His defensiveness interests me, and the fact that he lied about Laura's visits.

Emma Horden peers up at me when I enter the living room, her bowl of treasures cradled in her lap. It looks like she's been playing with her make-up box; dark red lipstick spiralling her mouth in a grotesque circle, peacock blue daubs on her eyelids. The effect is clownish without being funny. She gives me a suspicious stare when her husband exits the room.

'Go away. I don't like strangers.'

'You've known me since I was a child, Emma. You told me you'd seen Laura Trescothick, on the beach the other night.'

Her small eyes peer at me. 'Who?'

'The pretty blonde girl who visited you sometimes.' She shivers. 'Was it you that let her drown?'

'I'm trying to find out who hurt her. Tell me about your friendship with Laura.'

'She sings, or tells me stories. She'll be on TV one day.'

'Does your husband like her too?'

'He always likes the pretty ones.' Her face falls. 'Poor Tom. Almost blind, he relies on me these days.'

'Is that right?'

'Both eyes failing. Can't see the wood for the trees.' She cradles the bowl full of glittering trinkets closer to her chest, a few clam shells dropping into her lap.

'What else do you remember about Laura?'

'Don't tell my husband.' She presses her finger to her lips, swearing me to secrecy. 'I gave her money sometimes, to spread her wings.'

'That's kind, Emma. Do you remember how much?'

'None of your business.' The old woman reaches up, fingers snarling in her coarse grey hair.

'Will you show me your treasures before I go?' Something in her collection has caught my eye.

'Look, but don't touch.' When the old woman removes her hand, a red, heart-shaped earring just like the one in my pocket lies on top of the pile.

'That was Laura's,' I say, pointing to it. 'Where did you find it?'

'It's mine. No one can take it away.' Her voice is rising now, shrill with anxiety. Suddenly she lashes out, her clenched fist bouncing from my shoulder.

'Relax, Emma. Just tell me where it came from.'

'The girl let me keep it,' she whispers. 'To remember her by.'

She cradles the bowl closer to her chest, then croons quietly, as if she's comforting a child. I leave her to enjoy a rare moment of peace. My visit raises plenty of questions, but proves that the Hordens' marriage is more balanced than it seems: dementia and poor vision creating a level playing field. Emma's admission that she gave Laura money explains some of the cash in the girl's room, but I doubt she could have accessed such a large sum. Her confused state of mind makes it impossible to learn how she came by Laura's earring; she may simply have found it on the beach. Tom's reaction to my questions bothers me more. His professional humiliation twenty years ago seems to have left him afraid of judgement. Whether or not he behaved inappropriately, people love rumours, always believing there's no smoke without fire.

I pass the old schoolhouse then carry on walking, determined to get some fresh air before facing my deputy's constant cheeriness, the peak of Gweal Hill rising ahead of me. Breakers are curling across Hell Bay, a line of yellow spume draped across the shingle. It's only when I glance up at the hotel that I see Zoe waving; arms zigzagging like she's performing semaphore. I jog up the steps two at a time. She looks striking as always, blonde hair deliberately messy, like she's just crawled out of bed, but her mile-wide smile is absent for once.

'What's wrong?' I put my arm round her. 'Come inside, it's freezing out here.'

'Nothing, really. I just wanted to see a friendly face.'

When I glance through the doors of the bar, Angie Helyer is busy covering furniture with dust sheets, so I lead Zoe to the breakfast room. The space is more intimate but shares the same ocean view, the water two shades darker than the sky. My friend stands by the window, arms folded as she watches the sea.

'Who was I kidding, anyway? My voice is crap these days, it's years since I practised regularly.'

'Tell me what's happened.'

'One of the entertainment agencies turned me down. Maybe I should forget singing and stick to being a hotelier.'

'Don't be stupid. They've just got shit taste.'

She gives a narrow smile. 'Thanks for the confidence boost, big man.'

'Look, there's something I should check, but I'll come back. We can talk about it later.'

'You'll be too busy.' Zoe turns to face me. 'Can you even remember the last time we got pissed and lay on the floor, telling bad jokes?'

'Tonight, I promise.'

'Be here by ten and all is forgiven.'

She's already rallying by the time I leave, reminding me why I admire her. Zoe's childhood dreams have been dealt a hammer blow, but after five minutes of self-doubt she's hurrying back to work, her trademark smile firmly in place.

I give Eddie a brief explanation at the community hall, then he sets to work checking the Hordens' bank accounts, while I read an email from Alan Madron. The DCI's terse message advises me not to upset the victim's family again. I roll my eyes. The man doesn't seem to realise that ruffling a few feathers to reach the truth is an occupational hazard.

'The Hordens couldn't have given Laura much cash,' Eddie pipes up. 'They're scraping by on tiny pensions.'

His computer screen proves that my old teacher and his wife are virtually penniless, so the mystery of Laura's two thousand pounds remains unresolved. I spend the rest of the afternoon writing up witness reports and arranging a press conference for tomorrow, but neither Eddie nor I can understand how Laura Trescothick's earring ended up in Emma Horden's bowl of treasures.

By the time I head back to the cottage, frustration and hunger are burning a hole in my gut, the dog bounding across the beach after going AWOL all afternoon. His barks graduate to a full-blown howl as I open the door. In the kitchen, I empty a can of food into his dish and watch him dig in. Maggie appears in the doorway while the dog gorges himself, dressed in a bright yellow wind-cheater and carrying a wicker basket.

'How did you know I was starving?'

'Sixth sense. Plus, I wanted to check you're okay. I've brought lasagne, salad and chocolate fudge cake, courtesy of Billy.'

'My love for you grows stronger every day.'

'Odd how food affects men that way. Got anything to drink with this?'

'Coke?'

She wrinkles her nose. 'I'd rather hang onto my teeth, thanks. Let's have tap water.' Maggie pushes back her cloud of grey curls, nut-brown eyes scrutinising me. 'Give me details, Ben. Rumours are flying.'

I swallow a mouthful of pasta. 'It's all speculative so far.'

'But you've arrested Sam Austell?'

'Who told you that? He needs to recover before we can interview him.'

'Rose is on the warpath. The hospital say she can't visit yet; she came to see me, ranting about injustice.'

I rub my hand across the back of my neck. 'I'll drop by her cabin tomorrow.'

'You seriously think her boy attacked Laura?' Her face is expectant.

'Stop it, Maggie. You know I can't give details.'

'There's something else I'd like to know.' She narrows her eyes at me. 'A little bird tells me you spent the night with Nina.'

'For God's sake, I only spent a few hours at her cottage.'

'The island thrives on gossip, my love. You know that.'

'Nothing happened.'

Her shrewd gaze fixes on me. 'Pity, she could use some affection. I can't see why such a beautiful girl's alone, or you for that matter.'

'Maybe we're built that way.'

'Some bastard left her high and dry, I'll bet.' She studies me again. 'It's good you're spending time together.'

Maggie covers a lot of ground in the half-hour it takes to finish our meal. She informs me that Billy is planning to move into her flat; they're tired of running two homes. Hugging her goodbye is like embracing a robin, her small form fluttering in my arms, system revving for her next task. After she leaves I stare out of the window.

The hotel glitters on the horizon, like Christmas decorations strewn across the beach, incongruously cheerful. Part of me wishes I'd never begged to run the investigation, but watching someone else flounder would have felt even worse. When I look at the sea again, the waves are smaller than before, the tide retreating from the land. The water has been my worst enemy so far, washing away evidence from Laura's body, leaving little behind except my suspicion that her killer was close enough to watch her movements for a long time. He knew exactly where to find her, his face so familiar that she didn't even run when he brandished a knife. Under normal circumstances, a surveillance team would keep track of Matt Trescothick and Danny Curnow's movements, until the truth emerges, but no such luxuries are available here. When I turn back to the table, I feel sure that a vital piece is missing from the puzzle. I switch on my computer and check the islanders' statements again, until my eyes start to blur.

22

When I arrive at Zoe's flat at ten, she's pouring tequila into shot glasses misted with ice, the Kaiser Chiefs belting out the loud, old-fashioned rock we loved when we were in our teens. Shadow bounds across the room to greet her, with far more affection than he ever shows me.

'Here's to drowning our sorrows,' she says, pressing a glass into my hand.

'I haven't got any.'

She snorts out a laugh. 'You're burying them in work, sunshine. Keeping busy lets you off the hook.'

'When did you become a psychiatrist?'

'Tell me why you came home, then I'll stop nagging.'

'I'm not in a talkative mood.'

'Dance then, for fuck's sake, and let off some steam.'

'This is your front room, Zoe, not a nightclub.'

She grabs my hand anyway, and the combination of raw booze, good music and her goading makes me revert to type. I loved dancing with her as a kid, even though

I lumbered like a carthorse, while she was a picture of lithe grace. Three of our favourite numbers pass before we collapse back onto the sofa, laughing like fools. The release of adrenalin makes the conversation flow easily again for the next few hours. She tells me that she plans to keep on singing, despite today's rejection.

'I can't let the bastards grind me down.'

'You wanted to be Blondie when we were at school, like you could turn the clock back forty years. Do you remember?'

'I prefer Madeleine Peyroux these days.'

'Your voice is way better.'

She looks amused. 'Why can't I fancy you, Ben? You're ideal boyfriend material.'

'You missed your chance in year eight.' The brutal crush I had on her at thirteen is common knowledge. Luckily, it passed in weeks and our friendship resumed, unscathed.

'That's true,' she replies, her voice starting to slur. 'What do you want from life anyway, big man?'

Her expression is suddenly so serious I end up fumbling for the truth. 'Love and happiness, I suppose, just like everyone else.'

'That formula hasn't worked for me.' She slides her empty glass back across the table. 'I'd like a kid before I'm too old to enjoy it, but my relationships never work. I'll have to find another way.'

'Time for bed, kiddo. You've stopped making sense.'

It's the early hours when I haul her to her feet and lead

her to her bedroom. She's too drunk to be left alone, but when I peer into her spare room, the bed is piled with boxes full of vinyl – jazz albums struggling for space alongside Emeli Sandé and Pharrell Williams. My only option is to use her sofa, but it's a losing battle. It's one of those shiny leather deals, so overstuffed that even my fourteen-stone weight fails to make a dent.

In the morning, my bones ache from head to toe. Shadow must have grown cold in the night, because he's stretched across my chest like a canine duvet, whimpering in protest when I nudge him onto the floor. It crosses my mind that I'll be having dinner with Nina Jackson tonight. The idea of seeing her again lifts my spirits, but Zoe's moans seep through the wall around 7 a.m., so I make coffee and carry it through to her room. We sit in bed to drink it, with backs against the headboard. The view reminds me of her conflict of interest. Singing may be her passion, but she loves it here too much to leave; miles of uncluttered ocean spilling across the beach.

'Christ, I'm a lightweight. I used to be able to hold my booze, back in the day.' She turns to study me. 'You look even worse than me.'

'The case kept me awake. You knew Laura pretty well, Zoe. Who did she trust most?'

'Get to know Dean Miller, he's the island's Pied Piper. Adults give him a wide berth, but kids always seek him out.'

Shadow sprints across the beach with his usual joie de vivre when I take him back to the cottage. Zoe's words stick in my mind, because they chime with Dean Miller's claims when Eddie and I visited him, but my promise to go and see Rose Austell has to be fulfilled.

Once the dog is safely locked indoors, I head inland, passing the natural swimming pool that islanders use at the end of summer, fed by the run-off from Gweal Hill. It stays warm long after the sea cools, flanked by tall rocks that are ideal for diving. I stand at the edge, staring at the weeds choking its surface, wishing for those childhood days when my only concern was summer-holiday boredom. There's no sign of Rose when I reach Green Bay. Knowing her tendency to shun visitors, I crouch down and call through the letter box, promising to take her to the mainland today to see her son, and telling her to meet on the quay at noon. My only reply is a muffled curse in the distance, but I'm certain she heard, so I straighten up again and head for the old schoolhouse.

Dean Miller appears as soon as I arrive. He's wearing frayed overalls and clutches a box of paints, his oddly boyish eyes peering at me. Up close, he looks tired, deep lines marking his skin.

'You're up early, Dean.'

'Best time of day for painting.' He nods at the sky. 'The light's at its clearest.'

'Can I speak to you about Laura?'

'I've got another visitor, but that won't matter.' He sets off towards his studio before I can ask who arrived before me.

Dean's workspace stands at the end of his overgrown garden, a crude wooden building with skylights cut into the ceiling, a heater in the corner releasing paraffin fumes. A slim figure is hunched by the window. Suzanne Trescothick looks startled to see me, the young girl scrambling to her feet.

'There's no need to leave, Suzie,' Miller tells her.

'I should go,' she says quietly. 'Dad'll be expecting me home.'

The girl slips through the door before I can say a word, but her haunted expression lingers in my mind. It intrigues me that she chose Miller's studio as her sanctuary, despite the man's offhand manner. He's busy poking through brushes scattered over his workbench, as if her quick departure leaves him unconcerned. The walls are covered with seascapes that are too garish for my taste. One of the paintings is two metres wide, waves crashing to the shore in a frenzy of colour.

'Is that your favourite?' He turns to face me.

'It's dramatic, that's for sure.'

'You hate it, I can tell. Don't you go to exhibitions?'

'Not often. I can't see why anyone would pay millions for a Picasso.'

'Proud to be a philistine?'

'Books are my thing, not art. If I was rich I'd collect signed first editions.' I turn in his direction again. 'Do you exhibit your work much?'

'There's no need. I've got loyal patrons in the States.'

Dean returns his attention to his easel. I can see why

Laura loved it here; bebop jazz drifting from the stereo, sun beaming through the skylights and the glamour of watching something emerge from nothing. Pale grey lines are threading across Miller's empty canvas already, as if he's sketching ghosts.

'Laura was fascinated by you. She said so, in one of her letters.'

His hand jerks back from the painting, but his eyes stay focused. 'Kids are easy to impress. She imagined I knew something about the world.'

'She must have confided in you, Dean.'

'Not really. She asked questions mainly, about old-time movie stars.'

'And told you her secrets?'

'Only her escape plans. She wanted to hitchhike down the west coast of America with Danny, when she finished college. Then they'd be actors in LA, and make a fortune. Easy as one, two, three.' Behind the cynicism, his tone is mournful. 'She worked hard to get that boy; we planned her campaign together.'

'Dozens of love letters?'

'The direct approach works wonders.'

I visualise the envelopes on my kitchen table, packed with dreams and fantasies, hundreds of tender words. 'Why did Suzie come here this morning?'

He carries on sketching. 'To escape from reality for a while, I imagine.'

'Can I see your paintings of Laura?'

'Feel free. Two unfinished ones are over there.'

He points at a pile of canvases propped against the wall. Most are his usual brash seascapes, but two smaller ones are hidden at the back, a couple of feet square. The images are stark enough to make my jaw drop. In the first, Laura stands naked in a pale blue room, her frame small as a child's, arms outstretched like she's begging for an embrace. Her gaze is so hard-eyed, I feel obliged to look away. The other one is even more disturbing. Sprawled on her back, one arm covers her breasts, the image graphic as a centrefold. When I stand up again, Dean is wearing a narrow smile.

'More to your taste, Inspector?'

'Do her parents know you painted her like this?'

He rolls his eyes. 'Laura was at ease with her body. That's why she'd have made a fine actor.'

'I'm surprised she agreed to it.'

'She always had a chaperone. Suzie came with her most times; I guess that's why the kid keeps coming back here. Those two were never apart. She sat in the corner, doing schoolwork while Laura modelled for me.'

'Did you pay her?'

'Fifty quid a pop. She did five or six sittings.' He looks at the paintings again, expression closed. 'I'll never finish them now. I may as well burn them.'

'Were you in love with her?'

His strident laughter ricochets from the walls. 'I've never slept with a woman in my life. You're more my type: tall, broad-shouldered, butch. I have to travel to the mainland for guys like you.'

I stand my ground, even though his stare feels invasive. 'Life here must get lonely sometimes.'

'No one makes judgements, that's why I stay.'

'Laura must have spoken to you, Dean. She came here dozens of times. You're protecting her killer by keeping the information to yourself.'

'I told you before, I've got nothing to say.'

The expression in his eyes is suddenly so hostile that I wonder if I've misjudged him as a harmless eccentric. Maggie may have been right about his loneliness souring into a toxic force. I feel certain that he and Suzie Trescothick could fill in some of the gaps about Laura's death, but they prefer silence. Dean returns to his painting, releasing a frenzy of brushstrokes onto the canvas as Dizzy Gillespie's trumpet soars. I take one last look at Laura's face before leaving – defiantly young and beautiful, as if nothing could get in her way.

23

Shadow trots peacefully at my side until we reach the community hall. Then he cowers behind me, releasing a series of loud barks, until a figure in dark jeans and a waterproof jacket emerges into view. Jim Helyer keeps his distance while the dog continues to howl.

'Calm down,' I mutter, grabbing Shadow's collar. 'Go inside, Jim. He's having a mad half-hour.' I crouch beside the dog, looking into his colourless eyes. 'What's your problem? Stay outside and keep out of trouble.'

The dog's odd behaviour continues; he loiters in the porch, instead of doing his usual vanishing act. When I get inside, Jim is making stilted conversation with Eddie.

'Recovered from your migraine?' I ask.

'It was a blinder. All I can do when one hits is lie down in a dark room ...'

His voice tails into silence as the Dictaphone whirs. I've set aside my discomfort about interviewing my old friend over the girl's murder, but I know it won't be easy. The best way to make him talk is to stay quiet, forcing him to share his thoughts, while Eddie scribbles on his notepad.

'Tell us about Laura Trescothick, Jim. Begin wherever you like.'

The request makes him shift awkwardly in his seat, fingers toying with the cuffs of his frayed work shirt. When I study my friend objectively for the first time in years, I see that he's on the cusp of middle age, tension apparent in his body language, his wind-blown hair as ragged as a scarecrow's.

'It started last winter.' He rubs his temple hard, like he's trying to dislodge a bad idea. 'She turned into this perfect beauty, pure and uncomplicated. I know it sounds crazy, but I didn't even care that she had a boyfriend. She was in my head all the time.'

'When did you tell her how you felt?'

'Christmas time. Angie had gone to the pub to meet friends, and I waited at the house for Laura. I tried to kiss her, but she slapped my face. She wouldn't let me explain.' He hunches forward, gazing down at his hands. 'Laura was right to push me away. It did us all a favour.'

'You must have hated her for rejecting you.'

'I deserved it. What kind of creep comes onto a girl half their age? She probably saw me as some sort of pervert.'

'Were you afraid she'd tell Angie?' I ask. 'They worked together, after all.'

'I thought she'd speak to her sister, or Danny. She would never have upset my wife deliberately.'

It takes Jim fifteen minutes to vent his feelings. He had fantasies about the pair of them fleeing the island, like his family didn't exist, but he claims that Laura's rejection ended it in its tracks. Her phone and email records support his statements. There's no evidence that he sent her a single message in the last three months. Eventually, my friend runs out of steam, his gaze flitting back to my face while he waits for my verdict.

'You had a motive to hurt her, Jim. An infatuation gone sour.'

His expression is imploring. 'Why would I be here now? I could have kept quiet and you'd be none the wiser. I just needed it off my chest.'

'Don't leave the island without my permission. We may want to speak to you again.'

Jim gives a curt nod before leaving the hall. Our thirty-year friendship may never recover from my accusations, just like his damaged marriage. When I look at Eddie again, he's shaking his head.

'That bloke's got the perfect life; a farm, a lovely wife, kids. Some people don't know when they're lucky,' he says quietly.

My deputy's expression is too serious for his boyish features, like a child pretending to be grown-up. I spend the next half-hour completing my case log, aware that every step will have to be justified to the DCI at the meeting I've arranged for ten o'clock.

Alan Madron arrives precisely on time, dressed in chinos and a sleek oilskin jacket, not a hair out of place.

'What's this about?' he asks coolly. 'You could have updated me yesterday.'

'We've been busy, sir. I needed to complete my report.'

'Go on then, I haven't got all day.'

'The press are baying for information. I'm giving them a briefing at Penzance station at noon; I'll catch the Sky Bus from St Mary's.'

Madron stares at me. 'You invited the media, without my permission?'

'As SIO, I decide when to involve the press.' Most of the journalists I've met are chancers and fantasists, paying their rent by flogging lies to the tabloids, but staying silent will result in outlandish stories flooding the internet. At least this way I can control the information.

'We'll discuss your actions later. Just give me your update, Kitto.'

'We've ruled out most of the islanders. Some have cast-iron alibis, others are too frail to harm anyone. Matt Trescothick relies on his wife financially, ego struggling with being unemployed. There's no hard evidence yet that he killed his daughter, despite his anger-management problems, but it's a strong possibility. They were seen arguing on the beach days before she died. Danny Curnow has kept a low profile since finding her body. We only have his mother's word that he was at home when Laura was killed. For all we know, she rejected him and he killed her in a fit of rage.'

Madron peers up from his notes. 'So the boyfriend, father and the ex are still suspects?'

'There are more distant ones too. Dean Miller spent time with her, and I'm certain he knows more than he's saying, but he's got no clear motive.' I hesitate before adding the last name. 'Jim Helyer's admitted to fancying Laura, but his wife's given him an alibi.'

'Are either of those two serious possibilities?'

'They can't be ruled out, but it's more likely to be someone closer to home. Families are so interconnected here, relationships can feel incestuous. I'll be taking Rose Austell over to the mainland later. She's been complaining about her son's treatment.'

'Sam Austell's still your main suspect, from my point of view.'

'He may know who hurt Laura, but they split up a year ago. That's a long time to wait for revenge.'

'The boy was out of his head on drugs.'

'It's more likely he was hiding from Laura's killer. I think both of them were running contraband round the island.'

'Don't go throwing accusations around without hard evidence. Her family have suffered enough already. When this case finishes, the islanders will have to put their lives back together and carry on, just like before.'

I check my watch. 'I should go, sir. Rose Austell is meeting me on the quayside.'

'Not on your own,' Madron says, rising to his feet. 'I'll lead the press conference.'

The DCI's intervention bothers me, but there's nothing I can do. He seems irritated by my desire to treat Sam Austell as innocent until proven guilty, just like all the other men who hovered around Laura like bees to a honeypot. At least Madron's presence could defuse some of Rose Austell's anger with me for admitting her son to hospital. I'd rather not share the boat and plane journey to Penzance with the boy's mother while she's in a state of rage, but it's par for the course. Nothing about the investigation has been ideal so far.

'What should I do while you're away, boss?' Eddie asks.

'Find out if anyone else has been seen wandering round the island at night.'

Madron wastes no time in haranguing me once we get outside, still furious that I contacted the media without his agreement. I hold my tongue until his tirade ends, his voice finally calming as we head for the quay. He asks how Eddie is performing, offering to bring a more experienced officer over from the mainland, but I reject the idea immediately. An enthusiastic sixth-former is better than a jaded old-timer who knows nothing about island culture.

Rose Austell's dyed black hair looks brittle in the winter sunlight, patchwork coat several sizes too big, a bitter look on her face. Maybe she thinks that Sam could have avoided hospital if I'd left him alone. She cowers in the wheelhouse as the ferry sets off and Bryher recedes into the distance, and is still shivering when we arrive at the minute airport on St Mary's. The hangar resembles a motorway service station, hunkered by the runway, covered in dull-brown roof tiles. The Sky Bus waiting to carry us to the mainland is little bigger than a helicopter. Madron marches onboard first, leaving me to deal with Rose. She leans towards me, releasing a waft of scented air, the aromas of mint and dried rose petals trapped in the folds of her coat.

'Sam's never hurt anyone in his life. Why did you arrest him?'

'He's not under arrest, Rose. I just need to speak to him. He was in contact with Laura before she died; we need to know why.'

'What's wrong with talking to your ex?' She tosses back her hair. 'People often stay friendly after a relationship ends.'

'Your son took some serious drugs. Do you know where they came from?'

'My boy would never harm himself deliberately.'

'He couldn't even say his name when I found him.' Her face is growing paler by the minute. 'When's the last time you flew to the mainland?'

Rose doesn't reply, but I'm certain this is her first time on a plane. Her eyes are wide with fear when it taxis down the runway, engine buzzing like an irate mosquito. Panic makes her forget our differences as it takes off, fingers clutching my wrist until the mainland appears on the horizon twenty minutes later. Even under these conditions the outlook is stunning. Cornwall's granite coastline is indented by hundreds of minute coves, perfect hiding places for smugglers.

DCI Madron stalks away when we reach Penzance, leaving me to deliver Rose to the hospital by taxi. Her frown deepens as Dr Lucas describes Sam's condition.

'He's responding to anti-psychotic drugs, but his condition's delicate. Any more stress could undo his progress.'

'Is he able to communicate now?' I ask.

'He still struggles with direct questions.'

'When can I interview him for the murder inquiry?'

'Not today, I'm afraid.' The consultant's eyes are calm as she holds my gaze. 'You'll have to take it gently, Inspector. Further trauma could jeopardise his recovery.'

A uniformed officer is still guarding his room, but Austell looks too weak to mount an escape bid. He's sitting by the window, dressed in an ill-fitting tracksuit, keeping his pinched face averted. I stay in the background while he answers Rose's questions in slow monosyllables; his physical gestures are sluggish too, as if invisible weights burden his limbs. I wait until his mother has covered his bedside cabinet with packets of home-made medicine, before drawing my chair closer.

'Remember me, Sam? I'm DI Kitto.' I can't tell if he's listening as he rocks back and forth in his seat. 'Can you tell me what scared you, the day Laura died?'

'I'm next on the list. The tide changes everything,' he whispers.

'Who sold you the drugs?'

His face splits into a grin. 'Friends in high places, over the sea and far away.'

'Listen to me, Sam. I know you were hiding from someone. You understand Laura's dead, don't you?' I lean forwards to catch his reply but Rose grabs my sleeve.

'Stop persecuting him,' she snaps. 'You've done enough damage.'

She stands by her son's chair, cradling his head against her chest. Sam carries on rocking while Rose strokes his hair. I stay for another quarter of an hour then slip away.

It's a relief to get outside, even though the sky is misting the town with fine grey drizzle. I turn up my collar and head for Penzance police station – a drab municipal building, one street back from the quay. A pack of journalists has travelled down from London, including faces I recognise from other murder investigations. They look like a funeral party, milling on the pavement, dressed in the black clothes that media types wear like a self-imposed uniform. The sight of them makes me choose the back entrance, to avoid the cameramen.

I make an attempt to smarten my appearance before the briefing, but it's a losing battle; I was born scruffy. All I can do is fasten the top button of my shirt, then smooth my ragged hair, as it dawns on me that I should have worn a suit. The story will open the one o'clock news. The room is already prepared, a table with two microphones, two dozen chairs laid out in rows.

'You've got a full house,' Madron says. 'The BBC are here, Channel 4, and all the local press. Why request that much coverage, without an arrest to announce?'

'Damage limitation, sir. It'll stop them paying the islanders for gossip, and printing any more rubbish.'

A flicker of disapproval crosses the DCI's impassive face. This must be his biggest case since taking over the island force; a world away from the petty crimes he deals with all year. 'Don't let them bait you, Kitto. I'll answer any difficult questions.'

Madron takes the seat beside me as the cameras roll. I've sat through enough press calls to know that you can never relax; even a small slip-up makes you look clueless. My new boss seems to understand the rules of engagement. He sits motionless, his expression grave. The first question comes from a BBC reporter, the woman's calm gaze assessing me.

'Can you describe your progress in finding Laura Trescothick's killer, Inspector Kitto?'

'We've been pursuing some strong lines of enquiry. The murderer was on Bryher, on Monday the first of March. That's why islanders can only leave with our permission and all visitors are barred.'

'Less than a hundred people live on the island. Why's it taking so long to solve the case?' The questioner's voice is an unpleasant nasal whine. It's one of the slea-zeballs from the tabloids, Steve Hilliard, inspecting me with distaste, as another camera flashes. His brown hair sticks up in uneven clumps, leather jacket stretched tight over his paunch.

'At the time of Laura's death, seventy-two people were on the island. We're interviewing them systematically.'

I explain that Bryher has been crime-free for years; the kind of place where people leave their doors unlocked and kids play in safety. A handful of journalists ask easy questions for the next ten minutes, allowing me to pretend the case is making progress. Hilliard begins talking again before I can gather my thoughts.

'You're on extended leave from your job in London, Inspector. Your colleagues say you burnt out and tried to resign. Are you really the right man to lead the investigation?'

The DCI delivers a sharp kick under the table to silence me. 'Inspector Kitto's seniors at the Met have authorised his role here. I'm pleased to have someone of his calibre in charge. His inside knowledge of the islands is valuable too. Now, ladies and gentlemen, we have a murder investigation to run. Thanks for your time.'

My respect for Madron increases as he refuses further questions with a firm head shake. In the staff room afterwards, he eyes me warily, as if I'm a loose cannon, capable of misfiring at any time. It's clear that his patience will wear out fast if I put another foot wrong. The police cameraman is replaying our interview on a computer nearby. We look like chalk and cheese: the DCI small and contained, me sprawling and chaotic.

I make a mental note to get my hair cut before facing another interrogation.

Rose Austell weeps silently during the short plane ride back to St Mary's, but her tears have dried by the time the launch drops us on Bryher Quay. When I look at her more closely, her face is pale, hands trembling as I help her out of the boat.

'You should be ashamed,' she snaps. 'Sam's too ill for your bullying.'

'I'm sorry, Rose, but a girl's been killed. I think he knows who did it.'

She stares up at me. 'My boy would have told you who hurt her, if you'd stayed to listen.'

'What did he say?'

'Ask him yourself. You can do your own dirty work from now on.'

Rose's frown feels like a witch's curse. I doubt that Sam made a single rational statement today, but pretending she knows the facts must give her a sense of control. I stand at the waterside with the day's events flooding my mind. It's only five thirty, but dusk has already fallen. The island's darkness is thickening rapidly as I stumble down the path, wishing I'd brought my torch.

24

Rose still can't believe the change in her son. Sam has become unrecognisable, no sign now of the free-spirited child that tore across the beach, kicking a football all day long. Toxic chemicals in his system have made him retreat too far inside himself for her to reach. She comes to a halt on the sand at Green Bay, hoping to inhale the sea's calmness. She's too distracted to notice a difference in the air when she unlocks the cabin, until a faint sound sets her nerves on edge. Shock almost makes her lose her balance when she sees Jay Curnow sitting at her kitchen table, watching her take off her coat.

'How did you get in?'

He gives a fake smile. 'Your back door needs fixing, Rose, like the rest of this hovel.'

'What do you want?'

'I've got some papers for you to sign. It's time you found somewhere decent to live, isn't it?'

'I'll never leave my home.'

'It's a breeding ground for rats. Environmental health

would throw you out in minutes. Put your name on this transfer form, and you'll have enough money for a nice bedsit on the mainland.'

Rose shoves the folder back at him, the gesture bringing Curnow to his feet.

'Sooner or later you'll give in, so why play hard to get?' Suddenly he lashes out, fist banging against the wooden wall. 'This place is falling apart. It won't need a wrecking ball, just a few blokes with sledgehammers.'

'Leave me alone.'

'No one's protecting you, Rose.' His hard face is inches from hers. 'I only have to call in some favours; Pete Moorcroft owes me a small fortune and so does Jim Helyer. Half the men on the island will do whatever I say.'

'I'll tell the police.'

Curnow gives a grating laugh. 'We're just two neighbours, passing the time of day. I haven't put a mark on you.' His hand hovers above her face, as if he plans to smother her. 'Sign the papers and no one will get hurt, if you keep away from my son. He doesn't need your old wives' tales poisoning his mind.'

The smell of the man's anger curdles with his expensive cologne after he leaves. Rose stares at the folder he has left behind, too agitated to sit down.

25

My mood must be affecting Shadow, who prowls from room to room as if he's looking for something valuable. The day's drama is still in my mind when I cook dinner: Dean Miller's disturbing pictures of Laura, followed by the awkwardness of interviewing Jim, and Sam Austell's drug-addled nonsense. But the simple actions of throwing a fish pie together and chopping salad help to calm me, while Scott Matthews plays in the background. He's been my favourite singer for years, his soulful voice and poetic lyrics helping me unwind. A fire is roaring in the grate when Nina taps on the door.

She's bundled in scarves and a long coat, clutching a box of chocolates. I watch her peel off layers until she stands before me in skinny jeans and a wide-necked jumper that's slipped down to expose one pale-skinned shoulder. For a moment I'm lost for words, so I kiss her cheek instead. She returns the gesture, then leans down to lavish attention on the dog.

'You prefer him to me, don't you?'

'Obviously.' Her smile flickers. 'You were on the news just now. Don't you get any media training? You looked like Heathcliff on a bad day.'

'It's not my job to placate journalists.'

She angles her head to one side. 'Want me to come back another day?'

'You're not leaving. I need you here to distract me.'

Nina seems at ease in my lacklustre kitchen. She stands at the Butler sink, rinsing wine glasses, then roots in the drawer for cutlery. By the time I take the pie from the oven, she's lit the candles I unearthed from the sideboard. When I carry plates through to the living room, she's inspecting my bookshelves.

'Hundreds of novels, poetry collections and one hell of a vinyl collection,' she comments.

'My parents were jazz fans, the books are mine. My brother and I spent our summers swimming, but in the winter we read, or made up games. Not having a TV made us pretty inventive.'

'I was a telly addict. I can recite whole passages of *Grey's Anatomy*.'

'Lucky you, I had to watch *Match of the Day* at a mate's house. By eighteen I was climbing the walls, so I moved to London. The city was like a giant shot of adrenalin after so much quiet.'

Her eyes are tarnished gold, not missing a trick. 'What made you become a cop?'

'I considered boatbuilding, but police work won

the day.' I study her again. 'Where did you grow up, anyway?'

'Bath; a refined city, full of retirees taking the waters.'

'Are your family still there?'

'Just my parents; I'm an only child.' She drops her gaze. 'To be honest, I'm more of a listener than a talker.'

When I lean over to touch the tips of her hair, she freezes. 'If you're expecting witty banter you're in the wrong place.'

The conversation gradually finds a rhythm as we linger over the meal. Our talk is light and impersonal, until she relaxes again. She teases me about my musical taste, which veers from gloomy northern rock to Motown and R&B, but the rules of the game are frustrating.

'Aren't you going to say anything about yourself? You could explain the wedding ring for a start.'

'That's off limits.'

'It'll be tough getting to know you if you don't open up.'

'Why not admit defeat?'

'It's not in my nature. A challenge only whets my appetite.'

I cart the dishes through to the kitchen for some breathing space. Our conversation is so finely balanced, one word could send her marching out the door. When I turn round, she's standing a few feet away.

'Why did you invite me here, Ben?'

Her insistent tone makes it impossible to lie. 'Because I fancy you, obviously.'

She holds my gaze. 'You still haven't explained why you left London.'

'It's a long story.'

'That's okay. I'm in no rush.'

The idea of opening up sets my teeth on edge, but Nina has already settled on the sheepskin rug by the fire, her face expectant, Shadow curling at her side. I've never felt less willing to expose my mistakes. 'I came back to fix this place up as a holiday home, and I wanted to work with Ray again, too.'

'But there's another reason, isn't there?' The lack of judgement on her face makes me carry on.

'When I joined the Murder Squad ten years ago, they paired me with a detective called Clare Kirkbride. She'd spent her career working undercover; a chain-smoking Glaswegian, unmarried, cynical as they come, twenty years older than me. The chemistry shouldn't have worked, but it did, from day one. She was a brilliant mentor and put up with my mistakes when we became work partners. Last year we worked on our hardest undercover case ever: sex trafficking, three women burned alive in a car, dozens more tortured. I knew it was getting to her, but missed the signs. I thought she could handle anything.' My voice runs out abruptly, forcing me to take a breath.

'What happened to Clare?'

'She was due to retire. After living for her job, it must have felt like stepping into a void. I got this message one night, six weeks ago, too garbled to understand. I thought she was out with mates, getting pissed. When another one came, I knew something was wrong. I broke into her flat too late. She'd taken an overdose.'

Nina studies my face in silence before speaking again. 'I'm sorry, Ben. Suicide's a brutal thing to do.'

'It's me that let her down. She'd been dropping hints about feeling low, wrapped up in her usual jokes. It was easier to laugh than take it seriously.' I rub my hands across my face, wishing the whole mess could be wiped away. 'Her note didn't say much, except asking me to look after Shadow.'

'If he was Clare's dog, no wonder you resent him.'

'How do you mean?'

'Shadow must remind you she's not here, every day.' The dog's ears prick up at the mention of his name.

'It felt wrong to work with a new partner, but my boss wouldn't accept my resignation.'

'She must value you.'

'There aren't enough idiots to do the job.' I attempt a smile. 'What about you? It's my turn to listen.'

'One revelation's enough for tonight. I should go, I've got a client for cranial massage early tomorrow.'

'Is that what you gave me?'

She nods. 'Dean Miller thinks it frees up his creativity, but I have my doubts.' She rises to her feet in a graceful movement that makes me want to touch her again.

It's only ten thirty, the evening soured by talk of the past. The bitter aftertaste reminds me of the night I found Shadow barking his head off in Clare's hall, sirens blaring from the street below. When I force myself back into the present, Nina is already fastening her coat, wrapping her scarf around her throat.

'I'll walk you home.'

'No need.'

'There's a curfew, remember? You shouldn't be out alone.' I pick up my jacket before she can argue.

The dog vanishes across the dunes as Nina puts her hand through my arm, but I know my chances are blown. What kind of woman would let a man with so much baggage within a mile? She seems oblivious to my bad mood as we head down the path.

'You were lucky, growing up here. My childhood was horribly suburban.'

'It wasn't all picnics and wild swimming. Kids don't notice beautiful scenery.'

'But you do now?'

'It keeps pulling me back. The place is in my DNA.'

We complete the walk in silence. I wait on the porch while she unlocks Gweal Cottage, then stands on the threshold.

'I won't invite you in, Ben.'

'Pity.'

I'm about to say goodnight when her hands rise to my face and she's on her toes, kissing me. It's not some half-hearted peck on the cheek either. Her teeth graze my lip, fingers snagging in my hair. The kiss is so thorough that all I can do is go along for the ride, clutching the slim curve of her waist. I'm speechless by the time she finally pulls back, her eyes a shade darker than before.

'I fancy you too, by the way.'

'No kidding.' I run my fingertip over the curve of her cheek. 'Lucky me.'

'I've always liked honest men.'

'I'll never tell another lie.'

She backs inside then shuts the door, leaving me alone on her step. The pain from talking about Clare has ebbed away; sooner or later I had to tell someone. The walk home seems to take seconds, wind scattering dry leaves across the shingle. Elation is still buzzing round my system, but Shadow is far ahead, howling loud enough to wake the dead. When I reach the house, his barking alternates with pitiful whimpering.

'Pipe down, monster. What's the fuss about?'

I circle the house, scanning the overgrown garden with my torch, until a glint of metal catches my eye. Shock makes me reel backwards at the sight of a knife with a nine-inch blade lying on my doorstep, gleaming in the moonlight. I yank my phone from my pocket and dial Nina's number, to warn her to stay indoors.

26

Rose is still fretting about Curnow's threats when someone taps on her door, the sound almost too quiet to hear.

Suzanne Trescothick is waiting in the dark. The child's face is as pale as candle wax, her eyes shadowed by adult suffering. Rose is so used to the girl's night-time visits that she welcomes her without hesitation.

'Come inside, sweetheart,' she murmurs.

The girl huddles by the kitchen window, weeping into her cupped hands. Rose keeps busy making her a drink of hot milk and honey. She understands that the child must cry out her sorrow; painful emotions need to be released, not held inside. It's only when she notices a mark on the girl's wrist that she feels concerned.

'That looks sore. How did you hurt yourself, Suzie?'

The girl fumbles with her sleeve. 'Please don't tell anyone.'

'It's your story to tell, but it's been going on too long. This arnica cream will help you heal.'

Suzanne slips the jar into her pocket. 'What should I do? I can't stand it at home without Laura.'

'Tell someone the truth. You could talk to me, or Dean, or the police.'

'I can't, Rose. I'd be in so much trouble.'

The girl seems calmer when she finally leaves, but Rose's thoughts are in turmoil. Someone on the island is preying on the young and vulnerable. Anger sends her outside with her torch. Removing the flint marker, she digs up the package she retrieved from the beach. Sam has never disclosed what the boatmen trade, but when she unwraps it, hundreds of transparent sachets are filled with a pale, chalky substance.

Rose yanks up the lid of her wood burner, without pausing to consider, then throws the sachets inside. When the chemicals vaporise in blue and yellow flares, she understands the consequences of her rash gesture. Her chance to return the package has burned away. The one thing protecting her from the smugglers' demands no longer exists, but she can't let another young life be ruined.

27

I stand outside the cottage making calls, reminding people to lock their doors. The idea of the killer stalking me across the island makes me angry enough to let rip.

'You fucking coward!'

The wind dilutes my words, but it feels good to yell the frustration out of my system. I use an evidence bag to collect the knife and dump it on the table. There are scrapes on the handle, the long blade scarred from repeated sharpening. Whether or not it's the murder weapon, the killer has upped the ante since leaving the chopped-up photograph. Tonight's unwelcome visitor might not be connected with Laura's death at all, but why would someone else threaten me? This guy's a game player, taunting me that he's out of reach. My gut tells me that the gesture puts Sam Austell in the clear, despite the DCI's certainty that's he's our only credible suspect. When I stare at the knife again, a memory surfaces of Billy Reese in the pub kitchen, chopping herbs with a red-handled knife.

It takes me less than ten minutes to jog to the Rock, with Shadow in hot pursuit. At midnight, light is still leaking through the curtains of Maggie's living room above the entrance. My godmother appears in a vivid green dressing gown, anxiety behind her smile of greeting.

'Can you unlock downstairs for me, Maggie? Shadow can stay here.'

My godmother looks bemused, but follows my instructions, the dog whining at being left behind. She stands in the doorway while strip lights cast a stark glare over the kitchen's industrial ovens and steel tables.

'What on earth are you looking for, Ben?'

'Billy's knives,' I reply, yanking open a cutlery drawer.

'They're on the wall, ahead of you.'

Red-handled knives hang from a metallic strip, organised by size. I can tell straight away that tonight's offering belongs to the set; there's a gap between a vegetable knife and a cleaver with a foot-long blade, handles worn from heavy usage.

'Is Billy upstairs?'

Maggie shakes her head. 'He's in his flat packing his stuff, so he can move in tomorrow. Aren't you going to say what this is about?'

'Soon, I promise. Now go back up and lock your doors. Keep Shadow with you till morning.'

Maggie asks another question, but I'm already jogging towards the two-storey block fifty metres away, used for staff accommodation. Billy has lived in the ground-floor flat for the past ten years. When he lets me in, he's leaning on his stick, the radio droning in the background, his books and CDs crammed into dozens of cardboard boxes. The chef is dressed in a tatty black T-shirt, jeans and biker boots, jaw rimed with grey five o'clock shadow. It strikes me again that this ageing Hells Angel is Maggie's new love interest, and his injured foot might be a convenient lie. The guy could easily have left his knife on my doorstep then returned home without anyone noticing.

'It's late for beer and a chat, Ben.'

'Someone left this on my doorstep just now.' I lay the knife on his table, still wrapped in its evidence bag. 'Recognise it?'

He turns it over in his hands. 'It went missing from the pub kitchen a few months ago; Sabatiers don't come cheap, so it pissed me off. Chefs get attached to their knives. They become like family members.' He gives an uneasy smile.

'You think someone stole it?'

'They must have. The kitchen door's always open when I cook, for ventilation. Someone must have walked in when I was on a fag break.'

According to his story, any islander could have entered the pub's kitchen and helped themselves from his collection of cutting implements, but something doesn't ring true. His arms are folded too tightly across his chest, his direct stare making him look defensive.

'Did you spend much time alone with Laura Trescothick?'

'Not that I remember. The kid came in the pub with her mum and dad, but that's it.'

'Listen, I'll be putting your name through the police computer system again tomorrow. If there are skeletons in your closet, tell me now.'

His fingers tug the shoulder seam of his T-shirt. 'Do you want a beer first?'

'No, thanks.'

'I bloody well do. This type of thing is exactly why I left the mainland.'

'What were you running from?'

'Nothing serious, just some trouble from the past.'

'You don't have a record, Billy.'

'I changed my name by deed poll twelve years ago, from Sutton to Reese. I decided to turn over a new leaf and use my mum's maiden name.' His gaze slips away. 'I hung out with the wrong people for too long when I lived in Plymouth.'

'How long were you inside?'

'Three months for handling stolen goods, after wasting years with arseholes who turned out not to be friends. Coming here put my life back on track, thank God. I've got a brilliant job, people accept me, and Maggie's been amazing.' His gruff voice tails away, as if his sudden show of emotion has embarrassed him.

'Anything else I should know, Billy?'

'That's the lot.' His gaze drops to the knife. 'Can

I have my knife back when you're done? It'll save me buying a replacement.'

'When it stops being police evidence, I'll let you know.'

I consider calling Madron to explain the turn of events, but it's too late. The tension swilling round my system won't let me relax, so I check Billy's story on my computer. The chef hasn't broken any laws by reinventing himself, but his past worries me, even when I discover that he was telling the truth. Billy could easily have left the knife on my step, but so could one of the other suspects. The killer must be loving his new-found power. Thanks to him the island is on red alert, people afraid to leave their homes, viewing every member of the community with suspicion. The man who killed Laura Trescothick seems to be an adrenalin junkie, prepared to risk being spotted, to leave his tribute. He drifts around my head as I fall asleep, his features refusing to take shape.

I wake to the bawls of Atlantic gulls. The sound stopped registering when I lived here, but now their calls sound raw as an infant's, guaranteed to penetrate my dreams. I make myself exercise before my eyes are fully open: press-ups, lunges and star jumps until my muscles burn. I hate every minute, but the discipline vents my frustration. Shadow appears when I step outside, looking pleased with himself, as if a night at Maggie's has set him up for greater mischief. He's swift enough to evade my attempts to lock him inside.

'You're a royal pain in the arse,' I say, but he's already flying across the beach like a speeding bullet as I head for the shop.

June is standing by her counter, lining up bottles of olive oil and salad dressing, then ticking items from her checklist. Her clothes are so immaculate, she looks more like a solicitor than a shopkeeper, silver hair perfectly groomed. She looks up from her flip chart with a smile of greeting.

'Come to help me count stock, Ben?'

I sit on a stool as she finishes scribbling. 'I need to ask you about Laura. We've spoken to just about everyone, except you.'

Her hands fall still. 'She used to buy sweets with her sister, a little blonde chatterbox. She grew into such a lovely, confident young woman. We worked some of the same shifts at the hotel, but didn't get much time together.'

'Had you spoken recently?'

'She seemed thrilled about going to drama college.' She shakes her head. 'To be honest, I think Sam's story's almost as tragic.'

'How do you mean?'

'Life should be easy for kids, growing up in a peaceful place like this, yet some still go off the rails. Sam's been struggling all year. I told Rose he needed help.'

'What did she say?'

'Nothing, she can't accept that he's an addict.' June raises the palms of her hands. 'Things have been hard for her since Sam was born. She met his dad at a dance on St Mary's, but their fling only lasted a few weeks. He never sent her a penny after he left.'

'Where do you think Sam gets his money?'

'Not from Rose, certainly. We give her food each week, in exchange for her honey and remedies.'

'Does that work out even?'

'Not always.' She gives me a steady look. 'She's a friend, Ben. Who's counting?'

'You're not a typical shopkeeper, June.'

She gives a quick smile. 'Certainly not, I'm a classically trained chef.'

Her comments confirm my picture of Laura as a popular young woman, ready to break her ties with the island. June describes Sam Austell's erratic behaviour, the look on her face sober when I leave her to complete her inventory. I'm starting to understand the fragility of Rose Austell's lifestyle. Maybe it's not surprising that after growing up poor, Sam couldn't handle the sudden influx of money from his football career, the pressure of his new situation tearing him apart.

For once I reach the hall before Eddie. He arrives at 9 a.m., looking sheepish.

'Sorry I'm late, boss. My fiancée was off colour.'

'Is she okay now?' We've never exchanged personal details, his choirboy looks making me assume he still lives with his mum.

'Morning sickness. Michelle's three months pregnant.'

'Really? Congratulations.'

222

The width of his smile forces me to make adjustments. The kid is ten years younger than me, but clearly overjoyed about becoming a dad. Maybe I'm the one with arrested development. It feels wrong to spoil his moment by mentioning the knife left on my doorstep, but there's no choice. He sets to work instantly, phoning the lab to arrange collection; I suspect that the killer's smart enough to have sterilised it first, but a single DNA molecule is all we need.

We spend the rest of the morning poring over names; the list of suspects is shorter now alibis have been checked. Tom Horden's doctor has confirmed that he's registered blind, with just twenty per cent vision. It's unlikely that a pensioner with failing sight could have found his way to the cliff and overpowered a fit young woman, without someone else's help. Sam Austell is still unable to explain what sent him into hiding on the day of Laura's death, and Danny Curnow has hardly been seen since her memorial. Matt Trescothick remains unwilling to discuss losing his daughter. It doesn't surprise me that the three main suspects all lie close to home, when the majority of fatal stabbings are crimes of passion. But there are some contenders outside Laura's immediate circle: Dean Miller and Jim Helyer. The rest of the names remain on the suspect list only because their alibis are unsubstantiated; Pete Moorcroft, Arthur Penwithick and my uncle, Ray Kitto. Instinct tells me to reject them out of hand, but no one can be presumed innocent without concrete proof. The ferryman and my uncle are both solitary, lifelong bachelors, the last people on earth I'd consider capable of violence, yet seemingly harmless lone males sometimes commit violent acts. It's equally hard to believe that Pete Moorcroft could open his shop for business so soon after committing cold-blooded murder.

'How come Pete's still on the list?' Eddie asks.

'June stayed overnight with friends in Penzance. The shop didn't open till ten the day Laura died; he says he overslept.'

Eddie looks sceptical. 'Wouldn't his wife have noticed changes in his behaviour?'

'Not necessarily. People only see what they want to see.'

'We still haven't traced the cash in Laura's room.'

'Dean Miller paid her three hundred quid to model for him.'

'Dirty bugger,' Eddie mutters.

'The bloke's gay, so I'm guessing his motives were artistic. We need to find out about the other seventeen hundred. I'm still sure Sam Austell's involved in small-scale dealing. It would help to know if Laura was connected with the drugs he's been handling. Have the NCA got back to us yet?'

'They're patrolling the local waters at night, but no one's been caught. There are hundreds of coves for the smugglers to hide their boats.' He shunts another sheet of paper across the table. 'The lab sent through the results on the banknotes. There are only two clear fingerprint matches.'

'Sam Austell and Danny Curnow,' I mutter, gazing at the printout. 'Why would either of them give her that much cash?'

'They only found prints on a couple of notes. Maybe the rest came from another source.'

We're still ploughing through evidence when DCI Madron makes an unannounced visit. His grey eyes study me intently as I describe finding the knife on my doorstep.

'Someone knows local folklore,' he says. 'Smugglers left daggers on their rivals' doorsteps as death threats, in the old days.'

'He seems to enjoy a bit of melodrama. At least this means we can cross Sam Austell off our suspect list.'

'It may not be the murder weapon, but you should stay on St Mary's till the case closes.'

'Running away won't help, sir. I can't leave the islanders to fend for themselves.'

'Top-level decisions are mine. Remember that, Inspector.' The DCI's tone cools by several degrees. 'I told you to meet regularly with Laura's family. You'll get more from them if they feel supported. Make sure you see them today.'

'I've already arranged a visit.'

Madron seems too measured for turf wars, but his message is clear. If I push too hard, he'll remove me from the case, destroying my chance to protect the people I care about. It's a relief when Eddie returns with the incident log. Even though my team consists of two men and a wayward dog, we're sticking to protocols. The DCI compliments him on his evidence files, my deputy basking in well-earned praise.

Matt Trescothick says nothing when I arrive at his cottage after my boss leaves. It must be painful for his wife to watch him floating, silent and dangerous as an iceberg, threatening to capsize the whole family. Jenna seems to be compensating for her husband's mood with unnatural calmness, her movements slow and deliberate. Matt remains standing, arms rigid at his sides, while she sits beside me at the kitchen table.

'Any news from the hospital?' she asks.

'I'm afraid Sam Austell's still too unwell to give us clear information.'

She stares at me again. 'But it could be him, couldn't it?'

'He hasn't been ruled out formally yet.'

It's the wrong time to admit that Sam isn't her daughter's killer. Someone else is roaming the island at night, leaving calling cards. Matt's jaw muscles tense when he faces me.

'How long do we have to wait?' he asks. 'We can't even give Laura her funeral.'

'We're making progress. But I still need to know where she got that cash.'

'It was probably tips, from her hotel work.'

'That's big money for a young girl to earn.'

226

His head jerks up. 'If you think she did something wrong to get it, that's bollocks. She had too much self-respect.'

'No one's saying Laura broke any laws.'

'That's what you're implying. You think she was some kind of tart.' Suddenly he's in front of me, face so rigid with anger it's easy to imagine him hurting anyone that stood in his way. 'Your investigation's a fucking joke.'

He turns on his heel before I can reply. The door slams so hard it sounds like the hinges are about to break. Jenna seems smaller than before, hunched in her seat.

'Forgive him, Ben. He's hardly slept for days,' she says quietly.

'Has he ever been violent towards you?'

She flinches. 'Matt struggles to control his feelings, that's all.'

My alarm bells all sound at once. Trescothick's descent has been steeper than most – from local hero to unemployed dad in a few short years. Domestic violence often starts like this: a man falls on hard times, then his whole family suffers. I check Jenna's appearance for signs, but her high-necked jumper gives full camouflage. I'm almost certain her husband has hit her at least once, but I'd love to be proved wrong.

'Anything else I should know, Jenna?'

She gulps down an extra breath. 'We're splitting up. It's been on the cards for months, It's harming Suzie to hear us arguing all the time. She's too upset to go back to school yet, I'll keep her here with me, till she's stronger.'

'I'm sorry to hear it.' Many couples separate after the pain of losing a child, but this is fast by anyone's measurement. 'Where's Matt going to stay?'

'At his mum's, for the time being.'

'Can I see Suzanne?'

'She's not in good shape. We only gave her the news last night.'

'Let me sit with her for a bit. I'll leave if she gets upset.'

The living room curtains have sealed most of the daylight outside. The girl is standing by the window, her tall, athletic build just like her mother's, but she crumples onto the sofa when I arrive. There's no response when I ask how she's doing, which doesn't surprise me; the kid must be reeling from watching her family fall apart. She was closer to Laura than anyone, and I'm still certain she's got secrets to share. It was there in her face the first time I visited. After ten minutes, she pushes back her long fringe to study me.

'Ask Danny about the money,' she whispers. 'They were saving, for Falmouth. He'll know where she got it.'

'Thanks, I was planning to see him soon. I talked to Dean Miller, too. You and Laura spent time in his studio, didn't you?'

Her eyes blink rapidly. 'She didn't do anything wrong.'

'I know, Suzie, it's okay, you're not in trouble. Did she mind posing for him like that?'

She shakes her head. 'Laura said it was good practise for being an actor.'

'It didn't bother you either?'

'She'd have done the same for me. I like Dean's studio, but it was weird when he painted her, he just went quiet. He never let us talk.'

I can imagine the artist slipping into a fugue state, but it strikes me again that his intense nature could easily turn violent, under the wrong circumstances. I want to ask Suzanne more questions about Miller, but she's already withdrawing. When her sleeve slips back, there's a mark on her forearm, dark blue and big as a fist.

'Where did you get that bruise, Suzie?'

Her gaze flits away. 'I bumped into a door.'

'It's my job to keep you safe. I can't just ignore it.'

She covers it with her hand. 'I'm clumsy, that's all. It was an accident.'

The girl presses her face to her knees again, body language impenetrable as a shield. There's no way to prove Matt hurt her, but someone did. I weigh up whether to report her injury, but it's clear the girl would never press charges against her dad, and there's an outside chance that the injury was accidental. My best option is to keep a protective eye on her until she trusts me enough to tell the truth.

28

There's no sign of Shadow when I leave the Trescothicks' house. He seems to relish long spells of freedom; until hunger strikes. It's only when I return home at lunchtime that he bounds up the steps, interrupting my train of thought.

'No pride,' I say as he nuzzles my hand. 'You'd sweet-talk anyone for a free meal.'

I feed him, then nuke last night's fish pie in the microwave, eating it straight from the container. It's easy to imagine my mother's ghost standing by the cooker, calling me a slob, with an amused look on her face. I dump the bowl in the sink before collecting Laura's letters to Danny Curnow, pulling one from the pack at random. I've read them before, but I'm hoping for clues about the source of all that cash. She mentions the 'monsters' at home, without being specific, but after seeing the bruises on her sister's arm, I'm guessing she means her dad. The rest of the letter could only have been written by a girl on the cusp of womanhood, reckless enough to burn all her bridges. I fold the paper back into the envelope then set off for the Curnows' house.

Another drone is hovering on the northern horizon, despite Madron's threat of injunctions and my efforts to quell press interest. It buzzes so low overhead, photographing every speck of island soil, that my hair stands on end. Laura's death seems to have gripped the nation, with pages of guesswork still flooding the internet.

It's 2 p.m. by the time I reach the Curnows' house, to find it gleaming with winter sunlight. Majestic isolation and uninterrupted sea views explain why Jay campaigned so long to build here. I listen for the tap of Patty's high heels on the parquet, but it's Danny who greets me. Days after losing Laura, his expression is still blank with shock, his elaborate haircut collapsing round his ears.

'My parents are out.'

'That's okay. It's you I came to see.'

We sit in the kitchen in silence. Danny looks out of place in such a slick environment, wearing trainers and a faded tracksuit, his expensive watch the only sign of his moneyed background. The room has been designed for elegance, not comfort. The stools we perch on are made of metal, the marble counter polished to a high shine. This kind of minimalism doesn't appeal to me at all. I'd rather have comfortable sofas for chilling out on rainy Sundays, but the space contains only a solid wall of glass and a huge industrial cooking range. When I hand the letters back to Danny, their splash of colour is the only cheerful thing in the room.

'How did you and Laura plan to survive in Falmouth? Life must be expensive in such a popular town.'

'We'd have worked part-time to cover the rent.'

'Why not tell me about the money in her room, Danny?'

His hesitation lasts a fraction too long. 'Laura did odd jobs sometimes. There was her babysitting, or maybe it was a gift.'

'Your fingerprints are on it.'

'We lent each other money sometimes.' His eyes harden, a man's gaze now, not a boy's. 'I don't know who gave her the rest.'

'Was Laura doing something you didn't like, to get cash?'

'She never said.'

'Don't you want to know who killed her?'

The question brings him to his feet at last, eyes burning as his fist flies at me, but my height advantage helps me to overpower him fast. The look in his face is a mix of teenage fury and undigested grief as I grip his shoulders.

'Calm down, Danny. Punching a police officer isn't the solution.'

'You never believe what I say. Why would I lie? I loved her more than anyone.'

'I know it's hard, but it's my job to find out why she died.'

The boy takes a long time to settle, still refusing to reveal the origin of Laura's money. He remains determined to protect his girlfriend, even though it's too late to matter. After twenty minutes of questioning he lapses into monosyllables. I could arrest him for attempted assault, but it would do neither of us any good: there's no concrete proof that he killed his girlfriend. Right now, it's hard to believe he could harm anyone. The boy seems broken by the weight of his grief, but I'm still convinced that it took the kind of passion he's just displayed to drive a blade six inches into her chest. I urge him to call me if he remembers anything, then leave his parents' glass-and-chrome palace behind.

The rest of the afternoon is a blur of tedious admin. When we close up for the day, I'm desperate for physical activity, before my brain implodes. I walk to the quay and find my uncle hauling wood from the steamer, watching me in silence as I pull on a pair of gloves.

'Long time no see,' he mutters as we lift the first piece.

'Believe me, I'd rather be here.'

He gives a narrow smile. 'You didn't have to take the case on.'

'I'll help you more when it finishes, but I've got time now. What do you want me to do?'

'Start the lapping, if you don't mind getting your clothes dirty.'

We stand side by side, overlaying planks. I test each seam with my fingertip, making sure it's properly sealed. When I straighten up again, the small of my back aches like fury, but my uncle seems immune to pain, kneeling down to wedge the next strake in place. It disturbs me that he's still on my list of suspects. All lone males are potential threats, but anxiety makes me blurt out a question that's bothered me for years.

'How come you never married, Ray?'

His hand movements slow down. 'I preferred my own company, I suppose.'

'Dad said you were a heartbreaker. You had plenty of offers.'

'Hardly.' He hammers in another nail. 'Your mother and I were together before college. When she came back, he swept her off her feet. He got the best girl.'

His expression doesn't change as he pushes the sanding block. Forty years have passed since that act of betrayal, but my memories jar. Ray ate Christmas dinner at our house every year. What must it have cost him to sit at our table, the eternal bachelor, refusing to accept second best? I keep my mouth shut as I drive resin into another seam, amazed that I never figured it out for myself. That kind of loneliness could easily convert into violence, but Ray's expression is calm when he finally turns round.

'I've been thinking about Laura,' he says. 'That money you found probably came from several people on the island. I gave her some myself.'

His sudden admission makes me look up. 'Did you?'

'The girl had talent, and she wanted to make something of herself. I've got more than I need.'

'How much did you give her?'

He shrugs. 'About four hundred. I'd just been paid for repairing a dinghy last time she called round.'

'Jesus, Ray, why didn't you tell me before?'

'You've hardly been here.'

'What did you get in return?'

'How do you mean?' His shoulders stiffen. 'It was a gift.'

I grit my teeth but manage not to snap. Ray has always done things at his own pace, following no rules but his own. 'That's a lot of cash for a young girl.'

'Not really. I helped you the same way, remember?'

The memory is crystal clear. He waited on the quay with my mother to say goodbye when I left for London, and pressed an envelope full of ten-pound notes into my hand. I realise that I never thanked him properly, but now it's too late.

'You'll need to make a statement tomorrow morning, Ray.'

'I've already told you what happened.'

'It has to go on record. I'll see you at the community centre.'

My thoughts whirl as I walk home. My uncle's gift to Laura could have been no more than generosity, but the fact that he waited so long to reveal it makes the gesture look suspicious. I shove the thought to the back of my mind.

The person I want to see most is Nina, hoping her calm manner will put me at ease, but paperwork from the case delays me. It's nine o'clock by the time I'm putting on my coat, Shadow insisting on tagging along.

'You'll be a gooseberry.' The dog refuses to leave my side. 'Have it your own way.'

I'm halfway down the path to the beach when footsteps race towards me, someone sprinting through the dark. A body barrels into me before I can switch on my torch, almost knocking me over.

'Thank God. I called you, but the signal's down.'

When my torch finally clicks on, Zoe's face is shiny with panic. She looks like an actor from *Scream*, eyes staring, while words babble from her mouth. I rest my hands on her shoulders.

'Breathe, Zoe.'

'Someone was breaking down the door. I couldn't see a damn thing; the outside lights didn't work. When the banging started again, I ran out the back way.'

'Did you see who it was?'

'Just a shape through the glass.' She exhales a ragged breath. 'Jesus, I can't stop shaking.'

'You're safe now. Do you want to stay at mine while I take a look?'

'No way, I want to see what the bastard's done to my place.'

We walk back to the hotel, Shadow chasing in circles like the whole thing's a glorious adventure. Zoe stays close as I check the site. Someone has severed the cable for the outdoor lights and a long crack zigzags through the safety glass in her external door. I carry on walking, to check the other entrances.

'Has anyone been hanging around today?' I ask.

'Only Angie. She helped me get ready for the decorators next week.'

'She's not likely to stage a break-in.' My mind flicks through my list of suspects, before I put through a call to the pub. 'Who's in the bar right now, Maggie?'

'Most of my regulars. Why?'

'Matt Trescothick, Danny Curnow and Dean Miller?'

'Dean's been here a few hours, reading his paper. I haven't seen the other two.'

I say a swift goodbye, then put through more calls. Patty Curnow tells me that Danny is taking a night-time walk, and Gwen Trescothick says that Matt left earlier, to go to the pub. I stuff my phone into my pocket, rage still bubbling inside my chest. This is scare tactics, like the knife outside my door. There's no way to prove which suspect came here in a state of rage, but after today's display of emotion, Laura's boyfriend seems most likely. The killer's conversation is gathering speed, proving that the people around me are all in danger. Zoe looks upset when I insist she stays at mine instead of braving the empty hotel. I've always wondered how she copes there out of season. The corridors remind me of *The Shining*: all they need is a kid on a tricycle, and Jack Nicholson with a manic glint in his eye.

Zoe parks herself by my fire, her resilience soon reviving when she tells me about a new song, convinced it's the best she's written. She sings a few bars, the melody slow and haunting enough to etch itself on my memory, but the peace doesn't last long. Around midnight the wind chucks fistfuls of sand at the windows, reminding me that someone on the island is causing mayhem, the attacks getting closer all the time. With luck, the bastard will keep on taking risks to goad me, and I'll be there when he trips up.

29

Rose sits at her kitchen table, suppressing her worries with simple tasks. Her mind is focused on the medicinal oils she's distilling: feverfew for migraines, herb of Jupiter to heal burns and stings, bitter orange for pain relief. She pours each essence into bottles then seals the caps with wax.

When the phone rings at midnight, her tongue sticks to the roof of her mouth. She's afraid it could be the hospital, to say that Sam is sicker than before, but all she hears is someone breathing, slow and loud, into the receiver. Soon the sound is replaced by a hiss of white noise. When the phone rings again fifteen minutes later, she takes it off the hook. The calls came every half-hour last night, wrenching her from sleep, like the slow drip of water torture. Rose considers running to Ben Kitto's cottage to confess her secrets, but night-time has wrapped the cabin in a grey shroud that conceals too many unseen dangers.

It's only when she looks up again that Jay Curnow's face appears outside her kitchen window. The sight of him makes her take a panicked step backwards, his features forming a narrow smile. He raps on the glass pane, but she refuses to open the door. There's no knowing what the man will do if she lets him inside. She has always been able to read people's intentions, and knows that he intends to harm her for getting in his way. She can hear his voice rising to a shout, behind the thin glass.

'Sign the papers, Rose. You don't want to make me angry, do you?'

The man stares at her again. He could easily break the window, or force the door, the cabin's protection gossamer-thin as she backs away.

30

Zoe is still out for the count when I peer into my brother's old room in the morning. It's unsettling to see a Marilyn Monroe lookalike asleep in a teenage boy's sanctuary, wardrobe door plastered with ancient Glastonbury memorabilia, a faded Plymouth Argyle poster on the wall. The dog lazes at her feet, trying to look innocent. I dump a mug of coffee on the bedside table, singing 'Sweet Child o' Mine' tunelessly until she wakes up.

'Only Ryan Gosling gets to serenade me this early.' Her voice is gritty with irritation.

'Be thankful I brought you coffee.'

She gives a cat-like stretch. When her dark eyes focus on my face, it's too late for evasion; she's always been able to read my thoughts. 'Did Nina Jackson put that scowl on your face?'

'She's a minor obsession, that's all.' I hold up my hands in defeat. 'She could use a friend. Why not invite her to the pub sometime?'

'That's a classic piece of deflection. You should use your legendary charm, have sex, then see how you feel.'

I suppress a laugh. 'If only her world view was that simple.'

'Maybe *you're* the complicated one.' She's already drifting back to sleep.

'Keep those eyes open.' I give her shoulders a shake. 'You're staying at the pub till this is sorted. Maggie's giving you her best room, free of charge.'

'There's no way I'm leaving home.'

'If you argue, you'll end up in Penzance jail.'

She protests, but I refuse to listen. The walk back to the hotel gives me a chance to inspect the damage by daylight, while she packs a bag. A crack jagged as a lightning bolt runs through the door's safety glass. Whoever did it must have a powerful kick, or know how to swing a sledgehammer. So much boldness reveals that it's someone in a state of fury, with luck on their side. The night's rain has left the path slick with water, footprints and evidence washed away.

It's a quick, bad-tempered stroll to the Rock. Zoe is so annoyed about being bossed around that she can hardly speak when I deliver her to the kitchen door. Billy is at his workstation, chopping onions, the fumes making my eyes water. He glowers at me, but produces a smile for Zoe. The knife clutched in his hand is a smaller version of the one left on my doorstep, its red handle riveted to a thin, tapering blade. For a second I picture him as the killer, before remembering Maggie's alibi that he spent the morning of Laura's death in her bed. He looks like a throwback to the eighties today – dressed in a Springsteen T-shirt, bald head covered in a baseball cap worn back to front. He limps over to peer at Zoe's face.

'What's wrong, darling?'

His sympathy triggers the anxiety she's been bottling. 'God, Billy. Someone tried to hurt me; anything could have happened.'

Billy wraps her in a hug, expression tense as he meets my eye; Zoe's always been one of his favourites. I steal out of the kitchen, confident that he's better equipped to comfort her than I'll ever be.

It's not yet nine, so I walk Shadow round the island's perimeter, past the Curnows' glass palace. There's no categorical proof that Danny has been leaving calling cards and damaging property, or that he killed the girlfriend he professes to love, despite his night-time walks. I'm almost sure the killer's steering me in the wrong direction. But which members of the island community are angry enough to kick through a solid glass door? Matt Trescothick remains close to the top of my dwindling list of suspects. The last time I saw him, frustration was eating him alive. I can't prove he's beating his wife or daughter, but the bruises on Suzanne's arm are my main concern. Many murder cases begin with a father attacking his child in a fit of madness. But why would Matt terrorise Zoe? Maybe his marriage breakdown has sent his emotions out of control.

I spot something moving on Badplace Hill as I leave the beach. The figure is too distant to identify, but I can see his raised arms and that telltale black coat. I'm almost certain it's the man who was on the cliff when Laura's body was found. Shadow chases past as I run up the incline. At the top of the hill I'm heaving for breath, scanning the rocky summit. The man's back is turned, face obscured by a woollen cap, but I recognise Pete Moorcroft's profile. His binoculars are raised to the sky. I watch him pull a notebook from his pocket before I step into the open, but the dog is misbehaving. He gives a low growl, jaws snapping. The shopkeeper swings round, gasping in shock.

'You almost gave me a heart attack.' He looks down at Shadow warily. 'Does he bite?'

'Not often, he's just highly strung.'

Pete gives a shaky laugh. 'Aren't we all? This is my first time up here for weeks.'

'You're a birdwatcher?'

'It's a little-known fact. June calls me a world-class geek.' His bland face suddenly brightens. 'There's a Sabine's gull down on the ledge. Want to take a look?'

There's a sheer hundred-foot drop below us. I accept the binoculars and step out of his range before looking. The gull is smaller than the Atlantic variety, with a sleek grey head, beak tipped with yellow.

'Beautiful, isn't she?' His face is animated.

'Do you ever watch from Gweal Hill?'

'Not in winter. More varieties nest here; firecrests and green-winged teals.'

'Funny, I saw someone with binoculars there the other day. He looked just like you.'

'People watch boats from that side of the island. It's closer to the shipping channel.'

Shadow snaps at him again. 'Pack it in,' I hiss, grabbing his collar.

'How's the investigation going? June's been having nightmares.' He drops his notebook back into his pocket. 'She's scared someone else will get hurt.'

'Try and reassure her. We're doing all we can.'

'Everyone's grateful you're working so hard.' His face is solemn. 'Let me know if I can help.'

'Thanks, Pete. I will.'

Shadow seems relieved to say goodbye as I head back down the hill. The dog's reaction surprises me; normally he accepts every friendly overture. Pete's black coat flapping in the wind must have spooked him, just like he baulked at the sight of Jim emerging from the shadows outside the community hall. It's possible that other islanders climb the hills to birdwatch, and it's hard to imagine someone so mild-mannered harming anyone. Discomfort nags at me again as I trudge down the steep incline: the investigation is making me doubt people who've lived here peacefully ever since I was a child.

I pore over Laura's mobile phone record again in the hall. She called the same numbers every day: Danny, her mum, Suzanne, a couple of girlfriends on Tresco. There was a flurry of brief calls to Sam Austell two weeks before she died, and several long conversations with Dean Miller. I need to find out who she was afraid of while I've still got teeth left to grind.

By the time my uncle arrives, I've almost forgotten last night's tense conversation. Ray's expression is neutral as Eddie leads him to the table. He's dressed in work overalls, a smudge of varnish on his forearm, blue eyes steady as he sits down. Maybe it's just me feeling uncomfortable about making him account for himself.

'How often did Laura visit the yard, Ray?'

'Every few weeks, I suppose. She'd sit in the corner, chatting away. Most times she was with her sister.'

'Did she ever come to your flat alone?'

'Not that I remember. She liked seeing the boats.'

'What did you talk about?'

'Countries I'd seen, mainly. She wanted to travel the world.'

'Is that why you gave her money?'

He shrugs. 'I help all the kids. Someone has to, don't they?'

My uncle's face is impassive. It disturbs me that he's still so mysterious, after all these years. I had no idea that he routinely gave gifts to the island's young, as if his hard-earned cash had no personal value. When the interview wraps up, I'm none the wiser. Ray has no confirmed alibi for the morning of Laura's death. It's possible that he killed her, then returned to the yard, knocking on Arthur Penwithick's door at 9 a.m., yet instinct tells me he'd never hurt a soul.

Eddie looks thoughtful as he packs the digital recorder away. 'Your uncle's not exactly an open book, is he?'

'Tell me about it.'

I know Ray's preferences almost as well as my own. He favours single malt whisky, action movies with an intelligent twist, classical music, Old Holborn tobacco. But I could count the personal statements he's made over the years on the fingers of one hand.

31

'Dinner? Eight thirty.'

The message arrives on my walk home, Nina's texting style is as clipped as her conversation, and it strikes me again that she's the opposite of the easy-going women I normally choose. I send back a quick acceptance then head for the shower. Ten minutes under the jet fail to dilute the day's frustrations. Someone is running rings round me, exploiting their knowledge of the island. I'm still brooding when I hunt for something to take round as a gift. Luckily, Maggie has left two bottles of good red wine lurking at the back of a cupboard. I grab one then set off, while Shadow races ahead, pausing every hundred metres to release a pointless but ear-splitting howl. He's sitting in the porch when I arrive, ears pinned back from running into the wind.

Nina crouches down to greet him, and for once I don't mind playing second fiddle. It gives me time to admire her. She's wearing a simple white blouse and leggings, chocolate-brown hair swinging back as she kisses my cheek. I can't explain why the fact that she seems to have made no effort at all seems sexy. The ghost of her scent lingers in my airways.

'Do you believe in telepathy?'

She looks bemused. 'Not since primary school. Why?'

'The dog always knows where I'm going, before I do.'

'That's his job. He's your shadow, isn't he?'

'More's the pity.'

Nina beckons me down the hall, where garlic, oregano and the pungent smell of cheese browning waft through the kitchen door. I watch her move round, movements languid as she pours the wine then puts down a bowl of water for Shadow. My mouth waters when she lifts a huge pizza from the oven.

'If you made that, I'm seriously impressed.'

'Food's a big deal in my house. My mum's Italian.'

'She must be missing you.'

Her voice cools as she slices the pizza. 'I came here to avoid thinking about my home life.'

'There's this thing called conversation, Nina. It's a popular social ritual. Fancy giving it a try?'

'It's not my best skill. When I'm out with friends, I'm always the quiet one.'

'I've only got one serious question.'

Her smile vanishes. 'What?'

'Do we have to use cutlery, or can I just dive in?'

The pizza is the best I've tasted in years, loaded with sundried tomatoes, black olives and serrano ham. Nina lets a few personal details slip as the wine bottle empties. She considered studying music at college, but surprised her family by opting for medicine instead.

'How come you like touching people, but not talking?'

She shrugs. 'Communication's physical as well as verbal.'

'I'll drink to that.' I lift my glass in her direction. 'It's your turn to spill the beans tonight. You still haven't told me why you're here.'

She studies her empty plate. 'It would spoil the evening.'

'You know I'll keep on asking.'

'Wait in the living room then. I'll make coffee.'

Nina's lounge is cooler than the kitchen, the fire low in the grate. Her bookshelves hold manuals on caring for joint and back problems alongside a few novels by Dickens and Jane Austen. She reappears before I can check out her CDs, movements grinding to a standstill as she puts down the coffee tray.

'I wasn't planning to do this. I'm not even sure I can.'

'You can stop any time, take a breather.'

'I got married at twenty-one.' Her arms are folded across her body as she stands by the hearth. 'Simon was training to be an architect. We were too young, but that didn't bother us. We had a big church ceremony, fancy reception, then a honeymoon in Paris.' She perches on an armchair, Shadow curling at her feet. 'Everything was fine until he had a seizure, five years ago.' Her voice has fallen to a whisper. I'd like to comfort her, but she's so pent-up, it would do more harm than good.

'Don't go on, if it's too hard.'

'The doctors said it was an aneurism, too big to repair.' She buries her fingers in the softness of Shadow's fur. 'We lived as normally as we could, knowing the next haemorrhage could be fatal. His bravery was amazing, but last spring it happened again, and this time he was paralysed. I cared for him at home until he died in June. After the funeral I felt hollow, some days I still do.'

'That's why you left Bristol?'

'It was too painful seeing his stuff everywhere, but I can't throw anything away. I planned to come here and read, play my violin, find my balance again.'

'Until I started pestering you?'

'You've been a good distraction.' She looks apologetic. 'In your shoes, I'd run for the hills.'

'That's not my style.' Comforting words would be pointless, but she accepts my embrace when I kneel by her chair, her cheek cool against mine.

'The island's stopped feeling peaceful. Death seems to follow me around.'

'Bad timing, that's all. It's just me pursuing you.'

'I noticed.' She manages a smile. 'You must be crazy.'

Suddenly Nina's mood changes. She tugs at my hands, pulling me to my feet. Her fingers chase across my back, desperate for human contact, but something's cooling already behind all that frantic touch. When I draw back, tears are welling in her eyes. She weeps in silence, with her face pressed to my shoulder, then she draws away.

'I shouldn't have told you, Ben. I'm sorry.'

'At least we've heard each other's stories now.'

'You don't need any more drama.'

'How do you know what I need?'

Her head tips back, letting me kiss her throat. She's so relieved to have shifted the sadness from her system to mine, I could easily take her to bed. Maybe she just wants to be reminded that she's still alive. The urge to take advantage is powerful enough to make sweat erupt on the back of my neck.

'I'd better go, Nina. It's late.'

'You could stay here.'

'Believe me, I want to.' The heat between us rises by another notch. 'We shouldn't go to bed the first time just because you're upset.'

She attempts a smile. 'Maybe you're not so macho after all.'

'Hell, no. I'm a big Jane Austen fan.'

'I'll test you next time.' She releases a laugh. 'Thanks for listening.'

'Any time. Remember to lock up after me.'

Nina opens the front door and her parting kiss has me questioning my resolve. Shadow lets out a bark of disappointment when the door finally closes, as if he's equally reluctant to trudge home through the cold. I'm still warm from pizza, red wine and desire, raising my collar against the wind coming off the sea.

The dog's barking gets louder as I cut through the dunes, but he's nowhere to be seen. My guess is that he's found something disgusting to roll in; it's in my interest to haul him out fast. But he's standing in a clearing, releasing a high-pitched howl. It sounds like something you'd hear in the forests of Wyoming at full moon. I crouch down to grab his collar, but he barks louder, like he's seen a ghost. When I spin round to find what's scared him, a sharp pain burns the back of my skull. The last thing I hear is the dog's fierce growl, then footsteps racing across the shingle, before the world clicks shut.

32

My mouth is gritty when I come round, my tongue coated with sand. I'm face down on the beach, torch beam burning my retinas. The dog is making things worse, whining pitifully into my ear.

'Shut up, hellhound,' I mutter.

The sound of my voice quiets him, but the effort of twisting my head almost makes me black out again. It takes three attempts to rise to my feet, vision blurred, but when I glance at my watch I've only been out a few minutes. There's blood on my fingers when I touch the back of my head, and a wave of nausea washes over me. My attacker could still be nearby, crowbar in hand. The effects of the blow are more obvious when I stagger drunkenly across the sand. I consider going home, but instinct draws me to the boatyard, despite today's tense interview.

Ray's light is still burning, the sound of his TV spilling downstairs. His door is unlocked when I use the back entrance, but Shadow is playing silly buggers, barking at full volume, refusing to come inside.

'Suit yourself,' I tell him. 'You'll freeze out here.'

The air in my uncle's hallway is tainted with cigarette smoke, gunfire echoing from his living room. Gary Cooper strides across the old-fashioned TV screen as Ray's stern face looms at me.

'What on Earth's happened?'

'I was attacked, on Gweal Beach. Phone the Curnows and find out if Danny's at home, can you?'

'Let's check where that blood's coming from first.'

Ray seats me at his kitchen table. It reminds me of being a kid again, having salve rubbed into my scraped knuckles after helping him in the yard. Listening to him chunter as he riffles through his first aid box is as restful as a lullaby.

'That bump'll swell like a hen's egg by morning.' He swipes disinfectant into the wound. 'Who the hell did this?'

'I didn't see, he got me from behind. Call the Curnows please, like I said.'

'Keep the bandage pressed over the wound till it stops bleeding.' When he reaches for his phone, I can hear the low growl of Jay's voice at the other end of the line. 'He says Danny's asleep in bed.'

Curnow's response fails to convince me. So far, all I know about him is that he's got no scruples. 'Why isn't your door locked, Ray?'

'It's stayed open sixty years. Why should I change?'

'I'm surprised you're still up.'

He nods at the TV. 'I was watching *For Whom the Bell Tolls.*'

'Must be good, to keep you awake.' Normally he's in bed by eleven, but he loves old movies. Like everything else, it's a passion he keeps to himself.

'Sleep in the spare room. I'll check on you, for concussion.'

Ray's spare room is monastic, containing only a narrow single bed, a wooden chair and an old-fashioned anglepoise lamp. I'm still processing who would creep up on me in the dark, certain that the killer is continuing our conversation. He's already left the photo and knife as tokens, and put his boot through a close friend's door. My last thought is that I was a fool not to accept Nina's invitation. By now I'd be in her bed, blissfully awake.

My uncle is up with the larks in the morning. The smell of bacon frying drags me to my feet, even though his coffee may cause more damage than last night's assault. Shadow has forgotten his bad mood and is sitting in the kitchen, eyes one shade paler than Ray's. My head is still pulsing when my uncle shunts a plate towards me. I can tell he's about to deliver a lecture, along with my meal.

'Head recovering?'

'It's on the mend. Thanks for letting me stay.'

He pours foul-smelling black liquid into my mug. 'You've got an island full of willing volunteers. Why the hell aren't you using us?'

'An islander killed her, Ray. That's the problem.'

His eyes snap wide open. 'So we're all guilty now?'

'That's not what I said.'

'Let us help you, then.'

I can see his logic, even though there's little he can do. 'I'll keep it in mind.'

We eat our breakfast in silence, Shadow crunching noisily on the biscuits Ray keeps for him, until we part company. My uncle's words stay with me, but I've been part of a double act for the past ten years, no one to rely on except Clare. I can't imagine leaning on anyone else. The clatter of Ray's hammer follows me down the path, as if he's venting his irritation on the boat's gunwale.

Eddie looks alarmed when I describe my attack. He contacts Madron straight away to alert him before making calls, checking to see whether anyone was seen wandering round the island last night. I leave the dog with him and set off to meet the Trescothicks. Jenna has already sent a text, saying that Matt will be at the house too, despite their troubles.

The atmosphere at Tide Cottage has changed since my last visit, anger replaced by tiredness. Suzanne sits in the corner, twisting her long hair between her fingers. Her grandmother looks exhausted, a small grey figure hunched by the window. Matt is watching me closely, arms folded, but at least he seems calmer than before.

'Is there any news?' Jenna searches my face.

'Did you hear about the break-in at the hotel, and me being attacked?'

She looks startled. 'Are you okay?'

'Fine, but someone seems to think I'm getting too close.'

'You know who it is, don't you?' Matt's gaze settles on my face. 'Tell us who the suspects are.'

'I can't, Matt. It would compromise the investigation.'

Suddenly his mood darkens. 'It's my daughter you're talking about. I've got a right to know.'

'So you can beat them up?' Jenna mutters.

He stares back at her. 'Is that all you expect from me?'

The atmosphere is so explosive, one badly chosen word could blow the roof off the building. Gwen rises to her feet, her hand on Matt's arm, the quiet gesture restoring his self-control.

'Laura needs a proper burial, that's all that matters,' the old woman says.

Right now, the girl's body lies in the tiny morgue on St Mary's. 'I'll contact the coroner, but I've got some questions first. Did Laura talk to any of you about her plans to leave the island with Danny?'

'Almost every day,' Jenna says. 'Nothing else mattered. She couldn't see that she was too young to leave home.'

'Suzie, did Laura mention anything else to you?'

'Only that she had to go. There was no work for her here; she wanted to follow her dreams.' The girl stares down at her hands, but my sense that she could unlock her sister's secrets is stronger than before.

'We think Laura was desperate for money, to support herself through college,' I tell them. 'She may have put herself in danger along the way.'

Matt glowers at me, but Jenna soon changes the subject. The meeting dissolves as she praises the local support they've received: food parcels are still being delivered, dozens of cards bearing messages of sympathy. I wait until Matt leaves with his mother, to make sure he doesn't make any more threatening gestures, the tension dropping away once they depart. After a few more minutes I say goodbye, Jenna thanking me in the porch before I leave.

Eddie looks intrigued when I tell him about the meeting, as if a new method of detection is being revealed.

'Madron was on the phone earlier. The tabloids are offering big cash payments for interviews with the family.'

I shake my head firmly. 'Keep them at arm's length.'

'That won't be easy,' Eddie replies. 'I heard the Trescothicks are struggling to pay for Laura's funeral. I'll get my mum to do a whip-round.'

I could insist he types up witness reports, but he's already on the phone, enlisting local support. It's a reminder that things operate differently here. My colleagues in the MIT would be amused by the thin line between policing and social work. He's still gabbling when I leave, the dog slinking after me towards Rose

Austell's cottage. News of my ambush on the beach seems to have circulated the island, texts arriving from a dozen people, checking I'm okay. The community's interest felt stifling as a teenager, but right now it's a comfort, especially when my wounded skull is throbbing in time with my pulse.

Rose peers at me from the window of her cabin. When the door finally opens, she brandishes a broom at me.

'Go away,' she snaps. 'You're not welcome here.'

'I've brought you a present, Rose. A bottle of burgundy.' Luckily I remembered her fondness for gifts before I left home.

She takes a grudging step back. 'Come in, if you must. But the dog stays outside.'

Rose is dressed in a rainbow-striped jumper, threadbare jeans patched with bright red wool and a necklace of large orange beads. Even in her odd outfit, she's a commanding presence, with her hawk-like features and imperious gaze. I follow her through the crowded sitting room, almost toppling a mound of dried heather, the air scented with the musty sweetness of honey. She points at the only empty chair in her kitchen. Despite her bluster, I notice that the tremor in her hands is worse than before.

'I'm sorry, Rose. I didn't mean to upset you the other day.'

'You've got a job to do, I suppose. Better have a drink and forget about it, hadn't we?'

The atmosphere is too fragile to survive a refusal, even though it's mid-morning. She pours wine into coffee cups and passes one to me. 'How's Sam doing?'

'The doctors say he'll be in hospital for weeks, but should make a full recovery, in time.'

'At least he's getting there.' I swallow a sip of burgundy, the flavour setting my teeth on edge. 'Rose, you said Sam knows what happened to Laura. Is that true?'

'It's not for me to say. There are dangers here that outsiders don't understand.'

'I was born on the island, remember.'

She stares out of the window. The sea is a hard line of graphite, pressed flat by the weight of the sky. 'I can tell you the most dangerous man on Bryher.'

'Who's that?'

'Jay Curnow,' she says in a loud whisper. 'Stand still long enough and he'll slap a price ticket on you. He's got the island in a stranglehold. He hated the Trescothick girl for taking his son and heir.'

'You're scared of something, Rose. Why not let me help?'

The holes in her claim are obvious. Jay Curnow is a respected landowner and member of the parish council. The idea that he would sneak out one morning to kill a young girl seems ludicrous. His face the day Laura's body was found held relief as well as concern, but resenting someone's existence is different from killing them.

'I'll have to leave this place soon,' Rose whispers.

'Why? You own the cabin, don't you?'

'Curnow wants to buy it, before the council force me out.'

'That's coercion, Rose. If he bothers you again, tell me.'

Her eyes are brimming when she nods at the window again. 'The worst danger I'm facing comes from the sea.'

I don't bother to reply. Her words are as cryptic and confusing as her son's. She drains the last drop of wine from her cup then slams it down on the table as if the matter's closed.

The sun is breaking through the cloud for the first time in days when I head back to work. I know the chances of Jay Curnow hurting anyone are negligible, but Rose may be correct about him behaving ruthlessly to acquire so much wealth. He seems like the kind of man who stops at nothing to get his way; but would that extend to hurting Laura, for spoiling his son's future? That would make his wife complicit. She might have lied by saying that he was still in bed the morning the girl died. When I run a search on Curnow, the extent of his empire interests me. He owns eighteen properties; including a villa in a renowned beauty spot on St Mary's, valued at a million pounds.

'What do you know about Jay Curnow?' I ask, turning to Eddie.

'He sponsors the rugby club, and gives money to local charities, but him and his wife are too flash for round here.' Disapproval shows in his face. 'Patty loves her spa breaks and designer clothes. They keep a sports car on the mainland, by all accounts.'

His description chimes with Maggie's view of Jay as a tough businessman with few scruples, but doesn't amount to a killer's profile. I spend the rest of the afternoon digging for dirt but finding none. When I look up again, darkness has fallen over the island like a blackout curtain, while Eddie uses his own time to make more phone calls, gathering donations to pay for Laura Trescothick's funeral. My impression of him has shifted from earnest choirboy to a young man with a conscience, prepared to stay late, even though his pregnant fiancée wants him at home.

'Get moving, Eddie. You've done enough.'

For once he doesn't argue, grabbing his coat and racing for the door. Something flickers in the corner of my eye soon after he's gone. There's a movement outside the window, but when I look again, the blank square of glass is empty, the dog asleep in the corner. The silence is so complete, I can hear my own breathing. I use my torch to scan the area around the building but find nothing. Back inside, I rub my eyes then carry on reading witness reports. There's no point in interviewing the Curnows again without proof of their involvement in Laura's death.

My torch fails on the way home, luckily the moon is

out in full force. The last breath of an Atlantic squall fills my ears with white noise and my mouth with the taste of salt. Memories of being attacked on the beach make me glad to get indoors, but Shadow's behaving oddly, prowling at my feet. Maggie must have used her key earlier today. There's a loaf of bread on the kitchen table, a shepherd's pie in the microwave. I hit the button and watch my unexpected meal rotate. Years ago, her attempts to mother me would have grated, but now I'm grateful to be remembered. Clare's suicide has taught me that independence is overrated.

The meal settles my mood, last night's aches and pains receding. The dog seems calmer too, stretched out by the hearth, even though the fire's unlit. I dump the dishes in the sink and think of Nina, moving round her rented kitchen with long-limbed grace. She's probably alone, dwelling on details I forced her to remember last night. Suddenly I want to see her so badly that I'm hunting in my pocket for my door key. When my wallet falls to the ground, a photo of me and Clare falls out. I could shove it back into place without looking, but that would be cowardly.

The picture is a year old, the pair of us in dress uniform. We'd just been to Scotland Yard to receive our commendations for helping to track down a contract killer who had claimed a dozen lives. I hold the picture closer, to study Clare again. Her short hair is the brassy blonde she always favoured, and she's wearing the half-smile that was her trademark, as if comedy and tragedy deserved the same response. She pretended to be cynical about the bravery award, but I think she was glad that her decades of graft had finally been noticed. It must have been impossible for her to imagine a life outside the force. Grief and shame curdle in my stomach, emotions so raw that it would be crazy to start a relationship right now, but after last night's exchange I should check on Nina's welfare. Clare's death has taught me the consequences of ignoring someone in distress. I open the sideboard and put her photo on the top shelf, where I won't have to deal with it.

When I set off, the dog stays so close he seems determined to trip me. At first the walk is peaceful, until an acrid gust of smoke catches the back of my throat. When another arrives, I run at full pelt across the beach towards Gweal Cottage. Orange light flickers from an upstairs window, smoke belching from the broken glass, the front door hanging open. There's no sign of Nina, but that doesn't mean she's safe. I grab my phone and call Maggie as I rush inside. Smoke wafts down from the landing, making me grab the fire extinguisher before running upstairs. Flames are licking the walls of the bedroom in front of me, but the house seems to be empty. A fireman once told me you should contain a fire, so I slam the door and spray foam under it, sealing the inch-wide gap. With luck, it will give me time to search the other rooms. I chase across the landing, yelling Nina's name. Downstairs I grab her violin case, then haul more of her belongings into the front garden.

My eyes are streaming, lungs raw with smoke, but the cavalry are already arriving. Billy, still wearing his chef's uniform, Pete Moorcroft, Jim Helyer and Arthur Penwithick. The ferryman is riding the island's only vehicle, a tractor, dragging a water tank that serves as a fire engine. The hose unwinds with the comical slowness of a *Carry On* film, but eventually the jet shoots through the upstairs window. The fire is so localised that it's extinguished by a single tank, smoke spewing from the open window. When I look back, Nina is with Zoe at the edge of the crowd. Relief hits me with full force; part of me had believed that she was trapped in the flame-filled room. The whole island population seems to have turned out to gawk. Rose Austell is loitering at the edge of the crowd, eyes glittering, clearly thrilled to see Jay Curnow's property damaged. It surprises me that she's talking to Dean Miller, but the friendship makes sense; they're two of a kind, both preferring to watch island life unfold from a distance. Nina appears beside me, staring at my soot-blackened hands.

'You gave me a hell of a scare,' I say. 'Where were you?'

'At the pub, with Zoe.'

'I salvaged some of your stuff, but the bedroom's a write-off. Someone started this deliberately.'

We walk closer to the building, surveying the damage, one of the downstairs windows smashed from its hinges. I find myself scanning the crowd again. Chances are the killer's gloating nearby, watching me chase in circles. There's no sign of Danny Curnow or Matt Trescothick, as I search for the source of the fire. It's easy to guess how the attack started. An empty can of paraffin lies on the grass behind the cottage, suggesting that the arsonist escaped onto the beach. I angle my torch at the ground then take a picture with my phone, dropping the can into an evidence bag. It was probably sterilised before use, but the killer may be working fast enough to make mistakes.

It takes me an hour to speak to everyone at the scene, scribbling down names and alibis. Maggie explains that Matt spent most of the evening in the pub. The news makes me wonder if he could have sneaked out to start the fire then coolly returned to the Rock for another beer. By now the crowd is thinning, and Nina looks pale in the glow from people's torch beams.

'Stay at mine tonight,' I say.

'All my stuff was upstairs. I don't even have a toothbrush.'

'We'll cope.'

People are waiting for my instructions. The responsibility would have fallen to me, even if I had nothing to do with the case. Being the biggest man in a crowd always makes people assume I'm in charge.

'Thanks, everyone,' I tell them. 'Let's call it a night. You've been brilliant.'

The islanders have stayed true to form, rallying together in a crisis; Nina's belongings have been carted away for safe storage at the shop. Smoke is still billowing from the open window, but no more can be done until tomorrow, when the fire officer from Penzance will give his verdict on how the blaze started.

Nina remains silent on the way to my house. Once we get inside she collapses into an armchair.

'Did you lose much?' I ask.

'Camera, photos, laptop. Most of what I brought with me.'

'How come you're so calm?'

She gives a shaky laugh. 'It's just stuff, Ben. It can all be replaced.'

Nina looks beautiful but frail as she gazes at the fire, with Shadow's head settled on her knee. Her blank expression convinces me to keep my distance; it reveals the depth of her grief. After losing the person she valued most, shedding some creature comforts won't rock her world. It takes effort to back away, mumbling an excuse about making her bed. When I return, she's asleep in my chair. She doesn't stir when I clatter the fireguard into place. It's tempting to lean down and kiss her, but the consequences could be disastrous. Shadow seems content to have her to himself, yawning widely as he settles by the hearth.

My skin's on edge when I step into the shower, grey swirls of soot vanishing down the plughole. My head's still reeling when I put out the light, rerunning the sequence of events. The causal link's unclear, but the killer seems to be acting in a frenzy: first a stabbing, then a break-in, a bludgeoning and a fire. The island is divided between people happily going about their business and a handful of eccentrics. Hidden among them is someone whose rage can't be controlled. My last thought as I get into bed is for Nina, curled up in my living room. It's tempting to steal out for one last look, but I force the idea back into its box before shutting my eyes.

33

A light glows inside Rose's cabin, even though she left the place in darkness. She hides in the dunes until she can gather enough courage to climb the steps, but once across the threshold it's clear the culprits vanished long ago. Trays of herbs have been scattered across the floor, wooden boxes trampled underfoot, broken glass littering the furniture. The mess in the kitchen is worse. Pots of honey have been upended, leaving sticky trails on the lino, and blinds ripped from the windows. There's no way of knowing whether Jay Curnow sent his lackeys to tear the place apart, or the smugglers came looking for their package.

Sam's room has suffered most. Photos have been torn down, his mattress slashed apart, the boy's trophies dented and broken on the floor.

'You bastards,' Rose hisses.

She would rather they had destroyed all her possessions but left his treasures intact. The only consolation is that Sam is safe in hospital, where no one can harm him; her

270

own life is far less important. She surveys the kitchen again, but can't decide where to begin. The scale of the damage is too much to comprehend.

She stands rooted to the spot, letting the facts register: the island is no longer her sanctuary. It would break her heart, but for the first time ever she can imagine abandoning the place.

34

The sight of Nina in my kitchen this morning makes me feel guilty. If she hadn't got involved with me, the killer would never have torched her rented cottage, warning me to keep my distance. It bothers me too that she's wearing one of my shirts, revealing mile-long legs.

'I borrowed this to sleep in. Is that okay?'

'It suits you better.' I'm distracted by her glossy hair and acres of smooth skin. I cross my arms firmly across my chest, determined not to touch.

'You seem tense, Ben. Is something wrong?' Her gaze meets mine again.

'I'm fine. What do you want for breakfast?'

'Whatever's going. Can I take a shower?'

'Feel free, there's plenty of hot water in the tank.'

Once she's gone, I let myself exhale. The sky outside the window is calm for once, winter sunlight spilling onto mid-blue sea, gulls wheeling in circles overhead. Last night's drama has made the scene look too good to be true. I search the fridge for something edible, and by the time Nina returns, I'm serving two halves of a mushroom omelette onto plates. She's dressed in the pale blue blouse and jeans she wore yesterday. The only effort she seems to have made is combing her hair, yet I can't stop looking.

'Did anyone visit your cottage yesterday?' I ask.

She looks thoughtful. 'Dean Miller came for another appointment, then Jay Curnow making a courtesy call.'

'No one else?'

'Danny walked by, around seven in the evening, but he didn't stop.'

'Where was he going?'

'He was climbing Gweal Hill, lost in his own world.'

I take a gulp of coffee, but it leaves a bitter aftertaste. Danny's endless night-time walks could be his way of scouring the island to find Laura's killer, or escaping from his guilt. He would have been in the right place at the right time to start the fire at Nina's cottage.

'Have any of the islanders behaved oddly towards you, since you arrived?'

She gives a rare smile. 'Apart from you?'

'No one else?'

'Pete Moorcroft, one time. But maybe I imagined it.'

'How do you mean?'

She looks embarrassed. 'He carried my shopping back to the house, the day I arrived. It felt like he'd never leave.'

Pete has slipped to the bottom of my suspect list, with no hard evidence connecting him to Laura's attack. I remember our conversation when he was birdwatching, his manner friendly but awkward. By carrying Nina's shopping, he was probably trying to be welcoming, unaware that he'd overstepped the mark.

'Will you go back to Bristol now?'

She shakes her head. 'Jay's going to find me somewhere else to stay, if the cottage takes more than a week to fix.'

'You're welcome to stay here till then.' The statement slips from my mouth before I can stop it.

'Are you sure?'

'If you promise to keep the dog with you. He's not much of a bodyguard, but he's better than nothing.'

Shadow doesn't seem bothered by my lack of faith. He's already stationed himself by Nina's chair, looking pleased with himself, as if his luck's about to turn.

The fire investigator arrives from the mainland mid-morning, complaining about his long journey. Officer Mike Ferris is a small, rotund forty-year-old, bouncing with repressed energy. He looks amused when I explain that the islanders rejected plans for a helipad, to protect the environment.

'My arse,' he replies. 'They're keeping tourists away.'

It takes him an hour and a half to assess Gweal Cottage. The ground-floor rooms are intact, apart from smoke trails on the stairway's white paint. Upstairs the air reeks of charcoal. The bed frame is charred to cinders, carpet scorched from the floor; the melted remains of Nina's computer lie among the ashes.

'Lucky you got here fast,' Ferris says. 'Any longer and the roof would be gone.'

He confirms that the arsonist climbed in through the kitchen window, then splashed paraffin across the bedroom's walls, furniture and floor. His intention was to destroy things Nina valued, instead of ones her landlord could easily replace. It seems ironic that Jay Curnow visited on the very day someone set light to his property. Ferris gives a cheery smile before heading back to the quay, promising to file his report by tomorrow. I feel a twinge of envy for the simplicity of his job. He only has to establish cause and effect; no need to find the culprit.

I arrive at the hospital by mid-afternoon after taking the Sky Bus, and a slow taxi from Land's End. Sam Austell is in his room, dressed in a T-shirt and jeans, his skin pallid. The constant babble that spewed from his mouth has ended, but he's fallen a long way from his halcyon days as a budding football star.

'How are you feeling, Sam?'

His reply is a dull murmur. 'Better than before.'

'Your mum'll be here tomorrow. Are you up to talking?'

'I don't know. Everything's a bit blurred.'

'Let's see what you remember. Were you in contact with Laura much in the past few weeks?'

'Not really. We stopped going out last year.'

'But she phoned you the day before she died. What did she want?'

'Nothing.' There's a pause before he replies. 'We stayed friends, that's all.'

'Come on, Sam. No one had seen you together for ages.'

'I bumped into her at Dean Miller's house, the week before she died. She said things were bad at home.' A flash of pain crosses his face. 'Laura needed money. She was desperate to leave the island.'

'Did she ask you for cash?'

'She wanted to borrow a grand, but it was more than I had.'

'Even though you've been running drugs round the islands?'

His face tenses, and I can see why; dealing carries a five-year prison sentence. 'You can't prove anything.'

'I think you gave her some resin to sell, as a favour. We found it in her room, with photos of you.' I study him again. 'You told your mum that you saw something, the day Laura died.'

'Like I said, my memory's screwed.' His cheek tics with anxiety.

'You're not under arrest, Sam. I know you didn't hurt Laura; I just need to find out who did.'

'She was scared of someone. I keep thinking it was my fault, I should have helped her more.'

'What did you see, Sam?'

'She asked me to meet her before she started work, on the beach below Gweal Hill.' He stops, as if the words are choking him. 'I saw her fall as I came round the point. She landed on the rocks. It was horrible, the sea dragging her away. There was nothing I could do.'

'Did you see who pushed her?'

'All I saw was her falling backwards. I thought she wanted me to watch her die. It looked like she'd thrown herself off the cliff deliberately.'

'Is that why you took the overdose?'

The boy doesn't reply. My frustration increases as I ask more questions. Austell's answers have dried up, so I leave him staring down at the cars circling the hospital forecourt in an endless chain. His motives are clearer now. He still loved Laura, even though she only wanted escape funds. All he could offer was a portion of the drugs he carried. Swallowing a chunk of cannabis resin must have been his way of numbing the pain of watching her die. It's lucky for him that there's no proof that he's been handling drugs, apart from the guilt on his face. But the conversation proves that the Cornish smuggling trade is alive and well. Eddie has already checked Sam's contacts on St Mary's, their homes coming up clean. The major dealers are skilled at disappearing into thin air when a runner gets into trouble.

Sam's consultant catches up with me afterwards. Dr Lucas gives a guarded smile when I ask about his progress.

'He's taking steps,' she replies. 'Sam's asked for a place on our addiction programme, but he'll need long-term commitment.'

Her subdued tone of voice makes me certain that her

job is harder than mine. She must have treated dozens of cases of drug-induced psychosis; I'm guessing it's easy to help addicts through the first stages, but a tougher challenge to keep them clean. She raises her hand in a tired salute when I say goodbye. The prospect of a long journey back to Bryher irritates me as I leave the hospital. In an ideal world, I could click my fingers and be standing outside Dean Miller's studio. I'm hoping the island's Pied Piper heard Sam and Laura's conversation, and that he'll let me under his defences at last.

35

It's dark by the time I get back to the island, the wide beam of my police-issue torch turning the path silver as I jog towards Miller's house. From twenty metres away, a man's voice pierces the silence. I can see the artist on the floor of his studio, arms limp at his sides. Matt Trescothick doesn't even glance up when I burst through the door, his voice a dull growl.

'You sick bastard. You fancied her, didn't you?'

I haul Matt to his feet, but Dean has lost consciousness. His face is as colourful as one of his canvases, yellow bruising on his temple, blood dripping from a cut lip, eye socket already turning blue. It doesn't take a genius to figure out the sequence of events. One of the paintings of Laura has been ripped in two, a jagged tear across the canvas, legs separated from her torso. The other picture is still propped against the wall. The girl's eyes meet mine, round and accusatory, begging me to find her killer.

I force cuffs onto Matt's wrists then phone Nina, asking her to look after Dean. She's had more medical training than anyone else on Bryher; at least she'll be able to check for broken bones. The artist's eyes are opening as he wipes blood from his face with his sleeve. I grab hold of Matt's arm to prevent him from lashing out again.

'I'm arresting you for assault.'

Matt stares back at me. 'I came for the paintings of Laura. I expected something beautiful, not bloody pornography.'

'She agreed to sit for him.'

'The bloke's a fucking pervert.' He spits the words in Miller's direction. 'Maybe he killed her.'

'Dean was here the morning Laura went missing, people saw him.'

'Get your hands off me,' Matt hisses, trying to twist free.

'Calm down. You're already looking at an assault conviction.'

'I won't press charges.' The artist is pressing a cloth to his eye, his voice muffled. 'My paintings upset him. I should have destroyed them.'

'You expect me to take pity from filth like you?' The look in Matt's eye is murderous as I walk him back to the community hall.

'You're lucky Dean's let you off, but the caution's still going on your record.'

'The old pervert was screwing my daughter.'

'That's unlikely.'

'Maybe she turned him down.' His eyes burn with conviction, even though there's no proof.

'He's gay, Matt.'

'There's no way he'd paint her like that unless he fancied her.'

I turn to face him. 'While we're talking about violence, can you explain the bruises on Suzanne's arm?'

He jerks his wrists, as if he's trying to break his handcuffs. 'If you think I'd hurt her, you're a worse arsehole than Miller.'

'You like using your fists to settle arguments. Who else would it be?'

'No idea, but when I find out, I'll take him apart.'

Matt seethes quietly while I write my caution report. He still seems furious enough to bounce off the walls when I escort him to Gwen's home, a shocked look on his mother's face when she opens the door.

My feelings are mixed as I head home through the dark. There's no way of knowing how I'd feel about Dean in Matt's shoes. The painter seems to draw the island's young to his lair with no effort at all, like moths to a flame.

For once there's no clamour from Shadow when I get home. He's stretched in front of the fire, only raising his head by a fraction when I arrive. The dog closes his eyes again immediately, as if my arrival bores him. Nina is preparing food at the kitchen table, wearing my dark red jumper, that sleek waterfall of hair hanging to her jaw. I keep my expression neutral, trying to ignore how good she looks in my clothes.

'Dean's got bruised ribs, a loose tooth and his eye

socket needs an X-ray tomorrow,' she says. 'I left Maggie with him at the studio. What made Matt attack him?'

'He painted some explicit pictures of Laura.'

She shakes her head. 'This place is falling apart. I think I'll just stay indoors.'

I drop onto a stool to watch her cook, the air spiced with wine, garlic and freshly grated parmesan. 'You didn't have to make dinner. We could have gone to the pub.'

'It's a reward for rescuing my violin. It's the one thing I'd hate to lose.'

Nina crosses the room in a few long strides to kiss my cheek, the scent of her cutting through the other aromas. Instinct takes over as I pull her into my arms, but I remind myself that she came here to recover, not be mauled by a virtual stranger. When I release her again, she stands her ground.

'All that advance and retreat must be tiring, Ben. The food's ready, you can come and eat.'

Her reactions mystify me. No one would guess that most of her possessions have just gone up in a puff of smoke, her calmness still intact. The pasta is coated in wild mushroom sauce, with ice-cold Sauvignon Blanc to wash it down.

'What was your childhood like?' I ask.

'Quiet, but I liked being an only child. It taught me self-sufficiency.' Despite her smile, her voice resonates with loneliness. 'Let's not talk about the past. How about some after-dinner entertainment?'

'Brandy and lap dancing would suit me fine.'

'Scrabble's my best offer.'

I could retreat to my room, but she's already cross-legged by the fire, laying out the board. A new side of her emerges during the game, softer and easily amused, the dog lolling at her side. I don't want to fancy her this much, but the feeling won't shift.

'I should sleep, Nina. It's been a long day.'

She gives a nod of agreement, but when she opens the sideboard to put the Scrabble box away, the photo I hid flutters to her feet. She looks fascinated as she picks it up.

'This is you and Clare, isn't it?' she murmurs. 'Shoulder to shoulder, wearing the same smile. You could be relatives.'

'That's how it felt.' I stare down at the image again. 'I still want to bawl at her, for locking me out.' I rub my hand across the back of my neck.

'More pain?'

Before I can reply, she's facing me, one hand at the base of my skull, the other on my shoulder. I'm expecting another of those lightning movements that release my tension, but her touch barely registers.

'We could both use some temporary comfort, Ben. Why not think about that?' She steps back before I can reply.

When I open my eyes again, the room is empty. The photo of me and Clare is propped on the dresser; we look pleased with ourselves, like nothing could ever go wrong.

36

Rose tosses and turns in her sleep. She has nailed boards over her broken door, but nightmares are coming thick and fast. Laura is trapped beneath the ocean's weight; she has become a mermaid, unable to surface, her blue-lipped mouth gasping for air. When Rose startles awake, the girl's features have been replaced by the boatman's. He stands over her bed in the semi-dark, his icy fingers grabbing her arms. It's impossible to fight back, shock draining her strength.

'Where did you hide it?' the man hisses. 'Only Sam knows our drop-off point.'

'I didn't take anything.'

'Put it back, or I'll break every bone in your body.'

Rose's vision blurs, panic making her speak her thoughts. 'Was it you that killed the girl? I have to know.'

'Why would I, for fuck's sake?' His blank expression shows that he's telling the truth. But if the boatmen didn't kill Laura, who did?

'I'll do as you say,' she stutters.

'You've got till the weekend.'

When Rose opens her eyes again, she's alone in her ruined bedroom, amongst piles of broken furniture. There's a rip in the seam of her nightgown, a bitter draught chilling her skin.

37

My phone wakes me before the alarm. The voice babbling in my ear is female, her words garbled. It takes me a while to realise that it's Danny Curnow's mother.

'Slow down, Patty, I can't hear you.'

'We need your help. Hurry, please.'

Her voice disintegrates into noisy tears as first light seeps through the window. When I peer inside the spare room, Shadow is lying peacefully asleep beside Nina, allowing me to exit the house alone. Most of the island is in darkness as I head across Shipman Down. I cover the ground fast, jogging north when I reach the eastern shore, with Tresco's black outline visible from the corner of my eye. The Curnows' house still resembles a futurist palace, enough light blazing from the windows to drain the national grid.

Danny's mother looks different when she rushes outside. Without make-up, Patty is more girl next door than glamour model. She's dressed in faded jeans and a black jumper, skin blotchy with tears. Her mouth flaps open, releasing a high-pitched moan that edges towards a scream.

'Come inside, Patty, we can talk there.'

She's already gabbling. 'Danny never came home last night. We've looked for him everywhere.'

'Try to explain for me, step by step.'

An acre of clear air hangs over us in the vast hallway, but the atmosphere feels leaden. Through the living room doorway, I catch sight of Jay in his dressing gown, ranting into his mobile, but Patty chooses the kitchen for our conversation. She pours coffee without asking how I take it, slapping the mug into my hands. The tension she's exuding makes the air feel electrified.

'When did you realise Danny was missing?'

'Around 5 a.m., when I used the bathroom. I saw his bed was empty.' She's on her feet again, struggling to keep still. 'Since Laura died, he's gone out on his own, almost every night. We couldn't stop him.'

'What did your son do yesterday?'

'He wouldn't come out of his room; it was driving me crazy. I told him to pull himself together.' She claps her hand over her mouth like the words could be reclaimed.

'Can you remember what time he left last night?'

'I heard him go out about eleven.'

'No boats have sailed since then, so he can't have gone far. Has Danny talked much since Laura's death?'

'Hardly at all, he just shuts down. He's in a terrible state.' She keeps her eyes fixed on the window. 'I tried to get him to see a counsellor, but he refused.'

'Chances are he'll be back soon. Let's look upstairs, you can see what he's taken with him.'

The boy's sheets and duvet lie in a tangle, a whiff of stale aftershave, musky and unpleasant, lingering on the air. Clothes litter the floor, beside used plates and mugs, proving that he's been eating his meals alone. Laura's letters are scattered across his desk. Even from this distance I can see kisses scrawled across each page, her favourite heart symbol, pierced by an arrow.

'What's missing, Patty?'

'His phone's gone, but he's not answering. That's his wallet on the table.'

'How about clothes? Do you know what he's wearing?'

She peers into the wardrobe. 'His black hooded coat, and I think his grey trainers are missing too.'

'Has his dad been able to talk to him about Laura yet?'

'Jay's not keen on discussing emotions. He and Danny are so alike, they row all the time.' The frustration on her face reveals that she's caught in the crossfire.

'I'll start looking for your son straight away. Call me if he comes home, okay?'

Jay Curnow has finished making his call when we get back downstairs. There's no sign now of the ruthless millionaire, willing to steal any property from its rightful owner at a knock-down price. Age has finally caught up with him, his skin ashen. He mumbles a few words of thanks, but the sounds are incoherent, his vocabulary unravelling.

There's a chance that Danny is walking off his nightmares, but if he was telling the truth, he could have run into Laura's killer. My first port of call is the pub, a five-minute jog away across the dunes. I gallop up the steps of the fire escape to hammer on Maggie's door. She's wide awake when she answers, her expression shocked.

'Wake Zoe and Billy, can you? I need a team searching inland and another on the beaches, looking for Danny Curnow.'

She rises to her toes to kiss my cheek. 'Thank God you're here, sweetheart.'

Her confidence feels misplaced, given my lack of progress. When I check my watch it's only 7 a.m., salmon-pink clouds streaking the horizon, the start of a clear winter day. I head south, collecting searchers as I go: Pete and June Moorcroft, Arthur, then Ray. My uncle and the ferryman walk in silence, but the shopkeeper's jabber is so grating it takes effort not to tell him to shut up. There's no sign of activity on the quay except the *Bryher Maid* breaching the sound. The air's so pure, I can see Eddie on the opposite shore, neat and upright in his black gabardine. I call his mobile to instruct him to wait at the hall, in case the search party needs help. By the time we reach the island's southern tip, we meet a dozen more islanders, dressed in outdoor gear. From their gloomy expressions I know Danny hasn't been found. Most of the island's families are represented, alongside Maggie's staff from the pub. I feel a wave of gratitude when she rallies her troops.

'Everyone back to the Rock for breakfast.'

At the edge of the crowd I catch sight of Nina's slim frame, drowned by my leather jacket, Shadow at her feet. Zoe bobs forwards to join me. She seems to have dressed in a hurry, white-blonde hair flying in all directions, a bright green scarf at her throat. I reach out and squeeze her shoulder, but her million-dollar smile is on half-strength today.

'Where do you think he is, Ben?'

'Keeping warm somewhere, I hope.'

I divide the searchers into two parties, sending them back to the pub along the inland routes, with Zoe still at my side. We keep silent as we scan the open ground. The island is free of litter, nothing to see except gorse bushes, bracken and marram grass. When I look down at Zoe, she's concentrating too hard to talk. The swimming pool by Gweal Hill lies on the horizon, a dark patch on the water making me increase my pace.

'Jesus,' I mutter to myself.

'What?' Zoe's anxious face peers up at me.

The pond is growing bigger with every stride. The water's murky today, half covered by the round leaves of water lilies. A black piece of fabric floats on the surface beside granite rocks I dived from as a kid. I can see that it's a jacket as I grab the sleeve, leaving it heaped on the bank. My eyes search the water again. Why would a boy choose to die in an inland pool instead of miles of clear ocean, without leaving a suicide note? It crosses my mind to dive in and search for his body, but it's so overgrown I wouldn't see a thing. Zoe comes to a halt beside me, panting for breath, and although I feel like sinking to my knees, I stay vertical for her sake.

'Is that Danny's coat?' she asks.

'I think so.'

'Want me to fetch his parents?'

'Not yet, let's search the area first.'

Zoe's eyes are wide with shock, but she follows my instructions. We spend the next twenty minutes pushing through brambles and ground elder, checking thickets either side of the pond. I stand on the bank to call Eddie, asking him to summon a police diving team from the mainland. My head keeps filling with memories of late summer days, when the pool was dredged clean so we could dive from the boulders. Some of my best childhood days were spent here, but it never felt the same after a kid from my year jumped in for a dare one winter, the freezing cold stopping his heart before he reached the bank. I photograph the coat, then send Zoe back to the hall for an evidence bag. The wait feels worse than my hours spent guarding Laura's body. I can almost picture the boy waking in despair before sunrise, leaving the house in silence, a determined look on his face.

The worst part of the morning is watching the Curnows fall apart. Patty keeps begging me to check again, even though their son's coat has been found by a pool where others have drowned. She's convinced he might still be sitting on a rock somewhere, looking out to sea. I don't have the heart to point out that no sane person would spend a winter day outside without a coat. Rational argument won't help; all I can do is reassure her that the island will be patrolled all day, no one is giving up hope.

Eddie deals with the two police divers who arrive mid-afternoon from the mainland, laden with kit. The leader is a skinny twenty-five-year-old called Trevor, equipped with lamps, wetsuit and flippers slung over his arm. A helicopter buzzes overhead as we talk, a huge mosquito threatening to bite. Someone must have a hotline to the press, alerting them to every new development. I turn my back on it, wondering how much the informant is getting paid for passing on everything they see.

Light is fading when the divers enter the water. The area's been cordoned off but Jay and Patty wait beside the pool, clinging to each other while the men slip under the water, flippers pointing at the sky, the yellow beam of their lamps flickering beneath the surface. They work for an hour then wade up the incline, the lead diver yanking his oxygen monitor from his mouth.

'It's too dark,' he says. 'We'll have to wait till morning.'

'Thanks for trying. We've got rooms for you at the pub.'

The Curnows are already turning away, Patty weeping as Jay leads her down the path. Back at their house we sit in the glass-walled living room, with no curtains or blinds to protect them from the world outside. It's the opposite of Jenna's claustrophobic cottage, but the atmosphere is the same. Jay and Patty sit huddled on the settee, fear imprinted on their faces.

'Can you describe Danny's behaviour since Laura died?'

Jay's jaw tightens. 'My wife's in bits. Can't the questions wait till tomorrow?'

'Any information you give me now could help bring your son home.'

'He's been so angry,' Patty says quietly. 'Danny's obsessed with finding Laura's killer. He goes out all hours, hunting on the beaches, even though I begged him to stay indoors.'

'Did he mention names of people he suspected?'

'He never said.' She lets out another sob. 'It's our fault, he stopped trusting us.'

'We've done our best, love,' Jay mutters.

Curnow's comment falls on deaf ears, his wife turning away. I leave them to resolve their differences just before 10 p.m.

The night sky is clearer than before, a canopy of stars poised above the sea, moonlight bright enough to dazzle. The conditions encourage one last search, so I set off across the shore. I'm planning to drop down the eastern side of the island, then walk home from Droppy Nose Point. Instinct still tells me that Danny would have chosen the sea rather than a fetid pool if he planned to end his life, stripping off his coat as he headed for the beach. But the boy didn't strike me as suicidal. He was on a mission to avenge his girlfriend, nothing else cluttering his mind. My eyes scan the tideline; seagulls bob on the water, keeping quiet for once. I don't look up again until the wide sweep of Green Bay comes into view. The peaks of Three Brothers Rock look like a triad of old men, heads bowed in conversation, behind them the jagged outcrop of Merrick Island. When I look back inland, Jenna Trescothick is crossing the beach, wearing a padded jacket, a woollen cap shadowing her face, hands buried in her pockets.

'What are doing out, Jenna?'

Her eyes are unfocused. 'I heard about Danny; I can't let it happen again.'

'You shouldn't be here after dark.'

Her stare hardens. 'I have to do something. There's no way I can sleep.'

'Leave it till tomorrow, it's not safe. Let's go back to the cottage.'

She falls into step beside me, maintaining her silence, emotions travelling across her face like a storm system. Danny's absence must have kick-started her grieving for Laura all over again. When we reach her house, she slips inside and shuts the door without saying a word.

38

Madron is waiting in his office when I arrive, his eyes small and focused as lasers. No doubt he's been poring over the email I sent him since the crack of dawn.

'The divers have found no trace of him yet, sir.'

'Suicide, you think?'

'That's too neat. First the girl's murdered, then this. He wants us to assume Danny couldn't handle the guilt.'

'That might be exactly what happened.'

'I've reviewed the evidence; a suicidal kid isn't that organised. I think he went looking for Laura's killer then ran into danger. His body could be anywhere.'

'The lad probably wanted to avoid judgement,' Madron says.

'There are some suspects who could have been roaming the island when Laura and Danny went missing.'

'You sent me the list.' He reads the names out in a sing-song voice. 'Pete Moorcroft, Dean Miller, Arthur Penwithick, Jim Helyer, Matt Trescothick, Ray Kitto.' He slaps his glasses down on the desk. 'Half of these men are pensioners. Why in God's name would any of them kill a pair of teenagers?'

'I'd lay odds on it being Matt Trescothick.'

His chin rises. 'Give me your rationale.'

'I've always believed it was someone close to the victim. Matt Trescothick's been under pressure for years, I've seen his violence first hand when he attacked Dean Miller. Maybe Danny ran into him last night and got the same treatment, if he thought the boy knew what he'd done.'

'It takes madness to kill your own child. Trescothick's got anger issues, but he's not a psychopath.'

'You don't have to be crazy to lash out, then cover your tracks.'

'I'm not convinced, Kitto. You've got till tonight, then travel restrictions will be lifted. The commissioner wants the island back to normal.'

'You can't do that, sir. The killer could strike again.'

Madron's stare hardens. 'It's obvious the boy killed his girlfriend then took his own life. You've worked hard, but you're too close to the case. I'll handle the wind-down.' He checks his task list again. 'Contact the coroner again, can you? See how fast they can release Laura Trescothick's body for burial.'

'It'll be the end of the week, at the earliest. What about the press?'

'Once the case closes, they can do as they please.'

The news is like a direct kick in the guts. Bryher will be open for business again from tomorrow, as if no threat exists. Journalists will flood the island once the embargo lifts, selling the story as *Romeo and Juliet*, star-crossed lovers from warring families who met the same tragic fate.

When I get back to Bryher, Eddie is keeping watch by the pool.

'No news,' he says quietly. 'The divers are just finishing.'

He looks stunned when I explain that the DCI is pressing for a quick conclusion, despite having no proof that Danny Curnow committed suicide.

'It's too soon,' he says. 'It took us days to find Sam Austell; Danny could still be hiding somewhere.'

We stand together in silence, watching the divers appear then vanish again, like performing seals. Eddie is starting to feel like an ally, now that he's stopped accepting Madron's edicts as the word of God. The two divers look exhausted when they blow water from their breathing gear, then peel off their wetsuits. Swimming is a passion of mine, but I wouldn't trade jobs with them for the world. Their best day's work involves hauling corpses from the water. Judging by their bleak expressions, they would rather deliver the boy's body to us than go home empty-handed. I leave Eddie to thank them and return to the community hall, more certain than ever that the killer is teasing us. He left Danny's coat floating on the pool's surface to give himself a head start, while the real clues went cold.

Someone is crouched by the side entrance to Hell Bay

Hotel as I walk back. When I get closer, Jim Helyer is battening wood over the broken glass door. He looks startled when he swings round, the smile I remember from our schooldays slow to appear.

'Did Zoe ask you to fix that, Jim?'

'She moved back just now. I'm making the place secure for her.'

I curse under my breath then jog upstairs. The door to Zoe's flat hangs open, I can see her through the gap, hunched over her computer, humming along to a song playing on her headphones.

'What do you think you're doing?'

'Choosing songs from my backlist. An agency in London might put me on their books, if I send them a wider selection.'

'Why are you so bloody keen to leave? I thought you were happy here.'

She blinks at me. 'You only live once, big man. This place is beautiful, but I have to spread my wings.'

'That's not relevant right now. You should stay at the pub till I give you the all-clear.'

'I'm perfectly safe here. Danny's been a lost soul ever since Laura died. He took his own life, didn't he?'

Hearing Madron's argument repeated makes me grit my teeth. 'Someone could have murdered them both.'

'It was a lover's tiff that got out of control, and now it's over.' Zoe's fixed expression shows that she'll never back down.

'Don't blame me if you get hurt. I'll be round later to check the place is safe.'

'Love you too, sweetie.'

She blows me a mocking kiss before returning to her music. Jim's gone by the time I get back downstairs, leaving the door neatly fixed. He's installed a new mortise lock and nailed sheets of wood over the broken glass, but the extra security doesn't reassure me.

I channel all my frustration into organising another search this afternoon. People's voices sound jaded on the phone, as if they're sick of constant worry, but a group of around twenty is milling outside the pub when we set off at two o'clock. The tide is so far out, Cromwell's castle seems within touching distance, battlements and turrets charcoal grey against the pale sky.

'Thanks for helping us again,' I tell the group. 'Search the high-water mark, please, for anything that could belong to Danny.'

Everyone on my suspect list is along for the ride. Dean Miller is wearing a bandage over one eye, still looking frail, while Matt Trescothick and Jay Curnow stay at separate ends of the crowd. Patty is clinging to her husband's arm, her face pinched. It's Pete Moorcroft who trots over as I lead the group down to the beach, his anxious voice droning in my ears.

'Sad, isn't it?' he says. 'As if losing Laura wasn't awful enough.'

'We don't know what's happened to Danny yet.'

'But we can guess. The kid was heartbroken, wasn't he?'

'There's no evidence, Pete. That's why we're here.'

He recedes into the crowd, leaving me to scan the tideline. My eyes keep being drawn to Tresco's inlets as we pass Frenchman's Point. Under different circumstances I'd love to stroll round the bigger island alone, calling at the pub later for a quiet beer. We sweep the curve of Green Bay, our boots crunching across gravel, passing Rose Austell's dilapidated cabin. We've been searching half an hour before a shout goes up. Billy Reese is with Maggie at the high-water mark, holding something aloft, like a trophy winner. The item in his hands is a grey trainer, bearing the Adidas logo. There's no need to ask if it belongs to Danny; Patty Curnow is already in floods of tears. Matt remains at the edge of the circle, head down, his expression bleak. If he's the killer, seeming concerned is a wise strategy, even though the missing boy's father is his arch-enemy.

Billy's find brings a new energy to the search, people fanning across the beach, checking the shingle. My uncle catches up with me as the group edges forwards.

'If Danny went into the sea last night, he'll have been dragged south.'

'How come?'

'Full moon,' he replies. 'The riptide was at its strongest, his body could be miles from here.'

Ray walks on slowly, still scanning the ground. The investigation may have added him to my list of suspects, but I still trust his judgement. After decades spent designing boats for local waters, no one understands the tides better.

Patty and Jay Curnow have gone home, but the dozen islanders in my team carry on searching until dusk falls. We meet up with Eddie at the foot of Samson Hill. The rest of the party traipse away, weary from the slow trudge across familiar terrain. When my deputy speaks again, for once his face is bleak.

'We're no further on, are we?' he asks.

'At least we know that he may have walked into the sea, or someone dragged him there.'

'What do we tell his parents, boss? We've covered the whole island, but the boy may never be found.'

Eddie seems embarrassed by the words escaping from his mouth. He probably knows that my father was lost at sea, his body never recovered. Family tragedies are always public knowledge in a place this small. He heads away, but I stay on the beach, watching the tide turn. The waves are racing in with a vengeance, making me step back to avoid a soaking. When I look up, Bonfire Carn is a black pinnacle against the sky. Someone is standing on Samson Hill, light glinting from his binoculars, coat flailing in the wind. I race up the incline, sending loose pieces of slate skittering down to the beach, but when I reach the top, only the carn is waiting for me, its stones piled three metres high. Whoever was on the summit five minutes ago must be thrilled to watch me floundering in the dark.

39

The Curnows are in no state for visitors, but it's my job to warn them that the DCI is closing the case tomorrow. Patty looks exhausted as we sit in their state-of-the-art kitchen, long hair ragged from searching the windswept beach. Jay's voice is gruff with anger when he finally speaks.

'There's no way my son topped himself.'

Tears ooze from Patty's eyes. 'Danny wouldn't be that cruel. He'd have left us a note.'

'It's possible your son caused Laura's death, then ended his own, out of guilt.'

Jay rocks forward in his seat. 'People are saying that?'

'I'm afraid so.'

'Idiots, the lot of them,' he snaps. 'Danny's as gentle as they come. That's half his trouble.'

'Can you think of anyone he'd argued with recently?'

His temper cools slightly. 'Matt Trescothick made snide remarks a few months back outside the pub, but my son walked away. That bloke's always looking for trouble.'

'No one else?'

'He doesn't like Dean Miller, but never said why.' Patty's voice falls to a whisper.

It's easy to see why Danny would have resented the artist's intimate paintings of his girlfriend, but there are no other reports of tension between them. I spend the next half-hour trying to find out who could have followed their son, but Patty retreats into her shell, dabbing her eyes with a screwed-up tissue. She only speaks again as I get up to leave.

'He could still be alive, couldn't he? There's no proof he's dead.'

The look on her face reminds me of my mother's expression, weeks after my father's boat sank, still clinging to the idea that one day he'd be found.

'He's been missing nearly forty-eight hours, Patty.'

She's doesn't seem to hear, hope still glowing on her face as I say goodbye. Jay is monosyllabic; he's hardly met my eye during the interview, and now he's rushing me out of the door. He fits the stereotype for a cold-blooded killer perfectly – ruthless and lacking in empathy, desperate to retain control. He even tried to implicate Matt during our brief conversation, yet there's nothing tangible linking him to Laura's death or his son's absence.

For once I could use Shadow's company on the walk home, to cancel the tension that's hung over me all day.

Music floats from an open window when I reach the cottage; there's a wildness to it, like a storm spinning inland. When I peer through the living room curtains, Nina is playing her violin, slim body swaying with the tempo, the dog lazing by the fire. The sight of her conjuring that pure sound keeps me rooted to the spot for a long time, but the music falls silent as I walk through the door.

'Don't stop on my account. I could use some harmony.'

'I should practise more. I keep hitting wrong notes.'

It calms me to see her face, tawny eyes watching me take off my coat. She follows me into the kitchen while I pour a glass of wine, then raid the fridge for bread and cheese, suddenly remembering how little I've eaten. My normal pattern is to isolate myself after a lousy day at work, but she's waiting for an explanation.

'Everything'll be wasted at this rate.'

'How do you mean?' she asks.

'Logic doesn't always produce the right result. I know the killer's still out there, getting away with double murder.'

'You could be right. Danny didn't seem broken, last time I saw him. He looked like someone on a mission.'

Gratitude washes over me. Apart from Eddie, she's the first person to believe my theory. She returns to the living room to let me eat in peace, the lilting sound of her violin drifting through the closed door. I'm about to give up on work for the night when the Skype symbol on my computer begins to flash. DCI Sarah Goldman's gaunt features appear on the screen; she's wearing a professional smile, grey hair scraped back from her face. My line manager has never skyped me before, preferring to send emails. She's calling from Hammersmith, her office so recently decorated the white walls look like a hospital waiting room.

'This is unexpected, ma'am.'

'Just a quick call, Ben. How's your busman's holiday going?'

'It's frustrating right now. The case isn't going to plan.'

'That's murder investigation for you,' she replies. 'I thought you'd want to know the results of Clare's inquest.'

The screen blanks, and time passes too slowly until Goldman reappears, her face dividing into abstract squares of colour. I pull in a long breath as her image sharpens again. 'Sorry, boss, I lost you. The signal's terrible down here. Can you repeat that?'

'Clare had end-stage pancreatic cancer. She took matters into her own hands, rather than facing months of palliative care. I'm amazed she carried on working for so long.'

'Why didn't she say anything?'

'I think it was a brave decision on her part, and no one was to blame. I want you back here whenever you're ready, Ben. You're a key member of my team.'

'Thanks for contacting me, ma'am.'

'We'll speak again soon.'

When I close my computer, my heart's beating like a snare drum and Nina has slipped into the chair next to mine.

'That sounded like a tough conversation,' she says.

Knowing the truth doesn't excuse me. Why the hell didn't Clare explain? 'The daft cow probably thought she was protecting me.'

'Have you talked to anyone about it?'

'The police counsellor told me not to dwell on it and get more exercise. The Met aren't great with anything touchy-feely.' I rub my hand across the back of my neck.

Nina studies me again. 'No wonder you're in pain. Your injury's emotional, not physical.'

'It's a trapped nerve, that's all.'

'That's a stupid piece of denial.'

'Thanks for the diagnosis, Dr Jackson.'

Her hand settles on my wrist. 'I'm going to see Zoe. Want to come?'

'Not tonight, but I'll walk you there. I need to check the hotel's secure.'

The wind picks up while we cross Hell Bay, Shadow barking at full volume as he races between the dunes. When Nina slips her arm through mine I feel a quick jolt of pleasure and realise that I'm on dangerous ground. I don't just fancy her, I like her too, and we're facing the same challenge; both struggling to make sense of a missing element. My secrets spill out whenever she's around, drawn by that half-formed smile that only appears when she's genuinely amused.

'Call me when you're ready to come back.'

'I can cross the beach alone, Ben. The dog'll be with me.'

'Someone attacked me half a mile from here, remember? I'll collect you.'

She gives a grudging nod, the look on her face half grateful, half irritated. When I whistle for Shadow he follows her up the steps, tongue lolling. I circle the hotel grounds after they've gone inside, checking windows and doors. It still annoys me that Zoe moved back before I can guarantee the island's safe, but at least the access points to her building are secure.

Back at the cottage I pour the rest of my wine down the sink, the puritanical streak in me rejecting easy comfort. I sit by the fire, remembering Sarah Goldman's words, the guilt I've carried for weeks gradually fading. I'm still so revved when Nina sends her text, it's a relief to stride across the beach again, the exercise allowing me to switch off my thoughts.

40

Rose stands alone on the beach below Gweal Hill. The sea has always been her refuge, but tonight its magic can't protect her. When she was a child she slept with her bedroom window open, the ocean's song lulling her to sleep. It's a harsher sound tonight, pebbles scraping over granite, a cacophony of waves pounding the cliff.

She glances over her shoulder again, too afraid to return home. Moonlight pools on the water, great orbs of white floating on the dark. She stares at the waves until her eyes glaze, fantasy and reality starting to blur. Wreckers' voices echo down through the centuries, calling for blood, before killing the lawmen who stand in their way. On the horizon, she glimpses a tall ship listing on the rocks, drawn by the beacons on Badplace Hill. The taste of gunpowder, dry and acrid, catches the back of her throat, but the beach is empty.

'Wake up,' she murmurs. 'There's no one here.'

Rose knows that she must find shelter. It's too cold to spend the night outside, but pleading for help from another islander feels impossible, until she remembers the one person who never asks questions.

Dean Miller looks disappointed when she arrives at his door, as if he was hoping to see someone else. The artist listens in silence to her request. She's grateful that he doesn't press for details, simply leading her to his untidy living room. He rummages in a cupboard for blankets and a pillow then leaves her to sleep.

Rose stretches out on Miller's sofa, but her body refuses to unwind. She longs to be back in her cabin, surrounded by familiar aromas; she tries to conjure the marine smells of wireweed and sea kale without success. Her only company is the wind gusting down the chimney, raw as an infant's cry.

41

There's no sign of Nina or Shadow in the kitchen when I get up in the morning. She must have taken him for an early walk, so I drag on tracksuit bottoms and put myself through a punishing round of exercises. My body complains with the first sit-up, but my head feels clearer after dozens of squats, jumps and lunges. I'm so focused on completing my last set of press-ups that I don't hear Nina return, a cold blast of air announcing her presence. I finish the set fast, then rise to my feet, aware that a sweaty, bare-chested man might put her off breakfast. By contrast, she looks good enough to eat in one swallow, pink-cheeked from the cold, hair ruffled by the breeze.

'I've never seen anyone do one-handed press-ups before.' Her eyes trail across my shoulders, then back to my face.

'They satisfy my masochistic streak.'

I'm about to head for the shower, but she blocks my way, expression determined. 'I could take a room at the hotel if you prefer, Ben.'

'Why? I'd rather you stayed.'

'Having me around seems to put you on edge.' That clear gold stare is impossible to avoid. 'I wish you'd explain why.'

'Let's talk tonight. I'll organise some food.'

She looks thoughtful when I turn away. The idea of her leaving makes me uneasy; I need to know she's safe, even if she's out of bounds.

I walk straight to Tide Cottage to fulfil my first unpleasant obligation of the day. Jenna says little when I give her the news that Laura's case is closing, but her expression contains a mixture of fury and disappointment as she wishes me a curt goodbye. It's a relief to escape into the fresh air again, passing the Helyers' farm as I head north, with their goats bleating loudly at me, hoping for an extra meal. Grief is still etched on Gwen Trescothick's face when she welcomes me to her cottage. Matt is standing in the kitchen, his sullen expression more suitable for a teenager than a full-grown man. His tense gestures remind me of a grenade about to detonate. It seems to require supreme effort to unbend enough to sit at his mother's table. He only meets my eye after I've stared at him for a full minute.

'Laura's case is closing today, Matt, after the public meeting. I thought you should know.'

He gives me a guarded look. 'You've found the killer?'

'Madron thinks Danny took her life, before ending his own.'

'You don't agree?'

'I can't challenge the decision, but we haven't found his body. There's no categorical proof that's what happened.'

Suddenly Matt pitches forwards in his seat, face two shades paler as I help him through to the lounge. The end of the case seems to have broken through his defences at last. His mother and I sit either side of him as he weeps openly, his sobbing powerful enough to convince me that this is the first time he's released his emotions since Laura died, whether he's guilty or innocent. The room still feels like a shrine; photos of his daughter crowding the mantelpiece between flickering candles. It crosses my mind that he could be weeping tears of relief that the police are withdrawing without anyone blaming him. After a few minutes, his outburst fades to a murmur and Gwen follows me into the hall.

'Thanks for telling us, Ben,' she says quietly.

'I was sorry to hear about Matt's marriage ending.'

'It's for the best.' The old woman gives a crisp nod. 'Jenna's made him miserable for years.'

After we say goodbye, I'm left to process my thoughts. Gwen Trescothick must be one of very few islanders to blame Jenna for her son's unhappiness, given the public falls from grace that have undermined his hero status. I'm still standing on the path when Angie Helyer beckons to me from her back door.

'Come in for a drink,' she calls.

I've kept my distance since Jim's confession about his feelings for Laura, but it's impossible to refuse her invitation. The farmhouse is far roomier than Gwen Trescothick's doll's house: the kitchen is high-ceilinged and airy by comparison, yet the atmosphere is suffocating. Jim is seated at the pine table, spooning cereal into his daughter's mouth, reluctant to meet my eye. Angie offers me coffee then asks for news of Danny, but I can only give the official version.

'That's so sad, Ben. He must have been unbalanced.'

'Whatever his state of mind, he's still to blame. Laura didn't deserve to die.' Jim delivers the words with a scowl.

'I know,' she snaps back at him. 'But Danny must have been ill to hurt her, mustn't he?'

My old classmate soon regains his calm, but his outburst makes me wonder if he's still brooding over the past, despite his confession. He could have crept out of the house to hunt for Danny, still jealous, even though the girl's dead. I finish my coffee fast and thank them, before getting to my feet. Whatever the outcome of the case, relationships I've trusted all my life are being tested to the limit.

Eddie is packing away evidence files, a dejected look on his face, when I return to the hall.

'Help me carry those boxes to mine, can you, Eddie? I'll tell the DCI I need another week to sign off the paperwork.'

His eyebrows rise. 'You think he'll agree?'

'He won't have a choice.'

We cart three large boxes to the cottage. There's

no sign of Nina or the dog, but her quiet fragrance hangs on the air. My deputy stands in the doorway surveying the evidence: her tennis shoes are paired by the door, a brightly coloured scarf draped over the arm of the settee. He's too polite to question our living arrangements. Those keen eyes would make him a good detective, but he's unlikely to progress if he remains in the islands' tiny force. The prospect of returning to his regular beat on Tresco tomorrow could explain his low mood. His expression only brightens when he pauses outside the cottage to check his phone.

'Good news?' I ask.

When he thrusts the screen at me, there are only a few whorls and scratches on the black background. But on closer inspection, I can make out the baby's head curling forwards, the vertebra's dotted line, minute fists raised high. The scan shows a child prepared to enter the world fighting.

'That's amazing, Eddie. Is it a girl or a boy?'

'Girl.' His grin widens. 'Michelle had her first scan today.'

'Why didn't you go with her?'

'My sergeant's exams are coming up; I can't skip work for every antenatal appointment.'

'I'd have insisted you took the day off.'

Eddie's shocked expression makes me wonder if he sees me as an automaton, coldly doing my job.

We work together, laying out chairs for the public meeting at the community hall. The fact that we can complete the task in silence makes me realise we've melded into an unlikely team, shared frustration bonding us at last. I should be relieved that our duties are over, but too many questions remain unanswered.

It's two o'clock when Madron arrives. The DCI seems so pleased with the outcome that he accepts me retaining the paperwork without complaint. When the islanders arrive, I try to be fatalistic; the case has no satisfactory resolution, but at least my protest has been lodged. My final duty is to keep the sneer off my face while Madron addresses the packed room.

'Your community spirit has been exceptional. I'm sure your support has helped the victims' families, but we may never fully understand why this popular young couple died so needlessly. Laura was stabbed then cast into the sea; days later her boyfriend left home voluntarily in the middle of the night, items of his clothing washed up on the beach. We have to assume that he took his own life after suffering mental distress. Given the circumstances, we have decided not to pursue the case further. From now on, the hall will return to general use and all travel restrictions are lifted.'

The islanders look stunned, as if the gangplank they've been walking has suddenly been withdrawn. Some of their faces register relief, others anger at being left without answers. My uncle is beside Maggie, his neutral expression indicating that he's accepted Madron's conclusions. Angie Helyer sits by herself, weeping quietly, exhaustion or the sadness of the case overtaking her. The grieving families are both absent. The DCI addresses me on his way out, voice so low only I can hear.

'It's finished, Kitto. If you carry on digging, I'll tell your seniors about insubordination. Let the island get back to business. Do you understand?'

Madron's eyes are as cold as permafrost when he says goodbye.

42

By dusk, I'm a free agent. I should be elated that the weight has suddenly lifted from my shoulders, but loose ends have always troubled me. I'm stranded in an empty hall, with my hands tied firmly behind my back. Soon the island will flood with journalists, keen to milk the locals for information. The idea makes me kick the wall hard enough to send a hairline crack through the plaster, a jolt of pain travelling up my shin.

The temperature dips sharply when I leave, darkness enveloping the island. I turn up my collar and consider going home, but there's no point until I've decided what to tell Nina, so I head for the pub instead. The bar is deserted, apart from Dean Miller in the corner, hunched over his drink. A raft of familiar smells comfort me: the sweetness of stale beer, furniture polish, meat roasting in the kitchen. Luckily, the one person I want to see is easy to find. Maggie is hooking a bottle of vodka to an optic, grey hair a riot of curls, her small hands a blur of activity.

'Drowning your sorrows, sweetheart?'

'That's my plan. Double whisky, please.'

She serves me cranberry juice. 'Booze won't help you tonight.'

'You're wrong, Maggie. I want to be comfortably numb.'

'That's no answer.' Her eyes sharpen. 'You need to stay alert. How can Madron just walk away? The families need answers, for God's sake.'

Her righteous indignation doesn't help. She's so angry her voice fills the room, but the DCI will get me sacked if I pursue the case. The cranberry juice is sharp enough to sour my mood even further.

'Can I have some food to take home?'

'For you and Nina?' Her eyebrows rise.

'Don't go there, Maggie. It's not how it looks.'

'I'm not saying a word. Give me a minute, I'll see what I can do.'

Dean Miller sways towards me when she disappears. It looks like he's been downing booze all afternoon, movements unsteady when he settles on a bar stool. Up close, the damage from Matt's attack still shows on his face; raw bruises shadowing his eye, cheekbone puffy, a cut healing on his upper lip. But his injuries haven't stopped him working, his fingers still grimed with a rainbow of stains.

'None of you do your damned jobs properly.' Behind the boozed-up rage, his tone is mournful. 'I'm too mad to think straight.'

'With Matt?'

'Of course not. Bruises heal, don't they?' He leans

forward, bloodshot eyes locking onto mine. 'People on Bryher are being terrorised.'

'Who do you mean?'

'Rose Austell stayed at mine last night, in a terrible state.'

'About Sam?'

'It's worse than that. No one's helping her.'

'I'll drop by her cabin soon. Her son told me he visits your studio sometimes. Is that true?'

Miller's forehead creases into a frown. 'The kid came to see Laura. It had nothing to do with me.'

'They were at yours a few days before she died. Did you hear them talking?'

'I never listen when I'm painting, that's why I play music. We only talk if they catch me on a break. Sam's a difficult boy, not like Danny.'

It looks like he's about to share something vital, but the moment passes when Maggie reappears. I make a mental note to visit Rose tomorrow, even though the case is over. My godmother passes me a carrier bag large enough to feed a large family, waving away my thanks. I offer to walk Dean home, still curious about his cryptic statements, but the artist loses strength as we leave the pub. I have to grab his arm to stop him falling down the steps. Our conversation comes to a standstill as we cross the shore, his eyes fixed on the sea. The tide is at its height, waves battering the granite.

'So much loss,' he mutters. 'I can hardly bear to look.'

The statement sounds odd from a man who's made

his living copying the waves, yet I know what he means. On a good day, the winter tide feels majestic, hurling itself at the island with full force, but the assault can feel relentless. It's a relief to deliver Dean to his house. He reels inside, too drunk to bother saying goodnight.

It's eight o'clock by the time I find Nina curled in an armchair at home, no sign of Shadow. A novel is balanced on her lap; she's wearing sensible black-framed reading glasses, which fail to disguise the sexiness of her face, especially that full-lipped mouth. When she studies me over the top of them, I'm lost for words.

'Food smells good, Ben.'

'Curry, I think, probably stone cold by now.'

She follows me to the kitchen, switching on the oven, laying the table with quiet competence. It's her silence that I find so unsettling. The meal Billy has provided is an Indian feast: chicken tikka masala, Bombay aloo, naan bread, daal. But Nina ignores the food on her plate, taking a slow sip of wine.

'You still seem angry, Ben.'

'I'm that easy to read?'

'Most times.' Her slow smile emerges. 'Your frown travels before you.'

'The reason's obvious, isn't it? A boy's missing and a girl's dead, but if I carry on hunting for the killer, I'll get fired. All I know for sure is that Danny was too focused on avenging his girlfriend to top himself, and someone saw Laura climbing Gweal Hill before work. The killer was familiar with both of their patterns.'

Nina listens to me vent my frustration as we finish the meal, the curry spicy enough to leave a tang of heat. 'The violence is so raw. Whoever did it must be in serious pain.'

'Or mentally ill?'

'Maybe a combination of both.'

'Great. So it's a nutter with anger issues.'

'We all lash out when we feel let down. That kind of grievance makes people lose control.'

'I hate leaving things unfinished.'

'Think you can forget it for a while?'

'It's worth a try.'

I follow her to the living room, watch her stretch out on the floor, back settled against the settee. It still strikes me as odd that she's survived so much pain unharmed. I want to touch her more than ever, to borrow some of that deep-rooted calm.

'You still haven't explained why I make you tense.' She faces me, eyes glittering with firelight.

'My timing's wrong, isn't it? I arrived too early. You don't need me pursuing you.'

The bravado of my twenties has deserted me, when I chased whatever I wanted without hesitation. I expected my statement to close the matter once and for all, but she leans closer, her forearm brushing mine.

'I can look after myself, Ben.'

'You've proved that already.' I touch the tips of her hair, my index finger following the clean line of her jaw.

'I did something today that I should have done weeks ago.'

'What?'

'Phoned my parents. Mum cried her eyes out; it made me realise I've been selfish. She must feel like she's lost us both.'

When I reach for her she slips into my arms without hesitation, but a sound picks up outside. I can hear Shadow scratching at the door, followed by an ear-splitting howl. Nina pulls away, laughing.

'He's got great timing.'

'I'd better let him in, or he'll wake the whole island.'

Zoe appears on the doorstep as Shadow bounds inside, wearing a broad smile, a bottle of champagne in each hand. She steals my place beside Nina, explaining that she's had good news. An international talent agency in London has agreed to represent her. Before long, she could be singing torch songs in some glamorous bar in New York, while a replacement manager runs the hotel. On an ordinary day I'd be delighted to have two beautiful women getting drunk in my living room, but right now one would be plenty. It's clear they've formed a connection, Nina greeting Zoe's excited gabble with a serene smile. It's one o'clock when I finally go to bed alone, leaving Shadow lying between the two women, paws in the air, as if he's landed in paradise.

43

Zoe is draped across the settee when I get up, a champagne bottle empty at her side, which makes me feel better. Her hangover will be fair punishment for spoiling my chances. The sky is playing make-believe when I exit the house at 8 a.m., its shade a pallid summer blue even though the wind feels icy. Shadow is at my side, tongue lolling. Being canine seems enviably simple; no loyalties, except to the last person that fed you a square meal.

'Stay indoors.' I open the door and nudge him back inside. Nina and Zoe will fuss over him for hours while I walk off my frustration.

Oystercatchers are out in force on the beach, mincing over the shingle on matchstick legs, releasing their high-pitched screams. The wind is gusting harder than yesterday, the sea ridged with whitecaps. I can't help wondering where Danny is now. Have the waves carried him deep into the Atlantic, or is he hiding somewhere, out of view? When I look up again, a light sparks in the corner of my eye. The black-coated figure is there again, on Gweal Hill, back turned. This time I'm determined to catch him, even though my job's over. I know from previous attempts that I can't outpace him, so stealth is my only option. I climb the hill slowly, to avoid startling him. The figure is still visible, but a single sound will send him running. I pick my way carefully through the loose shale to avoid sending rocks skittering down the cliff face. When I reach the top, he's standing in the same spot, his hair concealed by a grey woollen cap, black coat flapping in the wind. I don't make a sound. He's so close to the edge, a sudden shock could send him tumbling off the cliff. My jaw drops open when the figure finally turns around. The baggy clothes had me fooled: it's Suzanne Trescothick, the girl's face blanched by the cold. I step out as she heads for the path, binoculars clutched in her hand.

'This is a surprise, Suzie.' She tries to escape, but I catch her arm, her shoulders twisting away from me. 'It was you each time, wasn't it? You were up here when we found Laura's body.'

Her voice sounds rusty, like a hinge creaking open. 'I climb the hill sometimes, to get fresh air.'

'What were you doing here, when your sister was found?'

The wind is stronger now, her coat billowing with each gust. 'I couldn't stay in the house, but when I saw her, my mind shut down. I just waited until someone came.'

'Why did you run away on Badplace Hill?'

'I'd gone out without telling dad. I thought he'd be angry.' Her face crumples into tears.

'There's something else.' It still looks like she could flee at any minute, so I settle my hand on her shoulder. 'I need to know what you and Laura were doing.'

'Don't make me say it.' She wipes her sleeve across her face, the gesture so childlike, pity almost dilutes my suspicions. 'They'll never forgive me.'

'Of course they will. At your age the worst I'll give you is a caution.'

'You won't tell mum and dad?'

'I'll try, but I can't promise.'

Her gaze drifts to the stony ground. 'Laura was calling in the boats, with a flashlight. She got paid for doing it.'

'She was working for the smugglers?'

'Laura shone the light from the cliff, or Badplace Hill, when the coast was clear. They left messages for her on the beaches.'

'And you've taken over since she died?' The girl's face is so strained, it's hard to feel angry. 'Sam Austell was the collector, wasn't he? Running their supplies to the mainland. That's why she phoned him.'

'Laura said I should do it, if she couldn't.' The girl is shaking now, fear of punishment making her whole body tremble. 'She said they'd hurt us all if she stopped.'

'It ends here. You can give me the flashlight now.'

'I'm sorry.' She hands it over without meeting my eye.

'Now tell me about those bruises your dad put on your arm.'

She ignores my words, turning her face to the sea. 'Laura was desperate to leave the island. I'll have to go travelling now, for her sake, see everything she wanted to see.'

'Where do you think Danny's gone?'

More tears slip down her face. 'Maybe people are right about him killing himself.' Her shivering's worse now, thin coat flapping in the breeze. She still looks burdened, even though she's finally revealed how her sister acquired her stash of money.

'How's your mum coping?'

'She wants the funeral soon, so we can say goodbye.'

Her answer doesn't surprise me. Jenna seems less volatile than Matt, more able to face emotional pain. 'Don't come here again, Suzie. Sam Austell could be facing charges for drug dealing when he leaves hospital.'

The girl still looks pale as she heads back down the path, but at least the facts are clear. Now I've got definitive proof that smugglers are using the island as a stop-off point. They could be running their supplies in on dinghies, from bigger boats moored at sea, making use of Bryher's deserted beaches. At present, I've got no hard evidence Sam Austell was their delivery boy. It's possible that Laura took packages over to the mainland too; she must have been desperate, to take such risks.

I walk back down the hill slowly, trying to make sense of what I've heard. Laura played a small part in the smuggling ring that the NCA are monitoring. I place a call to regional headquarters and speak to the same officer as before, asking him to send more patrol boats to guard Bryher's shores, his voice non-committal as the conversation ends. Dean Miller's words about Rose Austell keep coming back to me too. If Sam was involved in the operation, she might be under threat.

I pick up my pace as I head for Green Bay, hoping for more than Rose's usual vague answers. Her cabin is in a terrible state when I arrive. One of the window frames has splintered apart, as if the harsh weather has taken its toll, but when I peer inside, the place has been comprehensively trashed, most of her furniture smashed apart. I hold my breath as I look through the other windows, afraid that Rose might be lying injured on the floor, but all I can see is more damage to her property.

My first impulse is to call Eddie, until I remember Madron's warning to leave the case alone. My concern for Rose is another matter; she guards her solitude so fiercely, I can't imagine her sleeping on Dean Miller's sofa for one more night. She could be hiding in a cave somewhere, or out collecting herbs, steering clear of whoever did the damage. All I can do is call back later to check she's safe.

Ray is on his knees beside the lapstrake when I reach the boatyard, and I'm amazed by how much he's completed in the past week; only the gunwale and deck waiting to be finished. He's made a fine job of the lapping without my help, the pieces dovetailed in a seamless line.

'Come to admire my craftsmanship, Ben?'

'I've got a question, about Danny. Can you spare a minute?'

My uncle watches me steadily. 'I thought the case was closed.'

'Where would the currents take his body, if it went in at Green Bay?'

'I'll show you.' He wipes his hands on a rag. 'Come up then, I haven't got all day.'

It's clear he's irritated by my interruption. Only ancient loyalties make him lead me to his living room, where we stand together, peering at his tide map. Each island is ringed by a frenzy of arrows and a circumference of pale blue sea. To a mariner like Ray, the picture must be easy to interpret; he consults his calendar, then traces lines on the paper with his index finger.

'The night Danny went missing there was a full moon, like I said. The riptide drags everything southwest. Boats have to find harbour instead of anchoring at sea.'

'So his body would have been carried down by the tide?'

'I dropped a barrel off the quay on a moon tide once, when I was young. It washed up on Samson Beach the next morning. He could have been carried further west into the Atlantic stream, but there's a chance he'd end up there.'

When I stare down at the map, Samson lies due south of Bryher, the smaller island's outline forming a thin figure of eight. 'Thanks, Ray. I'll be back soon to give you a hand.'

'That's what you always say.'

'It's a promise this time.'

I step out of the yard, then freeze on the spot. The ferry is mooring on the quay, most of the passengers green-faced from the rough crossing. Steve Hilliard, the sleazeball journalist, is first off the boat. He's walking with renewed energy, like he's planning to squeeze every ounce of scandal from the granite landscape. A thin-faced blonde is at his side, a heavy-duty camera slung over her shoulder. I duck back into the doorway until they've passed. Steve and his crony will be the advanced guard, more hacks on their way. They must be staying at the pub while the hotel's closed, forcing me to avoid it like the plague.

I tap on Jenna's door when I reach the village, to warn her about the invasion. She seems calm when she answers the door, but her eyes are hollow. We stand in the hallway as she listens to my news about the influx of journalists.

'I'll send them packing if they come here.'

'Suzanne should take care too. Pumping kids for information is their speciality.'

'My girl's not stupid. She won't give them the time of day.'

'I saw her on Gweal Hill this morning. Is she okay?'

She glowers at me. 'She needs answers about her sister, Ben. You promised not to stop looking.'

'The decision was taken out of my hands. I'm sorry.'

Jenna's aquamarine stare freezes me to the bone, no words required to damn me, and I understand how she feels. After Clare died I felt the same, passing on my fury to every uniform that arrived at my flat. Anger always feels better than admitting you carry part of the blame.

An unwelcome visitor is waiting outside my cottage. Steve Hilliard must have raced across the island to find me. There's a sour look on his face, as if he's still bilious from the crossing.

'I'd like a word, Inspector.'

'The case is over. Didn't you hear?'

He edges in front of me. 'You screwed up, didn't you? This is your chance to set the record straight.'

I keep my mouth shut, while the skinny blonde points the foot-long lens of her Pentax at my face, shutter clicking madly, capturing my scowl. It's a relief to get indoors and lock the door behind me.

I spend the afternoon riffling through boxes of evidence at the cottage, looking for missing clues, but Eddie has been admirably thorough. The vast majority of islanders have an alibi for both Laura's attack and the night Danny went missing. I've got no way of proving which of the remaining suspects is capable of violence. But by the time Nina returns with Shadow, I've converted my frustration into action, preparing for my boat trip tomorrow. The clothes she's borrowed from Zoe are a size too big, yet she still looks stunning. Right now, that feels like another good reason to punch the wall.

'Where've you been?' I ask.

'Treating Angie's sciatica, the poor thing's in agony. Did you know there's a photographer outside?'

When I twitch back the curtain, the blonde woman is still perched on the garden wall. It's tempting to hurl stones and send her scurrying into the dark like an unwelcome cat. God knows what stories Hilliard will concoct by morning. I go from room to room, pulling down blinds, making sure there are no gaps. Nina seems oblivious to the intrusion, lighting the fire as the dog curls in an armchair. Once the kindling's blazing, she rocks back on her heels.

'Want to tell me what's wrong, Ben?'

'Not really. I'm taking a holiday from problem-solving.' I don't want to admit that this is my first professional failure in years; walking away feels like a dereliction of duty. 'I should take a long bath, instead of sharing my lousy mood.'

'It's never a good sign when you rub the back of your neck.' Her gaze holds mine. 'I could give you a massage.'

'Sounds tempting.'

'Or we could go to bed.'

'Sorry?'

'You heard me.'

'Are you sure?' Despite my words, I'm reaching for her already, unable to stop myself.

Her hand settles on my arm. 'It was going to happen, sooner or later.'

'Sooner works for me.'

Her invitation makes me stumble from my chair, thoughts spinning. She laughs at me when I lift her off her feet, but her arms hook round my neck as I carry her down the hall. The bedroom's so dark I light the candle on the bedside table, reminding myself that I'm the first man to touch her since her husband died; she's more fragile than she seems. My hands feel clumsy as a giant's when I unbutton her blouse, soft light accenting her pale-gold skin. She's ridiculously beautiful, a rapt look on her face as her fingers travel across my torso. Then instinct takes over and there's no need to think any more; she's tugging at my belt as I pull away the clothes that separate us. There's no trace of coolness now, her head flung back across the pillow as I explore those slim curves, with my hands, then my mouth. I don't know if she's laughing or crying when she finally loses control, but I wait until her eyes focus again before moving deeper inside her. The next time she calls my name, I let myself follow.

44

Rose spends the night in an outbuilding. After fifty-five years of independence, it feels wrong to rely on the mercy of others. Exhaustion hits her when she returns to Green Bay at dawn, senses so dulled that the footsteps trailing behind her go unnoticed. Someone grabs her before she has time to fight, an arm tightening around her throat. Her vision clouds as the heavily accented voice mutters in her ear.

'Tell me where the package is, Rose.'

'I don't know.' A sharp pain pierces her shoulder, making her cry out.

'Who's hiding it for you?'

'I burned it, so no one else gets damaged.'

'It's worth thousands. You wouldn't be that stupid.'

Now he's dragging her across the shore. All she sees is a flicker of winter sunlight before she's plunged under the waves. Brine fills her airways, memories surfacing as she loses consciousness: Sam built sandcastles here, long after-noons hunting for vetch and mermaid's purse. Now there's nothing except the freezing cold, and the waves crashing in her ears.

Rose's eyes blink open again when rain pelts her skin, her teeth chattering. She moves her limbs slowly, testing their strength, thoughts slow to arrive. She's still lying on the sand when a face looms over her. Laura's long hair brushes her cheek.

'Thank God, you're alive,' she murmurs.

The girl looks different when her features come into focus, brown-eyed instead of blue. It's Suzanne touching her arm, not Laura.

'Who attacked you, Rose?'

'They'll do worse, before they're finished. Will you help me back to the cabin?'

Rose leans on Suzanne's shoulder as the cold freezes her wet clothes to her skin. Less than fifty yards away she can see the colourful outline of her cabin, overlooking the beach. She walks slowly, the child's arm supporting her waist.

'You've always been a kind one, haven't you?'

'I'm so scared, Rose. I can't go home again.'

The girl's panic is visible, her face older than her years. Rose's distress burns more sharply behind her bruised ribs. She wishes she could offer the child sanctuary, but the men attacked her as a warning. Next time she won't be so lucky.

'Go to the schoolhouse, sweetheart,' she whispers. 'Dean will take care of you.'

45

I'm warm instead of cold when my eyes open at 5 a.m. Nina's face is inches from mine, chocolate-brown hair spilling across my pillow, her arm draped over my ribcage. I pull back the duvet as the dawn light filters through the curtains. Her body's beautiful, long legs tangled with mine, lithe as a dancer.

'Peeping Tom,' she murmurs.

'I thought you were asleep.'

'That's no excuse for ogling a naked woman.'

She drops a kiss on my shoulder and it's tempting to touch her again, even though I've kept her awake most of the night. But I need to leave early to avoid rousing the other islanders' attention.

'Where are you going?' she asks.

'Boat trip, no need to get up.'

I expect her to snuggle back under the covers, but she's drinking coffee in the kitchen when I finish my shower. I steal the mug from her hands and take a long swallow.

'There's more in the pot, Ben.'

'I haven't got time.'

She rises to her feet. 'I'll come along for the ride.'

'You're better off here, with Shadow. The water can be choppy between the islands.'

Nina ignores my advice, even though my chances of finding Danny are worse than locating a needle in a haystack. She keeps pace with me as we cut inland, Shadow leaping ahead.

No one's stirring when we reach the quay, even Ray and the ferryman's windows are in darkness, pink light blooming over Tresco's hills. My uncle has left his dinghy moored to the jetty and the dog jumps onto the bow confidently, as if boat rides are a daily occurrence. The water is uneven as I row through New Grimsby Sound, cold air chilling my face, waves slowing my progress. Once we're a hundred metres offshore, I yank the cord to start the outboard motor, hoping not to alert the journalists staying at the Rock. The wind's battering my face as we approach Samson. It's so near, you can wade over from Bryher at the lowest summer tide, but the place still looks ghostly.

'Does anyone live there?' Nina asks.

'Not for two hundred years. There's no fresh water supply.'

Anthracite clouds are gathering as we moor on the landing quay, North Hill rising above us. Samson is less than half the size of Bryher, but it still attracts plenty of visitors. People flock here in high season to photograph the deserted beaches and ancient tombs chiselled into the cliffs. My arm slips round Nina's waist. We must look like any other couple, strolling in a renowned beauty spot, the dog gambolling across the sandy beach.

'We need to circle the island, checking the tidemark.'

'Suits me. I like an early walk.'

When I glance down, her hair is swept back from that clean oval face, her smile relaxed. 'You survived a night with me then. No visible trauma.'

'Are you digging for compliments?'

'A few wouldn't hurt.'

Her smile widens into a grin. 'I'm just glad everything's in working order.'

'I can check again later, to make sure.'

'Kind of you to volunteer.'

We walk on in silence. Shadow is pawing through seaweed, chewing every stick he finds, but there's nothing on the tideline except razor shells, slivers of fishing net and the Coke cans yachtsmen lob overboard. We circle the island in half an hour without seeing anything suspicious, apart from an Atlantic squall brewing in the distance. If Danny's body went into the sea, it must have been dragged further south.

I nod at the boat. 'Want to go back?'

'Can I see the ruins first?'

It's a long time since I visited these deserted fields. The island fascinated me as a kid; its perfectly symmetrical, conical hills marking either end, prehistoric farmland edged by crumbling drystone walls. It's easy to imagine Bronze Age families huddled around their fires. Nina takes her time studying the abandoned homes; their structures still stand proud, door frames splintered away, windows gaping like startled eyes.

It's at the top of South Hill that I notice something unexpected. There's a white patch on the sea's surface twenty metres out from shore; gulls are landing and diving, wings forming a pale cloud.

'They've found something.'

'What?' Nina screens her eyes with her hands.

'Fish, probably. Let's take a look.'

We walk back down the hill, leaving the granite carn behind, passing the open mouths of rock tombs. Once we reach West Par Sands, my pulse quickens. The birds are squealing in protest as they fight over a new food source. I can't use the boat in such shallow water; it would run aground and damage the motor. I take off my coat then drop my shoes on the sand, Nina's eyes widening.

'You can't skinny-dip in sub-zero temperatures, Ben.'

'There's no other choice.'

I strip down to my boxers, then wade into the sea, with the dog splashing after me. It feels like stepping into a bath full of ice cubes, the chill fierce enough to hurt. By the time I'm thigh-deep, my feet are numb and the gulls are massing overhead, sizing me up as a potential meal. At first I see only the birds surfacing, black-tipped wings in constant motion. The water's waist-high when I glimpse his hair, waving like the tentacles of anemones. The smell of brine is replaced by the stench of human decay, but it must be imaginary. Danny's body lies under four feet of water. Shock and cold have frozen my movements, waves slapping my chest, as the tide rises. I turn back to the beach and call out to Nina that I've found him, watch her press her hands to her mouth, then fumble for her phone. My teeth chatter when I dive below the surface, hands catching his wrist. It takes effort to pull the boy's body clear of the seaweed that snares his limbs. I try not to look too closely, but my empty stomach churns as the advancing waves push me ashore.

Nina is pacing across the shingle, phone pressed to her ear. I remember the official advice on dealing with the drowned: leave them in the water until the police surgeon arrives. Oxygen speeds up decomposition, saturated skin peeling from water-logged flesh. I let Danny's body lie at the tidemark, waves nudging him further up the beach, and it's only now that I realise that the sea has treated him less kindly than Laura. Birds have feasted on his face, cheeks a tattered mass of sinew, his eye sockets stripped bare. They've damaged his torso too, surface wounds across his abdomen. But when I look more closely, the cause of death is obvious; there's a puncture mark in the centre of his chest that matches Laura's, too neat to be self-inflicted.

'Get dry, Ben, you're turning blue.' Nina hands me the woollen jumper she borrowed from my drawer.

My body is still aching when I'm dressed again,

huddled inside my padded coat. When I turn round, Nina is on her knees beside the boy's body. I want to yell at her to stay away and avoid nightmares, before remembering that her medical training would have exposed her to plenty of corpses. Her expression is intense as she makes me walk up and down the beach, warm blood spreading through my veins, diluting the shock. I'd never confess to my mates in the murder squad how much I hate fatalities. Everyone in the MIT prides themselves on being macho, including the women. Nina has caught me at a moment of weakness, teeth chattering from the shock of seeing the damaged body of a seventeen-year-old boy I should have protected.

I phone Eddie to keep myself occupied. His voice is upbeat, while a boat's engine grinds in the background; discovering the body will liberate him from tedious duties on Tresco. He's persuaded one of the local fishermen to drop him at the landing quay. Fifteen minutes later he's scurrying towards us over the dunes. I can imagine what kind of father he'll make, attending every sports day with that same hopeful expression. His smile of greeting vanishes when he leans down to inspect the body.

'Someone's gone to work on him, haven't they?'

'Seabirds,' I reply. 'He was in the water a long time. But you can see he's been stabbed, through the heart by the look of it. Same killer, same MO.'

It's another half-hour before the police launch delivers Madron from St Mary's. He's brought Dr Keillor, the elderly pathologist who carried out Laura's autopsy. Both of their faces are sombre, as if neither man can believe that a second corpse has been fished from the sea. Nina keeps Shadow occupied while the pathologist kneels on plastic sheeting to complete his examination. The tension on the DCI's face reveals that he's hoping Danny committed suicide. He looks more like an ageing librarian than a police chief today, dressed in a duffel coat, black trousers grimed with sand.

'What brought you here on a winter day, Kitto?' he asks.

'Nina wanted to see the ruins, sir. We borrowed my uncle's boat.'

'You were searching for the boy, weren't you?' His frown deepens. 'At least he's been found. That's something to be grateful for.'

The pathologist walks over, yanking off his plastic gloves. 'He was killed before he hit the water.'

'You're sure?' Madron asks.

'The stab wound would have caused massive internal bleeding.'

The anger on the DCI's face warns me that he's not planning to eat humble pie, no matter that he's been proved wrong. The sound of another engine whines in the distance – paramedics sent from St Mary's to deliver Danny's body to the mortuary. Madron's tone is severe when he addresses me again.

'You're back on the case, Kitto. This time I expect a quick result.'

I give a nod of assent, but even if he'd refused to make me SIO, I would still have felt obliged to deliver my promise to Jenna. 'What about the press?'

'Give them a briefing, before the rumour mill starts churning.'

I consider arguing, but his grey stare is as chilly as the brine. Now that the embargo has been lifted, journalists are free to turn over every stone.

It's 2 p.m. when I meet the Curnows outside St Mary's Hospital. Danny's parents have insisted on seeing him, despite the severity of his wounds. I'd have preferred to ID him through dental records, but a teenager's death is so hard to accept, they need to see the evidence for themselves. The sky is overcast, but Patty's opaque sunglasses would suit a movie star. When she removes them, her eyes are so swollen she can hardly blink. Jay looks almost as bad, a sheen of sweat forming on his upper lip.

'You can still change your minds,' I say quietly.

Patty shakes her head. 'We need this, for Danny's sake.'

The temporary mortuary is so small, my back presses against the wall when we're shown into the tiny room where their son's body lies on a gurney. The duty doctor asks whether the couple are ready for the identification, then draws the sheet back from Danny's face. Patty remains standing while her husband's legs buckle. I have to move fast to stop him hitting the floor, half carrying him out into the corridor. His voice is groggy when he finally speaks. There's no sign now of the man who thought he could buy the whole island for a song.

'That can't be Danny,' he murmurs.

'I'm afraid we think it is.'

I leave him to recover. When I get back inside, Patty is holding her son's hand, and it occurs to me that Danny's TAG Heuer watch is missing. The sea has taken the one possession that marked him out as a millionaire's child.

'My beautiful boy.' She keeps on repeating the words.

From her glazed expression, I can tell she's super-imposed how he used to look over that raw mess of wounds.

We travel back to Bryher on the police launch, sitting in silence in the cabin. Jay's reaction is the opposite of his relief when Laura was found. All his face shows today is a numb resistance to the truth.

46

I chuck an armful of logs on the fire back at the cottage, hard rain battering the windows. The sea's chill has entered my bones, leaving my skin sticky with salt. I'm longing for a shower, but Eddie sits opposite me at the kitchen table, pencil hovering over a sheet of paper. He looks expectant, as if I might be about to dictate the correct answer.

'Whoever killed Danny left home late Sunday night, without being spotted.'

'So it's someone who lives alone?' he asks.

'Not necessarily. Matt's mum's deaf, she wouldn't have heard him leave. It has to be someone with strong feelings for Laura and Danny. Smugglers have been running drugs through the island, and Laura was mixed up in it. There's a chance Danny was too, but I've never heard of drug runners being killed round here. Suppliers want to stay invisible; they hate taking risks. I'm still sure both victims knew their killer well.'

'You think it's Matt Trescothick?'

A pulse of heat passes through my chest. 'Jenna was on the beach alone, on Sunday night. She's been under stress for months, just like Matt. Maybe she resented her daughter leaving Bryher badly enough to kill her.'

Eddie gapes at me. 'That's pretty far-fetched, boss. Jenna seems desperate for the killer to be found.'

'It's the perfect smokescreen.'

'You're going to walk in there and accuse her of murder?'

'I'll talk to Suzanne first. She can give us more details of the trouble Laura was facing.'

We're still poring over the suspect list when I remember the press briefing Madron insisted on. Journalists have been arriving from the mainland on each ferry since the embargo lifted. Maggie has already corralled them at the pub; with luck, my formal update will stop them hassling the islanders.

Seven reporters are waiting when I arrive at the Rock. The function room Maggie keeps for private parties smells of stale air, the ceiling stained by a history of tobacco. Steve Hilliard and his emaciated sidekick look sceptical when I start the meeting.

'You'll have heard that Danny Curnow's body was found on the island of Samson this morning. We'll need a post-mortem to understand how he died.'

'But you think it's suicide?' Hilliard watches my reactions like a hawk.

'The pathologist will determine cause of death. Right

now, we need to find out why Danny left home on Sunday evening, or the early hours of Monday morning.'

A dark-haired woman raises her eyebrows. 'Laura Trescothick's case has been reopened, so you must think the two deaths are linked.'

'I'll be checking for any connections.'

'You're such a professional, Inspector.' Hilliard gives a rasping laugh. 'We've heard about your whirlwind romance. It's amazing you've found time to work on the case at all.'

'My private life is irrelevant.'

The terse reply shuts him up for an instant, letting me focus on the job in hand. I offer only the bare facts and warn them not to doorstep Laura or Danny's families. My teeth are still on edge when I leave the pub, half expecting to be followed.

Jenna's cottage is in darkness when I arrive. She listens to me say my piece without responding. Any trace of softness seems to have vanished since my last visit, anger written across her features.

'Can I come in, Jenna?'

'Not now. Suzanne's ill, I don't want her disturbed.'

'What's wrong with her?'

'Exhaustion, she just needs to rest.' Clearly she's cast me as the villain, until the killer is brought to book.

'You must be relieved that Laura's case has been reopened.'

Jenna folds her arms. 'It's disgusting that it was ever closed. I don't want you hassling Suzie again; you'll give her a breakdown. She's told you everything she knows.'

The door shuts in my face before I can ask another question. An irrational part of me considers shouldering it down, to check on Suzanne's welfare, but I walk to the back of the building instead. The light is on in the girl's room. When her outline appears behind the curtain, my heart rate calms. Jenna's reactions to Laura's death have veered from one extreme to another, shifting from hysterical grief to drug-induced calm, then hostility. The likelihood of a mother killing her daughter is thousands to one, but her behaviour increases my need to speak to Suzanne again.

My next port of call is Rose Austell's cabin, but there's still no sign of her. My concern is rising; between us, Danny and I have contacted every household on the island, but there have been no sightings of her today. The beach is deserted as I head through the dark, sea wind attacking me as I reach Hell Bay. There's a surprise waiting for me at the cottage, something glittering on my doorstep. When I crouch down, the object is easy to identify: Danny's TAG Heuer watch, absolute proof at last that the killer is leaving the calling cards, not someone else getting in on the act. I scan the outside of the building with my torch, but my visitor has vanished into thin air. My only welcoming committee is Shadow, who stirs himself to follow me into the kitchen. He stands by his bowl, ears pricked, waiting for food. Once I've packed the watch in an evidence bag I drop a handful of biscuits into his bowl, disappointed that Nina has gone to bed early, when I could use her calm intellect. The light's already out in her room and it feels wrong to wake her. Maybe last night was a one-off, to prove that she's recovering, after months of grief.

I take my time in the bathroom, showering away the salt from that morning's freezing dip, then find a second surprise waiting for me, but this time I'm not complaining. Nina is curled up asleep in my bed. Her breathing changes as I settle beside her, moonlight filtering through the curtains as she touches me. The sex is gentler this time, moving together like night swimmers with a distance to travel, pacing ourselves. Afterwards she rests against me, her hand on my chest. My body's glowing, but the case won't leave me alone; there's no way to forget the killer's taunts.

47

Madron drops a copy of the *Mail* in front of me at the community hall on Saturday morning. The headline shrieks SCILLY ISLAND MURDER MAYHEM. They've taken pictures of me and Nina, guaranteed to end our relationship before it's begun, the story written in comic-book language. Nina is described as a 'tragic beauty', and I'm the 'rugged island cop' tasked with finding Laura's killer. Steve Hilliard must have grown tired of chasing facts, settling for fantasy instead. He's magnified the one low point in my career a hundredfold. They've even found pictures of Nina on her wedding day, her face glossy with happiness. My first impulse is to track the lying scumbag down then chuck him off the quay.

'You played right into their hands,' Madron snaps. 'A murder investigation isn't the time for flirtations.' Argument would be pointless, my only choice to hear him out. 'You've resisted orders from the start. Do you even remember who's in charge?'

'You are, sir.'

'We'll do it my way from now on.' The strain of keeping my mouth shut while the DCI barks out his lecture makes my jaw ache. 'Jenna Trescothick says her daughter's mental health's suffering. Don't question that child again.'

'If anyone knows what happened to Laura, it's Suzie. Those girls were inseparable.'

'Disobey me and I'll have you replaced. Do you understand?'

I give a slow nod of agreement, before pulling Danny's watch from my pocket. The DCI peers at it through the evidence bag, the rest of the meeting passing without incident. He marches away after my update, shoulders back like a general inspecting his troops. It's only when he's gone that I kick my chair across the room. Why would Jenna suddenly raise her defences, unless she's got something to hide? The meeting with Madron confirms the need to interview her daughter again, even though she's out of reach.

I decide to clear my head before Eddie arrives. To kill two birds with one stone, I set off for the shop, to collect groceries and get some exercise. June and Pete Moorcroft are busy stacking their shelves. The shopkeeper's grey hair is neatly combed, his wife decked out in a floral shirt, Radio Four playing in the background. The place is the epitome of calmness, smelling of fresh bread and lavender soap, everything so orderly I can feel my blood pressure dropping. June gives a nod of greeting as I pack a cardboard box with bread, cheese, oranges and cartons of cereal.

She looks amused by my purchases. 'Shopping for two these days?'

'Just restocking my kitchen.'

'In a big way, my friend.'

I'm about to reply when my own face stares back at me from the newspaper rack, windswept and harassed, reminding me to warn Nina that she's front-page news. I'm so preoccupied that I miss the tension in Pete's manner until he follows me outside.

'A quick word before you go,' he murmurs as we stand in the porch. 'I remembered something about Danny. I saw him with Arthur the night he went missing, around nine o'clock. They were talking on the quay. It didn't strike me as odd at the time.'

'But it does now?'

'Our ferryman's not the chatty type, is he? Sometimes he hardly says a word when he comes here to shop.'

'Thanks, Pete, that's useful.'

He gives a gentle shrug. 'Could be nothing.'

I'm torn in two directions when I leave. My first impulse is to protect Nina from the scandalmongers, but duty wins by a hair's breadth. Arthur Penwithick's ferry is returning to the quay. It doesn't take long for the *Bryher Maid* to chug back across New Grimsby Sound, releasing a plume of smoke. I dump my box of groceries on the slipway and wait for him to moor. Penwithick is still wearing his skipper's cap, yellow oilskins protecting him from the cold, his small eyes wary.

'Have you got a minute, Arthur?'

'Not now. I'm due at St Mary's.'

'It won't take long. You spoke to Danny Curnow on Sunday night, didn't you? Can you remember what he said?'

A look of distress crosses his face. 'I was fixing a lamp on the boat and he started telling me his woes. The lad wasn't making sense. He kept ranting about who could have hurt Laura. Most of it went over my head, he spoke so fast.'

'It could have been his last conversation. Can you write down anything you remember for me today, please?'

He gives a slow nod. 'I'll do my best.'

I thank him, then hurry away. There's no movement when I pass Jenna's house again, curtains still drawn, a light glowing in the kitchen behind lowered blinds. I wait a few minutes, hoping Suzanne might emerge, but there's no sign. Sooner or later I'll have to break through Jenna's layer of protection to get the information I need. All the islanders have given me so far are hints and half-truths. The longer their smokescreen clouds the air, the harder it will be to find the killer. Frustration makes me head for the boatyard: Ray is one of the few islanders I can trust for a direct answer. Maybe that clear-sighted gaze of his can spot something I've missed.

A sound picks up when I reach the boatyard, almost as high and keening as Shadow's howl. Suzanne Trescothick is hunched on the bench inside Ray's workshop. My uncle looks oddly calm, as if comforting distressed teenagers is part of his normal routine. He beckons for me to enter, so I pull up a stool, digging in my pocket for a tissue. When the girl's weeping quiets, Ray slips away, to let me speak to her alone.

'Try and tell me what's wrong, Suzie.'

'There's no point. No one can help me.' She wipes her face with the tissue, exposing a fresh bruise on her wrist.

'You could say who's been hurting you, for a start.'

She shakes her head vehemently. 'That's not why I'm here.'

I rest my hand on hers. 'I promise to keep you safe.'

'Laura's the only one I could trust.'

'Your mum's been hitting you, hasn't she?'

The girl keeps her face averted, a wall of silence surrounding her. Logic tells me that Jenna must be responsible for the new marks on her daughter's skin; the kid's been locked inside for days, with no contact from anyone else.

'It only happens if I do something wrong.' Her voice is a dry whisper. 'She's been worse since Laura died.'

'Did she punish your sister too?'

'Once, for staying out late. The next time, Laura hit her back.'

The statement fits my image of the older girl; a free spirit, feisty and confident. It also explains why Suzie stuck to her side, hoping for protection. It's hard to accept that the golden girl of my youth has been raining abuse on her youngest child.

'Does your dad know?'

'Mum made us promise to keep quiet. I knew she'd lose it if I told him.'

'What kind of things set her off?'

Suzanne gives a tired shrug. 'Talking back, not helping her enough, leaving my room messy. Pretty much anything.'

'Where do you go to escape?'

'Dean's studio sometimes, or Rose's cabin.'

'Can I see your arm?'

She doesn't move at first, then slowly pulls back the sleeve of her jumper. Large red welts mark her inner arms, already turning blue. It looks like she's been beaten recently with something straight and solid, the bruises big enough to make me angry with myself for not springing her out of there sooner.

'That looks painful. You'll need to see a doctor, Suzie.'

The girl's eyes are terrified. 'Don't tell Mum, please. She'll be so angry.'

'I can't let her hurt you again. You can stay at your gran's tonight.'

More tears leak from her eyes, then she's on her feet, running outside. I call after her, but it's too late. The kid is probably desperate for comfort from her grandmother. If Jenna's angry enough to wound her youngest daughter, she could have stabbed Laura in a fit of rage. The older girl wasn't passive and accepting like her sister; her defiance might have been the catalyst that flipped Jenna from domestic abuser to murderer in a few short seconds.

Eddie is waiting for me in the freezing community hall, fiddling with a radiator. 'The system's buggered, boss. I'll ring round for a portable heater.'

'Not now, I need you with me. I'm about to make an arrest.'

He stares at me open-mouthed as I tell him that Suzanne's mother hits her regularly, and Laura was beaten too. He calls the station on St Mary's to request a boat immediately, then follows me to Jenna's cottage, his non-stop chatter quiet for once, as if the gravity of the situation is taking its toll.

Jenna opens the door by a crack when we arrive, clear blue eyes judging us through the gap. I can feel Eddie hanging back, reluctant to get involved.

'This is harassment,' she says. 'I've already made a complaint.'

'It's an urgent police matter, Jenna. You need to let us in.'

Her kitchen is a mess, dishes stacked high in the sink, empty tins and soup cartons strewn across the counter, but Jenna doesn't seem to care. She's wearing worn-out jeans and a black roll-neck jumper, staring at us like we're the wrongdoers as I explain her rights.

'I'm arresting you for assaulting Suzanne. You're also being arrested on suspicion of murdering Laura.'

She gapes at me as I explain that she'll be detained on St Mary's. Her eyes glow with outrage, but she doesn't move a muscle. It's growing easier every minute to see her as a potential killer. She has stored her anger behind that blank mask so effectively, it never revealed itself fully until now.

'My daughter's been murdered, and you're wasting time with this nonsense.'

'Physical abuse of a child is serious, Jenna. You could get a prison sentence.'

'What rubbish has she been telling you? I should see her before this goes any further.'

'That won't be possible for a while. Pack some clothes, please, then we'll get moving.'

It's a brief but choppy ride to St Mary's. Jenna sits in the small cabin, posture rigid as a figurehead. It's too late for a solicitor to travel from the mainland, so she'll spend the night in one of the tiny holding cells. It's eight feet by six, holding only a narrow bunk, toilet and sink, a window too high to see through. My pity evaporates when I remember the bruises on her daughter's arm – so much violence directed at a fourteen-year-old child. There's no sign of Madron, but I can imagine his reaction to the news. He warned me not to harass Suzanne, yet I've taken the radical step of arresting her mother.

Things don't improve when I return to Bryher. Steve Hilliard is waiting by the quay, swaddled in a thick coat. It crosses my mind to tell him exactly what I thought of the story he concocted, but I keep my mouth shut, ignoring his flurry of questions.

It's already dark when I visit Gwen Trescothick's house to check on Suzanne. The girl is huddled on her grandmother's settee, pale-faced with distress, the TV burbling in the background. Her dad stands with me in the kitchen when I inform him of Jenna's arrest.

'You think she killed Laura?' Matt's voice is flatlining.

'She'll be questioned tomorrow. Did you know she'd been hitting Suzanne?'

'Of course not. I'd have brought her to Mum's straight away.'

'You didn't see the bruises?'

He winces. 'She told me she'd fallen on the stairs.'

'Her mum may have given her more serious injuries, Matt. She'll need a medical.'

I explain that a doctor will examine Suzanne tomorrow, before saying goodbye. Mrs Trescothick appears to have aged several years, shoulders so stooped that an invisible weight seems to be resting on her. Shock has wiped Matt's expression clean, as if he can't believe the information he's been given.

48

There should be a sense of elation after an arrest, but too many questions nag at me as I follow the inland path towards Hell Bay. The walk feels peaceful at first, stars pulsing overhead, the moon playing hide-and-seek behind a bank of cloud. Then I feel it again, someone's gaze slithering up my spine. I yank my torch from my pocket and spin 360 degrees, trailing the beam over trees and bushes, tall patches of wild grass. No one's there, yet the sensation grows stronger all the time.

'Show yourself, for fuck's sake.' The words blast from my mouth at full volume.

Right now, I'm in such a foul mood I'd happily smash my torch into the face of my invisible companion, but nothing stirs. The noise of waves scattering shingle across the beach whispers in the background. It should be soothing, but it has the opposite effect. I'm certain another set of footsteps was echoing mine, even though the sound has fallen silent.

My spirits improve when I reach Hell Bay. The lights are on at home, smoke pouring from the chimney. I still haven't figured out why it feels so good to know Nina's waiting there, the dog keeping her company. My last attempt at cohabitation was a disaster. I was twenty-six, way too selfish to accommodate anyone else's needs; after a few months she grated on me, even though we limped on for another year. Since then I've lived solo, tolerating bouts of loneliness rather than facing another mistake. My happiness soon fades when I find Nina poring over a copy of the *Mail*.

'I wanted to tell you about that first.'

Her calm eyes scan my face. 'Maggie came by to drop off your groceries, so we went through it together. Most of it's nonsense.'

'You're not upset?'

'I hate personal information being made public, but I can handle it.' She drops the paper on her chair. 'Someone delivered a letter for you earlier.'

She points at an envelope on the sideboard. It contains a sheet of A4 paper, half covered in dense scrawl. It looks like ants have rolled themselves in ink then marched across the page. Only the signature is legible: Arthur Penwithick. I'm guessing that it's a transcript of Danny's last conversation.

'A graphologist would have a field day.' Nina peers over my shoulder. 'Want to try some of Maggie's emergency rations?'

Her cool expression twists the knot in my gut even

tighter. I was expecting tears and soul-searching about the newspaper story, but all I see on her face is the battle-worn strength that attracted me from the start. We sit in the kitchen, eating lamb tagine with hunks of fresh bread. Nina has already heard about Jenna's arrest; the news crossing the island like wildfire. By tomorrow the tabloids will have decided she's guilty, before she's even been interviewed.

Nina meets my eye. 'You really hate the press, don't you?'

'I don't mind people in war zones posting films on YouTube. Professional freelancers don't give a shit about the truth.'

'And you do?'

'Of course, it's why I do my job.'

She shakes her head. 'I've never met anyone so convinced they're right. I spend most of my time sitting on the fence.'

'You like fixing people. We're not so different.' I'm on the verge of explaining why we're compatible when her expression changes. She shifts back in her chair, shoulders tensing.

'I've decided to go home early, Ben.'

'Because of that rubbish in the paper?'

'I have to face reality sooner or later. My parents need me, and so do my friends.'

I suppress my urge to beg. 'When do you leave?'

'Next week, I'll move back to Gweal Cottage tomorrow.'

'One goodbye after another.' The statement comes out tinged with bitterness.

'What did you expect? Your flat's in London, mine's in Bristol. We knew it was only temporary.'

'Why are you leaving straight after we slept together?'

'That's not the reason.'

'No?' I put down my glass. 'Do you want my opinion?'

Her face is glazed with anger. 'You'll give it, no matter what I say.'

'You're protecting yourself, because you felt something. Why not follow your instincts, instead of running away?'

'Are you calling me a coward?'

'That's not what I said.'

'But it's what you meant.'

She turns away before I can build another line of defence. The door to the spare room slams shut, leaving Shadow confused. He stands in the corridor, whimpering. It takes most of my willpower not to drop to my knees and follow suit. I wait all evening for her to emerge, tempted to barge in and convince her she's wrong. In the end, I slope off to bed alone, too distracted to sleep.

The doctor who arrives from the mainland in the morning is called Holly Portman. She's around my age, and so petite I have to stoop to meet her eye. Her streaked blonde hair is drawn back from her face in a severe bun, but her expression is gentle as she addresses Suzanne.

The girl is reluctant at first, but eventually agrees to be examined in the living room, with her grandmother present. The doctor's face is tense when she joins me in the kitchen afterwards. She passes me a sheet of paper, carrying an injury diagram. I've seen hundreds over the years; they show an outline of the human physique, with individual wounds from an assault marked by a cross. Over a dozen injuries are scattered across the girl's body.

'There's moderate to severe bruising on her arms, back and torso, no broken bones. She's been attacked over a sustained period. Wounds like this are typical of domestic abuse.'

'How do you mean?'

'They're hidden by her clothes, so no one spots them.'

'It's that well planned?'

'Abusers enjoy the power, DI Kitto. They hate being stopped.'

'Jesus.'

'My thoughts exactly.' She gives a narrow smile. 'I'll email my report today. I hope there's a restraining order to protect Suzanne.'

'Her attacker's in custody.'

Dr Portman gives a brisk nod. 'There's a high incidence of self-harm in these cases. The child often feels guilty about blowing the whistle, especially on a parent. She'll need long-term counselling. Don't let Suzanne spend time alone until her emotions stabilise.'

The doctor's words stay with me when I catch the ferry an hour later. Steve Hilliard and his photographer step on board, just as the boat casts off. In an ideal world I could tell them to get lost, but it's better to keep my distance, even when they trail me along the harbour to the police station. I have to remind myself that they haven't yet crossed the line into harassment.

Madron's expression is thunderous when I arrive. He's halfway through his lecture on obeying orders when I slap Dr Portman's diagram on the table.

'Jenna's been beating Suzanne for months. Now I need to find out if her violence drove her to kill Laura, too.'

My statement removes the wind from the DCI's sails, his mouth flapping. He waits in silence when Jenna is brought from her cell. Her solicitor looks little older than Eddie, dressed in a sleek grey suit that must have cost several months' wages. His smile indicates high excitement about representing a client on a case that's making international news. Jenna looks like she's been starved of sleep for days, deep hollows under her eyes, her hard-edged beauty fading. No one says a word until I hit the button to record the interview.

'My client is requesting immediate release,' the solicitor says. 'She's been wrongfully detained.'

I turn to Jenna. 'A doctor examined Suzanne today; her injuries are consistent with regular beatings. Your daughter says you tried the same on Laura, until she turned on you. We'll submit the evidence to the Crown Prosecution Service, but the most important question is whether you killed your older daughter, on Monday the first of March.'

The lawyer whispers something to Jenna, but she ignores him, her eyes chilly with contempt. 'I never touched Laura. Suzie self-harms; she's got emotional issues, it's been a problem for years.'

'The doctor says none of her injuries are self-inflicted. What's wrong, Jenna? Physical abuse is nothing compared to killing Laura.'

Her anger suddenly crumbles into tears. 'Don't talk to me like that, everyone knows I love my girls.'

'You've been under strain.' I try to soften my tone. 'Losing the house, Matt out of work, money worries. It's been a bad year, hasn't it?'

Her fingers are shielding her eyes. 'It's always me, carrying everyone.'

'Why not explain what happened, in your own words?'

I wish Clare was with me now. She taught me that the gentle approach works best in interviews. Make someone believe you sympathise and they'll open up twice as fast. Judgement only makes a suspect pull up the drawbridge. I keep my eyes on Jenna's as she talks, coaxing her to reveal more, until she's a rabbit in the headlights. She confesses to the beatings, but denies responsibility.

'I do everything for my family, working myself to the bone. But one time, Suzie stood there, hands on hips, yelling at me. She had to be taught a lesson.'

I don't know if she realises that she's sleepwalked into a confession of assaulting a vulnerable minor, but her lawyer does. In a loud stage whisper, he counsels her to say 'no comment'.

'What about Laura?' I ask. 'With two strong women under the same roof, there must have been conflict.'

'I loved her more than anything. I never laid a finger on her.'

Maybe Jenna has finally realised that she's given too much away. I call the interview to a close, saying that she'll be interviewed again tomorrow. The excitement has vanished from the young solicitor's face as he withdraws his bail application. Madron gives a slow nod of approval after they leave, complimenting me on my interview technique, but he keeps me in his sights like I'm a dangerous reptile, curled in the corner of his room, ready to strike. His face remains tense when we say goodbye.

Jenna stays in my mind as I head for the harbour. Her voice was chilling as she spoke of punishing Suzanne to teach her right from wrong. For a second, I picture her and Matt two decades ago; young, beautiful, carefree. Broken dreams might have made her vicious, repeated disappointments piling on top of one another. But would all that loss make her kill her daughter? I'm so preoccupied that I almost trip over Steve Hilliard at the harbour. He's sitting on the jetty, tapping on his iPad.

'Ready to talk yet, Inspector?'

'There's nothing to say.'

'This story will keep me busy for weeks anyway.' He gives a leering grin. 'Mothers don't often kill their daughters in cold blood, do they?'

It's clear he's made up his mind, even though Jenna's arrest hasn't been formally announced. I keep my mouth shut and step onto the boat, to check a dozen texts that have arrived on my phone. Most of them are from Eddie, but Nina's silence makes me feel like chucking the handset overboard.

49

It's dusk when Rose arrives at Dean Miller's home. She has brought a thank-you gift, for her night of shelter: two pots of wildflower honey and a tea infusion made from spearmint and camomile. When she peers through the window of his studio, he's standing at his easel, dashing paint onto a wide canvas. His movements are quick and uncontrolled, a wild ocean rising before him to a blackened sky. He swigs from a bottle of vodka on his work table, then carries on, his movements frantic.

Rose waits in silence, unwilling to break his concentration. When she finally opens the door, the creaking hinge makes him swing round, his expression filled with fury and pain. It crosses her mind to run away; she has known him for thirty years, but never feared him until now.

'I brought you this, Dean, for letting me stay the other night.'

'There's no need for gifts.'

'I'm grateful anyway.' She puts the package on his table. 'Have you seen Suzanne?'

Miller's gaze sharpens. 'Not since Laura's memorial. Why?'

'She's having a bad time. I thought she might come here.'

'I'll help her, if she needs it.' He nods rapidly, but his frown lingers. 'Now you'd better leave, Rose. You shouldn't be around me in this mood.'

Rose quickly slips away. The artist's temperament has always been mercurial, but she has never seen so many raw emotions on his face before. The thought slips from her mind as she focuses on where to hide now darkness has fallen. She will have to sleep in one of the boat sheds, because the smugglers will never tire of hunting her down. She may be forced to sell her cabin to Jay Curnow after all, the prospect of leaving the island making her feet drag across the sand.

50

Arthur Penwithick looks more like a scarecrow than a ferryman when we dock on the quay at Bryher. His frizzy hair spills from his cap, gangling arms reaching for the mooring rope, rabbity teeth protruding from his lip. Kids used to tell cruel jokes, calling him the village idiot, but he's been savvy enough to run the island's only taxi service successfully for thirty years. He gives a grudging smile of thanks when I help him tie up on the jetty.

'Can I have a word, Arthur?'

He checks his watch then gives a slow nod. 'I've got half an hour.'

I follow him up the slipway to his narrow house. He's been Ray's neighbour for decades, but it's years since I last visited. The lounge is unchanged since his mother died; doilies on the coffee table, lamps fringed with tassels, a row of china figurines filling his mantelpiece. The room looks more suitable for an ancient spinster than a man of fifty, but Arthur seems oblivious, dropping his cap on a hook behind the door. When he returns from the kitchen, Scillonian hospitality has triumphed over suspicion. His tray is loaded with biscuits, a coffee pot, and two mugs bearing the face of Princess Diana.

'There was no need to go to any trouble, Arthur.' I produce his letter from my pocket and explain that his handwriting defeated me. 'Can you talk me through what you remember?'

'Danny kept ranting about blokes that fancied Laura. Jim Helyer, Dean, and he even mentioned Pete Moorcroft.'

'Try and be specific, please.'

Arthur frowns in concentration. 'He said something about Jim trying his luck with her all the time.'

'Danny thought Jim Helyer had approached her more than once?'

The ferryman nods. 'Couldn't keep his hands to himself, apparently. There was stuff about Dean and Pete looking at her too.'

'What did he mean?'

'How would I know? The boy was beside himself.'

The ferryman can offer no more details, so we finish our coffee in silence.

Eddie is working on St Mary's while I trudge home. He's busy processing Jenna's case for the Crown Prosecution Service, which gives me the last hours of the afternoon to consider the remaining suspects, but concentration deserts me once I open the door. Shadow almost knocks me over in his desire for escape. He bowls away without a backwards glance, in the direction of Gweal Cottage. Nina has tidied the kitchen as a farewell gesture, scrubbing the table clean, dishes stowed away. The place smells sterile, no sign of her anywhere, the picture of me and Clare staring down from the shelf. I've never needed my old colleague's advice more, but it dawns on me that she would be thrilled if I closed the case successfully. Missing her only increases my determination to discover who killed Laura and Danny.

I sit at the kitchen table, clearing everything else from my mind. Jenna's the first name on my list. I'm convinced that the killer knew both teenagers intimately, aware of their patterns and secrets. Her relationship with Laura was volatile, and now she seems to be in the grip of a breakdown, unwilling to accept that assaulting a child is a criminal offence. Her violence lasted months, but could it have caused a double murder? Jenna seemed detached this afternoon, unwilling to accept responsibility. I've seen that disconnection on killers' faces before; it allows them to commit monstrous violence. Mothers often turn on their daughters in a tense relationship, but why would she harm Danny? Maybe Jenna carries so much resentment towards Jay Curnow for stealing her home, she targeted the boy through no fault of his own.

The other names on the ferryman's list are less convincing. It's understandable that Danny would resent Dean Miller's closeness to his girlfriend, particularly when he heard about the paintings, but he must have known that the American would never obsess over a teenage girl. Pete Moorcroft seems just as unlikely to harm anyone. His awkward manner appears to stem from shyness, his relationship with his wife quietly affectionate. Thinking about Jim Helyer makes me more uneasy. If Danny and Arthur are correct, my friend lied about approaching Laura just once. He may have attacked her boyfriend for stealing the one thing he coveted.

I'm still staring at my notes when I notice that dusk has fallen, and there's still no sign of Shadow. A few weeks ago, I'd have been glad to lose him, but his boundless enthusiasm has grown on me. He's probably asleep on Nina's bed, exactly where I'd like to be. There's little I can do about the case until tomorrow. The killer is probably already behind bars on St Mary's, even though she's refusing to confess. Suddenly the prospect of an evening alone feels impossible, so I grab my phone and fire off a text.

Zoe arrives in double-quick time. It reminds me of childhood summers, when we shuttled back and forth between the cottage and hotel, playing elaborate games on the beach, or daring each other to swim to Merrick Island. She's wearing the same look of curiosity she wore then, always ready for new adventures. She drops into an armchair by the fire, her keen gaze assessing me.

'Start talking, big man. It's time you spilled the beans about whatever's getting you down.'

I take a gulp of water. 'Me and Nina had a misunderstanding.'

'A row, you mean?'

'She moved out today.'

Zoe shakes her head. 'If you've got feelings, you'll have to tell her. She's not clairvoyant. Women need words as well as sex.'

'She only lost her husband six months ago. Maybe I'm rushing things.'

'What do you want from her anyway?'

'I'm not sure, but I don't want her to leave.'

'She's going home on Wednesday. You'll have to act fast.'

I gaze down at my clenched fists. 'Brilliant.'

'Where's Shadow, anyway?'

'At hers. She's his new soulmate.'

She beams at me. 'That's the perfect excuse. I'm going to Tresco for film night, and you're collecting your wolfhound.'

Zoe is already on her feet. She waits while I pull on my trainers, then hands me my coat. I give her a hug before heading outside, the wind as sobering as a slap in the face. Courage deserts me within ten paces. I've dated plenty of women in my time, slept with more than my fair share, but rarely said how I feel. This time Nina has left me with no choice. More than anything, I'd like to get to know her properly, away from the pressure of the case.

I stand at the high-tide mark, watching the sea reposition itself against the land. At the end of the bay I drop down onto the sand, protected by the breakwater, to gather my thoughts, until a man's raw cry rings across the bay. I'm on my feet in seconds, racing towards the inlet where Laura's body was found. There's nothing here except waves pushing further inland. I hear another moan and vault over a granite wall to the next cove.

Matt Trescothick is doubled over on the shingle. His eyes clear when he sees me, as if he's been waiting for me to arrive.

'Suzie's gone,' he says. 'I can't lose them both.'

I crouch beside him. 'Tell me what's happened.'

'She's been taken, just like Laura, hasn't she?'

'Maybe she had cabin fever. Come on, we need to find her.'

A rush of panic hits me. Now a third teenager is missing; I can't let her meet the same fate as Laura and Danny. When I call Eddie, he promises to come over immediately. There's a clattering sound as he exits his house at speed, too flustered to switch off his phone.

51

Matt goes back to his mother's cottage reluctantly, following my instruction to call round the island for sightings of his daughter. My first port of call is Gweal Hill, hoping to find Suzanne on the cliff with her flashlight. But there's nothing except a thousand-mile view, and lights from cargo ships threading the horizon. My heart sinks when I turn back to scan the valley. Most of the islanders have taken the ferry to Tresco for a film screening at the Abbey Hotel, their houses in darkness. On the far side of the island, Arthur Penwithick's boat is missing. I head towards the boatyard, remembering that the girl sees it as a safe haven.

The doors are open as usual. My uncle is in his armchair, reading a book on maritime history, glancing up when he sees me.

'Good timing. I was about to pour myself a whisky.'

'Suzie Trescothick's missing, Ray. Have you seen her?'

His pale gaze sharpens. 'Not today. How long's she been gone?'

'An hour or so.'

'We can't let it happen again,' he says quietly, already on his feet, reaching for his oilskins. 'I'll check the beaches.'

He's gone before there's time to remind him to take care. His heavy boots thump down the stairs, the radio still pouring Mozart into his spartan living room.

Few lights are on in the village, but I knock on every door. The islanders react with shock, followed by offers of help. But the truth is, I'd prefer everyone to stay at home – just me and the killer roaming the island until he's caught.

I head north towards Gwen Trescothick's cottage, passing half a dozen unlit homes. It feels like the island is in lockdown, guarding its secrets too closely. To find the girl, I'll have to rely on my wits alone. A flare of light appears in the distance, coming from Jim's farm, encouraging me to make a detour. The doors of the chicken shed are wide open, and my friend is inside, raking straw across the ground, weariness evident in the set of his shoulders. I stand in the doorway, wondering how our childhoods have vanished so fast.

'You look busy, Jim.'

He turns round, offering his tense smile. 'No rest for the wicked.'

'Been here all evening?'

'Most of it. Why?'

'Suzie Trescothick's missing.'

His eyes blink rapidly. 'I saw her leave her nan's by the back door, around seven. She was heading towards the village, running at full pelt.' He walks over to join me. 'You don't think she's been taken?'

'Let's hope not.' I turn to him again. 'Why did you lie about Laura? She told Danny you hassled her loads of times.'

His face blanks. 'I was an idiot for a few weeks, that's all. I wanted to protect Angie.'

Jim's voice hits the wrong key. My alarm bells are ringing so loudly that I scan the barn for evidence of Suzanne's presence. But all I see are sacks of maize, the roosting house closed for the night, straw crunching underfoot as I walk away. Angie seems oblivious when I find her in the farm kitchen. She's rocking the baby, pink-cheeked from the open fire.

'There you are, Ben. You've been avoiding us again,' she says, smiling.

'Life's been busy, that's all.'

'Tell me about it.' She nods at the baby, gurgling in her arms. 'I can't remember the last time I had a full night's sleep.'

'Have you seen Suzie Trescothick today?'

'Is she missing?' She looks concerned. 'I've been indoors all day. All I've seen are Lego bricks, nappies and ironing.'

I head back into the dark, my frustration coming to the boil. It takes less than a minute to reach Gwen

Trescothick's cottage. The tiny proportions of the place make me feel like a giant, her sitting room airless when the three of us sit down. The mantelpiece carries the same photos of Laura, votive candles flickering between the images. A dry lump forms in my throat when I realise that her sister's face could be added to the shrine unless I act fast. It's clear that Gwen is feeling the strain, hands bunched tight in her lap. She almost jumps out of her skin when the phone rings on the coffee table. Matt utters a few gruff monosyllables before dropping the receiver back onto its cradle.

'Eddie says Rose Austell's seen Suzie on Green Bay.'

'How long ago?' I ask.

'Half an hour.'

They both scramble for the door before I can insist that one of them should wait at home, in case the girl returns. The look on the old woman's face is so determined, I keep my mouth shut. If anyone had told me to stay indoors when Clare didn't show up at work, my reply would have seared the paint from the walls. We set off at a brisk march, the sea glittering like onyx. All I can hope is that the girl hasn't met the same fate as Laura and Danny, the retreating tide dragging her body far from shore.

When we reach Green Bay, Matt and his mother begin combing the long sweep of sand. Rose Austell is standing on the beach, close to her cabin. She looks more witch-like than ever in a long grey coat, scarves billowing in the wind, black hair drawn back from her bird-like face. I can tell at a glance that she's in a bad way, movements jittery, shifting her weight from foot to foot.

'You should be indoors, Rose. It's cold.'

She shakes her head. 'I'm better off out here.'

'Someone broke into your cabin, didn't they? I saw the mess. Who do you think did it?'

'Not an islander, that's for sure.'

'Why not let me help you?'

'I brought it on myself.' Tears well in her eyes. 'It can't be changed.'

'We'll get this mess sorted out, then I'll come back, I promise. Tell me where you saw Suzanne.'

'On the tideline, alone, about nine o'clock. She had binoculars in her hand.'

'Did you talk?'

'Just a few words. It's not the first time I've seen her upset.'

'Where was she headed?'

'Inland, along the path.'

'Can you think where she'd go?'

Rose hesitates; I can almost see her fear of authority warring with her conscience. 'Try Dean Miller's house.'

I leave her on the shore, clearly afraid to return to her empire of potions and herbal cures, the honey-scented air of her kitchen. Matt and his mother are still patrolling the beach with Eddie when I walk inland. It crosses my mind that Suzanne may have run home, now that her mother's under arrest.

It doesn't take me long to get inside Tide Cottage. I clamber up a drainpipe then jemmy a bedroom window, but the place is empty when I turn on the lights. I'm desperate for clues by the time I enter Laura's room. My eyes catch on a photo of her and Danny. It must have been taken last summer, their skin tanned, smiles warming their faces. But when I study it again, the girl looks strained, her boyfriend's arm tight round her shoulder, protecting her from danger. Danny may have known that Laura had problems at home, increasing his desire to escape to Falmouth. I stare at the photo again: two infatuated teenagers, dreaming of a shared future. Danny's looks were almost as perfect as the girl's, with the type of classic bone structure that improves with time. My thoughts click into place with unexpected clarity.

Maybe I've been looking in the wrong direction all along; the killer's main focus may not have been Laura after all.

52

My ideas race as I march through the deserted village. What if the killer was obsessed by Danny, not Laura? Killing his girlfriend would be the worst punishment imaginable. I jog through Dean Miller's garden to his studio. The space is lit up, but no one's inside. The air smells of turpentine, paraffin and linseed oil. Tubes of paint lie open on the artist's table, pigment staining the surface, screwed-up paper mounded on the floor. A huge canvas propped in the corner shows a new seascape. Even I can see that it's arresting. The colours are so vivid, I can almost smell the ozone. He's caught the aftermath of a storm, the sky empty, tide quieter than before. I close my eyes to absorb the silence. What did Laura gain from coming here, apart from pocket money and an old man's tales of Hollywood?

It's only when I scan the room again that I realise the paintings have been reorganised. Fewer canvases are stacked against the wall, more hanging in long rows, as if he's been tidying the place. They vary in size, from small sketches to paintings several metres wide. Some are incomplete, while others are awash with colour. Dean has pictured the ocean in every season, as a stripe of winter grey, or azure blazing with sunlight. The damaged paintings of Laura still lie on his table, despite Matt's attempt to destroy them, the girl hard-eyed and mysterious as a mermaid. I flick through a pile of seascapes, but don't find what I'm seeking, until a new portrait confronts me. Danny Curnow stares out from the canvas. Miller has pictured him sitting on a stool, dressed casually in jeans and a sweatshirt, scuffed trainers on his feet. Another shows a close-up of his face, tense with boyish determination, uncannily lifelike. The next shows him lying naked on a chaise longue, face averted, impossible to guess how he felt about the artist's gaze caressing his skin.

'How did I miss it?' I mutter, under my breath.

Footsteps startle me while I'm still studying the image. When I stumble to my feet, Dean Miller is standing there, in his paint-spattered uniform, holding a glass bottle full of white spirit. His expression is so tense, it looks like he's deciding whether to attack me with it or run away.

'Are you leaving, Dean? I've never seen the place so tidy.'

'I'm thinking of taking a vacation, that's all.'

'I found your pictures of Danny.'

'So I see.' He stands beside me, still clutching the bottle, staring at the boy's image.

'I like them better than your seascapes. There's so much emotion on his face: anger, excitement, longing.'

'He was perfect. Like a young Leonardo DiCaprio.' Miller's voice is loaded with sadness.

'Did he know how you felt?'

'Of course not, he'd have been disgusted,' he says quietly. 'The boy came here for money, so I paid him well, to keep him coming back.'

'That explains the cash in Laura's room.'

'It was their escape fund.'

'You didn't want to be left behind?'

He gives a wry smile. 'You took your time figuring it out. I've been waiting for you.'

'Explain what happened then, Dean. I'm listening.'

'I had a boyfriend on the mainland, years ago. No one's tempted me since then, except Danny. He'd have sailed to the mainland with Laura, forgotten all about me.' There's a note of disbelief in his voice. 'I followed her to the cliff. Pure jealousy, I suppose. With Danny it was harder. He guessed what I'd done; I killed him in self-defence. Watching the sea take him hurt me more than anything.'

His tone sounds too casual, the confession slipping out so easily. Why would he just admit to his crimes after weeks of cat and mouse? 'That's not the full story, is it?'

'If you take me to the station, I'll tell you more.'

'Not yet. I need to know Suzanne's safe first.'

The girl steps through the doorway at the mention of her name. A surge of relief arrives once I see that she's unhurt. This man has claimed two young lives already; there's no way I'll let him take a third. Suzanne's eyes are out of focus and she's soaked to the skin, as if she's been caught in a storm. She stands at the painter's side, barely any clear air between them, her affection for the old man filling me with concern. I'm about to tell her to step back for her own safety, when something glints in her hand. The girl's knuckles are chalk-white, her fist bunched tight around the handle of a knife.

53

The girl raises her fist, the blade pointing directly at my chest.

'Calm down, Suzie,' I say. 'Drop the knife on the floor.'

Her facial muscles spasm. 'You can't make me live with Mum again.'

'No one's going to try.'

'You're lying. I'll end up in prison.'

'There are better places for people your age.'

'That's a lie too.' She steps closer, the weapon angled towards my face. 'No one ever tells me the truth.'

'Give me the knife, then we'll talk.'

A tear slides down her cheek. 'Laura said she'd stay with me, till I was old enough to go travelling with her.'

'Danny spoiled everything for you, didn't he?'

Her teeth are bared as she suddenly lunges at me, a flash of light as the blade slices through the air. I have to move fast to knock it from her hand. When it spins to the corner of the room, the girl casts around for another weapon, but Dean grabs her wrists. She tries to break free at first, then gradually responds to his hushing. Her arms stop thrashing as his grandfatherly murmur calms her. Once all of that vengeful power has drained out of her, she's no more than a tearful child.

The next hours are spent getting her into custody. Arthur Penwithick ferries us across to St Mary's, but the last Sky Bus to the mainland flew hours ago. It's agreed that Suzanne's interview must wait until her psychiatric assessment is completed tomorrow in Penzance. That will give us time to track down a solicitor with experience of representing juveniles. Dean agrees to talk immediately, even though the harsh overhead light in Madron's office reveals his exhaustion. Eddie's at my side as I read the artist his rights, the old-fashioned recorder whirring quietly.

'Talk us through what happened this evening, Dean.'

His stained fingers splay across the table's edge. 'That's obvious, isn't it? I was working in the studio. Suzanne came to see me, terribly upset. She asked if she could stay at mine.'

'She confessed to the murders?'

'The kid told me yesterday.' The artist's gaze drops to the floor. 'Laura had her own dreams to follow, but being left with her mother was more than Suzie could stand.'

'What about Danny?'

'Suzie hated him for taking her sister. Laura might

have carried on protecting her, if Danny hadn't tempted her away.'

'Why did you pretend to be the killer?'

He gives a tired shrug. 'I've got nothing to lose. Suzie's just a young girl.'

I carry on interviewing him for another half-hour, but little fresh information emerges. The artist states that he hadn't realised how much Laura and Suzanne were suffering. The older girl was too afraid of what Jenna might do to Suzie to tell the truth about her violence. He says little about Danny, face grave when I ask questions. Apparently, the boy had turned up at his studio unexpectedly, offered to model for payment. His feelings are unspoken, but the regret on his face is easy to read.

Eddie and I decide to sleep in Madron's office, so we can take Suzanne and Dean over to Penzance on the *Scillonian*'s first crossing, but the only comforts available are a couple of blankets and the hard floor. Despite the rudimentary facilities, Eddie's choirboy features blaze with excitement.

'Why would a fourteen-year-old girl act like that?' he says.

'Push anyone too far and they'll snap,' I reply. 'Violence was the norm in her house. When her mum beat her, there was no one she could tell.'

Eddie shakes his head. 'It's still hard to believe.'

I drift off to the sound of his voice, rehashing details, as if he's trying to pinpoint the exact moment when we should have realised the child was at breaking point. The concrete floor and an overactive brain makes my sleep fitful. The first sound I hear when my eyes open is Eddie's chatter, as if he's been ranting all night on a continuous loop.

We spend the morning phoning ahead and completing arrest reports, before boarding the *Scillonian* at noon. Sleep deprivation makes it feel like time is slipping backwards, as we handcuff Dean and Suzanne to chairs in separate rooms below decks. When I leave Eddie to guard them, the same teenage brunette who served me weeks ago is standing behind the bar.

'You again, Inspector Kitto,' she says. 'Where's Shadow?'

'He ran away.'

'But he was so devoted to you.' The girl looks concerned as she slides two coffees into my hands. 'He'll come back. Dogs are smarter than you'd think.'

My young assistant is out for the count when I return, slumped in his chair in the corridor. It's a relief to digest the facts in silence, drinking first his coffee then mine. Dean Miller seems an unlikely hero, prepared to sacrifice his freedom for a young girl. It's Suzanne's actions that leave me reeling. She seemed like a vulnerable child, broken by her sister's death. Her mother's violence must have unhinged her, Matt's unhappiness taking its toll as well. Storm clouds hang over the Atlantic when I look through a porthole, the sea one shade lighter than black, nothing like the slew of colour Dean Miller favours. Relief should be hitting me, but I'm still reckoning with the human damage to a single family. The mother will be sentenced for assaulting a minor, one daughter dead, the other arrested for double murder. My eyes fix on the horizon, longing for sight of dry land.

54

I expect to see Steve Hilliard and his sidekick on the quay when the *Bryher Maid* takes me home hours later. No official statement has been released about Suzanne, but they must know she's been detained. With luck, they've chased the story back to the mainland, the island finally free of the rubbish they've been printing. The afternoon air feels heavy as I step off the boat and thank Arthur Penwithick. His buck-toothed smile makes me feel guilty about suspecting him and so many other islanders during the investigation. It's Ray I feel worst about, the case making me doubt people I've respected all my life. It feels like lead weights are lining my pockets as I trudge to Rose Austell's cottage.

When I arrive at Green Bay, the door to her cabin hangs open. She's scrubbing stains from wooden furniture, trying to bleach away signs of the recent break-in. The smile she gives me is half relieved, half wary.

'Why don't we sit down, Rose? It's time we had a talk.'

It takes patience, tenacity and repeated promises that Sam won't be arrested before she tells her story. The details come slowly at first, then she gains confidence and her words flow like water breaking through a dam. Jay Curnow has been calling in favours from islanders who owe him money. He expects people like Pete Moorcroft to do his dirty work, and help build his property portfolio, by fair means or foul. But the information Rose gives about the drug smugglers explains why she's so afraid. I listen in silence as she describes their night-time visits in unlit boats, endless threats and abuse, the damage to her property.

'They won't disturb you again, Rose. A Latvian boat was caught last night, not far from shore. Green Bay will be patrolled until the rest of them are caught, but you still haven't told me how Sam got involved.'

The wary look is back in her eyes. 'He was too scared to refuse.'

It's clear she has no intention of admitting that her son has been their runner for over a year, but her information should help the NCA track the drug boats' circuitous route from Riga to the Scilly Isles' deserted beaches. All I can hope is that Sam will benefit from rehab, instead of breaking his mother's heart again. Jay Curnow's coercion will be easier to stop. I'll pay him a visit after Danny's funeral, to remind him that threatening behaviour to extort a property sale is against the law.

My phone vibrates in my pocket once I return home, Madron's voice jubilant.

'Congratulations, Kitto. You seem to have a knack for being in the right place at the right time.'

'Thank you, sir.' It's hard to muster much enthusiasm for an outcome that will condemn a fourteen-year-old girl to a long custodial sentence in a juvenile detention centre.

There's a pause before he speaks again. 'I should apologise. The case is the worst I've seen; my tone may have been too harsh on a few occasions.'

'No offence taken, but it's not over yet. I'm going back to Penzance tomorrow to interview Suzanne.'

'Why not let the mainlanders do it? She'll be needing psychiatric care.'

'With respect, sir, the final interview should be mine.'

'Stubborn as ever,' he replies, sighing. 'Have you heard I'm appointing a deputy?'

'That's news to me.'

'It's quiet here, compared to London, but you could fill the vacancy.'

His suggestion leaves me speechless. I've never considered coming home permanently, but an alternative future rolls out before me. I could slumber through a lifetime of neighbourhood policing, say goodbye to the stress of undercover work.

'I've got commitments in London, sir.'

'Think about it before you turn me down.'

He rings off before I can reply, leaving me amazed that after so many stand-offs, the DCI has offered me a job. It's been thirty-six hours since I had any decent sleep, but my body's still racing, excess adrenalin making me feel like I could run a marathon in record time. I should visit Maggie for a dose of common sense, but an idea is nagging at me. My only choice is to deal with it once and for all.

Nina takes so long to open the door of Gweal Cottage, I'm afraid she's already left. Her expression's neutral as she stands on the threshold; only the dog seems glad to see me, rubbing his muzzle across my palm.

'Have you come for Shadow?'

'Just to talk, Nina.'

She stands her ground. 'I don't want another argument, it's too tiring.'

'I agree. Just hear me out, that's all I ask.'

Nina leads me to the living room, the air still tinged with smoke. Her calmness is missing for once, hands fidgeting at her sides, and I'm wishing I'd planned a better speech. I feel like a giant with nothing to say. Words clog my mouth, until I remember that she appreciates honesty.

'Why not stay here with me, for a while? See how it goes.'

'You're going back to London soon, Ben.'

'I'll be here till spring at least. Now the case is over, things will be peaceful. I can show you the islands. You can relax and play your violin.'

'That's the longest speech you've given.' There's still no sign of a smile. 'My parents are expecting me this weekend.'

'Visit them, then come back.'

'You've only known me a few weeks.'

'Who cares?'

Laughter slips from her mouth. 'You're making this up as you go along.'

'I know what I want, Nina. Let's find out if it works.'

'I'm not ready. You can see that, can't you?'

'You'll recover better here.' I keep my hand on her arm. 'You like sleeping with me.'

'I won't deny it. Are you always this relentless?'

'Only when I'm chasing something important.'

She takes a step backwards. 'Let me think about it.'

'How long do you need?'

'I'll let you know. Shadow can keep you company till then.'

The dog traipses after me with his tail between his legs, equally reluctant to be sent packing.

55

Rose finishes Sam's room first. She has reattached his shelf to the wall, trophies pieced together with glue, stains scoured from the carpet. She will use her meagre savings to buy a new mattress for his bed, before he comes home from hospital. His health matters more than any of the possessions the smugglers destroyed. But when he returns, they must think hard about his future. The boy needs to recover fully and follow his dreams, even if that means leaving her behind.

She opens her front door to watch cold sunlight blessing Tresco's fields, the calm water of the sound turning silver. For the first time in weeks, she can breathe easily, with pure air filling her lungs. After facing so many threats, she will not be forced from the island after all. When spring comes, she can search the beaches for badderlocks, laver and sweet tangle, without having to look over her shoulder. She will tend her bees when their long hibernation ends. Emotions rush at her as the light patterns change. She sheds a few quick tears for the dead girl and her boyfriend, their chances stolen before they reached full bloom. If she could pray, she would say a few words for them, but faith lies beyond her reach. Instead she shuts her eyes and imagines the island in high summer, when honeysuckle riots in the hedgerows, Atlantic terns floating overhead, children flying kites on the beach.

Rose feels calm again when she steps back inside her cottage, humming to herself as she puts her small empire to rights.

56

The DCI at Penzance station isn't thrilled by my arrival the next day. She's a stout brunette of indeterminate age, expression sour enough to curdle milk. Her lapel badge tells me she's called Kathy Tremayne, but I doubt we'll ever be on first-name terms.

'You could have saved yourself a trip, Inspector.'

'I'd like to hear her statement first hand.'

She gives a heartfelt sigh. 'The girl's in the interview room. Her entourage is ready and waiting.'

Suzanne is surrounded by the full battery of professional support: a young female solicitor, an advocate and a psychiatrist. Carers always flock round juvenile murderers, years too late, as if it was possible to reel back the damage. The girl is dressed in a pale grey tracksuit, looking younger than ever. Without make-up, she could be a nervous twelve-year-old rather than a teenager, her face shiny with anxiety. At first, she seems unwilling to answer my questions. When she finally meets my eye, her voice is little more than a whisper.

'My sister said we'd always stay together, but she changed her mind.'

'And you couldn't accept that?'

'Laura knew Mum hit me all the time, but she was leaving anyway.' A spasm of rage crosses her face then vanishes again.

'Can you tell me exactly what happened?'

She presses her hands to her cheeks. 'When I heard her singing in her room that Sunday it was the final straw. She was so happy to be going, I knew she wouldn't change her mind. So I followed her to the cliff the next morning, with Billy's knife under my coat. I was going to threaten her, to make her stay, but she just stood there grinning. I saw her fall onto the rocks. The sea carried her away.'

'And what about afterwards?'

'I couldn't believe what I'd done. That night I went down to the beach and saw her lying on the sand.'

'You bumped into Emma Horden there, didn't you?'

'How did you know?'

'She's got one of the earrings Laura was wearing when she died.'

'I gave it to her, and told her to forget what she'd seen.'

'Shock has made it stick in her mind, even though she remembers so little. It must have been her that attacked me on the beach, thinking I was the killer.' I study the girl's tear-stained face again. 'Why did you leave me messages and start the fire?'

'To keep you away. I thought it would scare you enough to stop you looking for me.'

'How did you leave the house without your parents realising?'

'They were too busy rowing to notice. I climbed down the drainpipe from my room, then let myself in the back way.'

'What happened with Danny?'

'I thought he'd guessed it was me, so I waited for him on the beach. That time the knife was from mum's drawer, not the pub. I took the watch off his wrist and left it for you.' Her voice has a sing-song quality, as if she's reciting a lullaby.

'You've just confessed to killing your sister and her boyfriend, Suzanne. Do you realise that?'

The girl doesn't reply, tears dropping onto the pale fabric of her tracksuit bottoms, like heavy splashes of rain. I feel shell-shocked after the interview ends. Normally it takes hours to drag out a murder confession, but the girl needed just fifteen minutes to admit to crimes that could see her detained for decades.

Before leaving the station, I request a meeting with Suzanne's psychiatrist, Dr Coren. He's a small-framed man with an Einstein frizz of grey hair, brows lowering over intense black eyes. I can tell he's uncomfortable, in case our discussion prejudices his report for the Home Office, but I'm longing for answers.

'Is Suzanne suffering from a mental illness?' I ask.

'We'll run the full battery of tests. She may have a

dissociative illness like schizophrenia or bipolar disorder, but it's likely to be situational.'

'Meaning what?'

'When symptoms stem from the patient's environment. It could be PTSD, because of the violence she's suffered.'

The news strengthens the link between Suzanne's fate and her mother's. Jenna's regime has taught her to use violence to control her feelings. Even though Suzanne's below the age of responsibility, she could spend years in residential care until she's judged fit to return to society. It seems wrong that Jenna will serve a much shorter sentence for assaulting her child. With good behaviour, she'll walk free in two years. The fact that her child will suffer so much more makes me question our judicial system.

There's no sign of Nina or the dog when I get back to Bryher, mist still drifting past the windows of my cottage. I loved this kind of weather as a kid; ideal conditions for playing hide-and-seek, but today I'd rather be found.

I'm halfway to Gweal Hill when Shadow bounds out of the mist, soon followed by Nina, wrapped in her dark red coat and carrying a suitcase.

'Coming to say goodbye?'

'That sounds too final.' She comes to a halt, several metres away. 'I need to go home, Ben. If I stay much longer, it would be a disaster. I'd fall for you when I've got nothing to give.'

'You're just saying that to numb the pain.' I attempt a smile even though there's a void where my stomach used to be. 'At least let me carry your bag.'

We head back to the quay, with the dog trotting ahead, nose to the ground, as if nothing bad was happening.

'How come he knows where he's going, even in a pea-souper?'

'Canine intuition. It's his best virtue.' I look down at that perfect oval face of hers, and realise she's been crying. 'Want to take him with you?'

'I'd love to, but he's yours.'

'He's more of a ladies' man. We should let him choose.'

When we reach the quay, she looks up at me. 'Visit me in Bristol, Ben. The timing's wrong, that's all. I want us to be friends.'

I kiss her instead of replying, because we're unlikely to meet again. Real life will take over when she gets home: friends, patients, new boyfriends as she heals herself. The ferryman is emerging from his house, ready to skipper the *Bryher Maid* back to St Mary's. I look down at Shadow as the boat prepares to leave.

'Are you going or staying?'

He whimpers loudly, chasing in a wild circle before finally jumping onto the boat. My heart sinks a couple of notches lower, but I can't blame him; in his position, I'd do the same. Nina gives my cheek an abrupt kiss then steps on board. I turn away immediately. I've got no intention of watching them vanish into the distance.

KATE RHODES

I march through the doors of the boatyard without greeting my uncle. He's on his knees painting duck varnish onto the boat's keel. It's lucky that he gauges my mood with a single glance, silently passing me a brush. It's a relief to have something to do with my hands, even though my guts feel like water spinning too fast down a plughole. After a couple of hours, I make my excuses and leave. What I need now is a long walk to steady myself. I've been trudging along the beach for ten minutes before I hear a sound on the shingle. When I look back, Shadow is running to catch up. His coat is saturated and his heart's kicking like a snare drum when I touch his chest. He must have jumped from the boat then swum back to shore, imagining he's Lassie.

'How many miles before you changed your mind?'

I rub brine from his lean face, those glacial eyes observing me. There must be some kind of affection behind that cool stare after all. My mood lifts as the Atlantic breeze rises. It's warmer than before, but its force reminds me of childhood winters, when it could knock me off my feet. Cromwell's Castle appears then vanishes again in the fog, proving that nothing stays the same. At least the dog chose me, the case is solved and a month's hard labour in Ray's workshop will put my head in order. I've got two jobs to choose between, but right now, I don't care. Maggie will serve me a dose of island philosophy with my cranberry juice at the Rock tonight. Chin up, she'll say; whatever life chucks at us, we mustn't weaken.

402

Acknowledgements

Many thanks are due to the highly encouraging and supportive team at Simon & Schuster, particularly my brilliant editor, Jo Dickinson, and Carla Josephson for her excellent support. Teresa Chris, my agent of many years, you continue to be an inspiration, a kind friend and the ideal lunch companion. Thanks to Miranda Doyle and Penny Hancock for excellent feedback at different points as the book came together. I am also grateful to constant support from all of my Killer Women writing pals. The friendly staff of the Hell Bay Hotel are owed my gratitude, for giving me so much useful information about the island's smuggling history, and its flora and fauna, as well as several perfect holidays on the beautiful island of Bryher. Twitter pals, particularly Julie Boon and Peggy Breckin, I salute you! Your encouragement really does keep me writing, on winter days when instinct tells me to stay in bed, eating chocolate. And finally, my husband,

Dave Pescod, deserves heartfelt thanks for helping me at every step. Without your encouragement, Dave, this story would still be a few garbled words on the back of a menu in a Cornish hotel.

Love DI Ben Kitto?
Read on for an exclusive extract
from the new thriller by Kate Rhodes,
coming soon ...

RUIN
BEACH

PART ONE

'How that personage haunted my dreams, I need scarcely tell you. On stormy nights, when the wind shook the four corners of the house, and the surf roared along the cove and up the cliffs, I would see him in a thousand forms, and with a thousand diabolical expressions.'

TREASURE ISLAND,
Robert Louis Stevenson, 1883

It's midnight when the woman begins her steep descent down Tregarthen Hill. Excitement washes through her system as she follows the rocky path, with the breeze warm against her skin, a kitbag slung across her shoulders. She pauses halfway to catch her breath, staring up at the granite carn that glowers over the bay like a giant's silhouette. When she drops down to the beach she can feel someone's eyes travel across her skin, but the sensation must be imaginary; if she had been followed, she would have heard footsteps pursuing her through the dark. The woman takes a calming breath, remembering why she must take this risk, as moonlight glances off the Atlantic's surface. Her family need her help, there's no other choice, and the tide is drawing closer. If she works fast there will be time to complete her task before the returning surge floods the cave.

She presses sideways through a chink in the granite, the temperature dropping with each step. A sense of awe overtakes her as the cave expands. Her torch traces a line of brightness over sea-scoured walls that soar like a cathedral's nave. The smell of the place intoxicates her, reeking of seaweed, brine and ancient secrets. When she catches sight of the black water at her feet, the cave's history fills her mind. Pirates were slaughtered here for stealing smugglers' cargo, their ghosts resonating from the walls. She has to suppress a shiver before retrieving the wetsuit and mask she hooked to the wall of the cave days ago, to prevent the tide from carrying them away. The woman checks the oxygen gauge on her aqualung, before clamping the regulator between her teeth. She takes the package from her kitbag then lets herself fall backwards into the water. After diving alone hundreds of times, she knows how to avoid unnecessary risks. Nothing can disturb her now, except the measured rasp of her own breathing and her lamplight distorting the velvety blackness. She lets herself float for a minute, enjoying the solitude. Few other divers have experienced the beauty of this hidden fracture in the earth's surface, extending far below sea level.

The woman understands that losing focus would be dangerous. She stops to check her pressure gauge at twenty metres, the beam from her headlamp catching grains of mica in the granite, glittering like stardust. She locates the familiar opening in the rock, then places the package in the crevice where it will be easy to find, her fingers gliding through clear water. She's about to swim back to the surface when a light shines beneath her, then disappears again. It must have been a reflection; the depths seem to extend forever, the water a dense, unyielding black.

She kicks to the surface fast, relief powering each forceful stroke. It will be days before she must dive here again, and tonight she can rest easily, knowing she's done the right thing.

The woman is about to clamber back onto the rocks when something hits her so forcefully there's no time for panic. The regulator is yanked from her mouth, a hand ripping away her mask. Her headlamp falls into the water, piercing the dark as it plunges. She lashes out, but someone has gripped her shoulders, her arms flailing as she's pushed under again. A face looms closer, its familiarity too shocking to register. She fights hard, but the breathing control techniques she has practised for years are useless while her lungs are empty. The woman's fists break the surface again, before something cold is rammed between her lips. Terror is replaced by a rush of memories. She pictures her daughter's face, until a last flare of pain stuns her senses, and her body floats motionless on the water's surface.

1

My day off begins with a canine wake-up call. Something rough scrapes my cheek at 6 a.m., and when my eyes blink open Shadow is sprawled across my pillow, his paw heavy on my chest.

'Get off me, you hellhound.'

I jerk upright to escape his slobber, wondering how he managed to break into my room again. Shadow skulks away to avoid my temper, a sleek grey wolfhound with glacial blue eyes. A stream of curses slips from my mouth as I emerge from bed, my lie-in ruined by an unwelcome pet inherited from my old work partner. Loyalty would never allow me to abandon him at a dogs' home but it crosses my mind occasionally, depending on how many rules he breaks. When I open the front door it's impossible to stay angry. The dog bowls across the dunes, the cottage filling with the cleanest air on the planet.

Bryher is at its best in early May, before the beaches are invaded by day trippers keen to photograph every bird, flower and stone. This morning there's not a soul around. Sabine gulls spiral overhead, the Atlantic a calm azure, no sign of the storms that thrashed the western coastline all winter long. This is the view that summoned me home from my job as a murder investigator in London. I took the quality of light for granted as a kid; it's only now that I appreciate the way it makes the landscape shine. There are no houses to spoil the scenery, except the square outline of the hotel on the far side of Hell Bay, ten minutes' walk away. My own home is much humbler; a one-storey granite box built by my grandfather, with extra rooms added to the sides as his children arrived. The slate roof needs repairs since last month's gales played havoc with the tiles, but my DIY plans will have to wait. I owe my uncle Ray a day's labour in return for hours of dog-sitting, and an early start will give me time for a swim afterwards. I glance at the letter that lies unopened on my kitchen table before I leave. My name and title are printed in block capitals on the envelope – Detective Inspector Benesek Kitto – and I already know what it contains. It's a summons from headquarters in Penzance, telling me to report for a review meeting, to decide whether I can continue as Deputy Commander of the Isles of Scilly Police, now that my probation period is ending. I've spent three months fulfilling every obligation, but the judgement is out of my hands.

Shadow traipses behind when I take the quickest route through the centre of the island, my walk leading me eastwards over Shipman Head Down. The land is a wild expanse of ferns and heather, the fields ringed by drystone walls, with flowers rioting among the grass. If my mother was alive, she could have named each one, but I only remember those that are good to eat – wild garlic, parsley and samphire. No one's stirring when I cut through the village, passing the Community Centre with its ugly yellow walls, stone cottages clustered together like old women gossiping. When I reach the eastern shore I admire the repainted sign above my uncle's boatyard. Ray Kitto's name stands out in no-nonsense black letters, as clear and uncompromising as the man himself. I can hear him at work already, hammer blows ringing through the walls. The smell of the place turns the clock back to my childhood when I dreamed of becoming a shipwright, the air loaded with white spirits, tar and linseed oil.

'Reporting for duty, Ray,' I call out.

My uncle emerges from the upturned frame of a racing gig, dressed in paint-stained overalls. It's like seeing myself three decades from now, when I hit my sixties. Ray almost matches my six feet four, his hard-boned face the same shape as mine, thick hair faded from black to silver. He looks less austere than normal, as if he might break the habit of a lifetime and let himself grin.

'You're early, Ben. Prepared to get your hands dirty for once?'

'If I must. What happened to the boat?' Its prow looks battered, elm timbers splintering, but its narrow helm is still a thing of beauty, just wide enough for two rowers to sit side by side. Gig racing has been a tradition in the Scillies for centuries, the vessels unchanged since the Vikings invaded.

'It needs repairs and varnish before the racing season starts.' He gives me a considering look. 'Ready to start work?'

'I'd rather have a full English.'

'You can eat later. Bring the delivery in, can you?'

A shipment of materials has been dumped on the quay that runs straight from the boatyard's back door to the sea. Three crates stand side by side, waiting to be carried into Ray's stockroom. It takes muscle as well as patience to heft tubs of paint and liquid silicone onto a trolley, then shelve them in the storeroom, but the physical labour clears my mind. I stopped clock-watching weeks ago, no longer measuring hours by London time. Days pass at a different pace here, each activity taking as long as it takes, the sun warming my skin as I collect another load. My stomach's grumbling with hunger, but the view is a fine distraction. Fishing boats are returning from their dawn outings, holds loaded with crab pots and lobster creels. Many were built by Ray years ago, when he used to employ shipwrights to help him construct vessels with heavy oak frames and larch planking, strong enough to withstand the toughest gales. I shield my eyes to watch them battling the currents that race through New Grimsby Sound, and an odd feeling travels up my spine. One of the fleet is approaching the quay at full speed, black smoke spewing from its engine, while the rest head for St Mary's to sell their catch. The boat is a traditional fishing smack called the *Tresco Lass*, with red paint peeling from its sides, skippered by Denny Cardew. The islands' permanent population is so small I can name almost every inhabitant, despite my decade on the mainland. I don't know Cardew well, but the fisherman's son was a classmate of mine twenty years ago. I remember Denny as a quiet man, watching football at the New Inn, where his wife Sylvia worked as a barmaid, but his composure is missing today. He's signalling frantically from a hundred metres as his boat approaches. As it draws nearer I can see that the decking is in need of varnish, and there's a crack in the wheelhouse's side window.

When I jog down the quay to help him moor, Cardew stumbles on to the jetty. He's in his fifties with a heavy build, light brown hair touching his collar, skin leathered by a lifetime of ocean breezes. I can't tell whether the man is breathless from excitement or because of the extra weight he's carrying, banded round his waist like a lifebelt. Words gush from his mouth in a rapid mumble.

'There's something in the water, north of here. I saw it when I was collecting my lobster pots.' His mud brown eyes are wide with panic. 'A body, by Piper's Hole.'

'You're sure?'

'Positive. I went so close, I almost hit the rocks.'

His tone is urgent, but I'm not convinced. Last week a woman on St Agnes reported seeing a corpse on an offshore rock. It turned out to be a grey seal, happily sunning himself, but the tension on Denny's face proves that he's convinced. The coastguard would take an hour to get here, so my day off is already a thing of the past.

'Come on then,' I reply. 'You'd better show me.'

Ray is standing on the jetty as I climb over bait boxes strewn across the deck. The dog tries to jump on board but I leave him on the quay, whimpering at Ray's feet. My uncle watches the boat chug away, his expression resigned. He's grown used to our time together being cancelled at short notice, even though I'd like to repay him for his support since I came home.

Denny Cardew's skin is pale beneath his year-round tan as he focuses on completing the return journey, the fisherman's silence giving me time to watch the scenery from the wheelhouse as we sail through the narrow passage between Bryher and Tresco. Cromwell's Castle hangs above us as the boat chases Tresco's western shoreline, its circular stone walls still intact after four centuries. The bigger island has a hard-edged beauty; its fields are full of ripening wheat running down to its shores, but the coastline is roughened by outcrops of granite, Braiden Steps plunging into the sea like a staircase built for giants.

Cardew steers between pillars of rock at the island's northernmost point, waves pummelling the boat as we reach open water, nothing sheltering us now from the Atlantic breeze. A few hundred yards away, Kettle Island rears from the sea. It earned its name from the furious currents that boil around it. I can see a host of gannets and razorbills launching themselves into the sky, then winging back to settle on its rocky surface.

'Over there,' Cardew says, as we approach Piper's Hole. 'I'll get as close as I can.'

The fishing smack edges towards the cliff, with the shadow of Tregarthen Hill blocking out the light. From this distance, the entrance to Piper's Hole is just a fold in the rock. No one would guess that the cave existed without local knowledge; it's only accessible at low tide, when you can scramble down the hillside, or land a boat on the shore. Right now, the cavernous space will be flooded to the ceiling, my thoughts shifting back to a local woman who died there last year, stranded by a freak tide.

I peer at the cliff face again, but all I can see are waves breaking over boulders, a row of gulls lined up on a promontory. Several minutes pass before I spot a black shape rolling with each wave at the foot of the cliff, making my gut tighten.

'Can you land me on the rocks, Denny?'

Cardew gives me a wary glance. 'You'll have to jump. I'll run aground if I go too close.'

'Lucky I've got long legs.'

My heart's pumping as the boat swings towards the cliff. If my timing's wrong, I'll be crushed against the rocks as the boat rides the next high wave. I wait for a deep swell then take my chances, landing heavily on an outcrop, fingers clasping its wet surface. When I climb across the granite, the soles of my trainers slip on a patina of seaweed. I give Cardew a hasty thumbs up, then turn to the wall of rock that lies ahead, marked by cracks and fissures. Below it a body is twisting on the water's surface, dressed in diving gear, too far away to reach. I can't tell if it's a man or woman, but the reason why the ocean has failed to drag it under is obvious. The oxygen tank attached to the corpse's back is snagged on the rocks, anchoring it to the mouth of Piper's Hole.

I dig my phone from my pocket and call Eddie Nickell. The young constable listens in silence as I instruct him to bring a police launch from St Mary's; it will have to anchor nearby until the tide ebbs and the body can be carried aboard. The breakers cresting the rocks are taller than before, but the *Tresco Lass* is still bobbing on the high water, ten metres away. I make a shooing motion with my hands to send Cardew away before his boat is damaged, but he gives a fierce headshake, and I can't help grinning. The fisherman is a typical islander, unwilling to leave a man stranded, despite risking his livelihood. I turn my back to the pounding spray, knowing the wait will be uncomfortable. It could take an hour for the tide to recede far enough to let me reach the body. When I lift my head again, the corpse is rolling with each wave, helpless as a piece of driftwood.

2

Tom Heligan reaches Ruin Beach earlier than planned. He looks more like a schoolboy than a young man on his way to work, an overgrown fringe shielding his eyes, his legs spindly. He pauses on Long Point to catch his breath, images from the sea cave making panic build inside his chest. From here he can see the black outlines of Northwethel, Crow Island, and the Eastern Isles scattered across the sea. On an ordinary day he could stand for hours, picturing shipwrecks trapped below the ocean's surface. Spanish galleons lie beside square riggers and tea clippers. He could draw a map of the wooden carcasses that litter the seabed with his eyes shut, but even his favourite obsession fails to calm him today. Tresco's rocky shores have destroyed hundreds of boats, their precious cargo stolen by the waves, ever since Phoenicians sailed here to trade jewellery for tin. Now his own life is foundering. He drags in another breath, weak as a castaway stumbling ashore.

The boy crosses the beach towards the café at his slowest pace. How will he be able to work after what he saw? He should never have followed Jude Trellon from the pub last night; it was a pathetic thing to do, especially after spending the day in her company, but he hates letting her out of his sight. Tom comes to a halt, eyes screwed shut, trying to erase the memory. The shame of his cowardice will last forever. He saw a figure emerge from behind a rock in Piper's Hole, but was too afraid to act: he hid in the darkness until the terrible cries and splashing ended, then ran for his life. Fields passed in a blur as he sprinted home to Merchant's Point. Last night he convinced himself that everything he saw was a waking dream, but now he's less certain. Surely the woman he's obsessed with is strong enough to defend herself from any threat? There might be nothing to fear after all.

THE
DARK
PAGES

Visit The Dark Pages to discover a community of like-minded readers and crime fiction fans.

If you would like more news, exclusive content and the chance to receive advance reading copies of our books before they are published, find us on Facebook, Twitter (**@dark_pages**) or at **www.thedarkpages.co.uk**